THE PERILOUS ROAD TO FREEDOM

BOOK TWO: THE ROAD SERIES

N. L. BLANDFORD

To those who fight the monsters of their past.

CHAPTER ONE

The pregnancy test sat on the bathroom counter. I sat on the floor, leaned against the faded brown wall, my knees pulled tight against my chest. I watched the timer on my phone count down. Ten...nine..eight. The plastic pink tip of the test hung over the edge, taunting me. You thought you escaped that life, escaped him. But what I will reveal to you will have you looking into the eyes of that world for the rest of your life. Every day you will see his nose, ears, or eyes.

The timer blared and brought me out of my spiraling thoughts. I silenced it and continued to sit and stare up at the stick which could change my future. Finally, I stretched from my seated position and pulled the test off the counter. I closed my eyes and said a small prayer, "Lord, I know you have a bigger plan for me than I could possibly comprehend. I would respectfully request that it does not include a child right now. But should you choose, may you give me the strength to love it, no matter who their father is. Help me to nurture it into the person you want them to be."

I opened my eyes. A blue cross taunted me.

As if on cue, I crawled to the toilet and vomited, the pregnancy test still in my hand. I washed the remains of dinner off my face and tossed the test in the trash. With a clunk, it landed on top of the other five tests I had taken this week. All had the same results.

The person reflected in the mirror was a stranger. I had barely slept in three months, couldn't keep much food down and, according to my psychologist, was suffering from Post Traumatic Stress Disorder. How could I possibly take care of a child, especially William's?

I had dismissed my skipped periods as a reaction to stress, and the trauma of captivity. I had not prepared myself for the possibility that I had been carrying a child inside me. Now, the past could not be forgotten. It would always be in front of me.

My phone rang. I looked down at it and saw Whitney's name and number in white on my black screen. I didn't really want to talk to her, but I knew she would keep calling until I picked up, so I bent over and grabbed the phone off the cold laminate floor.

"Hey. Can we talk later -"

"Turn on the tv to channel 64," she said.

"What? Why?"

"Trust me. Just do it." I could hear her sniffling.

"Okay, one moment, I have to get to the living room. Are you crying?"

Whitney ignored my question and changed the subject, "How'd today's test go? Get a different result?" she asked.

"Same as yesterday," I said disappointedly. I grabbed the remote and turned on the tv, switching the channel to 64. "What am I looking at?"

"They are about to provide an update on the fire," Whitney answered.

"I thought they had wrapped everything up. What more can they add?"

"I don't know, but Detective Teller just called me. She said she didn't have time to explain, but they had an update and to watch. She said she tried to reach you and you didn't answer."

"Well, I would really just like to try and get on with my life. Here she comes."

Across the screen walked the assertive Detective Teller. She wore her dress uniform and stood behind a wooden podium, the blue Los Angeles Police Department crest on the front. Once she had settled her notes and looked into the camera, Whitney and I stayed silent.

"Thank you all for joining me today. As you know, on August 11, 2018 there was a fire which consumed the entirety of 1258 Holiday Drive. After a long investigation, it has been discovered that this house was an unlawful brothel which trafficked women and forced them to perform sexual favours for wealthy and powerful people across the city. We will not be releasing the names of those individuals at this time, however, we are in the process of speaking to many of them right now. Charges are pending for some, based on what we found during our investigation. Once charges are laid, their names will be released. The operation was run by a large organization, with William Hammond at its helm."

My legs went weak seeing William's picture pop up on the screen. As I sat on the arm of the chair closest to me I could hear Whitney pacing in her apartment. Her heels clicked on her hardwood floors.

Detective Teller continued, "We previously reported Mr. Hammond was in the house at the time of the fire and died. However, after further examination of the scene, the Fire Marshal has concluded there were no human remains on site."

My heart stopped. "What did she just say?" I asked Whitney, my eyes glued to the television screen.

"They think William is alive, but that can't be right. Can it?"

Detective Teller continued, "As the majority of the house had collapsed, there was a large volume of rubble and ash to sift through. Which is why it has taken three months for the Fire Marshal to conclude their investigation. We are both confident in the results. Therefore, if anyone sees this man, they must not approach him but call the police immediately. He is considered armed and dangerous. I will now take questions." Reporters lobbed questions at her, but my focus was on William's picture, so their voices became muffled.

"Whitney, he was still alive when I left him. Maybe he snuck out the back of the house? Fuck! Just when I thought things couldn't get worse." I was nauseated again and put my head between my knees.

"It's going to be fine. No one knows where we are." The crackling in Whitney's voice told me she didn't believe what she was saying.

"Reyna knows, and she turned pretty quick last time." Whitney didn't respond right away. She knew I was right. "Okay this is what we do. We get you out of town as soon as possible, change your number and we don't contact any of the group again. We can't create any trace between us and them, alright?"

"Right." My hands started to tremble. Would William's torment never be over? Would I ever be able to live without looking over my shoulder?

"Start packing now! I am going to make a few calls and see if I can find us a place to stay. Once I have a place, I will come and get you. We will leave your car behind, ditch mine when we are on the road and get a new one. Any questions?" Whitney always sounded so sure of herself when she made a plan.

"I don't know if I can do this. I had to be so strong for so long, I don't know if I can do it again." I started to cry.

"Olivia, everything will work out. I will be there with you. We will find a nice house in a quiet town and live out the rest of our lives as two crabby old women with an adorable baby, okay?"

"The baby, oh my God. What if he finds out about the baby? Whitney, I am freaking out. Please hurry up and come get me."

"I will. Talk soon." I heard a beep and the call disconnected. My hand gripped my phone as if it was the only thing that would save me.

I noticed missed calls from Jessica, Saria, Fay and Lily. Other survivors from L.A. I ignored the notifications and walked across my tiny living room to grab my suitcase from the front closet. I struggled to get it out, the wheels snagged on the rolling panel door. I yanked on it and it released, but both it and I fell hard onto the floor. My phone flew into the living room.

There was a knock on my door. I used the suitcase to prop myself up, and rubbed the bruise that was sure to be forming on my ass. Jessica lived down the street and likely came over to check on me after she couldn't get through.

I opened the door and a familiar cologne filled the air. I froze. It wasn't Jessica in front of me. It was the face that haunted my dreams every night. Instead of the evil red eyes, and torturous grin, the face was calmly smiling as if his presence was the most natural occurrence in the world.

"Hello Olivia."

CHAPTER TWO

I could not speak. My chest tightened. I had forgotten how to breathe. My tight grip on the door handle was the only thing that prevented the weight of the world from crushing me. The round metal knob dug into my palm and pinched nerves against bone. The pain masked my fear.

Before me stood a monster in an immaculately tailored black suit. The button of his collar was undone. William's wavy brown hair, piercing pale blue eyes, chiseled jaw, and well kept body, looked as though it suffered little from the fire poker I had stabbed him in the back with, almost four months ago. His visible skin had not been kissed by the ravaging fire I had left him to die in.

The sound of my name on William's lips had me frozen in place. A hint of rage flickered in his eyes, and an uncanny calm smirk crossed his face, which ignited my safety instincts. I pushed the flimsy wood door and tried to lock it. I wasn't quick enough. William had wedged his foot between the door and the door frame. I put my whole body against the back of the door and gave it a shove; however, the morning sickness had weakened me. My strength would not exceed his. With all the power I could muster, I gave it one last shove and ran.

There was nowhere to run to. My 800-square-foot, one-bedroom apartment was so small I could cross it in about fifteen strides. There was no other exit except out a window. A fall from the third floor would be survivable, if I could get the windowpane out before William got to me. I doubted my bones would remain intact. Not to mention the thing inside me. A moment of relief fluttered at the thought of its death.

The apartment door quietly closed behind me. The lock clicked and I was just outside the galley kitchen when William's hand wrapped itself around my wrist. He flung me around and pulled me toward him. I wrestled to free my arm. William's calm smile had vanished and had been replaced by fury. With one hard pull, my shoulder socket screamed and I collided with his chest. The rich, smoky cologne suffocated my senses.

William's mouth opened but I did not wait to hear words. I kneed him hard in the groin. William doubled over but remained on his feet, his grip on my wrist tightened, and I was bent awkwardly on top of his back. I used my free hand to grip William's shoulder, pushed him away and pulled my captured arm. This time it released and William fell to the fake hardwood floor with a thud.

Undeterred by his fall, my ankle became ensnared in his long fingers. My upper body toppled forward. My arms took the brunt of the impact against the floor. Still in his grasp, I rolled onto my back and kicked William in the face with my free foot. Blood started to pour from his nose, down his face, on top of his suit and onto the floor. He instinctively reached for his nose with both hands and gave freedom to my ankle.

"Bitch!"

I scrambled to my feet and had almost made it to the bedroom, at the back of the apartment, when a bullet whistled past my head and splintered the closed bedroom door. A small ray of light filtered through the hole. I detoured into the bathroom. My hands trembled as I fumbled with the cheap, rickety, silver metal lock of the pocket door. I knew it would not hold long, but I needed something between me and him. Anything.

The sound of William's heavy footsteps encroached on my racing thoughts. I gripped the lid of the toilet, and my shoulders tightened at the shrill sound of ceramic being scraped against the tank. I was not going down without a fight. Not now. Not after everything I had been through. Not after promising the memory of Claire, or maybe it was myself, that I would push past the horrors of being trafficked. I would live and I would be happy. One day.

The footsteps stopped and shadows crept under the door. My heavy breathing was the only sound. I hugged the wall beside the door, ceramic weapon at the ready.

Suddenly, the metal lock shattered with a loud crack. The bullet that caused the damage, lodged itself into the bottom of the mirror. The glass fractured into hundreds of pieces and yet remained intact - a puzzle of reflected light.

The door rattled along its tracks. I changed tactics and jumped into the bathtub. I would not let him get behind me. William's looming figure stepped into the room, blood caked on his face, and I swung the heavy tank lid at his head. Before impact, William caught it in his free hand. I struggled to keep my weapon, but even with the use of only one hand, he easily unarmed me. William tossed the lid aside and a loud thud marked it's collision with the wall in the hallway.

I prayed my mostly-deaf, 80-year-old neighbour below me had somehow heard the commotion and called for help. The unit beside me was empty and the occupants of the one across the hall worked nights. My life depended on someone who required a hearing aid they never wore.

Flat against the cream tiled wall, I glared at William. He raised his gun and the silencer emitted a metallic smell.

"How convenient of you to choose the bathtub as the location of your death," William said. "Very little fuss about the mess this way. In fact..." He bent over the sink, and smashed the butt of the gun into the mirror. Pieces rained into the sink. William grabbed a large piece, pointed the gun back at my head, and demanded, "Sit down."

He did not take kindly to my hesitation, angrily repeating "Sit down!"

I slowly slid down the tile until I was seated in the bathtub.

"Hold out your arms. You know, it really is tragic you just couldn't handle everything that happened to you. But, I guess, taking your own life was the only way you saw to let go of it all."

His condescending tone made my skin crawl. It also reinvigorated my hatred.

"You'll have to shoot me or fight me, as I will not let you stage this as a suicide. You will not get away with taking another innocent life!" I was trapped but not defeated.

"The more difficult you make this, the more I will enjoy it." A sly grin blossomed on his face. "Now, it's up to you, if you want to prolong the inevitable. I can wait here as long as necessary." Without removing his gaze from me, William sat down on the toilet, propped his elbow on his leg, yet the gun remained on target. "Give me your arm."

I pulled my knees to my stomach and wrapped my arms around them. "You think you know everything, but you don't understand -"

"What's there to understand? You wanted revenge for your sister. What was her name again? Right, Claire. Sad one that Claire. It's a shame you could not save her."

William knew exactly how to get under my skin. I had been close to locating Claire on multiple occasions, only for her captors to have moved her. I was devastated to learn Claire had been brutally murdered only days before William traded my imprisonment with his brother, Adam, for confinement with him in Los Angeles. The very same place Claire was last seen alive. For years, she had protected me from our abusive father, yet I failed to protect her when she needed me most. I had not been able to safeguard her from the drugs, her persuasive and detrimental boyfriend, or from the Hammonds. My failure would haunt me the rest of my life, and William fed off it. Anger boiled inside me.

William's grin widened as he continued, "Well, you wanted revenge for her death and got it. Now I will get revenge for Adam. One way or another." He motioned with his gun for me to stick out my arm.

William would wait as long as he needed to win, and with each minute my strength dwindled. Adrenaline would not save me this time. There was only one way I would get out of this bathtub alive.

"You can't kill me"

"I can and I will."

After three months of trying to come to terms with all the death I witnessed and the violence I experienced, it took everything I had to muster my courage, look this monster in the eye and admit, "I'm pregnant."

CHAPTER THREE

All the expression faded from William's face. No sly smile. Blank eyes looked right through me.

He leaned against the back of the toilet, zombie-like. William's brow furrowed. His face scrunched, as though he could extract information from me telepathically. Resigned, he sighed and the familiar, knowing grin started to form.

"I will hand it to you. You had me for a minute. But you would say anything to buy yourself more time. It's not going to work. This is it, Olivia. *You* do not win this time." William stretched the fingers holding the grip of the gun and then settled them back into place. He leaned over, his arm stretched as far as it would go, as the warm barrel of the used silencer kissed my forehead. "Hold out your arm!"

Unphased, I pointed to the corner opposite the sink. "Look in the trash bin.".

William wavered on whether he should get up. Curiosity won. He stood, backed up a couple of steps and looked down into the trash bin. He looked back at me and then back at the bin. He gently placed the piece of mirror from his left hand on the counter, careful not to cut himself. Gun fixed on me, William squatted, grabbed the bin, and stood up. The bin rested on the counter and he pulled out test after test, looked at it and then tossed it into the sink. With every test, William's face displayed a different emotion: confusion, disbelief, anger, worry, and finally defeat.

William's emotional journey allowed me time to regain my wits and courage. I considered seizing the moment. I could lunge at William, and try to get the gun, or get to the shard of glass. However, I feared both could also be used against me, if I was not quick enough. Instead, I stayed where I was and played out what I started.

"How? And more importantly who?"

"I am about four months pregnant. Adam raped me 7 months ago so that, thankfully, rules him out. The only nicety Mr. Y gave me, was that he actually wore a condom, so unless it broke, the child is not his. That only leaves you." William's face contorted and he looked skeptical. I continued, "You don't actually think I would willingly allow a man to touch me after what your family put me through, do you? As for the how, you tell me. I was too intoxicated the one night we were together to notice if you wore a condom."

"But...I...no..." William ran a hand through his hair and gripped the ends before he let go. The release of the hair acted like a switch, the confusion and defeat gone. Determination in its place. William took a deep breath, placed the gun on the counter furthest away from me and turned on the taps. The pieces of mirror in the sink chimed as the water stirred them. He put his thumb on one side of his nose, his pointer finger on the other, and with a quick turn of the wrist reset his nose. Not a wince from the inevitable pain. With the blood washed from his face and hands, he took another deep breath, grabbed his gun and turned to me. "Out of the tub." He waved the gun towards the hallway. "Let's go!"

I pushed myself up and stepped over the side of the tub. William grabbed my forearm with his free hand and he guided me into the living room.

"Pick up your suitcase."

Now was not the time to protest. William had been determined to kill me and had now chosen to extend my life. If I wanted to get out of this mess, I needed time. I would not jeopardize that. Not yet. As I bent down to grab my toppled suitcase, my cell phone dinged with another notification. I looked over, and before I could move, William had my phone in his hand.

"Whitney will be here in a couple of minutes. Perfect! That will save me a trip." William tucked the phone into his pocket. "Put the suitcase upright by the door. Good. Now sit on the couch and when she knocks, invite her in." William unlocked the apartment door and stood in the space behind where the door would open up. Whitney would not know he was there.

An overwhelming silence filled my apartment. The dried sweat from my fight with William created a layer of film on my skin. Nausea lingered at the bottom of my throat.

The cheap apartment walls were thin and it was not long before the thunderous stomps on the hallway stairs notified us of a visitor. The loud thuds told me whoever it was had taken the stairs two at a time. There was a rapid knock on my door. I wished I could warn Whitney but when I opened my mouth all that came out was, "Come in."

In slow motion, the golden doorknob turned, and Whitney stepped in. Her eyes widened as she registered my disheveled state. Her gaze traveled along the toppled furniture and the trail of blood caused by William's nose. William stepped out from behind the door and reached his hand around her face and covered her mouth. The gun pointed into her side, as her eyes swapped concern for fear. William closed the door with his foot, walked Whitney over to the chair beside me, and tossed her into it. He stood on the other side of the small wooden coffee table, fully visible to both Whitney and I.

"One word from you, Whitney, and both Olivia and the baby don't live to see tomorrow. Now, are we expecting anyone else? I know Jessica is also in Toronto. Should we be waiting for her before we get started?"

"Jessica's not coming." I was confident William loved to prove how smart he was, and I needed to buy time to come up with a way to get Whitney out of here, so I was not afraid to ask, "How did you find us?"

William had an uncanny way of reading my mind, "Don't even think about it. The sooner you realize you can't save her," he nodded towards Whitney, "the easier this will be. But back to your question, to be honest, for a former detective I thought you would have made it more difficult to find you. Despite changing your names, you actually made it very easy.

Toronto may have millions of people, but I knew you would return home and try to hide among them. Try and find a semblance of your old life."

He was right. I hated when he was right.

"I reached out to my contacts here, and within a week they had tracked you down. I only wished I had healed faster, before the LAPD discovered I had not actually died in that fire you started. It was harder to get out of the country than I anticipated. The delay allowed me to tie up some loose ends in the States. When everything was in order I made my way to you."

My voice trembled as I feared the answer to my next question, "What loose ends?"

William pulled the coffee table out and sat on the edge closest to me. "There were a couple of rats that needed culling. I couldn't keep those who knew the secrets of my business alive, could I? I hate to admit it, but I should have seen Jack or Kevin's betrayal coming."

Whitney whimpered. William's pleasure in her reaction displayed itself through clenched teeth. The intensity between their stares was palpable.

"Before my father died, he had told me there was a mole. Funny enough, Jack and Kevin both tried to help me track them down. Killed everyone who had worked for us in Michigan, so we thought we got them. I guess not. The two of them bided their time and now look where we are at. My standing over you too and both of them dead.

"Now, Jack had been easy to find. Hiding near a beach in Florida. A little carbon monoxide poison and no one was the wiser. Now Kevin... Ah yes." William patted Whitney's leg with the gun, and she recoiled from its touch. "Your long-lost lover. I thought I had ensured my workers would not entangle themselves with the product, however the heart wants what it wants. Or at least the cock does. Him, I played with. He was always a tough one and held out for quite a while. But once I switched, from a baseball bat to fingernail removal, he begged for death.

"You bastard!" Whitney slapped William across the face. Whitney could usually hide her emotions, however in this moment her tears escaped.

William had not flinched, his smirk remained and widened as he stood. He moved beside Whitney and rested the barrel of the silencer against her temple.

"I told you not to say anything."

Whitney looked to me, but her eyes did not plead for help. Rather, they had clouded over with acceptance that today she would die. She rested her head against the back of the chair, defeated.

My tears erupted. I wanted to hold her. Help her. Whitney had been my best friend through the horrors of L.A.. After we were free, we had supported each other through nightmares and panic attacks. I needed her.

"Please, you don't have to do this!" I said.

William pushed the gun harder against Whitney's temple, "Do you still think there is a way to have a fairy-tale happy ending? I would be foolish to let either of you two live. There is nothing left to do but this! Olivia, *you* have put me in a predicament I am still working out how to handle. However, Whitney here, well I don't see a way she survives this, and by the look on her face, neither does she. So why don't we just get this over with, as you and I need to get going."

"Going where?"

"That is information you do not need to know. Now, come over here, right in front of me."

I inched myself off the couch. I tried to grab the gun, but William caught my wrist and through gritted teeth said, "Stop trying to beat me. It's not going to work."

William kept hold of my wrist with his left hand, and turned me to face Whitney. He stood directly behind me; his chest touched my back, and I felt his warm, stale breath on my neck. He brought the gun toward my clenched fist. "Put your hand under mine."

My jaw slacked and I looked up at him in horror. I wanted to protest but I was at a loss for words.

He whispered in my ear, "You have no power. Hand. Now."

I struggled with him as he forced the gun into my hand, both our fingers on the trigger. Tears streamed down my face. I mouthed, "I'm sorry" to Whitney. She took my left hand, squeezed and held on. We both closed our eyes.

CHAPTER FOUR

The gun recoiled, but William's tight grip on my hand, and the closeness of our bodies, kept me steady. The smell of sulfur and burnt flesh surrounded me. My eyes remained shut. I couldn't look at Whitney. At what I had done. Forced or not.

William lowered our arms and removed the gun from my hand. It took little effort, as the gun felt like fire against my skin. I wanted it gone.

William stepped back, my knees buckled and I fell to the ground. I hunched over in a ball of tears. The scent of rust tickled my nose. I had smelled blood many times before. My own, others', and it rarely bothered me. Except today. It might have been my sensitive stomach, or the fact I had just killed my best friend, but today, the combination of rust and gunpowder made me feel sick and powerless.

My stomach churned. I turned my head to the side, my throat contracted, but nothing came up. I gagged as the emptiness that was in my stomach tried to escape. Behind me, metal scraped against metal as William unscrewed the silencer from the barrel of the gun.

"Get up, tears won't help you or your friend."

I unclenched my eyelids, stared at the faux wood floors and reached for the arm of the chair for some leverage, careful to avoid Whitney's arm.

My peripheral vision prevented me from avoiding the sight of Whitney. Rather my eyes were pulled directly to her. Blood oozed out of her head and I could see bits of brain matter on her and the chair. Even with the hole in her head, she looked as though she was asleep. Peaceful.

I took comfort that her past would no longer cause sleepless nights. The fears of what a strange man standing close to her in the grocery store could do had been abated. Therapy, with a doctor who placated her, was over.

I peeled some hair off her blood-stained face, and brushed it behind her ears. My lips pressed against her warm forehead and I whispered, "I love you. I am sorry."

"Get me your passport and wallet," William said. "Quickly now, we don't have all day."

I kissed Whitney one more time and stepped over her legs, towards the small table beside the couch. The wood drawer of the second-hand furniture stuck on itself. It happened all the time, and I knew the particular way to free it from its own grasp. However, I stalled it's opening in the hope I could come up with a plan. Any plan.

My synapses were clogged with fear, but I knew any attempt on William's life, here and now, would only result in my own death. I resigned myself to the fact I would have to wait.

William towered over me. "Opening a drawer is not rocket science. Stop trying to delay the inevitable."

As defeated as I was, William's nonchalance about the events that happened only moments ago was chilling. As I wiped my tears, Whitney's blood transferred from my hand to my face. I tried to rub it off, but was certain I had only smeared it around. The thick blood that had resided on my hand had diminished to a thin red smear.

William grabbed my wrist, "Drawer. Now." He said firmly as he placed my hand back on the black diamond-shaped handle.

If he was so desperate for my things, why did he not just get them himself? He let go and typed on his phone. I glared at him and pulled the drawer slightly to the left and it opened with ease. My passport and wallet sat on top of a bundle of old letters wrapped in yellow ribbon. They were old, covered in dirt, and their tears taped together. I pulled out my passport and wallet and stuck my arm out towards William. My eyes still focused on the letters. He took the contents and, without moving my eyes,

I saw he placed them inside his jacket pocket. I wanted to bring the letters with me to whatever new hell William would take me to. Even just hold them and feel Claire in this moment. My hand hovered.

If William knew what they were, their destruction would become another weapon in his arsenal of psychological trauma. I closed the drawer. I hoped leaving them behind would signal to police that there was more to what happened here. If Detective Teller became involved, she would know I would never leave without one of the few remaining pieces of Claire I had.

Oblivious to my train of thought, William clicked off his phone and put it into his pocket. "Get Whitney's keys. We'll take her car."

Demand after demand made my blood boil over. "You grab the keys if you want them so badly, you vile piece of shit!"

William laughed, "There she is! I was wondering when the mouthy woman I had known was going to come out to play." His tone went back to stone cold, "Now, here is how this is going to go. You're going to get me the keys, we will pack a few things, and then leave. I can physically force you to do all of this. I have no problem with that. Or...you can follow my instructions and have less bruises to show for it. Your decision."

"You think you are so tough, forcing people to do your bidding. I may not have succeeded in killing you before, but you can bet I won't fail again."

"We will see about that. Keys, now!"

I muttered, "Yes, we will" under my breath, turned, and faced Whitney. I could see the keys bulging from the pocket of her jeans. I tried to get them out without actually touching her but her pants were tight and the keys were jammed between the fabric. I fit two fingers into the pocket and weaseled the keys out. The irony of the yellow and black key chain which said Freedom was not lost.

I flung the keys at William, which he caught, and I stomped loudly to the bedroom. William followed closely behind, suitcase in tow. He lifted the suitcase onto the bed, slid the rickety closet door open and pulled clothes off hangers. The force caused some of the hangers to fall onto the floor, while others swung on the rod. William tossed my stuff into the suitcase and however it landed was how it stayed.

I rummaged through my drawers and paid no attention to what I packed. I grabbed the pajamas off the bed and William's eyes rested on my stomach, but he quickly diverted his gaze and finished zipping up the suitcase.

"Let's go." He motioned for me to walk in front of him.

As I re-entered the living room, I digested the entire picture of disarray for the first time. Furniture on its side, strewn around the room, and trails of William's and Whitney's blood. There were obvious signs of a struggle. Would the police put together what happened and find me before it was too late?

I turned to William, glued once again to his phone. "You won't get away with this. Not this time."

He smiled, "Yes I will." He walked past me and into the front entry. He pressed the button on the intercom in the wall to open the front door. He saw that I looked perplexed. "You didn't think I would leave the place looking like this, did you?"

That is when it dawned on me. William had no intention of trying to frame me for Whitney's murder. William had me take Whitney's life as he knew my actions would eat away at my soul for the rest of my life. He was also aware that I would torture myself with any hope that I could have saved her by fighting back. William's manipulative mind games were often more damaging than his hands.

William opened the apartment door just as two large men stopped in front of it. Each wore painter's coveralls with the drawstraps of the hoods drawn tight, construction goggles, and gloves. They were fully covered. One man had brought what looked like paint cans, however the stench of the contents told me they actually contained bleach. A roll of plastic was tucked under his arm.

The men stepped into the apartment, the one with the paint cans leaned into William and whispered something I could not hear. I noticed the man without the cans wheeled a large black case behind him. He placed it on the coffee table, clicked open the clasps and revealed an array of tools. They were not painters' tools.

He pulled out a saw, while the other man spread out some thick plastic and dragged Whitney to the floor. I instinctively moved towards her, but William held me back. "It's time to go and let these men do their work."

Pulled forward, towards my own destruction, I desired to go back towards Whitney's.

CHAPTER FIVE

William, my suitcase, and I trudged down the three flights of stairs to the apartment building's front door. The compilation of sweet and savory aromas from the tenants' cooked dinners made my stomach grumble. We stopped at the large glass front entrance while William looked around.

"Stay here. One move, one word, or one pleading look for help, and we will be paying a visit to Joe and Sally."

It was like I had been punched in the stomach. The blood drained from my face. William knew about Joe? Joe had been my rock when I had tried to help Claire navigate her drug addiction. He was the one who did the impossible and tracked me down in L.A. His wife, Sally, put up with my late night calls for help before, and after, I had been kidnapped. Was I really surprised William had learned they existed?

"Are we going to have any problems?" William pushed open the door.

"No." I would not risk the lives of the only family I had left. I had escaped before. I would again.

"Good. Stay right here, where I can see you."

William emerged from the building, turned right, and ducked behind some large pine trees. Through the glow of the large parking lot lights, he maneuvered through the trees that lined half the parking lot. When he ran out of foliage, he hunched over and weaved through the parked vehicles. Behind trucks he disappeared. William approached a black sedan at the far side of the parking lot. Two shadows appeared to sit in the car but I could not make out who they were.

The street lights followed William like a spotlight, but I seemed to be the only person watching the show. A glimmer of black materialized in William's hand. I squinted and stood on the tips of my toes. He held a gun by the barrel, instead of the grip. Crouched down, he snuck up on the driver side door, rested his hand on the handle for a moment, swung open the door, and jumped to his full height. While William's body blocked my view, my mind filled in the scene. Within seconds, half of William's body was in the car, his feet firmly planted on the ground. A few more seconds and William was out of the car, the driver side door closed and he strolled towards me. There was no longer a reason to weave or hide behind vehicles.

At the end of the walkway, William waved for me to come out of the building. I didn't know what was about to happen to me, or where I would end up, but I figured that as long as I was pregnant William was less likely to kill me. It was this thought that gave me the courage to push the door open and walk to William.

"Which car is Whitney's?"

I pointed to the third visitor parking stall and advised, "The green Cavalier."

William found the appropriate black-topped key from the keyring and inserted it into the driver side door. The vehicle unlocked, he bent down and the trunk popped open. He left the car door wide open and tossed my suitcase into the trunk. William placed his hand on my lower back, which sent a chill up my spine, and led me around the rusted shell of a car, to the front passenger door. He unlocked it and held open the door for me. The gentlemanly act felt out of place. My muscles screamed from the battle that had raged upstairs and my legs and lower back resisted bending to get into the car. William closed the door and I tugged on the torn grey seatbelt. I pulled too hard and it got stuck. Frustrated, I pulled harder which did nothing. I let go and caught a glimpse of myself in the side mirror.

I looked nothing like Olivia from seven months ago. Adam, L.A., and William had forever changed me. My eyes were encased in dark circles and soulless. Whitney's blood still kissed my cheek. I could have used a tissue from the glove compartment, instead I left it there. I wanted a part of her close to me.

William contorted his frame into the driver seat, reached under the seat and found the lever to move the seat back. His discomfort eased. He looked over at me, "Seat belt."

Really, you care about a seat belt? "It's broken."

Annoyed, he climbed over me. I pressed myself into the seat as much as possible and turned my head away from him. The gap between us was so small, the smell of cologne and whiskey that had become synonymous with William, encircled me. He lingered for a moment but I avoided his gaze. He grabbed the seatbelt and gently eased it out of it's casing. The fastener clicked and William plopped back into his seat, and secured his own seatbelt.

William turned the key in the ignition. Click, click, click. He released the key and tried again. Click, click, click. His hand tightened around the key and I prayed the car would not start. Maybe it knew it's beloved owner was not the one willing it to go. The engine finally turned over and the vibrations from the chugging pistons moved through the car. A sigh of relief was released beside me. I hung my head and rubbed my hands on my pants. Nothing was going to go my way today.

We drove past the black car William had snuck up on. The driver's head leaned back against the headrest. It appeared as though the person was sleeping. I suspected William had also knocked out the passenger.

"Who are they? What did you do to them?"

William glanced over at me, then back to the road, "People sent to watch over you. My men you met upstairs informed me they were positioned outside your place. They were not here when I arrived, so I suspect they showed up after Detective Teller's little announcement. Don't worry, they aren't dead. I don't need bodies marking my trail, now do I?" He winked.

I was still amazed, even with his line of work, and the death that encompassed it, how indifferent William was to death. Only 15 minutes ago we pulled the trigger to kill my best friend and he sat beside me joking about it. I clenched my fists as the urge to bash his head against the steering wheel filled my body. I closed my eyes, and silently said the Confucius quote my therapist had given me to deal with my anger towards William, "*If you hate a person, then you're defeated by them.*" I would not let him defeat me. I repeated it again. Even if I wanted him dead, with my luck my desired actions would only result in injury.

My anger downgraded, slightly. "Where are we going?"

"Somewhere-"

Before he could finish, a siren blared, and the dark evening that enveloped us was pierced by blue and red lights reflecting off the review and side mirrors. I turned around in my seat to watch, as a Toronto Police Service car approached from behind. The small silver car directly behind us yielded, and the police car came within two car lengths of us.

"Shit! We must have been seen exiting the building, or there was more than one car watching you." William slammed his foot on the gas pedal, the momentum from the drastic increase in speed pushed us back against our seats.

My knuckles turned white from my grip on the door handle. William started to weave through traffic. He handled the old clunker like a state-of-the-art race car. Although William maneuvered the vehicle with ease, as horns blared around us, his skill did not diminish the danger each swerve created. On multiple occasions cars in the oncoming lane had to abruptly dodge out of the way. With each close call I yelped, closed my eyes and braced for impact.

"You are going to get us killed!" My grip on the door was not enough, I secured myself further with a hold on the grab handle on the ceiling.

"You worry too much," he said. William's focus remained on the road, the traffic around us and the police vehicle now sinking behind us in the distance. "Besides, I would rather be dead than in jail. If I need to avoid a cell, I will make sure death is quick."

I could see a large steel cement truck barreling towards us and, for a moment, wished William would pull in front of it. Make it quick, as he said. That thought was quickly replaced by the fact that William would likely only guarantee it was quick for him. Even in death, William would try his best to achieve revenge. If he could plan it perfectly, I knew he would leave me to live, seriously injured or incapacitated.

The number of police cars behind us increased. William pulled onto the 401 highway. It was rush hour but it was Remembrance Day, so the normal volume of vehicles were parked in garages across the city. However, traffic still scattered our path. As he had done on the city streets, William easily maneuvered around them. He pulled onto the 407 toll road, which had even less traffic and accelerated. The pedal was literally on the floor.

The police cars kept back, and other than sirens, did not engage. This was normal procedure to avoid the risk of injury to innocent bystanders. However, if they got any indication of where William was going they would barricade him off as he exited the highway.

I suspected we were headed to an airport. I doubted William would stay on roads long, even if the police had not been chasing us. But which one? There were at least ten private airports in, and around, Toronto. The Toronto Police Service did not have the capacity to position themselves at all of them. The fact they had seven cars behind us astonished me.

Vehicles ahead of us, signaled by sirens and flashing lights, pulled over to the outer lanes, which cleared the middle lane of obstacles. With the imminent danger of an accident decreasing, I reduced my grip on the door handle and grip bar. My heartbeat remained heightened as scenarios of how this could play out raced through my mind.

The aforementioned car accident, with me badly injured. William dead. A shoot-out where either William or the police killed me. The scenario which caused the most fear, was if the police somehow captured us without incident. I would be forced to grapple with the loss of Whitney and bearing William's child. I would live in fear of William's reach from prison and likely wake up one day to hear that Joe and Sally had been killed. Thankfully, that scenario was unlikely. William said he would rather die than go to prison, he would not easily give up unless he knew he would win in the end.

The last scenario that my mind conjured up was one where we would make it outside the city limits, and I would be faced with a torturous future, of unknown length, with a manipulative and deceptive monster. Somewhere I could not escape from this time.

I looked over at William, focused on the task at hand, his square jaw clenched. His knuckles white as he gripped the steering wheel. He no longer looked like he was enjoying himself, as he had when the chase started. Now, he looked determined and calculated. That was the William I feared most.

His eyes darted from between the mirrors and around his surroundings. I could tell he, too, was playing out scenarios in his mind. I doubted he knew exactly how to get where we were going. Although he may have anticipated some roadblocks, the likelihood he could maneuver and change course on a dime was unlikely.

I turned and looked out the back window. The police cars kept pace. The highway was lined with slowed or pulled over vehicles. I resigned myself to the fact that for me to survive, and however unlikely it was - have a chance of freedom, we needed to outsmart the police.

Police vehicles lined an overpass in the distance. They were too far ahead, and too dark, for me to see if there were guns drawn; however, I suspected as much. I also knew that if they were prepared, there was a spike strip waiting for us. My gut told me if we hit that spike, William's gun would be out as quick as a gunslinger, and I would be dead.

When William pulled onto the 407, I don't think he realized it would be harder to leave it. The purpose was to get from Point A to Point B faster than the 401. This meant less entries and exits. William peered around for an exit. The next one would be after the overpass, unless we could somehow get back onto the 401. Then I saw it.

I pointed and, to ensure he heard me, yelled, "There is a gap between those orange construction barriers and the regular cement one on the right. Right by that street light. Do you see it?"

William didn't answer but moved over to the furthest right-hand lane. There was no need to shoulder check. The road and its drivers had conceded. The plastic barriers, which should have been lined up with the cement ones, were crushed, which told me they were weak. I wasn't sure a Cavalier would survive hitting them head on; however, the barriers had moved and a small gap had been created. If we could fit we would be out of the grasp of the police. At least for a little while. If we could not, we would be wedged and trapped.

William had already been at full speed but he pushed his foot down harder, trying to get as much out of the vehicle as it would give. As we approached the barrier, I closed my eyes, gripped the grip handle with one hand and then the center console with the other. I moved as close to the center of the car as I could, and made myself as small as possible.

A loud screech and crunch of metal reverberated through the vehicle after the passenger side of the vehicle scraped along the barrier. As quick as the sound hit my ear drums it was gone. I opened my eyes, the crushed door bent inward beside me. The car moved at top speed, unaware of the damage. The police cars which had been tailing us stopped. The collision had barely widened the gap and their oversized vehicles were too big to pull through. The police on the overpass scrambled into their cars. William weaved his way across four lanes of traffic to the off ramp.

"Give me a phone and tell me where we are going! Or we might run out of gas before you find your way."

William pulled out a phone from his inside jacket pocket, unlocked it, and before he handed it to me, said "You make any calls, texts or find a way to contact anyone. Joe and Sally are dead. You got that?"

"Yes," I grabbed the phone and opened up the map feature, "Now where are we going?"

William rambled off an address. When it came up on the map it did not look like an airport. It appeared to be a large piece of land. William was a calculated man and the use of an airport required paperwork. Wherever we were headed, paperwork would not be required. Why, then, did he need my passport? He wanted to ensure it was in his possession so that I couldn't use it. I guessed I would need it to get out of wherever we were going.

I refocused. As quickly as the map was updated, I alerted William where to turn next. The bottom of the screen displayed a green 15 minute trip to our destination. Plenty of time for the police to catch up. And they had started to. Two cars came over the hill behind us and there were sirens to my right.

William narrowly avoided a pedestrian in a crosswalk. Curse words flooded in through the open windows as we passed.

When we got onto the final stretch of road and the map said two kilometers remained, I debated trying to get a message to Joe. Maybe he and Sally could get away before William or his men could find them? Doubt devoured my courage. William had found Jack and Kevin, who were experts at disguise. He would find Joe and Sally too. It would be selfish of me to try and warn them. Instead, I held out the phone for William to take.

"It's just a couple kilometers up the road."

"Find S. in the contacts and put it on speaker."

I turned the phone back towards me and hit the blue contacts button. There were two letters. H and S. I wondered who these people were that William considered them the only ones important enough to have their numbers in his phone. I pressed S, then Call and held out the phone. It rang a couple of times and then dead air.

William spoke, "We have company."

The phone beeped to signal the call had been terminated from the other end.

I was not sure how this was going to end. What I was sure of was that whatever happened next would not be easy.

CHAPTER SIX

The Cavalier's brakes screeched as we took the corner at full speed. Only a few blades of grass were between us and the ditch. Tires squealed behind us as the police vehicles, which had closed in, made the same tight turn. My ears had become immune to their sirens, but not to the sound of gravel that belted the undercarriage and sides of the car.

My breath became heavy and I started to panic. We would have to get out of the car at some point. What would happen then? Bullets would invariably fly. I had never faced a similar situation during my time with the Toronto Police Service. I had no idea, in the heat of the moment, what would happen. Protocol for a man of William's reputation was to capture or kill. Especially with the lack of innocent bystanders around, I didn't see them working too hard to capture.

We approached a tall chain-link fence that two large men dressed in dark suits, feet dug into gravel, shoulders braced against the edge, pushed open. Once the gate was opened the men ran and took positions behind a row of vehicles lined up horizontally - a blockade of metal. A gap sat in the middle of the line. William did not slow down as we approached the gap. Once the front doors emerged on the other side of the barricade William slammed on the brakes. Unprepared, I was flung forward with the sudden stop. The seatbelt William had fastened for me prevented me from smashing through the window. My hands slammed against the dash and kept my head from colliding with it.

"Get out!" William flung open his door, pulled his gun and exited the vehicle.

I released my seat belt and tried to open my door, but the impact with the construction barrier must have jammed it shut. On either side of the car stood men and women, all in black, with guns rested on the tops of the vehicle blockade. Some held nine millimeters, others had semi-automatics. I tried the door again. It didn't budge. Behind me the sound of rapid gunshots pierced metal. The police had arrived.

I scrambled across the driver's seat and fell out of the car, hands first. I gathered myself to my feet, but crouched to my knees just as quickly. Bullets flew around me. A woman on my left collapsed with a thud. Blood poured out of her chest. She looked over at me, no fear in her eyes. No emotion at all. She got up as if nothing had happened, like a toy soldier who had lost its balance. She went back to her position and continued to fight those she deemed the enemy. A robotic guard willing to sacrifice herself for William.

William hunched over me and pulled me away from the gunfight. I managed to get to my feet but stayed as low as possible while we ran towards the back of a large metal airplane hangar. Shouting and the cracks of gunfire filled the air around us. We left the suitcase William had packed for me in the trunk, no doubt riddled with bullets.

On the other side of the hangar sat a private plane. Engines roared to life. We were protected from the bullets by the building, so we both straightened up, but didn't slow our pace as we ran towards the plane, William's grip tight around my arm.

We boarded the plane and a young, well-built man, dressed in the same black suit as the others, pulled up the stairs and locked the door. He banged on the cockpit door and the rumble of the engines filled the cabin. I stumbled as the plane moved along the makeshift grass runway. William put me into a chair beside a large circular window and then sat across from me with a loud sigh. No words were spoken. We were engrossed by the scene beside, and below, us.

The property was scattered with police vehicles. They too had formed a barricade. Two lines drawn in the gravel. On one side, those who tried to uphold the law. On the other, those who defied it. Both blockades were decorated with bullet holes. A few bodies, both officers and dark suits, were strewn on the ground. Puddles of blood surrounded them.

The nose of the plane pointed upward and the force of ascent pinned me against my seat. A helicopter hovered over the scene below. William must have noticed it too, as he got up and entered the cockpit. He left the door open as he spoke to the pilot. However, I could only hear muffled voices. The plane continued to rise and then veered to the right, away from the destruction in its wake. The helicopter was not equipped with weapons and would never keep pace with a jet. It wouldn't follow us. The officers would be restricted to the deadly scene playing out on the ground. Observe and report.

I leaned my head against the back of my seat and closed my eyes. The adrenaline that had coursed through my veins started to wane. Even the fear subsided as exhaustion overtook my body. I don't know how long I sat there. Alone. My eyes fluttered between the land of awake and sleep. William's dominating figure emerged from the small cockpit door and leaned against what looked to be a closet. He stared at me. I willed my eyes to stay open. I needed to know what was going to happen next, but try as I might, my body pulled me towards the dark of sleep.

The last thing I heard was William whisper, "Sleep now. It is going to be a long flight."

CHAPTER SEVEN

J ostled awake, I reached out for something to hold on to. My hands were sore from the tight grip I'd had during the car chase and they were arguing with my attempt to hold on to the arm rests. I rubbed them on my legs to try and calm the pain.

"It's just a little turbulence. Nothing to worry about. Should be over soon." William said.

The blur of sleep faded. William put his phone on the table between us and walked into the galley. Could I get the phone without detection?

Ice clattered into a glass, a seal cracked and liquid poured. I shifted in my chair, curious what was behind me. The young man, who had closed the plane door when we boarded, was seated behind me and to my right. His sandy blond hair shaved close to his scalp, his face made of stone and his arms crossed in front of him. If I had not seen his forest green eyes continue to look between William and I, I would have sworn he slept with them open. Another loyal soldier waited for orders. The phone would have to stay untouched.

The plane was different from the one William had brought me to Los Angeles in. It was smaller, but no less luxurious. Cream leather seats lined most of the cabin, with a matching couch behind me. Rustic wood accented the ceiling and matched the pull-up tables between the cabin chairs. I suspected the wood was oak, based on a table my father proudly displayed when I was a child. The orange wood carried through to the cockpit door and into the galley. The carpet was cream with grey triangles intricately woven.

My stomach turned, as though I rode a rollercoaster. For the past month, no matter how long I had slept for, I was always nauseated when I woke up. I stood up slowly, the young guard's arms unlocked and moved to his sides. He leaned forward as if about to stand and turned to William, who had also noticed I had moved.

William advised, "The washroom is up front."

I ran towards the front of the plane and the young guard settled back into his seat. I opened the door and gold and black beauty surrounded me. I crouched on the cream tiled floor in front of the toilet and lifted the lid. The roller-coaster still traveled my stomach but nothing disembarked. When my cheeks started to feel flush, the nausea started to settle a little. I used the counter as leverage to pull myself to my feet. I dampened a cloth with cold water and patted my face and neck.

Refreshed, I removed the cloth from my face. I looked ragged from the lack of sleep and stress since returning to Toronto. My auburn hair was a disheveled bush after struggling with William earlier, and the breeze from having the windows of the Cavalier down to listen for sirens during our tumultuous escape. I washed the remnants of Whitney's blood off my cheek, along with the caked-on dirt. I opened a small cupboard and found an unused hairbrush. I took my time and worked my way through the knots and tangles until my hair looked somewhat tamed. I brushed some dirt off the knees of my tights and looked myself in the eyes.

Freedom had not brought back the Olivia from April, before Claire had gone missing and before I learned how she was brutally murdered. Freedom had not erased the memories of the beatings and rapes. Freedom had not cleaned off William's touch from my skin, after a night I would like to forget most of all. A night that resulted in a child I feared would be just as monstrous as its father. A child I was not sure I wanted, but was thankful had saved my life, for now.

I splashed some more water on my face, dampened the towel again and sat back down on the floor. I rested my head against the wall and covered my face. The coolness from the towel gave me what little comfort I could get out of this moment.

A knock on the door churned my stomach. A male voice, in an Irish accent, asked, "Ma'am, you okay in there?"

"Yes, I'm fine, just a little nauseous."

"Mr. Hammond would like you to come out when you are able. He has prepared some food for you." Contrary to his stern exterior, the man's voice was kind. "I will be right here if you need any assistance."

"I can manage. But thank you."

Silence, instead of footsteps, hovered outside the bathroom door. Although the nausea remained, I was not fooled by 'come out when you are able'; one did not keep William waiting. One hand on the lid of the toilet and the other on the counter, I maneuvered myself to my feet. I folded the towel neatly on the towel rack and opened the door.

Sure enough, the guard stood before me. He stretched out his arm to direct me back to my seat and followed behind. William was seated and staring at the white billowing clouds which navigated the starry blue-black sky.

I took my seat and the guard went back to his. The smell of the buttery baked potato overpowered the rest of the food on the plate in front of me. Even with the somersaults in my stomach, I was famished.

"Eat," William said, cutting into his chicken.

The water was a sweet relief to my parched mouth. The clanking of silverware on the plates and soft chewing were the only sounds until the meal was over. The muscular arm of the guard reached for my plate. A small pale scar on the inside of his wrist crept out from his shirt cuff. It looked eerily like an H. He quickly covered it, took the plates, and the sound of dishes being washed echoed out of the galley.

"Is that an H on his wrist?"

William tilted his head without a response.

"You brand people now? When did this start?" No one in Los Angeles had an H anywhere I had seen. I couldn't recall anyone at the airfield with one, but they were fully covered and everything had happened so fast.

"I don't brand anyone. However, not every Hammond operates in the same manner."

"So, he doesn't work for you then?"

"Not exclusively, but he knows what will happen if he disobeys."

"Right, heaven forbid anyone have a mind of their own."

"Don't start."

I would get nowhere right now fighting about free will, so I didn't push it. There were more important things to figure out. "Where are we going?"

William rested his elbows on his armrests, put his fingertips together in a steeple shape and brought them to his lips. He pondered his response. "Somewhere we will be safe," he said softly.

"WE will be safe, or YOU will be safe?"

"For now, WE."

"Does this place have a name?"

William's voice became harder, "Does it matter? It's not like you have a choice where we go. Or are you already trying to plan how you will escape for a second time?" William shuffled forward in his seat, "If you try anything, I won't be the only one you will have to answer to."

"I see, so we are going somewhere where you are not in charge?" I wanted answers and I was not going to back down until I got them. If William hurt me, it would be nothing more than a few punches. Not enough to hurt the child. I had survived my time with him and his brother. I could survive whatever he might do to me in my current state.

William was caught off-guard by my question and waited a moment before responding. "Technically speaking, you are correct. However," he emphasized, "I won't have any less power than I had before. The only difference, where you are concerned, is that there will be more eyes on you. And no friends to help you this time." Satisfied with his answer, he got up, grabbed his glass and went to the galley.

I followed him. The guard watched from his seat. As William prepared himself another drink, I continued to question him. "Why won't you just tell me where we are going? It's not like I can really do anything with that information, now can I?"

William turned to me with hostility in his eyes, "You do not deserve to know where we are going!" He stepped so close to me that I was backed against the counter and he continued, "In fact, you do not deserve to be alive. However, until I can find out if that...that thing in you is mine, I will let you breathe." The familiar smell of whiskey on William's breath wafted over me.

"Oh, it's yours. But what happens to me when it's born? Will you take me out to the back pasture like Old Yeller?"

William rested his hand against the cupboard, getting as close to me as possible. Nose to nose. The veins in William's temples throbbed and his blue eyes pierced mine. I held his stare. "Your future is for me to decide. You have no say in what I may or may not do with you. Now...go...back and sit...down." He backed away just enough to give me room to leave the galley.

I had not felt or seen William's gun when his body was pressed against mine. He must have hidden it. As much as I wanted to, now did not seem the right time to attack. The guard would quickly be on top of me and I did not know how long the flight was. Whatever damage I might be able to cause could very well be cleaned up, or recovered from, before we landed.

I slid along the oak counter and came face to face with the young guard, blank stare and all. He stepped aside to let me through. Behind me the words "watch her...careful...devious." filtered out of the galley. I rolled my eyes, dropped into my chair and stared at the fiery stars. They burned for thousands of years and then one day ran out of energy and died. I would not run out of energy. I would not die.

One thing was certain, I would likely be alive as long as this child was inside me. I had about six months to figure out how to get away from whatever new hell awaited me.

CHAPTER EIGHT

M y determination of the length of time I had been on the plane was hindered by my walk between sleep and wakefulness. My eyes fluttered to reveal different scenes. William in the leather chair opposite me, his eyes focused on me. The young guard crouched in the frame of the cockpit door. An empty chair across from me. William with eyes closed and arms crossed.

Today's dreamland was a black void. No thoughts, no nightmares, nothing. I was removed from the void by a gentle shake of my shoulder and muddled words. Words with no meaning. As I came out of the haze of sleep, the words of the young guard became understandable.

"Ma'am, we are going to land momentarily. You should get ready."

The crevices of my eyes were crusted with discharge. I rubbed away the flakes and was drawn to the orange and red painted sky. The beauty outside the airplane window was a stark contrast to the reprehensible darkness inside. William's ungodly presence did not occupy his chair. Instead, his voice drifted through the cockpit door.

"What time is it?"

He pushed his shirt sleeve back, "Just after 7 a.m."

I stretched my arms wide and pretended to yawn, "Where are we?"

"I can not tell you that Ma'am."

I dropped my arms. Of course you can't! "What is your name?"

"I cannot tell you that either."

"What can you tell me?"

"Nothing Ma'am." He looked out the window and my eyes followed his. The beauty of the land above the clouds was replaced by the congestion of tall buildings, thousands of cars and smog. "We are about to touch down. You might want to put on your seatbelt." The young man went back to his seat.

Two buckles clicked as I braced for the landing.

The landing was smooth and once the plane had decelerated, William exited the cabin. He had changed while I was sleeping. He now wore a light grey suit, tailored to an exquisitely fit physique. He buttoned his suit jacket, ran his fingers through his hair and waited for the plane to stop before he spoke.

"Some clothes will be brought on board for you to change into. We cannot have you arriving looking like you slept in a garbage bin."

"Remind me the next time a barrage of bullets is coming at me to protect the cleanliness of my outfit."

"Let's not start with the attitude. You are to be on your best behaviour. Understand?" William stepped aside, as the young man with no name opened the plane door and walked down the stairs. I monitored his actions through the window. He took a black clothing bag from a small man standing beside a vintage black car. The white-rimmed tires sat beneath a wave of metal. It reminded me of a vehicle a gangster in the 1950s would use. How fitting it would be here for William.

"My *best* behaviour, is it? What happens to you if I am less than my best?"

William yanked the bag from the guard, who had emerged from the stairs, and threw it at me. "I do not have the patience for this right now. Put on those damn clothes, make yourself presentable and shove whatever hate you have for me into the deepest pits of yourself. Your survival is on the line. Now, you have ten minutes to meet me in that car. One second over, and I make a call to a friend who owes me a favour in Toronto. He is fond of making house calls."

No further explanation, or motivation, was needed. To protect Joe and Sally, I did what I was told. I followed William to the front of the plane.

He exited down the stairs and I entered the bathroom. Through the crack of the closing bathroom door I saw the young guard take up a position beside the exit. Even with one exit from the bathroom, let alone the plane, I needed a chaperone.

I hung the clothing bag on the back of the door and unzipped it. I could not believe what I was looking at. A baby blue skirt, long sleeved button jacket with a closed neckline to match, with a built-in belt that sat just above some sort of frill that lined the bottom of the jacket. If confusion was not what overtook me, I might have laughed. The outfit would not have been found in the curated closet back in L.A.

I found some new undergarments and cream coloured shoes at the bottom of the bag, along with some newly purchased cosmetics. None of this made sense, which was normal for situations involving William, but something weird was going on. If I was being taken somewhere to be held until the birth of this child, I would not be dressed like a Stepford Wife.

Reluctantly, I removed my clothes and washed the stench of sweat off with a small cloth. The new clothes swallowed me in a sea of pastel blue. I had to admit the colour was nice. However, I still looked like I had a secret stash of pills to get me through a life I could never make perfect. The frill of the jacket hid the small baby bump that my oversized sweater had concealed. My hair fell on my shoulders. I was never good at styling it in anything other than a ponytail, which my gut told me would be unacceptable. I ignored half the makeup and, based on what Whitney had shown me, put on just enough to cover the dark circles under my eyes.

The thought of Whitney made me shake with sadness. She had taken me under her wing when I first arrived at William's. She helped me plan Adam's death, and she helped me transition to life outside of the world of human trafficking. What did she get for it? A bullet in the head. A bullet by my own hand. Tears streamed down my cheeks and smeared what little makeup I had on.

Pull yourself together! I doubted I had much time left to get ready and I was determined not to give William a reason to go after any more of my friends. I put myself back together, shoved everything into the clothing bag and walked out of the plane with it over my shoulder.

The guard moved aside and allowed me to disembark the plane. The cool morning breeze kissed my cheeks, and even with the rancid smell of pollution, revitalization surged through me. My view did not yield any clues as to where I was, other than another airport. A steady stream of planes landed and took off. The passengers, and workers, came and went without notice of me. Not a single eye turned my way. I was just another invisible person in the sea of the rich. It was no wonder people could be moved around the world with ease and without questions.

Uncomfortable in heels, I grabbed the railing and carefully made my way down the stairs. The short man, in a suit and driver's cap, held the car door open. I stepped away from the last step, and expected the young guard to be right behind me. Instead, he had started to pull up the stairs to close himself in. The engine of the plane rumbled to life.

I contorted my body into the vehicle so that I would not bust through the seams of the outfit. The skirt was a little tight and hugged me close.

William inspected me. "Good."

"I look like socialite Barbie puked all over me. What is going on? Why do I look like this?"

Before William could answer, the driver had gotten into the car and sat in front of me. My eyes squinted as I took in this unusual information. I looked around the vehicle and noticed there was no steering wheel on the left side. "Wait, why is he...?" Pieces started to come together. The long flight meant we were not in North America. A driver on the opposite side of the car meant we were likely somewhere in Europe from what I could recall from school. I didn't think I had been asleep for twenty-four hours, so the flight wasn't long enough to be in Australia or New Zealand. William's father, Douglas, had grown up in England. A falling-out had relocated him to the United States. That meant William likely had family who remained in England. Who better to shelter you from the police than a criminal family?

My chest tightened and my breathing laboured. I had hoped I would have ended up somewhere alone with William. A small island. Some quaint little town. William was often different when we were alone and there would be plenty of opportunity for me to finish what I had started. I hadn't thought about the possibility William would showcase the woman who had caused his Los Angeles network to crumble. If he had brought me to his family, I was either being led to the slaughter, in an expensive blue dress, or William had another devious plan up his sleeve.

CHAPTER NINE

The car pulled out of the airport, the luxurious brown leather stuck to the underside of my legs. I cursed myself for being so stupid. I had been in danger with William, but I had taken him on before and survived. I believed I would be able to do so again. However, now I faced the unknown of his family. They would know I killed Adam and not be keen to keep me alive.

I was in an unfamiliar country and about to face a new set of monsters.

William nudged my arm with a bottle of water, the plastic cool against my skin. The cap fought back and I struggled to get it open. William took the bottle back, easily cracked the seal and I gulped down half the bottle.

"You will be fine." William said softly. The change in his tone caught me off guard.

"Fine. How exactly am I going to be fine? And why am I wearing this...this outfit. I am surprised I don't have one of those funny little hats on."

William laughed. I had seen him laugh a few times in L.A., back when I thought there might have been a heart under his cruel exterior. I had been proven wrong, and I wasn't going to be mistaken again.

"What's so funny?"

"You are." He unsuccessfully hid a smirk behind his hand. "You do look a little absurd and the outfit does not match your attitude."

"Please tell me I don't have to act like some sort of lady or whatever women are called here. You and I both know I would not be able to pull that off."

"Do I! However, as I said, you need to be on your best behaviour. No hate-filled or snarky remarks. My family, like some wealthy Britons, are very protective of their status and try hard to find fault with everyone. I need them to like you. At least for now."

"Wait...What? Why would you need them to like me? Do they not know what I have done?" My mind raced with questions. Who did they think I was? What the hell was happening?

"They know Adam is dead. But not how. They know what happened to me. But not who did it."

"Why?"

"If you told your family, who entrusted you with a billion dollar business, that you failed because a cop got the better of you, how would you look? Not only would you be chastised, you would be set to the most menial and pointless tasks, never to be trusted again. As far as my family is concerned, Kevin turned on me because of his relationship with Whitney, and he convinced Jack to join him to bring me down. The family knows nothing about you, and will only know what I tell them."

Fields of green hills rolled past as I let what William said sink in. William, the skilled liar and manipulator, had kept close to the truth. Kevin and Jack had turned on him. Although, their deaths meant I would never know why. Now, William needed me on his side in order to maintain his rank in the family. This could work in my favour. It meant I would not be locked up like a full-fledged prisoner. I took a deep breath and let an ounce of relief come over me. I was confident I was somewhat safe, for the time being.

"If they don't know what I did, who do they think I am?"

"They don't know you are here."

"Unexpected visitors are always appreciated, I'm sure. Sorry, less snarky, right. But, they know you are coming?"

"Yes. But my original plan was not to bring a guest." The revenge William wanted for his brother's death lurked behind his blue eyes. A shiver went down my spine as he continued, "I had made travel arrangements...well...before..." He pointed at my stomach and I guarded it with my hand. "Now, we are just going to have to play it off as a surprise."

"And does your family like surprises?"

"Not exactly."

"I didn't think so. You want your family to like me, but they are not going to like the fact I have shown up unannounced. How exactly am I to get them on my side?" The last thing I wanted to do was help William, but I knew I would be better off, if I played along.

William fussed with his suit jacket, "I will tell them you are my girlfriend."

My jaw dropped and my eyes widened, "Your girlfriend? Ha! You said it yourself back in L.A, you knew who everyone was that walked through your door. Am I to believe your family would be any different?" I did not know what William was playing at, but I could not believe he actually thought the girlfriend ruse would work.

William's hand touched mine and spiders tickled my skin. I pulled away.

"Olivia, it has been a very unforeseen eight hours for both of us. Right now, what we both need to do is convince my family we are in a relationship. If you have a better plan where you are not immediately killed, and my future is not ruined by the one person who can make or break me, I'm listening."

The hurt in William's voice made me turn to him. A pull inside me urged me to reach out and comfort him, but I quickly pushed it aside. William was an expert at appearing genuine but inside he was cold as ice. I reminded myself the fake relationship was only a stepping stone on a path to freedom.

"What do you need me to do?"

This time I ignored the spiders and allowed William to take my hand in his.

"Just be as quiet as you can and show an ounce of affection towards me. And only an ounce. The good news is, showing one's true emotions, or affection, are rare in this family. Unless it is anger or disdain. So you should not have to do much."

My palms leaked and I wiped them on my skirt. "Oh, well, that sounds easy enough. I mean, pretend to love the man who took my sister from me. Sure, no problem." Tears pricked my eyes. One escaped, William noticed and wiped it away. He held my chin.

"This is not easy for me either. I would rather strangle the very last breath out of you, but for now I need you alive. To keep you that way, we both need to put on this charade. Do you think you can do that?"

I didn't answer. William's grip on my chin tightened. "Well?" .

I pushed his hand away, "Yes."

"Good, because here we are."

CHAPTER TEN

G iven the luxurious accommodations in Los Angeles, I was not surprised to find the same, or greater, here in England. Large, immaculately cut fields of emerald green hugged the brown gravel path we drove down. A large cream house in the distance reminded me of the Von Trapp family home. At least the one in the movie, and with more of a modern take on ancient Roman architecture. However, I doubted there would be a family sing-along in this house.

Near some brush was a pond with a couple of ducks, and a vast forest blocked my view past it. Secluded, just how William liked to keep his prey. I rested my head against the back of my seat and tried to pull myself together. In moments, I would have to pretend to be in love with a man I loathed.

William broke the silence, "Welcome to Hammond Manor."

Of course the place had a name. I closed my eyes so William could not see them roll. I shot straight up in a panic. The house was gigantic. How many people lived there? I foolishly thought I would meet one, maybe two relatives. It was highly unlikely only a couple of people lived in the mansion that towered over us. Was this place like William's? Did they work women here too?

"William, how many people am I about to put on a show for?"

"That all depends on how many guests Aunt Helen, Lady Hammond to you, by the way, has, at the moment. Typically, there could be anywhere from four to fifteen people, not including the servants. Last time I was here, there were at least ten of them."

"So just a couple of people then."

William shuffled over and leaned against me, his lips close to my ear, as he too looked up at the mansion. "You managed to stab me in the back with a fire poker, burn down my house, and plan my brother's murder. I think you can handle this lot."

William was right. I had made it through hell. I may not have completely escaped it, but determination and perseverance got me through once and it would get me through again. I had taken down part of Hammond's network, maybe I could do it again?

The driver pulled around a large, ornate fountain and stopped at the front door. Beefy gentlemen dressed in black suits, with ear pieces, opened both passenger doors. I said a little prayer, swung my legs around, and grabbed the offered hand of the man in front of me.

Unlike the smell of pollution at the airport, the country air was filled with the smell of flowers, freshly mowed grass and the occasional waft of animals. Had my situation been different, it would have been quite enjoyable.

Instead, I was in an unknown nightmare. Before me, in a straight line, stood four men, ranging in ages and sizes. I presumed they were butlers, or whatever fancy word the British had for them. The line continued with five maids who were a range of diversity, and just off the parking area, beside a well-trimmed hedge, were a handful of gardeners who balanced themselves on rakes and shovels. They appeared to be around to watch the show of our arrival and not part of the reception party.

An older butler stepped forward, bowed slightly, and formally addressed William, "Mr. Hammond, it is nice to see you again."

"You as well, Caldwell."

A slim woman in her sixties emerged with a flourish, and hurried down the three front steps. She wore a royal blue pegged dress, her dark brown hair tied back into a stylish low bun. The unexpectedness of my presence caused her steps to falter, but she recovered. Her green eyes pierced mine and she stopped in front of me, looked me over, and continued to William. They cordially embraced.

"Now, William, who do we have here?" Her British accent cut like a knife.

I mustered a smile, rather than the sneer I wanted to deliver.

"Aunt Helen, this is Olivia. I apologize I did not advise you she would be joining me. It worked out at the last minute and then I thought it might be a nice surprise."

"Surprise indeed. I don't have a room made up for her, but I suppose Charlotte can put something together before dinner."

A young woman with toasty topaz eyes, in a black and white maids uniform, stepped forward in response. Her blond hair was tightly pulled back, not a hair out of place.

"That will not be necessary. Olivia can stay with me," William said.

Share a room! William said nothing about cohabitating. Yet, it made perfect sense. How else would he monitor my every move, make sure I kept up the charade and didn't try to escape?

"Well, if she must," Helen said.

"It's 2019, not 1919. One would think there would be less judgment around two people in a relationship sharing a room."

"No judgment," Helen replied. "You had not mentioned Olivia before and with everything that happened in Los Angeles, I had not realized you had time for a girlfriend." With that, she turned on her heels and walked back into the house.

Had Helen not been a Hammond, I may have respected her tenacity. However, I could tell she was not to be trifled with. It would be an uphill battle to get this woman to like me, even a minuscule amount.

William placed his hand on my lower back, which garnered a small twitch. If he noticed, there was no acknowledgement. My skirt confined my legs and only allowed for small steps. We slowly made our way into a large reception hall and I was amazed at the opulence. Five or more of my apartments could fit in this one room. Large black and white marble floors were accented by black diagonal lines. A large, round, wooden table with claw feet stood in the middle of the room, a vase of flowers in the center.

Golden papered walls, decorated with a white Egyptian design, encased us. Four closed wooden doors lined both sides of the room. Two large gold-framed mirrors, on opposite walls, hung above sets of blue suede chairs. A grand staircase, which split into two on the second level, stood tall at the far side of the room. Red carpet drew the beholder's eye. All of this had been paid for on the backs of women who had been kidnapped, raped and murdered. I could never forget that.

I remembered feeling small when I first walked into William's L.A mansion, but it was incomparable to the grandness of where I stood. I was amazed at how the rich fed their egos by amassing space and things they didn't need.

Helen stopped beside the stairs and turned towards us, "I am sure you are tired after the lengthy flight. I have to take care of some business, so why don't you two make yourself comfortable and get some rest. I will see you for dinner." A large arched entryway behind the stairs swallowed her.

William led me up the carpeted stairs. My legs weak with trepidation, I gripped the wooden banister for stability. Caldwell followed behind us with another man. Both carried luggage I hadn't seen before. The second floor only had one door open, at the end of a long hallway.

We were welcomed by warm rays of sunlight which beamed in from the six casement windows that ran along two sides of the room. They were adorned with heavy cream-coloured curtains that had a blue floral pattern. Beautiful antique artwork hung on all of the walls. There was a small sitting area with a chaise and armchair which matched the blue in the curtains. I looked at the one bed and took in its small size, for such a large room. It appeared to be a queen, at best. Caldwell opened a pair of wooden doors and he and the other man walked in. I craned my neck and my eyes followed them. The luggage was placed onto benches in the middle of a closet half the size of the bedroom itself. Finished their task, Caldwell and the man bowed to William and left.

"What do you think?" William asked.

"It's nice. For another prison."

"It is nice, isn't it?" William's eyes turned a familiar cold, "Unless you would prefer the stables. Or in the ground. Either could be arranged."

"Both could be more comfortable than sharing this space with you."

William rushed over to me, grabbed my shoulders and slammed me against the wall. The back of my head bounced off it. "I could have killed you, but I didn't. Just because I need something from you at the moment does not mean you have any power. You are in a house full of people skeptical of you. Especially Aunt Helen. It would not take much to have everyone turn a blind eye while I finish what I started. Child and all."

The colour drained from my face and I opened my mouth but no words came out.

"Mine or not, the child is not your saviour. This family comes before everything else and on occasion sacrifices have to be made." He stepped back. "Do we have an understanding?"

"Yes."

"Good. Now rest and get cleaned up. Someone will come get you for dinner."

Fixated on the subtle cream wallpaper pattern, which danced on the walls in the sunlight, I stood tall and unmoved against the wall. Annoying beeps signaled William had set the alarm clock on the bedside table. It was followed by the release of a zipper's teeth from around a suitcase. Moments later, William left, his arms full of clothes.

I waited until the footsteps faded into nothing. Strength gone, my legs buckled. I slid down the wall, and cried into my knees. I tried to muffle the tears and screams of frustration. Not to protect William, I could care less if his family thought we were an unhappy couple. More to protect myself. If I showed weakness, I would be devoured.

Pent-up emotions released, I tore off my jacket and skirt and climbed into the bed. Exhaustion quickly took over as I was enveloped in the soft covers. The last thing I saw before I entered the world of dreams were the faces of Claire and Whitney. I missed my sister and friend. I hated myself for not saving them.

CHAPTER ELEVEN

T he wail of the alarm clock startled me. In my scramble to figure out how to stop the piercing noise, I had forgotten where I was. The room filled with silence, my head back on the pillow, and the last twenty-four hours rushed back. I felt like the weight of it all pushed me down inside the mattress. But just as that feeling pushed me, I pushed back. I buried the fear and summoned courage. I called on my hatred for the Hammonds to make me steady.

The bed creaked when I swung my legs over the side. My spine and hips popped as I stretched. With purpose and determination I strode to the full-sized ensuite. The luxury of the rest of the house did not stop in the bedroom. I took advantage of the opulent shower and stood under the warm stream of water, from the rainfall showerhead above me, grateful it subsided my morning sickness. When I finally emerged, the desire to crawl back into bed and sleep for days was strong.

With a monogrammed hand towel, I cleared the steam off the large mirror and surveyed myself. The nap and shower had made a remarkable difference from how I looked on the plane. Add my tenacity on top of that, and I started to recognize myself. Small bruises had formed on my arms where William's strong grip had taken hold. Nothing too noticeable, but I noted to cover my arms for dinner. My stomach had started to harden and protrude. I doubted anyone else would notice, unless they looked for it. Even then it was not obvious.

I tapped my fingers on my stomach and, for the first time, spoke to the child inside of me, "Well...this is awkward, given you can't actually understand me, but I heard somewhere talking to you is helpful or something. Maybe it'll be a little cathartic for me, so here it goes. Life has thrown your..." The word mom sat on my tongue and refused to jump, "me...some shitty obstacles, one of which I...well we, are facing right now. Things are going to be scary for a while but I'll do whatever it takes to get out of it. It just means you might be under some stress. So I apologize now, but I might have to take things slow while I make a plan. I can't have your...William...show up at my door again."

"I should probably get ready, but you should know that the fact that you exist is terrifying. Please don't judge me for not understanding how I feel about you. It's not your fault, I just...well you're part me and part...him. The moment that test was positive I lost all hope that I would ever be able to bury the memories of what happened. Knowing that he is now forever with me and seeing how my parents' shitty upbringing impacted how they raised children, haunts me. Don't hate me if I can't love you like I should."

I dropped my hands to my sides and shook them to release the nerves, not only around the pregnancy, but about the entire situation I found myself in.

Wrapped in a grey house coat, from the back of the bathroom door, I stepped into the bedroom and was taken aback. Someone had laid out an outfit on the bed and shoes on the floor under it. I looked in the closet, but no one was there. I was unnerved to know that someone had walked in and I had been unaware. Had they heard what I had said?

A barely audible knock at the door interrupted my thoughts. Was I late for dinner? I turned the brass doorknob and the young blonde maid from my arrival stood before me with an innocent smile. Charlotte? Yes, Charlotte.

"Miss Olivia, I am here to help you get ready for dinner."

"Thank you for the offer, but I am sure I can manage on my own." I started to close the door but her hand fought against it.

"I am sure you could Miss, however, Lady Hammond would be quite upset if I don't. You don't want to make her upset."

"Well, alright. Come in."

Charlotte entered carrying a small black case, and walked over to the wood vanity that sat in front of one of the windows. She unzipped the case and started to remove creams, make-up and brushes to apply them with.

"Once you have your undergarments on, come sit over here and I will help you with your hair and make up. Then we will get you into that dress. It looks like it might be a bit tricky with the lace. You don't want to snag it."

So Charlotte was the mystery intruder. I didn't know why, but I felt a little better. With discretion, I put on the bra and underwear. It was unnerving that they fit perfectly. I re-wrapped myself in the housecoat and sat on the small stool facing the oval vanity mirror.

Charlotte tugged my hair into a simple up-do. She turned me around and got to work with the make-up. The brush strokes were softer than her skills with a comb. It was my first night here, but I couldn't pass up the opportunity to gather information.

"How long have you worked for the Hammonds?"

"Three years."

"Do you enjoy it?"

"As much as anyone can enjoy being ordered around and looked down upon. But, I need to work, so here I am."

"Helen does seem very...what's the word?"

"Demanding, strong-willed, nasty?"

"I was going to say uptight, but let's go with those."

We smiled at each other.

Was Charlotte just a good actor who wanted to lull me into a false sense of security? Could she be an ally?

"Do you help her get ready as well?"

"Rarely. Lady Hammond is shockingly self-sufficient when it comes to her beauty regime. She is also very particular about who touches her stuff. At a party, she requested a previous maid bring her a very rare and vintage hand-sewn silk scarf. The maid did as she was told; however, had not thought to transport it in its box or on a clean platter. When Lady Hammond saw that the scarf was draped over the maid's arm, she loudly humiliated her in front of one hundred guests. Apparently, the improper transport of the garment created an unacceptable wrinkle. After the maid was dismissed, Lady Hammond put on the scarf and created her own wrinkles."

"She was fired over a scarf? It's not like she stole it." I shook my head in disbelief.

"Not only was she fired, Lady Hammond actively ensured she couldn't work in domestic service again. That is why you don't want to make her angry."

"Helen is a fan of vendettas, great. Is there anything else I should know about her, or her family? I feel like I barely know William, and yet he has whisked me off to meet everyone. It's a little unnerving."

Blush brush in hand, her elbow rested in the other, a small scar peaked out from her sleeve. Charlotte stared at me for a moment. Her eyes squinted as though she tried to see the real me. "There is a lot you should know."

CHAPTER TWELVE

Charlotte helped me into a maroon, floor-length dress. If she noticed the baby bump, she didn't let on. I felt like I was going to the opera, not a family dinner. It fit well, without being too tight - unlike the awful blue dress from earlier. Charlotte had done a great job at making me look like I belonged here.

Charlotte had gone silent after she had advised me that there was a lot I should know about the Hammonds. She would not answer any of my questions. I needed to get her to talk, but how? I put on the shoes that had been set out for me as Charlotte cleaned up the makeup and hair products. Afraid to sit on the bed and be scolded by Helen for a wrinkle, I paced in a circle.

"Charlotte, you don't know me and likely don't trust me. I get that. Revealing Hammond family secrets would be a fireable offense, and I am not asking for secrets. I guess...well...what I am asking for is just to understand who this family really is. Maybe I'm skeptical, but sometimes I feel like William puts on a facade and I don't actually know him. Everything is moving so fast. I just want to make sure I'm not getting in over my head, if that makes sense."

The teeth of the zipper on the make-up bag stopped chattering, "We don't have much time. I have to get you to dinner."

"Please, just give me something. Am I safe?"

Charlotte's topaz eyes turned sad, and she rubbed her apron between her hands, "No."

"No! Why?"

"I can't."

I would have to risk Charlotte was a test sent by Helen. How else would I know? I took her hands and gently squeezed, "I know what William does for a living." I would have thought that information would have been more shocking, however Charlotte's eyes remained unchanged.

"I see. And you stay with him?"

"Not exactly."

Now Charlotte's expression changed, "Then why are you here?"

"Let's just say, I did not have much of a choice."

"Oh, so you are William's current favourite? He has never brought one of his workers home before."

So Charlotte knew about the business. This was good. "I don't think he would describe me as a favourite. I used to be...before..."

"Before what?"

"Before, I ruined his life." I could see questions formed in her mind, but would she ask them?

"How?"

I pointed to my stomach. If Charlotte was a trap, Helen would find out about the pregnancy anyways so I had not completely jeopardized William's plan. Whatever that was.

"You're pregnant?" her feigned surprise told me she had noticed the bump.

I nodded, "Not exactly on William's to-do list."

Charlotte removed her hands from mine and sat on the vanity stool. "How do I know I can trust you? That you won't tell William or Lady Hammond what I tell you?"

Yes! I had gotten somewhere. I crouched down in front of her. "I could ask you the same questions. I only just met Helen, but I would not put it past her to send you in here to retrieve information. I am an unknown in a family full of secrets." Knots formed in my stomach. "So, here is one of my secrets. William had my sister killed."

"He...oh...I'm so sorry." Her eyes welled with tears.

"Thank you, so do you see why I need to understand this family?"

Charlotte nodded and took a deep breath, "I want to help you. I can help you. How, I can't say. What I will say, tonight, is that you need to be careful. Helen is in charge of everything and she did not get there by being nice. It takes years of work to try and earn her favour, and even then some of us still haven't received it. Do not contradict her, go along with whatever she asks and keep your head down. The less you say, the less likely you will get yourself in trouble."

Time to go all in. "How much do you know about the business?"

"Quite a bit, but I can't get into that now. I need to determine if I trust you before I say anything further. But first, I have to get you to the drawing room. You can't be late."

Filled with both dread and excitement, I followed Charlotte down the darkened second floor hallway. The sun had started to set and the lights had yet to be turned on. The shadows cast around me by the large skylight looked like long thin fingers. They reached out to try and capture me but I slipped through each one.

Unease cloaked me. What would dinner entail? How would I meet his expectations, let alone be able to share a room with him? Then there was Helen. We were both unknown to each other and until I could formulate a plan of escape, I needed to heed Charlotte's advice and try to play it safe. I prayed my mouth would not get me in trouble.

My heels clacked loudly on the marble floor of the reception hall. Those in the drawing room would have been signaled about my arrival. We stopped outside a closed wooden door and I steadied my nerves. The turn of a brass door knob and I would enter into a den of monsters.

CHAPTER THIRTEEN

T he drawing room door itself was not intimidating. The occupants
on the other side were. Voices tried to permeate the door, however I
could not make out the words. The tone, on the other hand, was
unmistakable. Anger.

"Ready?" Charlotte asked.

"No, but that won't change anything," I joked, and smoothed out my
dress.

"Just be yourself. They can tell when someone is trying to deceive them.
You won't be aware that they know and they will use that to their
advantage. You don't want that."

"Be myself. That tends to get me into trouble."

Charlotte put her hand on the doorknob, "In that case, don't act like
you are the happiest person in the world. Lady Hammond hates bubbly,
happy-go-lucky people. Especially women. Just be calm, collected and
laugh politely when the moment calls for it."

I nodded in agreement, put a fake smile on my face, and she opened the
door. The room was long, with multiple gathering areas. There was a shiny,
black, grand piano across from where we entered. A green, vintage Chinese
carpet was bordered by hardwood floors. A large, white, stone fireplace
dominated the center of the main wall. The remains of the evening sun
spotlighted it from the floor-to-ceiling windows opposite. At the far end of
the room stood a billiards table.

Charlotte nodded and backed out of the room. Without hesitation, and with my head held high, I crossed to where Helen and William stood. Helen's green eyes tried to bore through me as I got closer. William must have noticed her distraction, as he stopped talking and turned towards me. Despite the anger heard through the door, William's eyes displayed kindness. He smiled and my cheeks became warm and flushed. Why, I don't know. I hated that William had that effect on me sometimes.

"Good evening, Olivia. I trust you slept well?" Helen asked. She had changed into a simple black dress that came just below the knee. Her jewelry was anything but simple. Diamonds danced around her neck and ears.

I stepped beside William, who now wore a sharp, navy blue, plaid suit. His white dress shirt was unbuttoned at the top, as usual, which gave off a casual yet fashionable look. Dark circles had formed under his eyes and told me he had not rested since arriving.

"I did, thank you."

"Good. William, you should get our guest a drink." Helen pointed to a gold drink cart beside the fireplace.

"Yes. Right." William left me with Helen. He picked up a bottle of vodka, unscrewed the cap and looked at his aunt. With her eyes focused on me, William promptly screwed the cap back on, not a drop had entered the glass. Instead, he filled it with contents from a metal pitcher. "Here you are."

The smell of whiskey on William's breath had grown stronger and told me he had continued his adventures with alcohol while I napped. How I longed for the memory-erasing effects of liquor.

"Thank you." Lemonade.

Helen sat down in a Granny Smith apple-green, silk upholstered, carved walnut chair. William and I took our cue and sat inches apart on a small red couch. Helen sat with the bearing of a woman used to prestige. Straight back, ankles crossed and hands folded around the glass in her lap. I tried to mirror her, as best I could. William slouched forward and rested his arms on his legs. His drink swirled as a distraction.

"William tells me you are Canadian, and that you met while he was working in Toronto. Tell me about that." Helen's crystallized eyes threw unseen daggers at me.

"Aunt Helen, I told you -" William said.

"I want her to tell me."

William kept his eyes on his drink. He appeared small. Powerless. I had only seen William like this on two occasions. Neither had other people present. My heart rate quickened. We had not coordinated a story and it would be my fault if Helen learned everything was a ruse. The longer I took to answer, the worse it would be, so I shared the first thing that came to mind.

"We met in Toronto, yes. A Hollywood meet-cute, as they say. I was being attacked by a vicious and vindictive man, and then, out of nowhere, came William. I heard his bellowing voice first, commanding the man to stop." I wanted to look at William for a cue I was on the right track, but decided better of it. "William pulled the man off of me, and while he dealt with him, one of his men stepped in to make sure I was okay. I was battered, but nothing was broken. When William returned, his kind blue eyes were filled with worry. I always found it weird when people said they had fallen in love at first sight. Now, I am not saying that was what happened, but it was definitely something. Something I had never experienced before." I rested my hand on William's arm. "On a whim, or maybe a desire to get out of the city I was attacked in, I agreed to go to L.A. with him. Now here we are." My lungs refused to breathe.

Helen's face was unchanged. Not a twinge of a reaction to let me know whether my story matched William's.

William looked at me with adoration and a hint of shock. A smile spread across his face and a weight lifted off my shoulders.

"Well, you two really do have a unique story. A regular saviour, our William." Helen finished her drink, stood, and, as she made herself another one, continued, "William also tells me I am to treat you like family." She loomed over us, "I do not treat people I do not know as family. So I will tolerate the fact you are here, until which time I deem you are worthy. You will also address me as Lady Hammond, as I am not your Aunt."

The door at the far end of the room opened and Caldwell, with perfect posture, walked in.

"Lady Hammond, dinner is served."

With Helen's back to us, I let out a sigh of relief as William helped me to my feet. I had passed test number one. Now for test number two. Dinner.

The dining room was an homage to the Hammond family. The dark-green walls were evenly covered with gold-gilded frames of all sizes. Each with a portrait of a different person. A single light mounted above each one. The paintings were all labeled and it did not take me long to find Douglas Hammond. He was prominently featured above the fireplace. Douglas sat on horseback in a black military dress uniform, a red stripe down the pant leg. His chest was adorned with medals and golden tassels. I was sure there was a proper name for them, but hell if I knew what it was. Douglas looked regal and I felt his dark eyes follow me as I moved around the room.

Across from Douglas' painting was Helen's. She was seated on a wooden throne, whose claw feet looked as though they dug into the platform it sat on. Her fiery red hair was accented by a diamond tiara lined with emeralds. The white dress she wore showcased matching emerald beading. Was it the fact one had to pose for hours, for a portrait, that the subjects never smiled? Or was it just Helen's natural demeanor?

A long wooden table filled the middle of the room and had twenty-two green and silver damask upholstered chairs seated around it. The green from the chairs matched the walls. A silver table runner sat in the middle of the table and was adorned with large crystal candelabras and an assortment of flowers. As with the drawing room, floor to ceiling windows took most of one side of the room, each framed with gold curtains. A set of French doors had been opened to let in the warm evening air. The fireplace was stocked with wood, but was unlit.

William held out a chair for me opposite Helen's painting. I would have her eyes on me from two different locations. Helen sat to my right. William took a place opposite me.

No additional guests joined us, which meant I could focus my attention on Helen, and do my best to make her believe I was in love with her nephew. However, it also meant her attention would not be taken up by others. William tried to steer the conversation away from me a couple times, but gave up after he was not successful. Why had he not prepared me for the questions I would get peppered with? Sweat built up in the crevasse of my back with each lie I told.

"Tell me, before William whisked you away to the sunset strip, how did you contribute to this world?"

"Well...I..."

"Spit it out girl!"

"I had been the Chief Operating Officer at a financial firm but found it wasn't right for me. Too stuffy. A couple of years ago, I switched paths and started to work with some charities. I worked to acquire new donors while keeping up relationships with existing ones."

Helen sliced her chicken and pursed her lips, "I see. Keeping the old clients satisfied, while finding ways to tempt new ones. Interesting. I am surprised you condoned William's line of work. Most women don't."

Okay, I was to know about the family business. That was good. "When I first found out, I wasn't. I was quite livid. In fact, I still don't approve of women being held captive and forced to have sex with the highest bidder."

"But you stayed?"

"I was only in L.A. for three months, before...everything fell apart. William said he would consider making some changes, so I gave him the benefit of the doubt."

"He did, did he? And how kind of you," she said. "Speaking of falling apart, William, exactly what happened? How could you let things get so out of hand?"

I was glad for the reprieve from the interrogation. I was also curious how William would respond. He was on his fourth drink since I had come downstairs and was visibly drunk. Would he be able to hold his tongue?

"As I mentioned when I called, Adam's death must have tipped the scales, as Jack and Kevin changed teams." He looked at me and continued, "All they told me, when I found them after the fire, was that they could no longer take the needless deaths or the mistreatment of the women by the guests." He turned to Helen, "After 10 years of hurt and death, much at their own hands, they each must have started to grow a conscience. Then, a new woman I had brought in started to stir up trouble. Working with Kevin, they quickly convinced the women to rebel and, next thing I know, my brother is dead."

Helen rapped her fingernails on the tabletop, "And you saw none of this coming? Unacceptable."

"I was focused on mending fences with guests after Adam destroyed our reputation. The less-than-ideal-caliber party he hosted, while I was away, had our regular, wealthier clientele spooked. Even with blackmail, I had a hard time convincing most of the guests to return. But I did. It was at that time that all of the deception and betrayal happened. I was wrong to trust Jack and Kevin. I take full responsibility."

Helen turned to me, "And you knew nothing of what was planned?"

I slowed my chewing to provide more time for me to think of a response. Helen's eyes widened with an expectation of urgency. I swallowed, "No. The women and I didn't really get along. Not that I didn't try. I got the feeling they thought of me as an enemy who would report back to William. They were very tight-lipped when I was around. I understood they were not living the life they wanted, so I decided to stay clear of them. Let them have what little freedom they could get."

Helen's eyes squinted slightly. She must have been satisfied, as she turned back to William. "Now, how exactly did that house burn down? That's thirty-six million dollars in insurance that we will never see, because of the police investigation. I thought you had the police taken care of?"

Caldwell came in with another bottle of wine, poured some for Helen, then before I could put my hand over top of my glass, it had been filled. He placed the bottle on the table and left. Alcohol had not crossed my lips since I had found out I was pregnant. As there was no mention of the baby, I presumed Helen was unaware. William shifted his eyes towards my glass. I guess I would have to keep up another charade. I took a small sip and let the flavour dance on my tongue before I swallowed. Given the immense amount of alcohol I had consumed in L.A. my taste buds savoured the moment and called for more. I ignored the temptation to finish the glass.

William addressed Helen's questions, "The women all attacked me at dinner one night. Knowing Kevin and Jack were on their side, I suspect they had no fear. One of them stabbed me in the back with a fire-poker and then knocked me unconscious. When I came to, the house was engulfed in flames. I barely made it out the back alive. I scrambled down the hill before the fire was out and the scene searched."

William finished off his whiskey and poured himself some wine, "Thankfully, everyone thought I had died in the fire. Unfortunately, no amount of threats to the fire inspector worked and I had no leverage. When the final report was issued, he noted a body had not been recovered. As for the police, those I had wrapped up tried to bury it, but Detective Teller wouldn't give up. She reminds me of someone else I know." He squeezed Helen's hand, but looked at me. "No matter what anyone threw at her, she kept digging. So it was announced that I was alive."

"I guess it is a good thing American news does not get much attention over here. I should only have to do a little bit of damage control with our good friends at Interpol and MI5. Not to mention, giving your cousin a heads-up just in case something comes across his desk at the defense department. I suspect the Americans will try and exercise their power to have you extradited." Helen patted the hand that was on hers, "But I will take care of it."

"Thank you, Aunt Helen." William sounded like a child who had been caught stealing a cookie before dinner.

"What is family for? At any rate, it is good to have you here. The business on this side of the ocean is expanding rapidly. We need all the help we can get."

William perked up with the news he would not be cut out of the business. "Happy to help. Whatever you need."

"Right now, I need a cigarette. Shall we retire to the parlor? I could get Caldwell to play the piano."

"I think Olivia and I might head upstairs. It has been a long day, and with the jet lag, we should probably get as much sleep as we can. We want to be fully functional tomorrow." William didn't wait for a response. He got up from the table, buttoned his jacket and came and pulled my chair out for me.

"Good night," I said.

Helen mumbled and poured herself some more wine. Caldwell stood at attention outside the door. He entered the dining room, and moments later walked out, with Helen on his arm. Both entered the parlour. When William and I were halfway up the stairs, piano music filled the air. It was beautiful, and if I could be that song I would have been happy. But I was not a song and I was not happy. I was a woman heading to bed with a man I loathed.

CHAPTER FOURTEEN

The lights on the bedside tables were on and the comforter turned down. A pair of silk pajamas had been folded and placed on each side of the bed. William's blue, mine cream. Without a word, William grabbed his pair and went into the closet, closing the door most of the way. I took mine into the bathroom.

It took a while, but I managed to work myself out of the dress. I could have called William for help, but the last thing I wanted were his hands touching me. The silk felt soft against my skin and freeing compared to the other chosen outfits of the day. I opened the bathroom door but remained and brushed my teeth. William entered and looked unphased by the interrogation at dinner. We stood at his-and-her sinks in silence. I avoided his gaze in the mirror, unsure what was expected of me next.

The silence continued as we exited the bathroom. William propped himself up on his pillow. I stared out into the abyss that was the bed, the blankets ready to ensnare me, like thick, unruly vines. I had already been as close to William as I wanted to be, throughout the evening. The thought of lying beside him appalled me. Instead, I grabbed a pillow and used the blanket strewn across the back of the couch to form a makeshift bed.

"What are you doing?"

"I'll sleep on the couch," I tossed the two throw pillows on the floor. "I am small enough it should still be comfortable."

"Why would you do that?"

"Are you serious? Why would I want to share a bed with you?"

"It's just a bed."

"Bah, just a bed."

"You can't sleep over there. The walls have eyes, trust me, Aunt Helen will find out." He patted the bed beside him.

Somehow, I knew he was right. I begrudgingly picked up the pillows from the floor and placed them back into position. I climbed into the bed, my arms still wrapped around the bed pillow, and held close to my body for comfort. I stared straight ahead, and the colours of the room melted into darkness.

I had been beside William most of the time since leaving Toronto, yet sitting beside him in bed caused my chest to tighten and I couldn't breathe. Scenes from the last time we shared a bed flashed before me.

I must have held my breath while the long scene replayed, as the next thing I knew, William had his hands on my shoulders and shook me violently, "Olivia, are you alright? Breathe!"

I exhaled a loud, long breath and coughed. My lungs tried to remember how to breathe.

"What happened? You became rigid and it was like you couldn't hear me calling your name." William started to rub my back. I twisted away from his touch and he removed his hand.

"I...I didn't hear you," I continued to take deep breaths and tried to slow my heartbeat. "I don't know what happened. I just...froze."

William had a faint look of hurt on his face. But, as quickly as it was there, it was gone. I wasn't sure what he had to be sad about. I was the one traumatized and had turned into a statue upon entering his bed.

William changed the subject, "You did well tonight. Really well. I thought it was all lost when Aunt Helen asked you about how we met. But you pulled through." William stared at the closed curtains. Charlotte, or someone else, must have closed them when they put out the pajamas.

I released my tight grip on the pillow, my fingers numb. "No help from you, might I add. You should have prepared me for that." I laid down, and brought the covers up to my chin. If the walls had eyes, they would see as little as possible.

"I'm sorry. I knew she would grill you, but I thought she would have waited until breakfast. How did you know what to say?"

"I didn't." I fiddled with the bedding under my chin to release the tension in my body, "I thought it would be best to stay as close to the truth as possible. As for the rest, I just made it up and hoped it worked. I take it our stories are aligned?"

"For the most part. I had added that you had recently lost your sister and that was part of the reason you wanted to leave Toronto. I am sure Aunt Helen will overlook that discrepancy, and chalk it up to you not wanting to talk about it."

I couldn't help myself, "And how did you say Claire died? Did you tell her that you had her killed?"

"What do you think? I said she died in a car crash. In fact, I used the lie you told me about her and the drunk driver going the wrong way on the highway. That should be easy for you to remember."

I longed to hurt William, for what he had done to Claire and I, but I restrained myself. I would bide my time. I needed to be more meticulous if I not only wanted to survive, but take down this part of the Hammond empire. Rather than hurl myself at William, I tightened my grip on the comforter and twisted it to release some of my anger. I would not respond to his bait, instead I moved onto something more important. "What will happen when your aunt does a background check on me and finds out who I really am?"

"I made a call while we were on the plane and had that taken care of. The Olivia Beaumont that she will find was an executive at a firm specializing in community outreach. I made another call when you were just in the bathroom to add the COO part. I really should have known you would take on your sister's life. Not sure how I had not thought of that." He ran his fingers through his hair.

"How did you figure out to use community outreach?

"Lucky guess. I figured, if asked, you would pick something on the opposite side of the spectrum as to what I do for a living."

"Lucky is right. This Olivia you have created is now supposed to be in love with a human trafficker? What in the world would make you think a person like what would..." Then it hit me, William made sure he had an out. "I see. If all of this goes wrong, you can play the whole I was trying to infiltrate the family to expose you and/or save the women. Smart."

"I thought so."

I had to hand it to William, it was a good plan. I hated that he was so adept at being two steps ahead.

"And what do I say when she asks me the same question I had?"

"You already laid the foundation tonight, when you talked about hoping I would change and go legitimate. Add in something about it being lucrative if the women had a choice to come or go. Hopefully, she will believe you."

"Do you think she will buy that?"

"I think she will question it, but I don't think she will worry too much about it."

Somehow I doubted Helen would dismiss me so easily. I had one more question that had been eating away at me since the night of the fire in L.A. "So back in L.A. you knew who I was the whole time, why would you bring me there at all or even let me live for that matter?"

"I was wondering when you were going to ask me that. You aren't the first cop to get caught up in our business and I doubt you will be the last. Most try to fight back; infiltrate the inner workings; or try to escape. Invariably they gave up and fell in line at Adam's hands. You are the only one who didn't become defeated. So when Smith called me to give his report, I decided to take matters into my own hands. I'm sure part of it, really, was to show Adam who was boss, as well."

"Then why were you, well, relatively - I hate to say it - nice to me? You let me heal when I was hurt. If you wanted to break me, why not force me to continue?"

"Ahh the million dollar question. We couldn't break you the normal way, and you quickly revealed your feisty nature, that I thought I would try another tactic. Ease you into compliance. We see how well that worked out, so I won't be doing that again." William winked and rolled onto his side, his face away from me. "We should get some sleep. Breakfast is at eight o'clock and she will expect us to be there." William turned off his light and slid down under the covers.

I turned over, clicked off my light and stared at the dark walls. I wasn't fully convinced by his answer, but I saw no point in pushing it. I had more important mountains to climb. "William?"

"Yes."

"What happens tomorrow?"

"Tomorrow, we survive."

CHAPTER FIFTEEN

The awkwardness of breakfast matched the moist, heavy air that filled the dining room. Heaviness caused, not by the morning dew that had kissed the top of the grass outside and levitated over the hills, rather, by the palpable discomfort of my presence. The eyes of the portraits put me more at ease than my companions.

We all avoided the eyes of the others as we forced down the food. Each chew, a chore.

Wildlife frolicked on the wet grass, as the songs of birds filtered through the French doors along the back of a warm November breeze. This was a stark contrast to the harsh, bitter cold, winters back home. However, Helen's eyes brought winter indoors, as I waited for the icicle stare to pierce me.

Once the food had been cleared, Helen spoke, "William, darling, your cousin Jasper will be here shortly. Why not take him on a hunt and catch up?"

"Oh...Well...It has been years since I have hunted, and it would be nice to see that bastard again. Um...What will you and Olivia do?" The irony of his words were not lost on me. William was always on the hunt. Today would just be different prey.

"I thought we would enjoy the fall day out by the pool. Maybe we will plan your welcome home party. It's been ten years since you spent any significant time here and there will be plenty of people who will want to see what you have become."

"I don't need a party."

"Nonsense. If you wish to be a part of the business here, or anywhere in Europe, you need to pay your dues. Those dues include reacquainting yourself with our business partners and guests over here. I could send you to Asia, but the customs there are even more formal than anything I could put together here."

"Fine, but please keep it simple."

"When have I ever been simple?"

William sighed, "Never." He tucked in his tall-backed chair under the table, kissed the cheek Helen had stuck out for him, and then kissed the top of my head. "Find a jacket to stay warm. Be nice, Aunt Helen."

"I am always nice."

Just like that, I was alone with the green eyes that I swore saw right through people's souls. Helen and I grabbed some jackets that hung by the back door. I drowned in the oversized black fabric that fell to my knees and well past my hands. I found comfort in being swallowed inside a shell; it felt like a shield of protection, although I doubted it would help.

We were greeted by a cloudy grey sky and the buzz of insects in the lush trees. The long walk, past a large building which matched the paladin decor of the main house, felt like I was being led to the gallows. With Helen and I alone, it felt as if a noose would tighten around my neck with her every word.

The patio was anything but simple, like the rest of the house. It featured an oversized pool lined with lounge chairs on one side. The sight of the water rippling in the breeze caused the hairs on my arms, and the back of my neck, to stand on end despite the warm jacket. I steadied my heartbeat and walked as far away from the edge as possible without walking into the wooden pergola or it's contents; a wicker and glass table and chair set for twelve. Helen walked past the table and sat down on a large brown patio couch with teal pillows. I chose a couch opposite her. The more distance the better.

We may have just finished breakfast; however, Caldwell brought out a tray of treats, some tea and wine. Caldwell poured Helen some wine, while I poured myself some tea. I swore there was a twitch of a smile hidden in the crease of his mouth. It went unacknowledged by Helen, who with a curt nod sent Caldwell and his flapping black tails away.

We were not alone, not really. Guards were positioned at the corners of the building and a team passed by on a sweep of the grounds, the occasional wrist brought to a mouth with unheard words.

"You and I have a lot to talk about," Helen said. "For starters, what is a person like you really doing with my nephew?"

"What type of person is that?"

"Charitable people work with us out of ignorance or blackmail. Does William have something on you? Or are you ignorant?"

I was prepared and would not let her words cut me. "I can't speak for William; however, sometimes you can't help who you fall in love with." Helen rolled her eyes and I continued, "However, love doesn't always conquer all. So, as much as I abhor his profession, I thought I might be able to help William change. His business model that is. He has made it perfectly clear he has no plans to leave the business."

"I am glad to see his loyalty has not waned. And what grand changes to our business model will you have William make?"

"Nothing he doesn't want to do, of course. But if the women had a choice in working for you, they would be happier overall. Happy workers are more productive workers, which then leads to larger profits. There is the added bonus of the elimination of bribes or other tactics to keep law enforcement in line."

"Let me see if I understand you, we make our venture legitimate and you think our profits will increase. How do you see that happening if we now have to pay our workers?"

"Less overhead in the precautions to keep everything hidden, or at least untouchable."

"The world is not ready to embrace sex work as a legitimate business, the protests prove it. Besides, it would take all the fun out of the illicit activity. People thrive off their secrets. We thrive off their desires."

"Someone has to be the first to make the change, why not you?"

"You have spunk, I will give you that. What I will not give you, is the ability to weasel your way into this business. For hundreds of years, this family has conquered the forbidden and built an empire doing it. We will not be the ones to pioneer its demise. You can try to change William, but be warned, if he deviates from the path this family is taking, he will no longer be a part of it. As for you, well, we have a way of handling unwanted infestations."

I expected nothing less than a slew of knives thrown at me from the hardened matriarch. I wasn't sure how long before one hit its target. "I wouldn't do anything to endanger William. You are a business woman, evolution is inevitable. The question is, will this family evolve or die off? You saw what happened in L.A."

Helen's eyes widened and her grip tightened on her wine glass, at my own knife being thrown. "You want me to believe that you have the family's best interests in mind, in order for us to make more money, all out of the goodness of your charitable heart?"

"I don't expect you to believe me or the fact I love William and want what's best for him." The words left a vile taste in my mouth. "I also don't expect you to trust me or ever think I'm good enough for him. I'm not blind to the fact that more goes on than just the trafficking of women. In fact, I'm a little afraid of the atrocities this family has committed. But, I also know that inside, William is a good man. A man who had his life shattered when Sharon and Penny were taken from him. A man who, since then, has only known anger and hate. I am not naive enough to think that I can miraculously change him, or the family that made him. But I am smart enough to know that he deserves to be happy, even if sometimes he does not believe that himself. If I can be with him as he discovers this, great. However, I also understand who runs this family. And it isn't William." Helen's eyes transformed from dark to light-green, but their fierceness remained. "I am actually quite impressed that a woman is at the helm of what, I can only presume, is a family filled with men eager to secure power. If you deem me a liability, I know what that means for me. I just ask you to let me live. I am not sure how useful William would be if another loved one died."

Helen twirled her wine glass and sat for a moment in thought. "The night's sleep must have done you well. Your meekness seems to have evaporated."

"I was only doing what I was told last night. William thought, if I showed you any strength, you would be less likely to warm to me. He wanted to play it safe last night, given my unexpected arrival."

"Well, he was right about that." She sipped her wine, "You alluded to other atrocities committed by this family. How much about our business has William informed you of?"

"I was present when he killed Jenna. Given how collected he was when he did so, I would say that wasn't his first kill. We haven't really talked about it, but the illegal nature of your business would also lend itself to arms dealing, drugs, tax evasion, the aforementioned blackmail and God knows what else."

"You have it all figured out don't you?"

"Not really. I'm just not an idiot."

"Apparently not. William's loss of family members aside, whether you live or die is not his choice. So you may want to be smart about how you answer this next question." She topped up her wine glass. "What really happened in L.A.? How did you get out unscathed and William was left behind to burn? It seems a little too convenient."

I had suspected the topic of Los Angeles would return. While William had slept, I had played different responses in my head. Before breakfast, I ran them by William, and we chose the one that he could take the necessary steps to cover our tracks.

"I wasn't at the house at the time. I had made friends with Dr. Boyden's wife and we were having a ladies' night. Dinner and dancing. When I arrived back at the house late that night, the fire trucks were dousing the smoke. Officers on the scene told me what happened. Scared, I went and stayed with the Boydens for a couple of days until I could get on a flight back to Toronto. Dr. Boyden told me what the police were saying about William, his illegal activity, and that he had died. I knew if the LAPD found out about me, I would be considered complicit with his crimes. I went back to my life and pretended nothing had ever happened. I knew William would want it that way. Then, out of the blue, he showed up at my door."

Helen pursed her lips and squinted, "You know I will check up on your story."

"I would do the same if I was in your position."

"If I wasn't so dubious about you, you would be a great asset to this family. You seem to have a head for business, and keep a low profile when needed. The problem is, my gut is usually right, and my gut is telling me you are hiding something."

I needed to divert her attention. If she kept digging she would figure out who I really was. "There is something we haven't told you. Not about the fire, but William wanted to be the one to share the news. I didn't want to overstep, but the later it gets, and the more wine that finds itself out here, you would figure it out anyways." I put down my tea cup and saucer on the table and cupped my stomach with my hands.

Helen took the bait, however there was no change in her tone. "You aren't?"

"Just over three months. Now, you have to act surprised when William tells you."

"Three months means..."

"The night before the fire. Fortuitous that he survived and can now rebuild a family."

Helen finished her wine and stared at me. Her face was just as cold as it was when we sat down. "Is it his?"

"Yes. Although, I understand your skepticism. William also wants to ensure he is the father and said he would make arrangements to get a DNA test done as soon as he finds a doctor."

"I see. Well, we will have to make that happen immediately." She pulled out her phone from a pocket in her pantsuit and started to type. "I guess that explains the lack of drinking last night."

"You noticed."

"I notice everything."

No matter what I tried, Helen would not loosen up. Time to play to her ego.

"May I ask how you have successfully managed to maintain control of everything? And keep the men in line? I doubt the world is any different over here, and where I come from it is rare for men to like women in complete power."

Helen looked me over. "Fear. Respect. Loyalty. In that order. If people do not fear the consequences, they will not respect the power and then there is no loyalty. My father taught Douglas and I that at an early age. We never forgot it. Did William tell you much about his father?"

"A bit. Seems to be a sore spot, so I haven't pushed him."

"Best not. Douglas is not to be mentioned around here and that is the last we will speak his name."

I poured myself some more tea and bit into a biscuit, the crumbs falling into my lap. "How did you come to run this empire?"

"Some things are family secrets, but it would help you to understand what I am capable of. This way, you can do away with any lofty ideas about what power you and William could achieve. Especially if that child does turn out to be his."

"I assure you-"

"Many people have assured me many things in the past. They now reside at the bottom of the Thames river."

I sipped my tea and shook the tea cup a little to feign fear. Helen smiled and continued, "I was not meant to run the family business. My role had been made very clear to me early on. I was to marry a rich and influential man, preferably interested in politics. He would then work to keep the family name off any government or law enforcement list. I obeyed and my husband complied with the tasks my father set. Then, my brother was banished, and father could not find a male relative he felt confident to leave the business to, should he die. He even considered my husband, but quickly realized his feeble mind would not be up to the task. Jonathan also did not have the stomach for the more gruesome part of our line of work. It took me two years to convince my father I was worthy enough. A woman was worthy enough. The things I had to do would make your skin crawl."

Helen finished off her wine. "Father became unwell and the jostling for power began. Relatives turned on each other to get ahead. In the end, after services rendered, and backroom deals made for what little soul I had, I killed my husband."

I choked on my tea at the unexpected information. "You...wait...why?" I wasn't surprised Helen was capable of murder. I was surprised she had revealed as much so quickly.

"For years, he had one affair after the other. The Hammond name was at risk of being disgraced. A name he vowed to take and uphold. Father was devastated at what I had let happen. Rightfully so. Not only was the Hammond name in jeopardy, but so was my father's legacy. Killing Jonathan showed that I would let nothing stand in the way of my family. Nothing."

Helen held my stare. "I was also now feared by those vying for power."

"I see. And no one has tried to take it from you since?"

"Tried, yes. Someone is always trying. But I have little birds everywhere. I get to the traitors before they get to me."

Her words hung heavy in the air. William was right. The walls would have eyes. I would need to be extremely careful about what I said and did if I wanted to stay out of the river.

CHAPTER SIXTEEN

The dark, grey clouds, which had threatened rain all morning, opened up. Large, cold drops pummeled the ground, as well as Helen and me. We ran inside before an outfit change would be required. Caldwell, on the other hand, was drenched, after he cleared up the remnants of our time on the patio.

Helen would not let me out of her grasp so easily, and we spent the time before lunch in the drawing room. Similar to in the parlour and dining room, a large marble fireplace encompassed most of a bright yellow wall. Today it was aflame. This room was smaller, but could easily have sat ten people scattered on antique furniture. With the location change, I distracted myself with one of the books that had been lying around. Helen had pressed me for information about my life back in Canada and, once she was satisfied she had gotten all she could out of me, we had sat in silence. For hours.

Caldwell knocked, stood at attention and announced lunch was ready. For a house so large, I had only seen four rooms of it. Laughter emanated from the back of the house and stopped Helen and I in our tracks. The source of the sound was revealed when William and another waterlogged figure emerged. Their hunting gear had turned a dark brown, almost black, from the rain.

"Olivia, this is cousin Jasper. Jasper, this is Olivia," said William. The smile on his face appeared genuine. It was a little off-putting and yet welcome.

Jasper stood a touch taller than William, leaner, and his black-rimmed glasses matched his curly dark hair, which peeked out from under a green, tweed, flat cap. The only family resemblance I saw was the mischievousness in his black eyes. A hint of kindness, followed by a dash of danger. Jasper stepped forward, extended his hand and then kissed the top of the one I gave him.

"So this is the new blood around here. Welcome. Please forgive my appearance." Jasper performed a small bow.

My cheeks warmed at his Scottish accent and charmed smile. "It is nice to meet you."

Helen was less impressed, "You two look like drowned rats, and you are forming puddles on my beautiful floors. Go and change for lunch. But be quick about it. We are not going to wait long. CHARLOTTE!"

Jasper tipped his hat and stumbled when William pushed him forward, to get him moving.

Charlotte arrived, out of breath. "Lady Hammond?"

"Get this mess cleaned up immediately!"

"Yes, Lady Hammond. Right away." She turned and headed back from where she came, without acknowledgement of my presence.

"Well, let's go have a drink while we wait." The echo of Helen's heels bounced off the walls.

Lunch had been laid out on the table. Salad, chicken sandwiches and some tarts for dessert were all displayed on tiered trays. I was famished, but refrained until I was told. Instead, I filled up on water.

Thankfully, it did not take William long to return. His hair was a messy wet mop, however he had exchanged the hunting outfit for khaki slacks and a black polo sweater over a white shirt. He gave me a half-hearted smile, poured himself a whiskey and, as he had at the other meals, sat opposite me. Jasper trailed in and I couldn't help but laugh.

"Am I really that funny looking?" He looked at William and realized they wore the exact same outfit. "I see that William and I shopped in the same closet this afternoon."

Even Helen could not contain a smile. "You two were practically twins when you were younger. Clearly, not much has changed. Now, Jasper, hurry up and finish making your drink. I would like to eat lunch before dinnertime."

Jasper obeyed and sat next to me. He placed his arm across the back of my chair and leaned in close, "Tell me, what is it you see in my mate here? From what I have gathered, you are too good for him." His accent tickled my ear. He shot William a sly grin.

"Ha. Well, let's see. Money, power, prestige. I think that covers it."

"That really is all he has going for him isn't it?" Jasper sat back in his seat and removed his arm from my chair. "I like her. I can tell she won't put up with your bullshit." He laughed and filled his plate.

"Jasper Hammond, if you care to speak like that you can take your lunch outside. Undignified words do not belong at this table," Helen said.

"Apologies, Aunt Helen. But, William, am I wrong?"

"No, she doesn't put up with my bull...stubbornness," William said.

"I have arranged for Doctor Harrison to join us for dinner this evening," Helen said. "She can examine Olivia prior to the meal. Unless, William, you have already arranged a doctor's visit?"

William looked up from his plate, mouth full of food.

"I'm sorry. Your aunt figured out I had a secret. I hope you aren't angry?"

William swallowed his food then spoke, "No. Of course not. I just thought we were waiting until we were more settled to announce the pregnancy." His timid eyes did not match the smile on his face. "Thank you Aunt Helen for arranging the doctor. It has been a rough few days. It would be good to know everything with the baby is okay."

The ingenuine smile faded from my face. William noticed and must have realized he had messed up. Before he could rectify the situation and share that he had concerns he may not be the father, Helen spoke.

"Don't play me for a fool, William. I know that you, as much as I, have doubts about this child's parentage." She looked at me, "Doctor Harrison will help us determine, in twenty-four hours, if someone has been lying to us."

A chill ran down the back of my spine. I continued to eat and, from the corner of my eye, watched as Jasper surveyed the situation.

"Just to make sure I am up to speed. Olivia is pregnant and William may not be the father? Well, my stay here just got a lot more interesting. And what say you, Olivia?" He finished his drink in one mouthful.

"There is no doubt in my mind that the child is William's. But, given everything that has happened, I can see why there may be questions."

"And tomorrow we will have answers," Helen said. "Jasper, why don't you take Olivia on a tour of the house while William and I discuss Doctor Harrison's visit."

I rose from the table, a flutter in my stomach. Helen seemed keen to keep William and I apart. Any coordinated effort thwarted.

I looked back at William. His face bore no expression.

CHAPTER SEVENTEEN

O nce we were across the threshold of the dining room, the air felt lighter and fresher. It may have been the array of flowers meticulously placed around the reception hall, or the fact that William and Helen had a talent for sucking the life out of a room. Even Jasper's quick-witted personality had not eased the tension.

"Well, now that we are out of that stuffy situation, how about you and I have a little bit of fun? I give entertaining tours, full of grandiose tales of deception, and cunning characters, at no extra charge." He smiled and held out his arm, like he would escort me onto a dance floor.

I put my arm through his and, with my best southern American accent replied, "Well, sir. I do say, I am rather intrigued and would gladly take you up on your offer. Where shall we go first?"

Jasper laughed at me, "To the library!" and pulled me quickly through a nearby door. The skirt of my white cotton dress trailed behind.

"This my lady, is the Library. Here you will find the Hammond family history, some books by a lot of dead people and, if you look in this cupboard, you will find," he squatted down behind a mahogany desk and opened the cupboard door. When he stood up he held a box that looked to have been made out of green and black granite. He placed it on the desk, opened it, and turned it towards me.

"The great Lord Jackson Hammond's 1861 Colt revolver. It's quite the antique, with the ivory handle, and intricately carved metal. The story is

82

that Jackson killed himself with it in this very room. In fact, guests have reported that if they are in here late at night, they were visited by his ghost."

"Well, then, I better let poor old Jackson rest at night and avoid the Library."

"I highly recommend that you do. Now, if you look out the window, from right here. . ." He waved me over, "Come on." Jasper stood behind me, placed his hands on my shoulders and moved me into position. "You can see the entire valley from here. Beautiful isn't it?"

His warm breath made the hairs on my neck stand tall. "It is." I said softly. The view was magnificent. All the different shades of green that made up rolling hills and forests. Even the winter rain had not dampened the picturesque view.

Jasper's hands remained on my shoulders. I kept crossing and uncrossing my arms, unsure what to do. As much as male hands on my body elicited fear and tension, I needed more information on the family. I stepped away and ran my finger along the gun, still in the case. "So who exactly was Jackson Hammond?"

Jasper leaned on the front of the desk, as close to me as possible. His dark eyes were inviting, and I was tempted to play his flirtatious game, but from a distance. I walked around the room and perused the thousands of leather-bound books that filled the floor-to-ceiling bookshelves.

"He initially worked as a coal miner, but quickly found there was more money in bootlegging and gambling. He started out small, having a few people at his lodgings for some cards. Within a few years, and a lot more players, he was making more money than he knew what to do with. He bought this estate, bought his title and started what is now known as Hammond Enterprises. Hundreds of years of Hammonds each building on the legacy of the one before them."

"And how do you fit into the legacy?"

Jasper walked over to me, hands in his pants pockets, "I am the future."

"Are you now? How does Helen feel about that? It seems to me she is pretty set on being the head of the family."

"True. Admittedly she does a great job. Eventually, she will have to retire. People tend to lose trust in the elderly after a while. Or, she will die. People in our line of work die all the time." He had an air of superiority about him. "Not that I would wish her dead, of course."

"Of course. And what part of the business do you manage now?"

"I'm not sure I should be telling you that. Aunt Helen was pretty clear that you were not to be trusted. What sort of loyal subject would I be, if I started spilling all of our secrets? Shall we make our way to the indoor pool?"

I would rather visit any place other than the pool. When I was seven, Mom, Dad, Claire and I had stayed at a hotel when visiting Grandma. One of the few times Dad spent money on such a luxury. The hotel had an indoor pool, where Claire and I spent the hours that we were not at Grandma's. One afternoon, Dad got angry at how loud I was, finished his beer and jumped into the pool.

Before I could get away he had dragged me into the deep end, let me go and told me to swim. I could barely tread water in the shallow end, and struggled to battle fear and water. My arms whipped the water and I kicked my legs, but my head could not stay above water.

Claire tried to come get me, but Dad kept her back. After what felt like hours, although I am sure it had only been minutes, my seven-year-old arms and legs got tired and gave up. Dad pulled me up and told me to keep swimming. This went on five more times. Each time my lungs filled with more water, my tears washed away by chlorine, and my pleas for help were ignored.

Eventually, Dad got tired, or thirsty, and got out of the pool. Ever since, I could only dangle my legs in water when I was alone. Otherwise, if I got close to the edge of the water, panic would set in.

The tour continued and we stopped outside closed doors, where Jasper advised what was on the other side. I tried to delay the visit to the pool and asked if we could go in the rooms, but he stated they were unremarkable and there was no point. As we passed the dining room, I could hear William and Helen's raised voices. My name was said a few times and I started to worry. Had the plan unraveled already?

"This way!" Jasper took my hand and pulled me down a long corridor. Windows took up one wall, the other had evenly spaced half-moon tables with artwork hung above, or statues sat upon them.

"Here we are," Jasper opened the double, glass doors and we stepped into a golden room showered in warm blue and yellow light. It reminded me of the Colosseum in Rome. I had never visited it, but the architecture was iconic. Stone arches with pillars framed each window along the side and end of the room. The large pool had a hot tub alongside it. There were three blue doors, with circular frosted galley windows, along the wall.

"This is my favourite room in the house. People rarely use it, so it is often peaceful. The servants rarely come in here, so you could be here for hours and no one would disturb you."

"It's nice." My heartbeat accelerated.

"Care for a swim?" He dragged me to the edge of the pool.

My playful smile would not stay plastered to my face, as I tried to remove my arm from his grip. If Jasper noticed, he did not let on. I balanced on the edge and, when I tried to move, he side-stepped, so I remained where I was. My arm still in his clutches. "I am not sure I am properly dressed for a swim. And don't they say you should wait 30 minutes after a meal? Looks like we are out of luck this time."

"Rules are meant to be broken, are they not?"

Jasper's eyes were playful but his grin was menacing. He wanted to prove he too had power in this family. He released his grip and his other hand pushed my shoulder. My arms flailed as my heels lifted off the deck. I could not keep myself upright and I fell towards the water.

SPLASH

I twirled around in the warm water, Jasper above me, as the waves enveloped me. He laughed. I was terrified.

The weight of my body pulled me to the bottom of the pool and water started to fill my mouth and lungs. The chlorine burned. Jasper's blurry figure danced on top of the water, now settled after my entry. My mind was yelling at my limbs to move, but they wouldn't. I closed my eyes.

An arm wrapped around my chest, and I opened my eyes to see the light blues of the surface getting closer. When I broke through the crest of the surface, I coughed up as much water as I could. Jasper stood where he had before, the laughter gone, replaced with worry. He bent down, grabbed my arms, and with the help of the person behind me, pulled me out of the pool.

Jasper carried me to a lounge chair on the side of the pool deck. William emerged from the pool with ease. This was the second time today he looked like an overpriced drowned rat. This time there was no smile or laughter. He rushed over and bent down beside me, "Are you okay?"

I nodded and tried to catch my breath and my bearings. William wrapped a large soft towel around me and brushed my hair behind my ears. "Are you sure?"

"Yes." The chlorine in my lungs burned and my throat was sore.

"Good." He shot to his feet and rounded on his cousin.

"What made you decide to throw her into the pool?"

"Look, mate, we were joking around. She was only in there for, like, thirty seconds before you jumped in. How was I supposed to know she couldn't swim?"

"And you didn't think to go in after her, when she was seated on the bottom of the pool?"

"Chill. She's fine."

"Fine!" William ran his fingers through his hair, then his fist tightened and collided with Jasper's face. Jasper fell to the deck, pressed his hand to his cheek and checked his fingers for blood. There was none.

"Overreacting a bit don't you think?" Jasper used an empty lounge chair to assist him to his feet.

I sat with the warm pool water starting to turn into a coat of ice, as the two men jostled back and forth. I tuned out their squabbles and focused on the rain pelting the windows. My heartbeat and breath started to slow back to a normal pace. Strong enough to walk, I made my way towards the exit, leaving the two men behind with their punches.

Halfway down the hallway, a path of water droplets behind me, William and Jasper caught up.

"Wait. Let me help..." William tried to grab my arm, but I pulled away.

"I'm fine." I glared at Jasper and both men backed off. Welcome silence walked with us.

We were part-way up the stairs to the second floor, when Helen caught sight of us.

"What the hell happened here?"

William responded, "Jasper pushed Olivia into the pool."

Helen's eyes lasered in on Jasper, "I suppose it is your intention to test my nerves and ensure water is traipsed around my entire house today? This time you get to clean it up. And with no help."

Jasper did not respond, he simply nodded, and headed in the direction of where he had told me the kitchen was. William addressed his Aunt, "It might be best if Olivia misses dinner. We don't know if anything has happened to the baby and further excitement may not be wise."

Helen threw up her arms. "Alright. I will have Doctor Harrison brought upstairs once she arrives."

"Thank you, Aunt Helen."

"I expect you to be there, though." She marched into her office. Another room I had not seen the inside of.

William and I continued up the stairs. I clung to the comfort of the towel. My hands had started to shake and I could feel a panic attack erupting. My breath had become rapid again, and, about to break down, I started to run. William's saturated footsteps tried to keep up. I arrived in our bathroom, and slammed the door, before the tears started. I shoved my towel into my mouth to muffle my cries. My knees throbbed from the impact of my weight onto the tile floor.

I was supposed to be stronger than this. I was supposed to keep it together so that I could get out of here. I was not supposed to unravel. It had only been forty-eight hours since William found me, and look at the mess I had become. How was I going to get through another twenty-four hours, let alone the remaining months of my pregnancy?

CHAPTER EIGHTEEN

B ANG!
"Olivia? Open the door!" William's voice penetrated the white wooden bathroom door.

I pushed myself up to a seated position and stared at the door. Thankfully, I had locked it, in my rush to close it. "I'm fine! Just leave me be." I wiped my tears and tossed the wet towel aside. The coolness of the tiles had seeped into my bones. I shivered so much that the removal of the wet clothes plastered to my skin was difficult.

"ARGH!"

William's body barreled through the bathroom door, which now dangled off one hinge.

"We need to get you out of these clothes and warmed up."

"I tried. They're stuck." A weight heavier than my clothes sat on top of me.

William pried my clenched hands from my clothes and gently took off my dress. The tears on my face made friends with the pool water on the floor.

"We should remove everything. Are you okay to do that, or do you need me to?"

The thought of William getting me naked propelled me to fight the shakes in my hands, and remove my undergarments myself. William had seen my naked body on multiple occasions but this time felt different, more vulnerable.

William's soft hand led me into the shower, where he warmed the water before he positioned me under the shower head. His body supported my weakness, as the hot water trickled over me.

"What happened? Did Jasper do something to you, besides throw you into the pool?"

I shook my head no. William's pale blue eyes were the kind and concerned eyes I had glimpsed on occasion in Los Angeles. I fought the anger I had towards him. All I wanted right now was to feel safe. Even if it was just at this moment. I leaned my forehead against his cold wet sweater, buried myself into his chest and wept.

William wrapped his arms around me. We stood together, the water coursing around us. With most of my tears released, I decided to open up to William, otherwise he would cause further trouble with Jasper. Trouble we didn't need. "I almost drowned, at my father's hands, as a child. Now I can't swim in a pool without an ensuing panic attack. They haven't been this bad, but, with the stress of everything else, I just couldn't handle it."

William's lips pressed against the top of my head, "You're alright now."

With my arms around his waist, I backed away. Using both of his hands, William wiped the matted hair out of my face. William hadn't hesitated to pull me out of that pool. Whether it was for me, or the child, he let me live. How could the different sides of a man be so drastic? One I loathed, and one I longed to help.

Our eyes locked. Was he going to kiss me? Did I want him to?

I grabbed the collar of William's sweater and pulled him towards me, our lips parted. William's hand removed my hands from his clothes and without a word he stepped back.

His silence cut like a knife. I dropped my hands and moved around William, "Right. Well, I'll let you get ready for dinner."

I didn't wait for a reply. I stepped out of the shower and closed the door without a look back. I grabbed the closest dry towel, wrapped myself and left the bathroom.

I rushed to dry off, I didn't want my exposed body viewed any longer. The silk pajamas danced against my warmed skin. My wet towel remained where I dropped it on the carpet.

The bedding took the brunt of my hurt and aggression. I tossed it, and myself around, until I was as comfortable as my anger would allow.

Bottle caps snapped open and closed. I curled up into a ball. The multi-coloured trees outside the window danced in the wind's rain. I was sick at the thought of what I had initiated with William. What would we have done if Doctor Harrison was not scheduled to see me?

The water stopped, the shower door creaked. I closed my eyes and pretended to be asleep. William stopped for a moment beside me, my ears attuned to his breath. The floor creaked under every careful step he took. Hangers gently collided and a drawer slid on its rails. The bed shifted and I opened my eyes slightly. William's reflection in the window displayed him seated on the edge of his side of the bed, his back to me. I closed my eyes again and willed him to leave me in peace.

A knock at the door signaled that peace was not meant to be. Charlotte's voice advised that Doctor Harrison had arrived, and that a few of the butlers would bring up her equipment. William thanked her, but I didn't hear the door close. He walked around to my side of the bed and gently rubbed my arm "Olivia, the doctor is here."

I inhaled, "Okay." I pushed myself up to a seated position and fluffed the bedding around me. I avoided eye contact with William and numbed myself to what was about to happen.

In walked, who I presumed was Doctor Harrison, led by two of the butlers whose names I had not been advised of. Doctor Harrison looked to be in her seventies and had taken good care of herself. Her long grey hair was curled back into a half ponytail. Her dark brown eyes were as ominous as her smile.

"Out from under those blankets. In fact, why don't we move this bench here from the foot of the bed out into the middle of the room?" She snapped her fingers and the butlers jumped to work.

"Bring my stuff around here to the side. Yes right there. Olivia is it?" She didn't wait for a response, "Take off your pants and lie down here." Again she snapped her fingers.

I obeyed, no longer concerned with strangers seeing me naked. Not after everything that happened when I was captive in Los Angeles.

William placed one of the couch pillows under my head. He towered over me as Doctor Harrison plugged in a portable ultrasound machine and retrieved her tools from her leather bag.

"We will start with a couple of ultrasounds and make sure everything sounds, and looks, fine. Then I will take a sample of yours and William's blood to run the DNA test. You should be very grateful modern science has pretty much eliminated the need for invasive needles to complete a paternity test during pregnancy."

I pulled my shirt up and Doctor Harrison squirted the ultrasound gel on my stomach, which flinched from the cold. It was not long before repeated thumps filled the room. I closed my eyes and felt disoriented.

"The heartbeat sounds healthy," Doctor Harrison said. "Now let's take a look at the little one."

More cold gel and I felt the probe glide along my skin. I took a deep breath and kept my eyes closed. It wasn't until Doctor Harrison said, "There it is," that I looked at the screen. A range of emotions overwhelmed me as I stared at a tiny head, hand and what might have been a foot. I was flooded with relief that William and Helen would not be able to deny the pregnancy. Relief was replaced with pride that I would bring life into this world. Then the ever-present fear took over. Fear of what having William's child could mean for my and the child's future. Fear that I would not be a good mother. Finally, I was overcome by love. I vowed to myself that I would do everything in my power to keep this child safe.

"Everything looks good. It's too soon to identify the sex of the baby. Another month and a half, based on Olivia's timeline. Should it be required after the DNA results, we can follow up on that."

It was a coin flip between relief and anxiety knowing it would be a while until I found out if there was a replica of William inside of me. Relief, as denial had become customary. Anxiety as it meant there was another unknown explosive in the minefeild of them.

For a man who had been so concerned about the baby yesterday, William looked unphased by anything Doctor Harrison had said. He simply stood behind me staring at the ultrasound monitor.

Doctor Harrison handed me some paper towels, "Now, sit up and wipe off the gel. William, sit beside her." She sounded like a drill sergeant as she tossed me a towel.

William rolled up his sleeve, sat down beside me and paid me no attention. Doctor Harrison drew his blood and then William left the room. Just like that. No words spoken. After my blood was taken, the doctor and butlers cleaned up, and I sat half naked in the middle of the room.

Left behind to stew in my own thoughts.

Tomorrow the truth will come out. I hoped it was only about the child's father and that my true identity would remain hidden.

CHAPTER NINETEEN

B reakfast the next morning was silent and somber. Even Jasper's jovial quips were nowhere to be found. William had moved from sitting opposite me, to beside me. Helen seemed to be filled with more disdain than usual. Caldwell either read the room, or was instructed not to make a sound, as the food was served without explanation or morning greetings. It was as though there had been a death in the family.

I didn't want to cause more trouble, so I had not asked about the DNA test. I figured the confirmed pregnancy was the culprit of the mood change in the house.

Once the plates were cleared, everyone else departed without so much as a 'Have a nice day.' The vastness of the room loomed, me a tiny, trapped animal. The tall walls started to close in. I needed fresh air. I would explore the grounds and determine if there was a way I could escape without being noticed.

The warm sun battled with the cool breeze to kiss my cheeks. The smell of winter was in the air. Time alone, outside of sleep, was a luxury I would finally have. I stepped off the veranda, but the crunch of grass under my shoes did not cover up the stomp of boots behind me.

Jasper, hands in his pockets, looked past me at the expanse of the property.

"Going somewhere?" I would not be fooled by his Scottish accent today.

"For a walk, if you must know."

He stepped beside me, "Then I will join you."

"I would rather be alone, thank you."

"I bet you would. However, that is not going to happen. Orders are orders. And you are not to be left alone." Jasper's eyes dawned a darker shade of brown than yesterday.

"Why?"

"Even with the DNA test results confirming it's William's child, Helen does not trust you. I'm also getting the sense you don't have William's full trust either. After all, he didn't protest when Helen demanded you be watched at all times."

Of course he didn't. "Was no one going to inform me of the results?"

"I just did."

"Nice. Is that why everyone was so morose this morning? Hoping for a different result?"

"I know Aunt Helen was. William wouldn't talk about it, so I don't know what has his panties in a knot. Shall we?"

Disappointed, I followed, as it looked to be the only way I would be able to canvas the area. "Why would Helen not want William to have a child? You would think having another Hammond around would be welcome news."

Jasper smiled. The genial host was back. "You have much to learn. Aunt Helen does not like anything or anyone that distracts from the business. A child would be a distraction. *You* are definitely a distraction. Especially, with your absurd ideas to make the business legal. A word of advice, don't speak further about those ideas to anyone. Not if you want to keep your head attached to your body. Aunt Helen is looking for any excuse to get rid of you. She had hoped the DNA test would prove you had lied about the parentage and solve her problem. Now, she will pay particularly close attention to you, in order to find a way to remove you, and the baby, from the equation. Anything to keep William's eyes on the business, and off of you and the child."

We turned down a path and ended up in the middle of a cobblestone square surrounded by stable stalls. Half of them were filled with majestic, large horses.

"Do you ride?"

"No."

"These are prize-winning thoroughbreds. One of the legal ways we make money."

The soft hair of a horse named Rebel tickled my fingers, as Jasper went on about horse racing. The words went in one ear and out the other, without a place to reside in my brain. I gave the occasional "uh huh" of feigned interest.

From the stables we passed some outbuildings. One of which, Jasper informed me, was Caldwell's residence.

"So, what's going on between Caldwell and Helen? Our first night here they seemed a little more...close than one would expect between a Lady and her servant."

"Ah, yes, the elusive tale of Aunt Helen's love life. She keeps quite tight-lipped about it but there has never been a man around long enough for the family to ever really know they exist. I suspect any relationship she has, if you can call it that, is strictly out of the desire for her to extract what she needs from them to support the business. But Caldwell has always been a different story."

"I knew it." I let a playful grin replace the annoyance of not being alone.

"Caldwell worked for Douglas, starting out as a young footman. The way I have heard it, back then he did not hide his desires as well as he does today. Rumour has it Aunt Helen and Caldwell have been, let's say, enjoying each other's company for years."

"Really? Just call it sex, I'm not a child."

"I was trying to be a gentleman."

"Ha! Do gentlemen throw women into pools?"

Jasper clasped his chest and wobbled backwards, "Ouch!" he joked, "gentlemen can have a little fun."

We walked through a magnificent winter garden in full bloom. Flowers of every colour painted the scene. I longed for the falls in Toronto to last as long as they apparently did here. We rounded a corner and came upon a large pond with two white swans and some ducks. I hesitated for a split second and Jasper noticed.

"Don't worry, I won't make you take another swim. I'm sorry about last night. No hard feelings?"

"That depends. Do you plan on trying to kill me - intentionally or not - again?"

"Only if so ordered." He winked at me, but I saw a familiar flash of evil in his eyes.

"And how many kill orders have you followed?"

"Enough to make your skin crawl." There was no denying he was a Hammond, and just like a Hammond, his personality flipped like a switch.

"Of course." I would not let Jasper distract me from learning more about Helen. "Let's get back to your story. I'm intrigued that with Helen's apparent desire for status and power, she would sleep with the help."

"Aunt Helen has always done what she wanted and keeps everything close to the chest. There is a good reason why there are only rumours and never any evidence. It was her husband's affairs that stirred up trouble, not hers. She was too smart to allow her desires to be displayed for anyone to see. Even now that she leads the family, she will not allow the veneer over her personal life to crack."

"Are they in love?" I doubted Helen had a heart, but if she did, I might be able to use it. Maybe.

"Oh you are funny. I don't think Helen has loved anyone in her life. I'm not too sure about Caldwell. It wouldn't surprise me if he pines for being by her side, more than just in her bed. Not much of a talker, that one, and so hard to read. Now, enough about them. You should see the view from the top of that hill," he said and grabbed my hand as he ran towards the faded green hill. I stumbled to keep up.

On the hilltop, I could see the kilometers that spanned in front of me. It was a very different view from the library. Here there were no buildings or other signs of human life. A couple of deer sprinted across the pasture and birds danced from tree to tree. They greeted each other with their songs. From what I could see there was a small ravine not far out. I squinted and tried to identify where it led. If I could follow the water off the property it might lead me to where I could get some help.

Jasper's voice interrupted nature's song, "I wouldn't do that if I were you."

"Do what?"

"Leave."

How did he know what I was thinking? "Why would I leave?"

He stepped in front of me and looked me sharply in the eye, "Because you want as far away from William as possible."

I could not stop my face from contorting into a question.

Jasper continued, "I know what William and Adam did to your sister."

My knees folded under me and they, and my hands, hit the grass. How did he know about Claire? If he knew about Claire then he knew...Is that why William was so distant at breakfast? He had been caught in the lie. My mind raced as I tried to determine my next steps.

Jasper squatted in front of me, took my chin in his hand and forced me to look at him. "My question is, what will you be willing to do for me to keep that secret?"

"Does anyone else know?"

"Not yet, but if you don't make it worth my while, they will. Aunt Helen will be so pleased to hear who you really are. I get the added bonus that William will never take the helm of the business from her." He brought his face closer to mine, "Who would trust someone who knowingly brought a cop into their home, let her burn everything down and then introduced her to the family?"

"How did you find out?"

"I have my sources."

"Sources Helen doesn't have?" I silently begged his ego to talk.

"I created a secondary network of contacts Aunt Helen only wished she had."

I thrashed his hand away and stood up. "Let me guess, this information you found would help solidify your rise to power before Helen dies?"

"You're on the right track."

"So then why keep it a secret? Why not use it? What could I possibly do for you?

Jasper's toothy smile widened, "Well, by lording this secret over you - you can provide me intelligence on any plans William may be making to be more...hands-on over here."

"Since you seem to know who I am, what makes you think that William would share anything with me?"

Jasper paced around me, "Oh I am sure he will. Eventually. I have seen the way he looks at you. I'm not sure if he knows it yet, but I would bet my last pound that he is in love with you. He always liked a challenge, and, well, you are just that."

"Ha! He tried to kill me a few days ago and you think he is in love with me! This family is a lot crazier than I thought." I shook my head as I grappled with what Jasper had said. Sure, William was protective of me, but in Los Angeles that was out of a desire to keep his asset safe and make money. Here, it was about keeping his child safe. Right?

"This is priceless. You didn't know, did you? Well, that just makes this more fun. The man who had your sister killed and is the father of your baby, is in love with you. And you can't escape him. At least not without my help." His laughter echoed off the hills.

"How exactly would you help me?"

Jasper reigned in his joy, "Well, you feed me information and once I have what I need to gain control of the family, I let you go. Simple as that."

"Simple. Right. And, let me guess. You decide once you have enough information. So I could be stuck here for years. Why wouldn't I take my chances and try to survive on my own? If you know who I am, then you know what I have been through and I will fight to get my life back or lose it trying. So what else do you have to offer?" He didn't need to know that I wanted to stay alive for the child.

Jasper straightened his jacket and patted his dark, bristled hair. My wrist became enveloped in his tight grasp and he pulled me against him. His breath seethed like a dragon on the verge of burning a city. "Don't try to be a hero. You are nothing. Right now, you have full access to the house and grounds, albeit, escorted. That could easily be taken away. You would be locked up, unnoticed by guests or staff, until the child is born. I would raise your son as my own, groomed to be my successor. During which time, you would be committed to an asylum nearby, highly medicated and left to rot. Because I am a gentleman, I would send you letters to apprise you of my son's first sexual exploit, his first sale of a person and how he learned to master the art of murder."

I tugged my arm hard and Jasper fell over. I stomped on his chest. He moaned in agony and curled over. I wrenched my arm free.

"I won't let you do that to MY son! He is not going to be like any of you." I ran down the hill, towards the ravine. My balance tested, I jumped over twigs and vines but caught my toe on a gopher hole. I tumbled down the hill, tossed around by nature. I scrambled to my feet, Jasper was halfway down the hill. Scraped and bruised, I sprinted along the river, and hoped it led me somewhere. I grabbed a small log, protruding from the bank of the river, to use as a weapon.

"I know this land better than you, you will not get away."

My legs burned. They had not seen this much exercise in almost a year, but I pushed on. I had to get out of here. The scenery had changed from lush grass, to dense bush and forest. Everything went silent. Not a crack of a broken branch, or the crush of leaves underfoot. Even the trees had stopped their rustle in the wind. I took each step as slow as possible. One wrong move and my position would be announced. I hugged a tree for balance as I rounded a sharp bend in the ravine.

Jasper's confidence radiated off the large rock he sat on, directly in front of me. "I told you there was no escape." He tossed a couple of pebbles in the water and pushed himself off the rock with his foot. "Why don't we try this one more time."

His large, yet slim body, pinned me between him and a large oak tree. He held my hands above my head and stood between my legs. I struggled but could not free myself. Jasper held my wrists in one hand and squeezed my neck with his other.

"I tried to be nice earlier. Give you the opportunity to decide your own future. But you are making it very hard for me to not just kill you. It would be so easy. Say you fell, hit your head. Yes, William might question it, but only briefly. Soon he would be overcome with grief from not being able to save his second child. This time he would succeed in his attempt to kill himself. He tried once, did you know that? After Sharon and Penny. That's where the scar on his arm came from. Tried to end it the same way his mother had, in a bathtub with a piece of mirror. It really was too bad one of his men found him. Now, what will it be? Death or me?"

My life in this moment, and the next, was in Jasper's hands. If I colluded with this new devil, the other one was smart enough to figure it out. If that happened I would be dead. Either way, the risk of death had increased and I only had one choice. I hoped I would be able to juggle the expectations of both men.

I strained to speak through Jasper's tight grip on my throat, "Okay" He loosened his hand.

"What was that?"

"Fine. I'll help."

"Good girl. Was that so hard?" Jasper lingered for a moment and a hard bulge in his pants pressed against me. "We are going to make a good team. In fact, I think we could make a good team right now." The hand from my neck ran down my chest and under the skirt of my dress. His touch was gentle, but repulsive.

I froze and stared off into the distance. I didn't want to be present for what would come next.

A loud voice bellowed in the distance.

CHAPTER TWENTY

My skin itched and burned from Jasper's touch. The booming voice got closer.

"You speak a word of this and I will kill you. Understand?"

I nodded. Jasper stepped away from me.

"Wash your face. When they ask, you fell, and we were just cleaning you up. Hurry!"

I splashed the cold ravine water on my face and my body temperature decreased. The bottom of my dress transformed into a cloth. I scraped off as much dirt as I could without a mirror. When I was done, one of the groundskeepers looked down at us from the tree-covered hill.

"Lord Hammond! Lady Hammond has been asking for you. You better come quick. She's very upset."

We scrambled up the hill, the branches my life line. The groundskeeper took a step towards me, eyebrows drawn together, but stopped.

"She fell. She's fine. Right?"

"I'm okay." The groundskeeper's eyebrows remained furrowed.

Jasper darted ahead to the house. I was positive he would relay the fabricated story about what happened, before I could tell anyone any different. I sauntered, in no rush to be consumed by the contemptuous stares. I needed time to think and went around the side of the house towards the doorway off the stables. The groundskeeper headed towards the pond.

Jasper would only keep me alive as long as it benefited him. Should I risk battling the devil I knew or the one who had just revealed himself to me?

I pushed the handle on the back door and was grateful it had been left unlocked. I stepped into a beautiful Victorian-style kitchen. Stacked, navy blue cupboards adorned the walls. Two candelabra chandeliers hung from the smooth ceiling. The cook and Charlotte stopped chopping vegetables at the long wooden island in the middle of the room, to see who had unexpectedly entered their habitat.

"I'm sorry, I didn't realize anyone was in here. I'm just passing through."

Charlotte came over, "Can I get you anything Ma'am?"

"No, I'm fine. Thank you. I'm just going to go get cleaned up."

"I will bring you some tea. It might make you feel better after your *walk*."

Had she heard what happened already? Jasper could not have been back for more than a couple of minutes before I walked in.

"It's really no trouble."

All I wanted was a shower but her persistence was palpable. "Fine, tea would be nice."

Charlotte showed me the stairwell tucked at the back of the kitchen. Grateful I would avoid the family, I trudged my sore body up each step.

The weight of Jasper's words pushed on every muscle. The bedroom was empty and I closed the door with quiet precision. Then I dropped to the floor, my body forming a barricade against the door. Jasper may not have had a fully-formed plan before we spoke, but he demonstrated how quickly he could piece together my worst nightmare. My eyelids were heavy and I let them rest as I leaned my head back. I was tired of being outsmarted. Tired of the evil in the world winning. Tired of having no power to do anything about it. And what was he saying about William being in love with me? What type of messed-up mind game was that? I couldn't even think about that possibility right now. As much as I hated myself for my weakness, all I wanted to do was curl up and let the grief for Claire, Whitney, and my old life wash over me.

A small rap of knuckles behind me pulled me out of my spiral. I crawled over to the bed, the desire to get off the floor nonexistent. Charlotte walked in, the clatter of cups and saucers followed her to the table in front of the coach. She smiled and nodded, walked into my closet and came out with a clean dress, laid it on the bed and reached out a hand.

"Let's get you cleaned up shall we?" she said.

Her hand hung empty. "What's the point? This family hates me, and I them. So what if I show up to a meal covered in dirt. It's not like they will think any less of me. I can't possibly sink lower in their eyes."

Charlotte retracted her hand, brought over two cups of tea, and sat down beside me. This casual act was out of place, but I was grateful the formality had dissipated. She sipped her tea and then spoke. "There is a way out of all of this," she said.

"Out of what? Here?"

"Yes. I can get you out of here and somewhere safe."

"I appreciate the offer, but I think I am probably safer right where I am." I heaved myself up and put my empty cup back on the tray.

Charlotte rose off the floor with less effort than me, "Olivia, I know who you are, what you have been through and I think we can help each other."

"You-"

"Just hear me out. I work for MI5 and they have worked hard to build a case against the Hammonds for the last four years."

This woman looked twenty-five at best and she expected me to believe she worked as an agent of the government? How would someone, almost as trapped in this place as I am, even receive training? Our conversation the other night had given me hope I had an ally, but whoever had come up with her cover story was not very smart.

She continued, "Your and William's arrival was quite fortuitous and could give us access to information we didn't have before. The North American authorities won't share much about the Hammonds' operation there. In fact, we are positive it was the fire and the escape of you and the others which meant they could no longer ignore what was happening."

Heavy footsteps came towards us from down the hall. Charlotte scrambled to clean up the tea and grabbed the tray. "You could be an invaluable asset. Trust me. I'm on your side."

"Why didn't you tell me this the other night?"

"I didn't know who you were the other night."

"But-"

The door creaked open and William stepped inside, his head tilted and eyes narrowed as he took in the scene.

CHAPTER TWENTY-ONE

William held the door open and tapped his finger on the doorknob. Charlotte scampered out of the room. The door closed behind her and William walked over to me, his hands clasped behind his back.

"How is it, whenever you are with Jasper you come out scathed? Look at you. Go get cleaned up, and then we can talk about what I just walked in on."

"You didn't walk-"

"Don't try to make excuses. Now, go wash up. Here." He tossed me the dress Charlotte had laid out.

I grabbed some clean undergarments and went into the bathroom. The floor creaked under William's footsteps as I closed the newly-fixed door.

As warm water rushed over my body, I replayed what Charlotte had said. Was she really a government agent? Or was this some ruse Helen or Jasper cooked up? If it was true, she could be the answer to my problems. But how would I be able to determine if I could trust her? I needed proof. But proof of what?

I still needed to figure out what I was going to do about Jasper. I doubted he would do anything right away, so I had time to do a little reconnaissance. William was skilled at the art of deception, both as a deliverer and receiver. He never let on that he knew someone was trying to get something past him. I would need to be careful. Even more so now that he was suspicious of Charlotte.

I put on the yellow and white floral dress and found William seated on the couch, legs crossed, with a book. He put the book down and pointed for me to sit in the chair opposite him.

"We don't have much time before dinner, so first tell me what happened with Jasper. It's not a coincidence that you once again found yourself disheveled after being around him."

"I think your cousin gets a thrill out of playing tricks on me. We were walking, as apparently I am not allowed to do that alone," my teeth ground together as I swallowed my anger. "And the next thing I knew, he scared me and I tumbled down the hill."

"Is that so?"

"Yes. Why, what did he tell you?" I prayed I had been vague enough to have not slipped up.

"He said you had tripped and fell."

"Given you punched him last time, can you blame him for not revealing the full truth?"

William uncrossed his legs and leaned his elbows on his knees. "What were you and Charlotte doing? We do not have tea with the help."

"I came in through the kitchen and she saw the state I was in. She tried to be nice and brought me tea. Maybe she thought you would be here too."

William rose from the couch, his stature cast a shadow over me. He leaned over, placed his hands on both arms of the chair, and we were almost nose to nose. My hands tightened around themselves, I moved as far back against the chair as possible while I maintained eye contact. William's eyes were cold and hard.

"Both tea cups had been used. Unless you were having tea with someone else, you might want to try telling me the truth."

Shit! He must have noticed the used cups when Charlotte passed him on her way out. "Fine, she poured herself some tea. What's wrong with that? And don't go spouting about paid to serve, etc. I have no friends here. Hell, I don't even know how long I will be alive here. So what, if someone is being a little nicer to me than your family."

William seethed, "You are only here because you are carrying my child. You are not in a position to have people be nice to you and I will make sure Charlotte is reminded of that." He pushed himself away from the chair and started towards the door.

Defiance filled me. "Do you get satisfaction from making people's lives miserable? You must, if you collect women against their will, blackmail people and show how powerful you are by hurting those around you. All for what? Your own greed? Charlotte didn't do anything wrong and now you are going to *remind her*. Are you feeling less powerful, now that you are no longer in charge? Need to show a little dominance, is that it?" Even if I didn't trust Charlotte, she didn't deserve what William would dole out to her.

William spun around, marched over to me and slapped me so hard I fell back into the chair. The ring on his hand split my lip open. Blood dripped into the hand I had reflexively brought to my face to ease the sting of the pain. William then slapped the side of my face that I had not protected. My cheek burned.

"Don't push me. I can still hurt you." He straightened his clothes. "Now, let's go!"

I laboured to get up. On the way out of the door I grabbed a tissue and wiped off the blood from my face and hands. Helen and Jasper would be pleased to see me battered. I hoped one day soon I could return the favour.

CHAPTER TWENTY-TWO

The next month and a half went by without much excitement. Even the once colourful leaves on the trees decided they had had enough life for one year and departed their hosts. December snow blanketed the beautiful landscape that surrounded me, and painted a warm inviting picture,quite contrary to the chill that ran through the house.

Christmas had come and gone with an air of obligation rather than festive enjoyment. The house was beautifully decorated, but Christmas dinner was so sullen any light-hearted jokes by Jasper fell on deaf ears. After dinner, we all went to Midnight Mass, where I almost fell asleep to the monotone voice of the priest. William had to continually jab my ribs with his elbow to keep me awake.

I was grateful gifts were exchanged after Mass, rather than on Christmas morning, as I would be able to sleep in after such a long day. William bought himself a very nice hunting rifle and put my name on the From line on the tag. I received first editions of the complete works of Jane Austen. The brown leather binding was in mint condition. At least William made it look like we were in a relationship.

Jasper thought it would be ironic to make a personalized gift card for swimming lessons. A computer printed coupon with tiny flailing women in a pool boarded the page. The instructor? Jasper of course. As if I would let him near me in any form of water.

To keep the irony going, Jasper gave William boxing lessons. However, the coupon explicitly stated someone else would provide the coaching. I guess Jasper didn't want to receive further blows to his face from William's hands.

I was not surprised when the holiday spirit did not stir Aunt Helen to give me a normal present. What surprised me was what resided under the lid of a pretty red box with a green ribbon. The deed, and key, to a property in Germany which had been put in my name.

"You wanted to provide input into the family business. Well, let's start small and you can own the property to one of our mid-echelon houses."

William looked pleased and Jasper couldn't stifle a laugh. I am sure the whole house heard his reaction.

I simply smiled, said "thank you," and put the lid on the box. I tucked the box away in the bedroom closet, and would show Charlotte the next time we were alone.

Outside of Christmas, I spent most of my time between meals alone in my room. It was the only place I was unaccompanied. The family, and staff, were so busy with Christmas and then plans for William's Welcome Home party that no one paid much attention to me, which I was grateful for. The less I had to fake happiness, the better.

William and I barely saw each other which meant we co-existed rather peacefully. We lobbed unpleasant comments at each other now and again, but our altercations were not violent as they had been in the past. I worked very hard to bury any feelings other than hatred toward him. Just because I tolerated my situation, did not mean I wanted to get used to it.

I avoided Jasper and was thankful to learn he had gone into London until William's party on New Years eve. I still grappled with what I was going to do about him and William. I needed out, not to entrench myself deeper. I would have to try and play nice until I could come up with a solid plan.

I had scoped out the deliveries, however, would not be able to escape in a truck as they were searched by Helen's guards before and after the delivery was made. Was it William or Jasper's idea for the departure search? Did someone want to ensure I stayed put? Like William's house in

Los Angeles, this one also had cameras everywhere, but they were camouflaged into their surroundings. Unlike Los Angeles, they appeared to be monitored twenty-four hours a day. I only found out, at dinner one evening, when Helen asked me if I had enjoyed my visit with the horses.

I thought I had been stealthy when no one saw me leave the house. I even used a side door. I wanted to see if there was a way for me to leave on horseback. To my detriment, the animals were all padlocked in their stalls and the keys had not appeared to have been kept near them.

I had become so enamoured with a golden brown horse, who stood under a sign that read Prince, that I lost track of time during my visit.

After Helen revealed my stable visit, William made sure I was reminded to not leave our room unaccompanied. After which, we needed new bedside lamps. I side-stepped both before either hit my head.

I had my nose in my fifth book for the week, and fifth cup of chamomile tea when, without a knock, the bedroom door opened and Doctor Harrison barged in with two butlers trailing behind. The ultrasound machine's squeaking wheels rolled along the carpet and took its place at the foot of the bed. Without being asked, the butler's moved the bench and placed it where it had been during the doctor's first visit.

William walked in, and annoyance masked his face. He had been spending most of his time with Helen in her office, focused on the business. Not having to spend time with him was a blessing, especially when he appeared looking as though he had a short fuse.

"Well, lady, you know how this goes, strip down, lie down and let's see how things are progressing."

I reluctantly closed the book I was reading and followed orders. The quicker I could get this over with, the quicker I could be alone.

A few minutes of the paddle careening around my skin and she finally said, with zero excitement in her voice, "Well, everything looks good. No change or cause for concern. Are you interested in knowing the sex of the baby?"

I forced myself to look at William towering behind me. He had his hand over his mouth and a tear caressed his cheek. He shrugged.

"Yes, please." I said. I never liked surprises and the more information I had around the Hammonds, the better.

"You see that little sprout right there?" Doctor Harrison pointed to a small dot on the screen, "It's a boy."

My heart skipped a beat and the fear I had rarely experienced over the last month and a half returned. My body contained a miniature William. I tightened the grip on my shirt, as I kept it risen off my stomach. I prayed this child would look like any image other than William, when he arrived in the world. William's heavy breathing reminded me of his presence. I kept my eyes fixated on the screen.

Doctor Harrison pressed a few buttons on the machine, "I have emailed William the image." The screen went black. "I'll see you in about a month." With that she was gone. The two butler's scrambled to clean up her stuff and keep up with her.

William grabbed me a towel from the bathroom, handed it to me and started to leave.

"You have nothing to say? I mean, I like the fact we avoid each other most of the time, but if you want people to think we are in a relationship, don't you think we should be planning a little more? Maybe act like we are excited about this child. From the look on your face I would say you are dreading its arrival." My survival depended on Aunt Helen's belief we were in love and I felt that belief slip away with every meal William and I attended where few words were spoken.

"Don't begin to think you understand how I feel about my son."

"Well, then tell me. If I was watching us right now, I would not be seeing two parents exuberant about their child. More like two people who are on the cusp of a divorce, but don't want to talk about it."

William opened his mouth, then thought about something and seemed to change thought tracks, "I've taken care of everything, so you just have to not disturb the peace around here and all will be well."

"Right. Well for you? The baby? Me?"

"Oliv-"

"All I am saying is it would be nice to know the plan. Are we living here? Somewhere else? Helen is always looking for a way to catch me in a lie, so unless you want to hang us both out to dry before the baby comes, a little more information would be helpful."

"As far as Helen is concerned, we will live in one of the family properties in London, so I can be closer to those I need to work with."

"And in reality?"

"You don't have to worry about reality. You just have to carry this baby to term."

"Ah yes, I am just a baby carrier to you. Not a human being who might deserve to live!"

"You deserve nothing but revenge for Adam!" William paced in front of me, his fingers pulled at his suit jacket. "I don't have time to fight with you."

The bedroom door slammed. I wadded up and tossed the gel stained towel across the room. I desperately wanted to strangle that man, but he was the only one keeping me alive. If I didn't find a way out of here soon, I wouldn't be leaving at all.

CHAPTER TWENTY-THREE

The boredom of the repetitive life I found myself in, and the grey snow storm outside, covered me in a blanket of drowsiness. As my eyelids fluttered and tried to stay focused on Elizabeth Bennet's distaste for Mr. Darcy, I had not noticed Charlotte was the one who had brought me afternoon tea. A cough drew my attention away from the land of sleep.

Charlotte wore the same tight blond bun, and black and white maid's uniform, but her eyes were different. The topaz sparkled and she bounced from one foot to the other.

"What is it?" I asked.

"Sorry I couldn't get to you sooner. William made it known to the whole staff I was not to be allowed near you. I am only here today because Janet is sick with the flu and everyone is run off their feet with this party. I need your help."

"You need my help. With what?"

"I need you to get into Helen's office and retrieve their banking records."

"Oh is that it? Why can't you do it, say, when you are cleaning?"

"It is locked and no one is allowed in that room. I have tried."

"How exactly do you expect me to get through a locked door and not be seen on camera?"

"I think I can get to the security office and, you know, bribe the guard," the wink she gave was unnecessary. I understood what she meant. "Distract him while you grab the information."

"And the locked door?"

"I will put the key under the vase on the table beside the door."

"Okay, the camera's and the locked door are taken care of. What about, oh I don't know, the guards, or the fact I am never alone except in this room?"

Charlotte removed a throw pillow from a chair, hugged it and sat down. "A middle of the night escapade. The night guard would be bored with nothing to watch and my distraction would be most welcome. The others are outside and won't see you."

"Let me get this straight. You want me to sneak out of bed, where a man who wants me dead sleeps beside me. Sneak down into Helen's office and pray you have distracted the guard. Get through the door, find this information you are looking for. Hide it somewhere and then sneak back into bed with William. All without him noticing I was gone. I give that a two out of ten chance of succeeding."

"Don't be such a worry wart. I noticed some sleeping pills in William's bedside table. Put one of those in his drink and you will be fine."

"I don't know if I like your over-enthusiastic attitude, or if I should be scared that you seem so nonchalant about the possibility of my death if your plan should fail."

"So you will do it."

"On one condition."

"Name it."

"Since you know who I am, you will know about my police partner Joe and his wife Sally, yes?" She nodded. "Great. I need them to be kept safe. Not surprisingly, they are a bargaining chip for William. As long as they are at risk, I can't begin to think about getting out of here."

"Done."

"Just like that?"

"Yep. Trust me."

"Trust is a strong word. So once I hear they are safe I will consider it."

"This can't wait."

"Well, I don't know if I can trust you, so it has to."

"Please. I overheard William and Lady Hammond talking about moving operations out of the house. I don't know when it will happen, but we need to get that information before it's too late."

"Then tell me this. That tattoo on your wrist, what is it?"

"Everyone who works for the Hammonds receives an H. A loyalty marker. Despicable, isn't it? It's meant to make people subservient, but it only invigorated my drive to tear this place apart."

"Who put it on you?"

"Caldwell."

"The butler?"

"He's more than the head butler. Him and Helen have been together since before I got here."

"Really?"

"It's a long story. Will you help me?"

"How do I know you aren't in league with the Hammonds and trying to lure me into a trap?"

"You don't, but I suspect you trust your gut. What is your gut telling you?"

"To take a chance and, if the opportunity presents itself, try."

"Thank you." Charlotte smiled, got up to leave.

"One minute, there are a couple other things." I went into the closet and retrieved Helen's Christmas present. "I don't know if this property deed is real, but Helen thought it would be fun, or some kind of insurance maybe, to put my name as the owner of a workplace in Germany. It could also be a trap to see if I am sharing any information, so please make sure your boss doesn't go knocking down any doors."

Charlotte found a pen in William's bedside table, rolled up her sleeve and wrote down the property address. "We will look into this." Again, she made to leave.

"Great. One last thing."

"I really should be going."

"I know, but trust me, this information will be useful. I don't know if they use it here, but in L.A., William had a phone app that people placed their bids for women on. It might lead you to where they keep their money. Especially if I can't get into Helen's office."

"I haven't heard of an app before but we will look into that too. Now I really have to go." Charlotte left without waiting for me to respond.

The rest of the afternoon was spent snacking on biscuits and staring at the same page of my book. I kept it open should anyone walk in, however my mind had wandered to how I would pull off the heist of information. How would I get a sleeping pill in William's drink? He had started to come to bed later. Most often I had fallen asleep before he joined me. I had been grateful for that, but his schedule would not work for this plan. He would be suspicious if I stayed up and waited for him.

Ever one with perfect timing, William walked sloth-like into the room and announced, "Dinner has been canceled. Aunt Helen is so stressed over the party, that it would be better to stay as far away as possible. I asked for it to be served up here. Far away from the stampede of people downstairs." He fell into a chair.

William and I had shared fewer than one hundred words over the last week. Now, we had the rest of the night together. Did this help my plan? Yes. Did I want to spend this much time with him? No.

"Oh, I brought you this." He handed me a 1930's hardcover *Anne of Green Gables* in perfect condition. The green cover was smooth to the touch.

"Where...How?" No offence to Jane Austin, but I was overwhelmed with a contentment I hadn't felt in a long time. In all my troubles as a child, and an adult, Anne would bring me to a world of adventure and love.

"My mother was a fan and my dad had found her this copy as a wedding present. I saw you pull out the copy I had in L.A. and thought you might like it. Someone had put it on a top shelf of the library, so I couldn't find it in time for Christmas."

"I don't know what to say." I put the book I had been reading on the table and with trepidation turned the pages of the beloved classic. "Thank you."

"How are you feeling?"

"I...oh. I am fine. The morning sickness is pretty much gone. Now if only I could go for walks by myself. Caldwell and his men are not exactly enjoyable company."

William rubbed his temples, "Please don't start. I have been working late to get caught up on the business over here and I am exhausted. I really do not want to fight with you. If you can't be civil, can we just sit in silence."

Taken aback, I turned to page one. William unfolded a newspaper off the stack he had not gotten to in a few days. The wrinkle from turned pages was the only sound that permeated the tense atmosphere.

The moment to drug William came in the middle of dinner. While he was in the bathroom, I tiptoed to his bedside table, careful not to disturb the floorboards. With caution, I opened the drawer, the pill bottle remained unmoved.

The pop of the lid made my shoulders tighten. I removed one pill, put the lid back on and closed the drawer.

The toilet flushed. I ran back to the seating area with no concern for noise. I would make an excuse should I need to. I used the back of a spoon to crush the pill against the table. Water collided with the sink. I brushed the powder into his wine glass. The bathroom door opened, the glass still in my hand.

"What are you doing?"

Shit! "I..uh..I was going to top up your drink." Powder floated on top of the wine.

"It's more than half full."

"Right, I-"

William grabbed the glass and my right leg bounced with trepidation as he stood before me, his eyes on the wine.

CHAPTER TWENTY-FOUR

William finished his glass of wine in one large mouthful. Relief flooded over me, and I cut my food into the smallest of pieces, chewing each piece ten times, as I waited for the drugs to take effect.

What I hadn't expected was William's sexual appetite to be ignited. Throughout the meal, he caressed my leg and tried to massage my shoulders, until I batted his hand away. I wondered if I had put the right drugs in his drink. I hadn't looked at the label on the orange prescription bottle, as I was not aware William took anything else. The pill was white, not blue, but then I didn't know what knock-off Viagra looked like.

When not a morsel remained on my plate, I put my fork and knife down. William's soft lips kissed my neck, and his hand crawled under my shirt. My body and mind became embroiled in a battle. One yearned to be touched, the other wanted to run. The body longed for William's hands, to relive the pleasure they had once created, while the mind yelled at me, no pleasure was worth being close to this monster.

If I pushed William away, I would be met with anger, or worse. He had not been this forward with me before and I feared if I said no, he would take what he wanted with force. I reasoned with myself, if I detached my mind from my body's desires, he would be gentle. I shut my mind down and hovered outside myself.

William led me to the bed and removed my shirt. "Is this okay?"

I heard myself say, "Yes."

William tossed my clothes aside and lifted me onto the bed. My eyes blurred his image. A belt buckle unclasped in the distance and clothes dropped onto the floor. The blurred image climbed on top of me, heat radiated from his body , his lips gentle to the touch.

William kissed my shoulder and then collapsed on top of me. The weight of a large boulder crushed me into the mattress and I laboured to breath.

"William?"

No answer. My pokes and prods also elicited no response.

Either the pill kicked in, or he had a heart attack. My life depended on it being the pill. My eyes refocused and the crystal chandelier above the bed came into view. The rest of the room started to eat away at the grey that had taken over my peripheral vision. I mustered all my strength and rolled William over. The snoring started once William was on his back. Not a heart attack.

I quickly got dressed and, inch by inch, moved William to his side of the bed. I would not be able to get him under the covers, so I laid the fleece blanket from the couch over him. It was only ten o'clock. I would need to hold off on going to Helen's office for at least two more hours.

I curled up on the couch and continued my adventures with Anne.

At midnight I crept past William, his snores masked the creaks of the floor. I slowly turned the brass door handle, stuck my head out of the doorway and looked around. No one. The house was dead quiet. I left the door open a crack so that I would not have to worry about the unoiled hinges upon my return.

I slithered along the hallway, as close to the wall as possible, and down the stairs. My stocking feet slid noiselessly along the foyer floor. Before I lifted the large blue and white vase I said a silent prayer. Please, Lord, guide me to the necessary information and quickly.

The lock clicked, muffled by my pounding heartbeat. I closed the door and scanned the papers strewn over her desk. Most were invoices for William's party. I tried the desk drawers but all of them were locked. I looked around the room. A tall bookshelf stood opposite the desk. One shelf held ledgers. I pulled one down, flipped through the pages, but could not make sense of the information. I pulled down another. More nonsense. The Hammonds had a system the average eye would not be able to crack with ease.

After the fourth ledger I decided, even if one had contained useful information, I would not be able to remove it without a noticeable gap left behind. There was no computer for me to look at. I had come up empty-handed. Out of desperation, I pulled the last ledger from the shelf and opened it to a random page. I found a ruler, placed it as close to the inside spine as possible and tore out a page. I turned to another random page and tore it out, then another page. Two more pages followed. I folded them up and stuffed them in the waist of my pants. I slid the ledger back and placed my ear against the door. I heard nothing and opened the door.

"AH!" I gripped my chest, as my heart stopped.

CHAPTER TWENTY-FIVE

C harlotte stood on the other side of the door with a satisfied look on her face.

"You scared me! What are you doing here? You are supposed to be on guard duty."

"Sorry. I was. Let's just say I tuckered him out."

"What if he wakes up?"

"He won't"

Oh to be young and cocky. "Well, here. This was all I could find. Hopefully, you can make sense of their code. There was a whole shelf of ledgers in the same lettering. No computer. Drawers locked. Without anything else to go on, I didn't want to grab anything that might be missed."

"It's a start. But we will need more."

"We? You know what, I don't have time to hang around the scene of the crime while you explain to me what more you need. Let's reconvene once you have Joe and Sally safe. I am doing nothing else until I have proof of that. Agreed?"

"Agreed."

"Goodnight." I ran up the stairs two at a time, down the hallway and threw myself into the bedroom. Out of breath, I closed the door.

"Where were you?"

"Fuck!" I whirled around and William, now in his pajamas, sat awake in bed. "I went to the kitchen and got a drink. I'm sick of water and tea."

"Where is it?"

"I...I drank it down there."

"Right. Anyone see you?

"Charlotte."

"Oh, your new Whitney."

Gut punched, I could not hold back. "You know what, I don't understand you. One minute you treat me like a human, seem to be worried about me and sometimes get all hot and bothered. The next you are as cold as ice and I am a piece of shit you step on to make yourself feel better. I swear you throw Claire's and Whitney's names around like a grenade and wait to see if I'll explode. I ran downstairs for a Goddamn glass of orange juice and ran back because I knew if you woke up you would be mad. Are you happy? You have me dancing around like your little puppet. What else would you like me to perform, my master?"

"Get in bed." He turned off his light.

"What, no witty comeback? Are you sure you don't want to slap me again? Maybe add a black eye into the mix?"

"Get in bed and don't make me ask you again."

"I need to put on my pajamas first." Without waiting for William to speak I went into the closet. Out of view of the bed, I bent over and put my head between my knees. Had I stayed any longer with Charlotte, William would have found us. How had the pill worn off so quickly? Had the wine diluted it's potency?

Covered in silk, I used the moonlight to guide me to the bed. I climbed in and turned away from William. He rolled over and moved so close that his chest pressed against my back. I had already been close to the edge and I had nowhere to go. William wrapped his arm around me. Unsure what he wanted, I stayed completely still.

"I'm sorry."

Did I just hear him right?

"You don't know how much stress I'm under. The business. Our lie. The baby. You have given me no reason to trust you, and then I wake up and find myself naked and you're gone. You can't blame me for being paranoid can you?"

"I guess not. But I've done everything you've asked. At some point you will need to loosen the leash, just a little bit."

"I will try, but there is a lot at stake and if one little thing goes wrong, this time the flames will consume us both."

We remained entangled and my adrenaline started to wane. Exhaustion settled in and it pulled me closer and closer to dreamland. A land of red clay, tall grass and fiddles were in sight when I was abruptly brought back to the present by a tumble in my gut. Then another one. Dazed, it took me a moment to realize it was the baby. I moved William's hand to where I had felt it.

My stomach fluttered and William shot up in bed. "Is that?"

"Yes." William's hand pressed against me and followed the flutters as the baby moved.

"William, may I ask you something?"

"Hmm?"

"If you could do anything differently with this child than you did with Penny, what would it be?" I watched the shadows of the trees outside dance in the moonlight through the window.

"I want to be there more. Not just physically, but actually present in his life. Like a respectable father should be."

Respectable? Really? I bit my lip so I wouldn't share my thoughts. I didn't want to fight. I rested my hand on William's. I had not felt closer to him than at this moment. No deception, just truth. I was still desperate to get away from Hammond Manor and all it's evil. But if I had no choice but to stay, I hoped it was with this William. Though I doubted it.

CHAPTER TWENTY-SIX

At breakfast, the day of the party, Jasper had returned and with smugness. He had a sly grin painted on his face.

"Jasper, what's with that look?" Helen asked.

"I ran into Emma last night at the Black Swan, and she mentioned she was eager to catch up with William." He winked at William.

Before I could ask who Emma was, Helen answered my question. "Emma has been a great help to this family. Albeit, she seems to have to help Jasper out of more legal situations than she should."

"What else are we paying her for if she doesn't keep us out of trouble?"

"She keeps us out of trouble by ensuring the authorities' eyes are pointed elsewhere. The more attention you bring to yourself, the more light shines on this family. You two were so close during your summers here. I bet it would be nice to catch up. She might even be able to help with our situation." She nodded towards me.

Had William told her who I really was? Had Charlotte?

"We don't have a situation here." William said. "Olivia can just forget her place sometimes and get a little hot headed. However, she won't going forward, will you?"

"No." I said.

William brushed my hair behind my ear, "See. No situation."

"All I am saying is Emma is loyal. I am sure Olivia is loyal to you, but is she loyal to this family?"

Everyone stared at me. I swallowed my toast, and took a long sip of tea. "Yes, I am loyal to William. But I am also loyal to myself. I don't see any advantage for me to not be loyal to this family. I understand your hesitation to trust me. But, I think, in time you will find me an asset." Out of the corner of my eye, I saw a small smile appear on William's face.

Helen continued, "The problem is, I trust five people in this world and I doubt you will be the sixth. Given your condition, you are here. But here isn't where you have to stay."

"Our house in Poland is nice. Rather run-down, but really what more do you need?" Jasper said.

"That's enough! Olivia is not going anywhere. Aunt Helen, I appreciate your concern for this family, however we do not have a problem, so let's move on."

Jasper and Helen looked between each other, and must have decided to give up on the subject, as Helen switched back to the topic of the party, which had taken up most of the conversation prior to Jasper's arrival. A number of dignitaries, politicians and business associates would attend, all of whom Helen wanted to ensure William met. He would need to know who was who, if she decided he would be responsible for important aspects of the business. Helen emphasized that she had not made up her mind as to William's role in the business.

"I'm heading to London for a few things," William announced.

"Now? The party is tonight, can it not wait until tomorrow?" Helen said.

"It's for the party tonight."

"Leaving things to the last minute, just like your father. Be back by five o'clock. We need to be ready to receive guests by seven-thirty."

"I promise to be back in time, Aunt Helen." William kissed her cheek.

"The guest of honour should never be late to their own party."

"I won't be." William's voice trailed out the door.

To avoid Helen's wrath, I went to the library. If the house wasn't a home of haunted dreams and villains, I would have loved to spend all of my remaining days surrounded by the voluminous collection. As I climbed down the ladder attached to one of the bookshelves, Jasper entered.

"Since your boyfriend is away, and Aunt Helen is yelling at the servants to perfect everything for the party, I think it is time we talk about what I need you to do."

"Lovely." I walked over and stood by the windows. If I was going to have this conversation, I would at least enjoy the view. Jasper's good looks no longer held appeal.

Jasper paced the room, "As you heard, there are going to be a lot of influential people here tonight. I need you to tell me how receptive they are to William and what they talk about."

"What makes you think I will be part of these conversations? I am sure Helen has other plans for me."

"She might, but I doubt William will let you leave his side, especially given all the trouble you seem to get into when you're around me," he winked. "Aunt Helen will not want to be your guardian. That leaves William. Besides, I doubt there will be any serious business talk, but if there is, you will report back to me. Immediately."

"How will I know what is serious and what isn't?"

"If they talk about William filling the capacity of leadership positions, or he commits to meeting anyone outside of the party. I need to nip those meetings in the bud. I can't have people turning to William for work when they should be turning to me." Jasper perched on top of the desk.

As much as it disgusted me to be close to Jasper, I wanted him to think I was on his side. Men like Jasper responded to flattery, and adherence to their demands. I wasn't good at flirting, but I could try and make Jasper feel powerful. "I am sure you thought about this, but what do I do if I do need to get you some information?" I smiled and leaned against the arm of the leather couch opposite him.

"The servers will be walking around with drinks; however, they will all be alcoholic. If you need to talk to me, place your hand on William's upper arm, tell him you are going to get a drink and head to the bar. I will meet you over there."

"You don't think William will escort me?" I ran my finger along the arm of the couch.

"Not if you do it part-way through a useless conversation. He will feel obligated to entertain whoever he is talking to. He will also be able to watch you."

"When he asks what you and I spoke about?"

"Tell him I, pathetically, tried to hit on you." He smiled. I forced a smile back.

"If I keep running to the bar after every conversation and talk to you, William will put two and two together. And what about the people around us at the bar, won't they overhear me relaying information and inform Helen?"

"I will handle those who may overhear us. Only meet me at the bar when you have information that must be communicated directly. Otherwise, whatever guests have committed to meeting William, just signal me when you are with them, and I will track them down later in the party."

"Okay. How about, if I brush the hair behind my left ear?"

"That will work." Jasper's eyes were enraptured by my hand as I practiced. He hopped off the desk and stood before me. "I am glad you came to your senses about my proposition. This will work out better for you in the long run."

Even when I stood up, I still needed to crane my neck to meet his gaze. "As I said at breakfast, I look out for myself." I ran my fingers along the buttons of his shirt.

"As long as that means you look out for me as well, I think we will make a good team." He framed my face with his cold hands and kissed me. I willed myself to not pull away from his slimy lips.

"Sorry, I don't mean to interrupt, but Lady Hammond would like to see you, Lord Hammond."

Jasper stepped back, smiled and trotted towards the door. Behind me stood Charlotte who looked innocent as ever. As Jasper passed, she told him Helen was in the parlor. I thought she was about to follow behind him, but instead she closed the door.

"What are you doing? Are you crazy to get involved with that man? You should be keeping a low profile."

"It's either that or raise suspicion by not playing his game."

"Well, be careful. Jasper has a way of turning people into his pawns and it never works out well for them in the end. Now, I don't have much time, but I have information about Joe and Sally."

"Are they okay?"

"Yes, but they do have people watching them. From what we have gathered, Joe has noticed, but has yet to make a move. We don't think Sally knows, as she seems all-too-happy to leave her house."

"Can you get them somewhere safe, forever?"

"We are putting everything in place now."

"What about getting word to Joe that I am okay. Well, not okay, but alive. He had beaten himself up after I had gone missing the first time. I can't stand to think about what he is going through."

"I'm not sure that's a good idea. What if he finds you and ruins everything I have been working towards?"

"If it is coming from MI5, he should respect your wishes. Please just tell him enough to be satisfied that I will be okay."

"Fine. I gotta go. Lady Hammond cannot stop finding something wrong with every aspect of the party. I have rearranged the flowers from one vase, to another and back to the original vase too many times to count. Good luck tonight."

Once Charlotte had left, I sat on the couch and rested my head in my hands. I was a strong woman, but had I taken on too much? I had to keep William's temper at bay, at the same time as I tried to decipher what it meant when he was vulnerable. I could not have Jasper turn on me, or Helen exile me, and, in a few hours, I would face a house full of guests who supported the cruelty this family imparted on the world.

One step out of line and everything would crumble down on top of me.

CHAPTER TWENTY-SEVEN

The party loomed and, with the requirement for me to put on a happy face, I avoided as many people as possible for the rest of the day. Most times the bedroom felt like a prison, but today it was my sanctum. No Jasper, no William and never Helen.

I fought back against the negative thoughts which tried to creep to the forefront of my mind. If I walked down that dark winding road, the tangled vines would ensnare me and I would become trapped inside the horrors of my past. Or my present.

My mouth watered for alcohol, or any mind-numbing agent, to prevent the synapses in my brain from firing arrows of regret, sorrow, apprehension and fear. Unable to alter my mental state with a substance, I put up my well-used shield of denial and repression.

I lost myself in the words of writers. A calm before the storm. A storm that started to brew when Caldwell opened the bedroom door, without the customary knock, and brought me out of fantastical worlds and back to the real one. Caldwell's lack of acknowledgment of me had become familiar and expected.

He carried a tower of three white boxes, each a different size and each wrapped in a gold ribbon. Caldwell bent over, like a robot, and placed the packages on the bench at the foot of the bed. Even when he stood directly in front of me, his eyes rested above me. I did not mind. The hardened face told me the less I interacted with him, the better.

Without another task to occupy him, Caldwell left and was replaced by William. His head was held high and his wide shoulders back.

"I thought you might want to wear something a little less stuffy than the clothes in the closet."

William sat on the edge of the bed and I untangled myself from the bedding. I rounded to the tower of boxes and hesitated. My life had been spent longing for presents that never came. When I received the random birthday or Christmas present, it was either hand-me-downs or practical items like socks. Not even fun socks, but plain white sports socks. Extravagant gifts would only be given with strings attached.

I understood what strings were attached to the boxes in front of me. Contrived affection and obedience. I undid the ribbon of the smallest box, on the top of the pile, and pulled out a black case. Inside was a beautiful V shaped diamond necklace. The diamonds got larger as they progressed to the bottom of the V. It was accompanied by matching diamond earrings, a barrette and tennis bracelet. I felt unworthy to wear such luxuries, even if it was only to make a good impression to the high-profile guests of the evening. To do so, I supposed I would need to look the part.

I put the case back in the box and set it aside. A pair of Alabaster Pink sling-back pumps filled the second box, Prada written on the bottom. I was grateful the heel was short. Standing all night would have been unbearable in anything higher. I put that box aside and struggled to undo the tight ribbon around the largest box. William rose off the bed, but the bow loosened and he sat back down. I put the lid on the floor and unwrapped a layer of pink tissue paper.

My jaw tightened. I looked down on a white nurse's costume, too small for the box, and eerily similar to the one Adam had forced me to wear at a horrific party five months ago. I glanced up at William, who wore a large grin and released a roar of laughter. I was less impressed.

William could barely get his words out."What? You would be a big hit with guests."

I shook my head, but I could not contain a small smile. There were worse jokes William could have played. I bundled up the outfit and tossed it at his face. William batted it out of the air before impact.

I opened another layer of tissue paper and was presented with a beautiful, royal blue, velvet dress. I pulled out the dress and the fabric released like an accordion. The top was made of floral lace, with some jeweled accents. The blue velvet from the flowing skirt criss-crossed over the chest and wrapped around the neck. William was right, it was a lot less aristocratic then the clothes I had been forced to wear to date. It was one of the most beautiful dresses I had ever seen.

William had regained himself, "What do you think?"

"I think you will look great in blue."

William laughed, got off the bed, picked up the costume and brought it with him to the closet, "We will put this in here for safekeeping." Hangers rustled, drawers opened and closed, and William emerged with an armful of clothes.

"I will get ready in one of the guest rooms, so that you can have this space to yourself. Be downstairs by 7:30 p.m. as guests will be arriving by eight, and some always arrive early."

I nodded. William rested his hand on the doorframe and turned back, his smile gone. "I don't have to tell you how important tonight is for me. Don't mess it up." The previous moment of normalcy was sliced into pieces.

I draped the dress over its box and had a shower. When I came back out, Charlotte waited by the vanity. She had hung the dress up on the closet door. The shoes were placed neatly under it and the jewelry was displayed on top of the vanity.

"Lady Hammond asked me to come help you," she said.

"And William didn't protest?" William didn't trust Charlotte, so why would he be okay with us being alone?

"I think William knows what battles to fight and given Helen's on the warpath today, this wasn't something to argue about."

"Right. Any news on Joe and Sally?"

"Arrangements are being made, but I have no other news at the moment. Sorry."

I sat down at the vanity and Charlotte styled my hair into waves that framed my face. The diamond barrette pinned up some of the hair behind my right ear. Silver and black eye shadow created a dramatic effect around my eyes. The rest of the make-up was subtle and based on natural tones. I stepped into the floor-length, empire-waisted dress. When I had removed it from the box, I had not noticed a slit which went up most of the left leg. The skirt fabric was loose and hid any sign of pregnancy. I was amazed at how beautiful I looked.

This was the first Hammond party where I did not feel like an escort. Even if the payment I received for my attendance was my life.

In all of my interactions with Charlotte, I had been so worried about me, I hadn't asked how she had managed to infiltrate the Hammonds. She clipped the bracelet to my wrist, and reflections of light danced on the ceiling.

"How is it that no one here knows who you are?" I asked.

"My mother worked for the Hammonds until she died, and I replaced her three years ago. I had helped out, on occasion, for larger parties when extra staff was needed, so the Hammonds already trusted me. Two years ago, MI5 approached me."

"I have to ask, how old are you? You seem a little young to be involved in all of this?"

"I'll take the compliment. I'm thirty-two, but my youthful looks are probably what helps hide me in plain sight."

"I can see that. Crazy question, how could you possibly have been trained as an agent when you are stuck here?"

Charlotte smiled, "Right, well, some errands I had to run in the city would take a little longer, or I would have a sick relative that required attention for a few days. Honestly, most of the time I just wing it."

"You wing it? My life, and the lives of those I love, are in the hands of someone who just wings it?" I was starting to lose faith in Charlotte's ability to help me.

"Okay maybe wing it wasn't the best choice of words. I follow my intuition, use the training I did receive, and am actually quite smart, so you have nothing to worry about."

"Right, no worries as I stare death in the face, but sure, I'll trust your weekend training has been adequate."

"Well, I am all you've got, which is better than no one at all."

She was right, at this point I would have to take my chances. To date, I had no reason not to trust her. "A couple more questions; knowing the Hammonds as you do, you had no misgivings about spying on them? If Helen is anything like William, there would be a high probability of death."

"It may be idealistic, but I would like to live in a world different from the status quo. A world where I can make a difference. I can make a difference through the destruction of this family."

"And you trust your boss?"

"A hundred percent. The Hammonds may have a lot of people in their pocket, but they don't even know who my boss is. Most people don't know he exists. It may all seem very James Bond to you, and in a way it is, but if you could see what we have put together you wouldn't second-guess our tactics."

"How big is the team that is on this? Are you sure you don't have a mole?

"There are only four of us. The four my boss thoroughly vetted. He, too, recognized that there would be a serious risk of a mole."

"It only takes one person to be a mole."

"True. We don't have a mole. I would be dead by now if we did."

"Would you?"

The question hung in the air like a cloudy mist. If a mole was flawless, no one would suspect them.

"Why haven't you gone after them yet, if you have been compiling evidence for two years?"

"We haven't been able to legally go after them for a few reasons. First, they are really good at covering up any paper trail. We still have not been able to decipher the pages you gave us, but we have people working around the clock trying to do so. Second, Emma is an impeccable lawyer. We tried to go after them a few times for tax evasion, but she handily had the cases dismissed, and not because she had a judge in her pocket. Third, we have never been able to find someone who would testify. A jury loves a witness." Charlotte repositioned some of my hair to fall over the front of my shoulder and stepped back.

"And you want me to testify? Are you insane? I may not know the plan for me after I give birth to my son, but it likely includes a grave if I am not careful. Now, you want to ensure that is the result?" I had asked multiple witnesses to put their life on the line and pretended the risk was minimal. Charlotte would not be able to use the same tactic. Not when I needed to protect my child.

"We can protect you and the baby."

"I get it - you need someone deep on the inside. But Helen would have no qualms about getting rid of me, and the child, if it meant protecting her family. I don't know if I could risk that. I also don't want to be on the front of every newspaper. Should this ever end, I just want to hide away somewhere, where no one knows who I am."

"Just think it over. If we can arrange it, I will get you to meet my boss, and you can judge our efforts for yourself. In the meantime, keep your eyes and ears open, as any little bit helps. Tonight's party will be a petri dish of information."

I still didn't have any proof that Joe and Sally were safe, so I withheld that Jasper had also asked me to relay information to him. "I will see what I can do."

Charlotte helped me into my shoes, opened the door and whispered, "Good luck."

I needed more than luck.

CHAPTER TWENTY-EIGHT

Helen's hostile voice ricocheted off the walls. Servants scrambled to follow her last- minute orders. I stopped at the top of the stairs, grateful to be hidden from view. My knees knocked against each other and my hands shook. I gripped the dark wooden stairwell railing and took the first set of stairs, one step at a time.

All sound ceased the moment I stepped onto the landing. In the middle of the reception hall stood all three Hammonds, their eyes fixed on me. The staff had stopped their tasks, surveyed me, and quickly returned to work. No distraction would be suitable for delayed perfection. Helen, in a silver, scoop-necked, knee-length dress, devoured me with her eyes and returned to her role as taskmaster.

Jasper had opted against a traditional black tuxedo and chosen one of burgundy, with black lapels and topped off with a black bow tie. Why were all the good-looking men in my life evil? I broke from his gaze and continued down the stairs.

William, who stood beside Jasper, looked very dapper in his black tuxedo. He had added some flair to his outfit with a blue paisley printed bow tie and accompanying pocket square. The royal blue made his blue eyes seem more piercing than ever. William's wavy brown hair had been tamed, but for a few stragglers. A charmed smile spread across his face, my heart fluttered, and I couldn't help but smile.

The reception hall no longer held signs of Christmas, and had been converted into an indoor garden. Bursts of pink, orange, yellow, blue, purple and green were everywhere. The winter weather did not hinder Helen's ability to bring in flowers from all over the world. A large stepping-stone fountain had been erected by the front corner. I did not think the house could become any more magnificent; however, in the few short hours after breakfast, the hall had been completely transformed. Caldwell's men stood evenly spaced throughout the room and held trays of champagne. They looked very stoic, almost statue-like.

I approached the group and Helen turned back around, gave me another once over, "Good, you look presentable. Now, when people start to arrive, we will receive them outside as usual. William, you stand beside me, Jasper, you will be on the other side of Olivia."

Resentment flashed briefly across Jasper's face. If anyone had noticed, it was not acknowledged. Before William and I had arrived, I was positive Jasper would have been positioned beside Helen, and now he had been relegated to fourth in line. I took pleasure in that thought.

Caldwell opened the heavy front door with ease and we stepped out into the cold winter breeze. Helen cared not if people froze; there would be no outdoor jackets, as we all needed to look beautiful and strong, while guests were greeted. The trees which encased the property had a thin layer of snow which reflected the fire from the torches that had been set up on both sides of the lengthy driveway. Everyone took their places, with Caldwell positioned just to the side of the front steps, to assist people as needed.

The first set of headlights appeared and for the next forty-five minutes there was a steady stream of arrivals. I plastered on a smile, hid my shivering as best I could, and said nothing when each person scrutinized me. Most did so with their eyes, others added a commentary to their stares.

I curtsied when William told me to and almost toppled over once. Thankfully, William supported me before I embarrassed myself, or the family. I could feel Helen's eyes of disgrace burrow into the side of my head. Jasper tried to make me laugh with appropriate remarks about the strangers I met.

Guests continued to arrive after forty-five minutes; however, Helen was adamant that if they had wanted to be greeted they should have arrived on time. William and I, arm in arm, followed Helen around the reception hall once and then she took off the leash so that we could mingle on our own. People rarely addressed me directly, but rather inquired with William. Normally, my feminist instincts would have kicked in, but I bit my tongue. I accepted the polite greetings and compliments on my dress. The less I said, the less trouble I could get myself into.

As William spoke to a member of the House of Commons about some controversial new law, heads around the room turned towards the front door. William and I mimicked the herd.

A tall woman, with long, brilliant red hair, and voluptuous curves walked in with an air of prestigiousness that captivated everyone's attention. If I thought I looked beautiful, she looked immaculate. She wore a black v-neck dress which impeccably hugged the top half of her body. The skirt had an opening larger than a slit that exposed her toned legs. Layers of fabric built off the next one until it hit the floor and flowed behind her when she walked.

William leaned over, "That is Emma." Admiration materialized in his eyes.

Every muscle in my body tightened and my chest burned. I had only seen William look at me that way. What was happening? Was I jealous? What was wrong with me? I tried to douse the fire in my chest as the crowd parted like the Red Sea and Emma made her way towards us, her eyes and smile locked on William. I looked up at him and could see his cheeks were flushed. The fire inside me grew hotter. Emma stopped in front of William, without a glance in my direction. She held out her hand, which William took and politely kissed the top of.

She kept hold of his hand, "How nice to see you after all this time."

William slipped his hand out from her grip, "Nice to see you again. Let me introduce you to my girlfriend, Olivia."

At least he recalled who I was.

"Yes, Olivia, I have heard all about you. William, I hear things did not work out too well in L.A. I do hope that means you will be staying here for a while. I miss our long, late-night walks." Emma leaned in and straightened William's perfectly aligned bow tie.

William's hand, which had been resting on my back, twitched and I leaned back and noticed his right hand mirrored his left. His jaw was clenched. William pulled me closer to him, which must have had the result he was looking for, as Emma stepped back and he relaxed.

"Aunt Helen tells me you built up a successful law practice in London. Congratulations."

"Yes, well, I could not have done it without her. She believed in me when no one else did. Other than you, of course. I finally managed to pay the last of my tuition debt to her, and, even with a portion of the profits landing in Helen's coffers, I live like a queen."

"You do not give yourself enough credit. Even without Aunt Helen, you would have succeeded."

"Before we get lost in the whole catch-up business, I just wanted to say how sorry I was to hear about Sharon and Penny's passing."

The smile vanished from William's face, his shoulders slumped, and his eyes went dead. The door to buried memories had been opened and, with it, a flood of hurt. William removed his hand from my back, looked at his feet and rubbed the back of his neck as he mumbled, "Thank you".

Emma pursed her lips and glared at me with a smugness I wanted to slap off her face. Did she view me as a threat? Or an obstacle to be removed? What better way, than to have William do it himself? She had reminded him of what he did to his family and William's anger at himself would only be quashed upon release against the one person he had control over. Me. I had to hand it to Emma, she was good.

Jasper joined us, handed William a drink and wrapped his arm over Emma's shoulder, "Glad you could make it. Love the dress."

Emma weasled herself from under his arm, "Jasper, ever the one for a dramatic outfit."

"Why be boring, when you can be fun? Why don't I take Olivia to get a drink, she looks a little parched, and then you two can catch up."

William looked as though he might protest, and I hoped he would. He regained his composure, but the hurt in his eyes lingered. Jasper dragged me away without objection and Emma took William by the arm and led him to the side of the room where less people had gathered.

Jasper weaved me through the crowd and over to the bar that was set up under the stairs, "An Old Fashioned for me, and some orange juice for the lady."

I had lost sight of William, so I thanked the bartender and addressed Jasper, "Why did you pull me away? How am I supposed to report to you what they talk about if I am not present for the conversation?"

"We have nothing to worry about with Emma. She works for the highest bidder, unbeknownst to Aunt Helen. I have enough on her that she won't be able to do anything but support me."

"And you don't think Helen has the same, or more, information?"

Jasper pondered for a moment, "Emma is a smart woman, she will see the tides are changing and roll with them." He finished his drink, got another and then we stepped away from the bar.

William and Emma were now within my sightline. They, and Helen, were talking to an older couple, mid-sixties, who wore blue sashes with medals on them. I had no idea what the medals were, but I expected they meant the people wearing them were important. I also noticed an alluring young woman dressed in a skin-tight, strapless, black dress, was part of the group. She flirted with the guests, who blushed profusely. When she brushed some hair away from her forehead, I noticed a scar on the inside of her wrist. I was too far away to make it out, but I knew what it was.

I looked around the room and noticed multiple women wearing the same dress, faces plastered with smiles and their hands suggestively on the body of another person. Men dressed in all-black suits, rather than the tuxedos of the attendees, were interspersed around the crowd. Their simulated smiles were a little more obvious.

This wasn't just a welcome home party for William, this was a business endeavor. A room full of masters and slaves. I counted twenty-five men and forty women. All of which I was certain had an H branded on their wrists. Why had William not told me the party would be worked? Enraged, I marched towards William, Helen and Emma.

Jasper gripped my wrist and whipped me around, "Where do you think you are going? I need my report."

"Your report, ha! Well, first you need to tell me what the hell is going on here. I thought that this was a party for William, not a buffet of sex slaves."

"I see you noticed we have extra, let's call them, appetizers, present. Right, you were not supposed to know about that."

"I...how would I not notice men and women scattered throughout the crowd all dressed more casually than the guests? What kind of detective would I have been if I did not pick up on that detail? And why in the world would I not be told?"

"One, you have no right to know what business decisions we make. Two, we did not want you to make a scene. Like you were about to do."

"Oh, I can make a scene."

Jasper's grip tightened, "How about you not get yourself killed, and just tell me what information you have gathered."

Infuriated, I pulled my arm loose but accepted he was right. Any rash outbursts and I would be buried before the sun came up. "I don't have much to provide." I wanted to keep my cards close to my chest. "That man over there, next to the painting of the battle of whatever, mentioned something about looking forward to working with William. Otherwise, most were either curious about L.A. or made small talk about nothing relevant. I suspect you kept tabs on everyone who approached us, so I don't have to try and recall their names or point them out?"

"I have, but you might want to work on your memory. The closer to the finish line we get the more important the people will be. Speaking of L.A., what really happened? William keeps saying one of the fireplaces was left unattended. That seems highly unlikely."

I prayed Jasper's deception-detection skills were less than that of William, "He hasn't told me any different. Truth be told, that was not the first time it happened. One night, we had thought we had doused the fire in the bedroom, but woke up to a room full of smoke. Thankfully, we caught it before it had spread outside the fireplace. It would be reasonable to believe the incident in the dining room was no different, except people were not woken by the smoke. Jasper appeared satisfied with my answer and I hoped he never found out William's bedroom had not had a fireplace.

A hand touched my back and, startled, I jumped. William came around beside me and firmly said, "I need to talk to you."

"Oh. Alright." I caught my breath, playfully twirled my hair and smiled at Jasper. William looked sullen and the last thing I needed was Jasper to follow. I hoped a little flirtation would do the trick.

William led me towards the Library. Before he could open the door, a resounding voice filled the room. The scratching of fabric, and the friction of leather shoe soles on marble, followed as everyone turned to find the source. Caldwell stood on the staircase, four steps below Helen. Once all eyes were forward, Caldwell stepped away.

"Damn it!" William took my hand and we weaved our way through the crowd that had closed in on the stairwell. We stopped at the front of the crowd, and settled beside Jasper and Emma.

"Most honoured guests, I humbly thank you for joining us here tonight to celebrate the return of my nephew, William. Many of you knew him when he spent his summers here on the estate. He has a brilliant business mind and thrived in the States. Due to some unfortunate, but maybe blessed, circumstances he has relocated here. As William adjusts to our way of doing business, I am sure many of you will be fortunate enough to collaborate with him. I graciously ask that you treat him as you would me. William, why don't you come up and say a few words."

William had not let go of my hand, and now led me up the stairs with him, much to Helen's dismay. We faced the crowd and I was amazed by just how many people filled the room. I had suspected the Hammonds' reach was wide, but I had not actually comprehended it in terms of numbers. And these guests were just those I presumed were in the area, and in a high enough echelon to receive an invitation. Jasper shifted from one foot to the other and tapped a finger nervously on his glass.

William cleared his throat and addressed the crowd, "Thank you, Lady Hammond, for putting together this impeccable party. Thank you everyone for joining us tonight, I do appreciate the warm welcome and wish you all a Happy New Year. I am not a man of many words, although my darling Olivia here would probably argue otherwise."

Quiet laughter filtered through the crowd.

"I do look forward to working with most, if not all of you, in the near future. I think, under Lady Hammond's guidance, we can bring even more success to the business."

I found it ironic that the baby started to kick at that moment. A battle in my womb against the aristocrats and their incessant need for power and money. The sounds around me dissipated while rage seeped out of my pores. I desperately wanted to lash out at the room, lecture them about how their actions ruined the lives of countless people. How their selfishness created systems of oppression, for the sole purpose of profit. The lucky few victims who did not end up dead, if they were anything like me, would be forever terrified of the people around them. Nightmares for dreams.

With heavy breaths, I found every piece of property dressed in a short black dress or suit and willed them to revolt. Maybe not tonight, but someday.

The hum of William's voice slowly filtered into my ears and I faintly heard a joke about my grip strength. He held up our interlocked hands to display his contorted fingers, the tips bright red. I loosened my grip and apologized, "Pardon me. I'm a little nervous."

A few in the crowd provided obligatory laughter and William continued, "I am sure you do not want to hear me ramble on, but before I let you get back to the party, there is one thing I need to take care of." He dropped my hand and walked down a few steps. When he turned back around, his face had transformed from jovial to stern.

I looked to Jasper for any indication of what would happen next, but confusion rested on his face. My eyes landed on Emma, who appeared exuberant about the turn of events. Helen, only a few body lengths to my right, stood with her hand resting on the banister. Added to her regular air of callous superiority, was a hint of malice.

A trickle of sweat voyaged down the valley of my back and the crevasse of my breasts. All eyes were on me. There was nowhere for me to run. My focus returned to William, who had a hand inside his jacket pocket.

I raised the hem of my dress, I had to at least try to leave. One against hundreds were not odds in my favour, but I could read the hostile mood around me and I could not stay put. My foot hovered over the front of the step I was on.

"Don't move," William ordered. "I had planned to do this a little more privately, but you and I both know how plans do not always come to be. In a way, handling our little situation in front of everyone feels a little more...what's the word...serendipitous."

William pulled his hand out of his pocket, the rays of light from the teardrop crystal Chandelier pieces kissed something black in his hand.

CHAPTER TWENTY-NINE

I had known the day would come when William would attempt to take my life. Every indication had been that it would occur after the baby was born. Had Helen won and William now wanted to sacrifice the child? Has Jasper revealed our partnership? It would only hinder his succession; however, it would ensure my downfall.

Whatever it was, I was done. Done pretending I could win. I was not strong enough to survive this place, or these people. I couldn't fight back. If I was meant to be sacrificed in front of a crowd of people, so be it. I would not put on a show of defiance for the crowd, just to be shot like an animal, like Claire had been. God, please just make it quick. The back of my eyelids were my only comfort.

"Olivia?" whispered William. "Please open your eyes. You are leaving me exposed here."

My curiosity gave in to the calm urgency in his voice. I cracked open my eyes. They had not been closed long, so the adjustment to the bright light was minimal. However, I was stunned just the same.

At the bottom of the stairs knelt William and he held an open black velvet box. My eyes bulged and my jaw dropped, at the sight of a large princess-cut sapphire perched on a band of white diamonds. What was happening? I must have missed the question, as, when I looked up from the box, William's eyes pleaded with me to say something.

"Third time's a charm? Olivia, will you marry me?"

The room had become a tomb. Rows of deathly still bodies stared forward. The only sounds came from a faint rattle in the air vents and the gurgle of the water fountain. Even the ice cubes stopped clattering against glass. My brain flipped a switch and rebooted. Marriage? What was William thinking? My life depended on adhering to his plans, and yet not once had he told me what they were. Sure, he got some sick pleasure out of manipulation, but this!

I had no choice. My throat tightened and I could not speak. Thankfully, I would not have to actually say yes to marrying William. I plastered a smile on my face and nodded. A collective sigh of relief emitted from the crowd below, William included. He walked back up the steps and put the heavy ring on my finger. It fit perfectly.

A few people in the crowd yelled "Kiss her!"

William put one hand behind my neck and the other on the small of my back and pulled me close. Our eyes locked, before our lips met, and I thought there was a reflection of actual affection. The kiss was supple and sweet. As we parted the crowd erupted in celebration. William laughed and bowed, so I played along and curtsied. We hopped down the steps and were greeted by congratulations from those in the front row. Everyone, that is, but Jasper and Emma.

The congratulatory line went on for more than an hour. People I had been introduced to earlier now acknowledged my existence. It was a complete one hundred and eighty degree turn, but I knew they only wanted to appease William. I continued to play along, now the dutiful fiancée. Ugh, that word, fiancée. It would not take residence in my vocabulary for long. Not if I could help it.

I spotted Helen, Jasper and Emma huddled at the other side of the room. Their noses wrinkled and lips pursed. William noticed as well, excused us from the group that had gathered around us, and led me toward the disdain. When we approached, obligatory smiles spread across all three of their faces.

"Congratulations, William!" Emma said. Her pretentious and yet playful voice did nothing to hide her contempt. "Olivia."

"Congratulations, cousin!" Jasper hugged William. "Are you going to make an honest man out of him now?"

"Yeah, sure. Any tips?" Only William laughed.

"You will not get a congratulations from me," said Helen. "You hijacked this party and had not informed me of your plans. Keeping information from me is unacceptable." Helen's voice seared through the tension she oozed.

"I apologize. To be honest, I was not sure if I would propose tonight. However, given certain conversations," his eyes rested on Emma as he continued, "I thought it best. Now, people will definitely talk about the party you put together."

"They were supposed to be talking about the prospects that would grow from having you here. Now, all they are going to talk about is you and this...this whore you think you are going to marry."

The volume of the voices around us lowered and, while the conversations continued, no one paid attention to anything but William and Helen.

The veins in William's neck throbbed. He reached out his hand towards Helen as if he wanted to strangle her, but pulled it back, "Don't you ever call Olivia a whore! She is not only the mother of my child, but she is stronger than you could ever realize. Now apologize."

Helen's mouth dropped, Jasper tried to stifle a grin, and Emma took a step back.

"I will not apologize."

"APOLOGIZE!"

The attention of the room once again directed itself at us. Helen's face turned scarlet and her eyes twitched from side to side as she calculated her move. Helen had wanted the guests to respect William, and to show her superiority, which had just been challenged. A quarrel with William would demonstrate there could be a rift in the family. Rifts would not be good for business. If she backed down, everyone would see that William held the power. Everyone waited with bated breath.

Helen finished her drink and spoke through gritted teeth, "Olivia, I am sorry. You are a wonderful young lady and I am sure you will make

William very happy." With that, she departed.

Emma turned and walked out of the house, not a word to anyone on her way.

Jasper laughed and patted William on the back, "I forgot how big your balls were, mate. Taking on Aunt Helen. Phew. You are in for it now. Good luck." He turned to leave but then pivoted around again, "I forgot to congratulate your lovely bride-to-be. How rude of me." Jasper wrapped his arms around me and whispered "We will need to take care of this." He nodded to William and joined a group of guests nearby.

William and I were unaccompanied for the first time all night. I didn't know what to say about any of the events of the evening, especially the engagement, but I was exhausted and wanted to be as far away from the party as possible. "Would it be rude of us to leave? I am tired, and if I have to keep this fake Barbie doll smile on my face for much longer, I might scream."

"I am sure the guests would forgive us for not staying until midnight. I expect they will presume we are going to celebrate."

"Ha! Very true."

William held out his hand, palm up, "Shall we?"

I smiled and put my hand in his. I prayed that when we got back to our room, away from prying eyes, the monster who lurked inside of William stayed hidden. I also prayed that the DNA that made William a sadistic monster, whose mood swings were abrupt and violent, did not reside within the child inside me.

CHAPTER THIRTY

I kicked my shoes off the moment I stepped through the bedroom door and welcomed immediate relief. They may not have been two-inch stilettos, but my feet were glad to be free. Pajamas had not been laid out tonight, the staff busy with the party, so I walked into the closet to change. William had just hung his suit jacket when I entered.

I removed the gifted jewelry and placed the pieces in their respective spots in their box, on top of the cabinet in the center of the closet. My hair fell to my shoulders as I released the barrette and I placed it in its predetermined crevasse. That was when I noticed the box had an opening I hadn't paid attention to before, for the engagement ring. I looked at my finger. The ring was beautiful. And heavy. Not just in physical weight, but the weight of what a marriage to William could mean - if it were to happen at all. For all I knew, everything was part of the charade and I had only just received the updated script.

I slipped the ring off my finger, put it in the box and started to fiddle with the three small buttons on the back of my neck. The buttons would not give.

"Damn it!" I slammed my hand on the dark wood cabinet in the middle of the room.

"Need help?"

"Ugh, yes please."

William stood behind me, fought with the buttons and lost. He maneuvered his fingers around the lace, and, with each tug, the neck of the dress got tighter around my throat. My airway started to get smaller. I choked for air.

"Fucking buttons!" William yanked the lace hard, and tore the dress. "I can get you a replacement."

The velocity of his dress destruction pummeled me against the cabinet. I caught myself before the top of it rammed into my belly. "It's okay. In another month, I probably wouldn't fit into it anyways." I needed to lighten the mood. It didn't take much to go from somewhat happy William to angry William. "I know you had a lot of fun with those buttons, but could I get your help with the zipper? I can't quite reach it."

I braced myself against the cabinet, in case the zipper was just as stubborn as the buttons. It released with ease.

Rather than stepping back and continuing to get undressed, William stayed put. His hands rested on my lower back, where the zipper ended. My grip on the cabinet tightened and the hairs on the back of my neck started to stand tall as William's breath danced across it.

The mirror on the opposite wall revealed a man, lost in troubled thoughts, his eyes fixated on my exposed back. In moments like these, where William looked more scared and unsure than terrifying and angry, my hatred for him melted. Was it my desperate need to redeem the lost? Or had I been around William so long that an inexplicable bond had formed? I pushed away my questions, and the feelings that had started to rush blood through my body; I would not think about any of that tonight.

I shifted my weight between my feet in the hopes that the movement or the rustle of my dress would bring William back to the present. It worked. William looked up and we locked eyes in the mirror. His sullen face was unchanged. William leaned his forehead against the back of my head. His cologne encased me and I willed away all of the memories attached to it. William swept my hair to the side and with the lightest touch kissed my neck.

My gasp at his touch startled him and he backed away, looking at me in the mirror with concern, and asked, "Are you okay with this?"

This was the second time William had asked me for permission. Neither he, nor any Hammond, had ever asked me if I was okay with anything. Now, it was twice in the span of a week. I still feared how he would react if I said no. I also didn't know if I wanted to. I nodded.

Nothing about my life with William had been straightforward. Now with Jasper and Helen added to the mix, I was exhausted, fed up, and after everything I had been through, I just wanted to escape my life. Even for a little while.

I faced William, his shirt half-undone and his wavy hair in disarray after the battle with my dress. There was only one voice inside my head tonight, it screamed "You need this! What's the worst that could happen? You are already pregnant, why add battered and bruised. Enjoy yourself!"

I slid my arms out of their lace and let the dress fall to the floor. William stepped forward, rested his hands on my hips, and kissed me. Our lips locked, we scrambled to remove William's clothes.

We took in each other's bodies, his well built, mine showing the beautiful signs of pregnancy. A small smile crept across William's face. Something about him was different. He seemed relaxed and, dare I say, happy. I was a mess of emotions, which I continued to ignore.

Rather than wait for William to make the next move, I took the initiative. I didn't want to stand around with time to second-guess my choices. I stood on my toes, wrapped my hands around the back of his neck and pressed my lips hard against his.

We became entangled in each other, and the clothes hung up along the walls of the closet, as we fumbled around the room. Each touch more satisfying than the last. My body pulsed in anticipation.

I guided William to a bench in one of the clothing alcoves and climbed on top of him. With each thrust of my hips, I released my pent up anger. Our groans of pleasure reverberated around the room.

As we neared the climax, William pulled me as close to him as possible. We couldn't contain the gratification any longer. William's sounds were muffled by my body, but mine filled the alcove.

Our bodies no longer consumed with desire, we sat silent in each other's embrace as we regained our breath and our heart rates slowed. Thoughts of hatred seeped into my head. I hated William. I hated myself.

CHAPTER THIRTY-ONE

T he wind howled outside. The low, grey clouds blocked out the moon and transformed the bedroom into a dark cavern. Music and voices, from the party below, crept through the crack under the bedroom door. Had the racket not kept me awake, my confused thoughts would have.

Awkwardness had filled the closet while William and I put ourselves together. We danced around each other to pick up the tossed clothes. Words were not spoken and gazes averted. We took turns in the shower, unable to be that close to each other for longer than we had to. William had climbed into bed and, without a glance in my direction, turned off his light.

I stared up at a dark ceiling I could not see. A movie reel of thoughts played above me. What transpired in the closet, William's blatant disregard for his Aunt in front of the guests, Jasper's threats, Charlotte an MI5 agent, and the unexpected engagement. All of that combined with a pregnancy and what appeared to be my permanent relocation to England. The memory foam of the mattress pulled me down into itself.

I was not naive enough to think the engagement had any basis in love, despite Jasper's declaration of William's adoration. Even if it did, what would that mean? Was that what I wanted? I tossed onto my side and then onto the other. Engaged, married, or neither, William would not hesitate to kill me after our son was born if he wanted to. It was all too much. A shot of panic overtook me. I flung the blankets off, for fear they would suffocate me, and pushed myself to a seated position, legs dangled over the side of the bed. Light-headed, I gripped the edge of the bed.

The mattress moved behind me. William's hand touched my back and I exploded. I jumped off the bed, wrapped my arms around myself and I paced the room, my breath short and quick. William turned on his bedside lamp, tossed his covers aside and came towards me.

"What's wrong?"

I was hyperventilating and my voice box contracted. My thoughts were all jumbled, so I would not have known what to say if I could talk. Each step William took closer to me, I took two steps backwards. He registered what was happening, stopped, and sat on the couch. I continued to pace the room in the hope my anxious energy would dissipate. My hands fought with my clothes, my hair and my skin.

"Should I get the doctor?" William's voice now matched his worrisome eyes. His hands twitched.

I shook my head no. I knew I would be fine. I had to be.

"I will get you some tea. Maybe that will help?"

William got up and had made his way to the door before I could muster a faint "No. Please...don't go..." and I fell back against the wall and slunk to the floor in a puddle of tears.

William rushed over, but stopped in front of me, "May I sit?"

I nodded. He watched me, as he used his hands to guide himself down the wall, unsure if a sudden move would cause more panic. I stared forward, tears a curtain over my eyes. I tried hard to get control of my breathing but it seemed impossible. William rubbed his hands. One would move towards me before it was pulled back. I took his hand, if only to make him feel better.

We sat together until I calmed my breathing enough to speak above a whisper. "William?"

Startled by my voice, his shoulders jerked, "Yes."

"I need to tell you something, and I need you to not get angry. At least not right now. I need you to stay as calm as possible, otherwise I might spiral again. Can you do that?"

"I can try."

My voice trembled as I verbally vomited my stress, "Jasper attacked me in the woods that day he supervised my walk. He said he was going to kill you and Helen and take over the business. He threatened to take my son and raise him in this life, as his own, if I didn't help him."

William's grip on my hand tightened, but he said nothing.

"I didn't know what to do. I was afraid of him, of you, of what could happen to me. To my...our son. So I went along. I signaled him tonight whenever you spoke to someone about business. Later, he spoke with them and tried to dissuade them from working with you."

William's teeth chattered, "Anything else?"

I hesitated. A thread of carpet was loose beside me and I picked at it with my free hand. If I left anything out, he would find out. "He forced himself on me in the forest, but a gardener came upon us before anything happened. Then, I let him kiss me in the library this morning. I had tried to fight him off in the forest to no avail, and I feared worse would happen to me if I did not play along today."

William let go of my hand, jumped to his feet, and punched the wall. Plaster landed on my head when he removed his hand from the hole he had created. William's face was flush with anger. He looked down at me, "I'm sorry. I tried to stay calm but...I...." He punched another hole in the wall.

I got up off the floor, brushed the white dust off of me and moved away from the wall and William. I did not want to be the next thing he punched. Without warning, William's eyes looked as though an idea had formed. He walked towards his bedside table, opened the drawer and pulled out a gun. A gun that was not there the night I had drugged him. He cocked it and made his way towards the door.

I sprinted across the room and spread myself against the door. "William, no. You do that and we are dead. All three of us."

"If Jasper thinks he can kill me, hurt you and take our child, I cannot sit around and wait for it to happen."

My eyes were focused on the gun, "I know. I know. But not like this. I admit, I don't know what you are going to do with me. But I do know you will protect this child." Slowing, I emphasized each word I said, "Shooting Jasper tonight would take away that protection."

William's steel blue eyes locked on mine and then fell to my stomach. Tears trickled down his cheeks.

I continued, "We don't know what contingency plans he has in place. We need to slow down and think about everything."

William walked over to me and dropped to his knees. He rested his head on my stomach, as he held it with both hands. The cold of the gun seeped through my silk pajamas. "I will protect you," he said.

I slowly eased the gun away from William's grip. He fought, but then let go. I held the gun in one hand and comforted William with the other. I slid my finger over the trigger. It felt nice. Adrenaline coursed through my veins. It would be easy to rest the nozzle against his temple and pull the trigger. Then, the man who ordered Claire's death would be dead.

CHAPTER THIRTY-TWO

My index finger massaged the curve of the trigger. My skin glided over the soft metal. I squeezed and released. Squeezed a bit further and released. The weight of the gun was unnoticeable.

My breathing became laboured as my desire for revenge grew stronger. One bullet would be all it would take.

My head rested against the door. William's soft cries were muffled by my stomach and the war of whispers between my ears. My fingers navigated thick waves on William's head. Could I risk it? Would I make it out of the house alive after a bullet found a home in William's skull? There were enough bullets for Helen and Jasper, but what about any loyal soldier that got in my way?

William cared about the child inside me, so he kept me alive. Without him, death was guaranteed.

My hand under William's chin, I guided him back to his feet. "I think I would like that tea now. It might help us think about our next steps." Two dark-grey house coats hung inside the closet door, I put one on, and handed one to William.

He nodded, reached for the gun and my grip tightened around the handle. One, two, three heartbeats. The heavy barrel propelled the gun forward and upside down on my trigger finger. William slid it off my finger and de-cocked it. The gun now resided in the pocket of his housecoat. If he had ever been without it, after tonight he would not be.

He stepped out into a silent hallway. All of the guests had left sometime during my panic attack.

The kitchen had been thoroughly cleaned after the night's events. One would never have known, only hours earlier, food for hundreds of people had poured out of this room. William found the kettle and put it on while I found cups and some biscuits.

"I'm going to do a quick sweep, make sure no one is lurking to overhear our conversation."

The shrill of the kettle voiced the ghosts of the past. I could hear Claire and Whitney pleas for me to stop pushing my luck by trying to juggle yet another plan on my road to freedom. I silenced the voices before they could travel out of the kitchen and infiltrate the rest of the house.

The pot of chamomile tea sat atop the long wooden table, while nerves prevented me from sitting still on the accompanying bench. Was telling William about Jasper the best plan? It had to have been the safest, right? Jasper had no loyalty to me. William's loyalty resided in his son, and for now, me as its carrier.

As I waited for William to return, I silently prayed.

God, we haven't spoken in a while. Again. But this plan of yours for me has to mean something. Right? Please tell me what it is, as my trust is waning. You've taken Claire, Whitney, and I don't know if Joe or Sally are alright. Soon, I will come face-to-face with William's child. Why is all of this happening? Please keep those I love safe. Please keep William's anger at bay and prevent him from doing anything hasty. Please send me a sign I am doing what you want me to do.

"Amen" had not whispered past my lips when a faint cough echoed from across the room. I unfolded my hands, opened my eyes, and Charlotte stood at the opposite end of the island, dressed in blue checkered pajamas. Her eyes drooped and her usual meticulous bun was a disheveled golden mane. I rushed over to her. "William will be back any minute. If he catches us together again-"

"Okay." She glanced up the back stairs, "Just tell me if you are okay. The marks on your neck. Did he do that?"

I touched my neck, "We couldn't get the dress unbuttoned. I am fine. Shockingly, it was completely unintentional. Look, if you can stay hidden, you will want to hear the conversation I am about to have with William." My eyes darted around the room "You have to promise me you will not interfere with whatever we plan, unless you can take down this entire operation. But only then."

Charlotte's eyes went wide, "What's going on?"

"You wanted me to work with you. This is me working with you. Now go. Before he gets back."

As if on cue, footsteps could be heard through the kitchen archway. Charlotte stepped inside the pantry and hugged the shelves at the back. I closed the door and made sure her shadow did not stretch itself under the door.

William rustled into the room and stared at me for a moment. I removed some milk from the fridge. The creak of the fridge door was overshadowed by the hinges on the back door. William scanned for people outside and checked the stairwell beside me. His eyes were ever curious.

"The place is quiet. We should be just as safe to talk here as in our room. The floors creak and should alert us to any eavesdroppers." William retrieved a small glass bottle from the back of an overhead cupboard, unscrewed the cap, and poured a shot into his steaming cup of tea.

William drew a long breath and released the tension in his shoulders.

I was unfazed by William's dependence on alcohol. With the pantry in my line of sight, I sat down. I wrapped my hands around my tea cup for warmth and waited for William to speak.

"Thank you for telling me about Jasper's plans. I forgive you for not telling me immediately."

"Forgive? What-"

"I just mean, I understand why you did not come to me. I won't hold that against you."

"Well, thank you?"

"If Jasper is planning to take over the business, he would want me out of the way first. Get rid of the competition to succession. The question is, do we risk telling Aunt Helen and let her deal with the matter? Or do we handle it ourselves?"

"I'm sure you are not surprised to hear this, but I don't trust Helen. Like all of you, protection of herself comes first. If I was in her shoes, I would want to secure my position with my contacts without giving any indication of dissension in the ranks. To do this would mean either the disposal of Jasper, without alarming others, or moving him and stripping him, piece by piece, of his power. My guess is Jasper's slow destruction would result in an irrational reaction and cause trouble for everyone. Again, if I was Helen, I would also use this as an opportunity to get rid of unwanted additions to the family, who may be perceived to be part of the plan. But what do I know, they're your family. What do you think?"

"I think it is a little scary how well you know them already. So we don't tell Aunt Helen. How do we take care of Jasper without raising suspicion?"

Was William trying to make me come up with the entire plan? Keep himself out of it? Or was he keeping his cards close to his chest, like usual? He would not have all the power this time. "How has it been dealt with in the past? I am sure this is not the first time you have had to handle an ambitious family member, or worker?"

William's eyes glistened, "And you are skilled at the art of poison so I think we will be a good fit."

"If only I wasn't pregnant and could get my hands on some more Oxy. Let's start with how we need it to look. Accident? Unknown cause of death? Rivalry? Scorned lover?"

"Did your detective school also teach you how to be an assassin?" He smiled and sipped his spiked tea.

"I have seen people attempt to cover up a murder in many ways. Most often, not very well." I yawned, my adrenaline dwindled. "So what do you think?"

"Rivalry would cause too much of a problem with the overall business. Unknown cause of death could draw too much attention to the family. Also, Aunt Helen might think it was a rival so we would be back to starting a war we don't want. A scorned lover would eventually talk, or we would need to get more blood on our hands, which I doubt you would agree to. That leaves us with an accident. We would need to do it off the estate, otherwise Aunt Helen will be on alert."

"A drunken night on the town could lead to many options?" I finished my cup of tea and poured another one. William held out his cup and I topped him off. This time there was no additive.

"Jasper does love a good party. There is a potential for a car accident, we just need to make sure there is no evidence of intent. I'll make some calls in the morning. I need you to keep going along with whatever he has planned. Just keep me updated as it happens. I guess the last thing to determine is the occasion?"

"The loss of your freedom due to a marriage? Which is something else we need to talk about, by the way. Or a simple guys' night out. I don't think Jasper will care. You just need to make sure he doesn't try to take you out at the same time." Although if that happened, maybe Charlotte would be alerted and I could get out of here sooner?

"Which means this has to happen soon, before Jasper can make a more permanent move against me. Tomorrow could be suspicious. Maybe Friday, take a little walk down memory lane at the Phoenix nightclub."

I choked on my tea, "I'm sorry, aren't you a little old to be going to a club? Even then, I cannot picture you enjoying the hot sweaty mess that is one."

"You'd be surprised at how often women are drawn to older men." William winked, stood up and held out his hand "and you'd be surprised how much fun I used to be. I'll show you."

I don't know if it was the pregnancy, or the English air, but the man in front of me was different. Was I getting too comfortable around him, that the simple gesture of asking me to dance pulled a curtain over the past? Only minutes ago I craved his death, now I was drawn to his embrace. The walls I had built were still strong, but if I wasn't careful pieces might start to chip away.

The softness of his hands did nothing to shield my confusion. We danced, cheek to cheek, in the middle of the kitchen. With every rotation, my eyes rested on the pantry. There were no sounds or movements. To minimize the risk of being caught, William and I needed to leave sooner rather than later. I would ask William about the engagement and the workers at the party another time.

"William?"

"Hmm."

"I think if we keep dancing like this, I'm going to fall asleep and you'll have to carry me back to bed."

"I suppose I have kept you up long enough. Let's get you and our son some rest." William kissed my cheek and led me out of the kitchen.

I dared not look back to see if Charlotte emerged from the room in which the next death in William's wake had been planned.

CHAPTER THIRTY-THREE

A loud knock at the bedroom door woke me from a dreamless sleep. Bones cracked and muscles objected to my attempt to sit up. William, already dressed in black suit pants and white dress shirt, answered the door. Charlotte wheeled in a cart full of fruits, breads, pastries, tea and juice.

"Good Morning, Mr. Hammond. Brunch delivery for everyone in their rooms today."

"Thank you. You can put the tray by the seating area."

I inched myself slowly to a seated position on the edge of the bed. I was prepared to make a run for the bathroom, should morning sickness hit me. Although it had dissipated over the last week, I was surprised the long day yesterday had not revived it. China plates collided with each other and the cutlery, as Charlotte set the table.

What would Charlotte do with what she overheard last night? I needed to find a way to catch up with her later.

William patted the stiff, cream couch cushion beside him. I obliged, he passed me a plate and I took a few of the lighter pastries from the tray. I slowly nibbled, unsure who sat beside me. I hoped it was the William of last night. He read the newspaper while he ate and I could not help but smile. Any unsuspecting person who walked in the room would think we were a typical couple enjoying a nice brunch.

But we weren't typical. My smile faded and I cursed myself for letting my guard down last night. I dropped the croissant back on my plate and, a little heavy handed, put it on the table. William folded the top of the paper down, his head tilted to one side.

"The whole engagement thing, what was that about?"

"I know it was rather sudden and I should have warned you first. I wanted to tell you you, in the library but ran out of time. To be honest, I was concerned if you knew about it much before that you would seize the opportunity to humiliate me in front of all the guests. Taking you off guard was my best bet, to have you agree."

William knew me well. I would have come up with a plan to curtail it. Especially, with how careful I had to be around Helen.

"Are you planning anything else I should be aware of? Or is this pawn only privy to information after the fact?"

Newsprint rustled with William's tightened grip, "The world may seem like a progressive place; however, reality is different. Most of the people you met last night support the old-fashioned, hierarchical system. The Hammonds included. They will have all the extra-marital fun they want, but have a child out of wedlock and the whole family's status diminishes. Hence, the engagement."

"You've got to be kidding me? There is no way any of those people don't have illegitimate children somewhere."

"Most likely they do, but, if I want to rebuild what you had me lose, I can't start off on the wrong foot."

"Oh yes, blame the victim and your soon-to-be wife apparently. I see how this is going to work." I tapped my foot rapidly to try and release my anger. The vibrations sent shock waves through the couch. "Helen was not impressed with the engagement. If what you say about the drop in status is true, why would she be so upset?"

"She was upset I stole the limelight away from her throwing a grand event. The party may have seemed like it was for me, but it was really for her. Remind everyone who is the queen of the empire. Also, the way she kept pushing Emma on me revealed she had other plans for me. And you."

I did not have to ask what Helen's other plans were. I was a roadblock. If I was her, I would not want me around either. "Would she not expedite her plans now?"

"As the proposal was public, Aunt Helen will want to protect her, and the family's, reputation. The last thing she would want would be the embarrassment of a broken-off engagement. She won't be able to fight it now. Not without a lot of attention and explanation. Even she would have a hard time hiding a missing wife of a prominent family member to those authorities not on our side."

"This is ridiculous. We can't get married."

"Why is that?"

"Seriously? In what world does it make sense for us to be married. We killed each other's siblings, for Christ sake. Not to mention the fact I DO NOT want to be here. I get the whole pretending to be your girlfriend thing, to hide what happened in L.A. But this! I don't know about you, but marriage to me is not just something you do to appease the upper echelon of society."

"You will do it if you want to stay alive."

"And how long does marriage buy me in terms of time? Until you can arrange a wet nurse? So that's what, four months, tops?"

The veins in his neck throbbed, his eyes aflame. "For someone so cunning, I am dumbfounded by your stupidity. Would you really rather die than marry me?"

I stared him down, "I would rather have a choice in WHO I marry. But you can't live in a world where others have choices, can you? You always-"

William grabbed my face with his hand and squeezed so hard my jaw flared with pain, "Heaven forbid I try to make your life as comfortable for you as I can! Maybe you would prefer if I shipped you to one of our houses in Bolivia, if what I am doing isn't enough. You would be locked up in a very lovely, albeit dingy, cell, provided shitty food and then, once you have given birth, set to work in a place that makes Adam's hellhole look luxurious. You would never see your son again. Would that plan suit you better?"

With both of my hands I pulled his hands away from my face, pushed him back against the couch and used the force to propel me to my feet. "There he is! I was wondering when the real William would make his appearance again. How often will you threaten me when I don't do exactly what you want? Why should I live in constant fear of death, or worse?"

"If you would rather die than help raise your son, I can make that happen."

"I just hope you have the balls to do it yourself. Unlike with Claire."

William came at me so fast I did not have time to react. Both hands wrapped around my neck, my feet scuffed backwards along the carpet until I slammed against a wall. The glass of the picture that hung beside me shattered on the floor, A large hole torn into the peaceful sunset beach scene.

"I don't generally take pleasure in killing someone. I only do what needs to be done, but I will make an exception." His grip tightened.

William closed the gap between us. I grabbed his arms for leverage, managed to get enough movement in my leg, and I kneed him hard. He let go of my neck and toppled backward. I bolted for his bedside table, for the gun. William jumped to his feet and wrapped his body around me from behind. My arms were pinned and my feet lifted off the floor, I squirmed to get free. I could not generate enough force to use the back of my head as a weapon. William pinned me down on the bed, his body on top of me, his arms still wrapped around me.

KNOCK, KNOCK, KNOCK.

Movement ceased. There was another knock and then Jasper's voice, "Are you two lovebirds okay in there?"

"We're fine." William huffed.

"Well that's good, as I could hear you fighting from the other room, so I wanted to make sure no one was dead. Just think of the poor maids who would have to clean that up. Anyhoo, Aunt Helen would like to see everyone in the parlor. Now."

Jasper's footsteps dissipated in the distance and William loosened his grip one arm at a time. The weight of his body lifted off my back. I rolled myself over, cautious about William's next move.

"Get dressed. Quickly." He flung on his suit jacket, ruffled out the wrinkles in his pants and scowled at me. "If you are not down in twenty minutes I will presume you have chosen death over marriage. I will inform Aunt Helen and Jasper of your decision, both of whom, I am sure, will be elated. Even if it affects Jasper's immediate plans." Then he was gone.

I stared up at the waves of the stucco ceiling. I did not want to die, but I did not want to live either. I dragged myself up and reached for the bedside drawer. My hand shook as it hovered over the handle. The drawer opened without a sound. William's gun sat on top of a Bible. One bullet and this would all be over. One bullet and I would be at peace.

CHAPTER THIRTY-FOUR

The pistol was heavy in my hands, heavier than last night. The ridged barrel and textured grip taunted me. Joe and Sally would be heartbroken when they found out about my death, but they would understand. Wouldn't they? William would be upset at the loss of another child, as Jasper predicted. He would spiral even further out of control with his drinking, but what did I care? He was a monster and deserved what he got.

The hollowness of my body swallowed my desire to live. It was better to stop my suffering and prevent the child inside of me from suffering at all. What life would he have anyways? Would a good mother bring him into a family of death and destruction? What lessons would he learn, if he saw me living a life that was a lie. No amount of acting would hide my unhappiness.

Yet, here I sit, the power to end it all in my hands.

Finger by finger I gripped the handle. The safety clicked off. Cold kissed my temple. The trigger accepted the pressure.

Click.

Nothing.

I popped open the cartridge. Empty. I checked the barrel. Empty. Fuck!

Nothing under the mattress or the bed itself. I ran to the bathroom and scoured the cabinets and even in the back of the toilet tank. Nothing. I tossed the contents of every drawer, checked each jacket pocket and every shoe in the closet. Nothing. Where the hell were the bullets? Why would William have a gun nearby without bullets?

The closet mirror reflected the disheveled shell of the women I once knew. Even though I was pregnant, I had lost weight. Any hope I had after I escaped L.A. had been extinguished. Charlotte's offer of help would no longer reignite it.

Tears, from my soulless eyes, painted my cheeks. I dragged my feet back to the bedside table and placed the gun in the drawer. I would find another way. The cool bathroom floor sent a chill through my bare feet. I ran my finger along the blade of a razor, blood stained my finger. The cut stung, but was shallow. The razor would not be enough. There were no scissors, or other sharp implements. I wrapped my hand in the gold monogrammed towel, clenched my fist and jaw. I pulled back my arm, ready to use all my force to break the mirror.

"OLIVIA!"

The haze around me faded to reveal Charlotte right beside me. When had she arrived? She grabbed the razor from my one hand, tossed it into the wastebasket and unwrapped my other hand. Her mouth moved but her words did not penetrate my ears. A cold cloth patted my face.

Charlotte bandaged up my finger and led me, like a child, into the closet. I stood stiff like a mannequin as she undressed and dressed me. Her mild-mannered demeanor eased into my focus.

"Olivia, you need to snap out of it. They are not happy you are keeping them waiting."

"What's the point? I'm dead either way. Why not be dead now?"

"And what about the child?"

"What about it? It will be just like William anyways. Do we want another one of him in this world?"

"Don't let him be like William."

"I'm powerless over who the child will become. It's not worth it. None of this is worth it."

"What about our plan? I need your help to stop this family. Isn't that worth living for?"

"And how long have you, or anyone else, been trying to do that? You haven't succeeded yet. I don't think I am the secret weapon that will keep these vampires from rising again. William rose out of the ashes once. There is no stopping them."

"You know, it's funny, Joe described you as a very determined, strong-willed and capable woman. Yet the person in front of me appears to be a weak and scared child."

The dark emptiness inside me saw some light. "You spoke to Joe? Where is he? Is he safe? When did you talk to him? How?" I had a million questions.

"He's fine. We have him and Sally somewhere safe. I spoke to him this morning, while I was in town doing some shopping for Lady Hammond. He also told me to tell you that watching hockey is no fun without you."

My heart swelled. I am sure Charlotte could have easily found out Joe and I bonded over hockey, but my gut told me she had actually spoken to him. Then I realized what else she had said, "He is here!"

"No, no. I was able to call him. Olivia, I know you are scared, and your situation is horrible, but I need your help. You're right, with just me in this house, we won't be able to make a dent in the fight against the Hammonds. But with you, the person who helped destroy the L.A. syndicate, the person who went through hell to try and find her sister? With her, I can do this! But I need that Olivia."

I inhaled and exhaled three large breaths. I stepped around Charlotte, and opened the black velvet box sitting on top of the waist-high cabinet in the middle of the closet. I stared at the engagement ring and could hear Claire's voice, "I love you. You took care of me at my worst. Now take care of yourself. Do whatever it takes, but don't let them win."

Revitalized by the belief Joe and Sally were safe, I found my strength. I slipped the ring on my finger. The Hammonds could not win. They destroyed what I loved and I would destroy them. If I could survive Adam, I could survive this. If William wants me to play his game, I will. This time, I will be the one to call check-mate.

CHAPTER THIRTY-FIVE

ead held high, I sauntered into the parlour with two minutes to spare. William shook his head and pressed his palms to his eyes, as if to push the tension back into place. I took particular pleasure in his annoyance with me.

Helen glared at me and checked her watch, "Finally decided to join us, did you? Well, let us get this over with. There are better ways I would like to spend my time, than planning a wedding."

It had been less than twenty-four hours since the engagement and New Years Day. I had expected more time to digest everything, better yet, time to get out of it. However, William was right, again. Helen appeared to be at the extreme end of acceptance of the inevitable. I wondered who she had to pay, and how much to work on a holiday. Or were there skeletons she was using to get what she wanted?

Helen almost shoulder-checked me when she rushed past, "William you ride with me, there are some things I want to discuss, and then, on the way back, you can ride with the other two. I will need the car."

"Yes, Aunt Helen."

Jasper grinned and held out his arm, like a gentleman about to walk a woman into a ball. I took it and smiled back. The game continued.

The sun bounced off the crisp snow and I had to shield my eyes. Birds sang to celebrate my ability to leave the estate. I had almost forgotten what it felt like to breathe in fresh air. A driver dressed in black held open the car door and I ducked inside, my back to the driver-seat. Jasper sat across from me, legs outstretched ankle over ankle. Our car followed the one that carried William and Helen.

"An eventful night. And morning it seems." Jasper said.

"That it was."

"The engagement was definitely unexpected. Although, the fact he brought you all the way here should have given me a clue it would happen. I just did not think he would ever try to steal Aunt Helen's limelight." Jasper shuffled in his seat, "I could have used that information. What else are you hiding from me? William has to have larger plans if he stepped on Helen's toes already."

"Believe me, I was not expecting a proposal, otherwise I would have told you. As for his plans, all I know is that apparently you all are very backwards over here and for him to have any sort of success, we have to be married before the baby arrives."

"True. Why have the announcement last night, though? That is the part that is bothering me. William has always been meticulous. Every move contrived towards a particular end. It has to play into his aspirations for the business."

I needed to tell him something. "We have been more focused on the baby, but what I do know is he plans to re-establish himself and to be in a place of power."

"I would suspect nothing less. What did you find out about the guests he spoke to last night?"

I forced myself to blush, "We didn't exactly talk last night."

Jasper winked, "Ah, yes, well, I might have to expedite my plans. Aunt Helen seems to have her clutches in William and I don't like all this time they are spending alone together."

Unsure if a response was expected, I remained silent. The power lines along the road reflected on Jasper's black-rimmed glasses. A sly grin crossed his face. He moved and sat beside me and crossed his legs. "Out of curiosity, how does the fight you two had this morning play into all of this?"

I forced myself to shield my confusion,"How do you know we were fighting? We might have an active sex life."

"Do you usually scream about death and murder during sex?"

The blood drained from my face and Jasper's smile told me he noticed. Had he heard everything or just the end? Did he know I was not at Hammond Manor by my own free will?

Jasper leaned in, "The house may be modern, but the walls are thin. I must say I enjoyed listening to you two last night. Thank you for that. Although, this morning's conversation, if you want to call it that, was much more, what is the word, enlightening." He leaned back against the seat and smiled. His eyes glistened with knowledge.

I turned the engagement ring around my finger. It felt awkward enough but now the heft of it seemed unbearable. There had to be a way to get out of this mess. Think Olivia!

"And how long have you been eavesdropping on our conversations?"

"Long enough to solidify my thoughts about you, since our stroll through the grounds. You were out for nothing but revenge. You just happened to get knocked up in the process."

"You think so? Well, your network of sources are amatuer at best."

Jasper's eyes narrowed, "I have some of the best hackers, who easily found out about Claire."

"But not me?"

"Well..." Jasper's eyes searched my smile for clues.

"I burned the place in L.A."

Jasper's jaw slackened "You are telling me that you are the reason we lost L.A? The millions of dollars that place brought in was lost because of you? William's move to England, and the threat to my succession, is all your fault?"

He laughed uncontrollably. "This is glorious. William will never survive this. And he brought the source of the destruction to the central hub. Oh man! Aunt Helen is going to hang him out to dry. Any plans I may have had are nothing compared to this gold you have given me." He rubbed his knuckles, glee emanating from his every pore.

"Given I'm the source of destruction, I suspect I won't survive the revelation if I am within the radius of Aunt Helen's wrath. As you said, this information is gold, so what do I get in return?"

Jasper's eyebrow raised and he took my hand, "Sweetheart, there is nothing I can do for you. There is no place you could hide where Aunt Helen's reach wouldn't find you."

Trap set.

I cleared my throat and hoped that if the driver had not heard everything already, he would hear this. I was certain Helen's reach included the front of this vehicle. "I thought you were going to get rid of her! Why not use this information to show her followers that she can't control her own network, humiliate William at the same time and then handle them both?"

"Why would I go to those intricate lengths, when I can have Aunt Helen on a rampage and clean house for me. It won't only be you and William who will be dealt with. Anyone loyal to William will be found and taken care of."

"How soon do you plan to share this information with Helen? Or, more matter of factly, how long do I have to live?"

"Well, you see...the wedding would be the obvious choice; however, that would give you and William ample time to find a way out. Or worse, turn against me. I could call her now, but I want to see both of their faces when the truth comes out. I guess the officiants' office will have to do, no sense in getting a marriage license if there won't be a wedding."

I had no way to warn William there were only hours, if not minutes, until death and destruction. I would have to neutralize the threat myself.

I curled my knuckles and with the heel of my hand struck Jasper's nose. Blood poured profusely down his face. I undid my seatbelt and jumped on top of him, his hands distracted by the broken bone. I grabbed the seatbelt behind Jasper and tried to wrap it around his throat but his hands were quicker than mine and he tossed me to the other side of the car. The scene played out for the driver in the rearview mirror.

Jasper lunged at me but I kicked him back against the seat. He grabbed my leg and pulled me onto the floor of the car. He was on top of me and we grappled. We both landed punches. His against my cheek, mine into his side.

"Aunt Helen would have loved to handle you personally, but I suspect she will understand why I had to do it." A knife snapped open beside my ear.

My eyes went wide, I dropped my arms and went docile. I laid prone, breathing heavily under Jasper. My reaction caught him off guard. He straightened his back.

"Now you stop fighting? Just as I am about to kill you, and this baby, you give up? Are you really going to let me kill you so easily?" His brown eyes were ice cold.

"I'm done fighting. If you don't kill me, Helen will. Why give her the satisfaction? Let's just get this over with."

"I don't think I have ever had someone just give up before." The sharp blade pressed against my throat. "Well, I guess it will make things-"

Like a flash of lightning, I grabbed Jasper's wrist with both hands and squeezed so hard he dropped the knife. He fell forward to grab it off the floor and I swung myself over and on top of his back. My knees pinned his arms to the floor. I took his head in my hands and slammed it hard against the car door, three times. Jasper stopped struggling. No noise emitted from him. I dropped his head and checked for a pulse. I had only knocked him out.

I took the knife from under him, kneeled on the seat behind the driver and placed the blade against the driver's neck. He was terrified. I looked through the front window, William and Helen's car was well ahead, on the other side of the bridge we had just entered.

"Have you notified anyone about what happened?"

He shook his head.

"Give me your phone."

The driver took one shaking hand off the wheel, and reached into his suit jacket. As he did, I removed the knife from his throat, grabbed the wheel and yanked it to the right. The crunch of bending metal caused the vehicle to shake as it smashed through the bridge's railing.

CHAPTER THIRTY-SIX

The car careened over the bridge. I let go of the steering wheel and pushed myself back into the passenger cabin of the vehicle. One hand clung to the seatbelt behind the driver, the other held the knife. I braced myself for impact. My fear of drowning stuck deep in my throat. I swallowed hard and buried it, while gravity pulled my feet off the floor as the car tumbled towards the water.

SPLASH!

The back of my legs slammed down against the seat and my head hit the window. Small cracks started to grow along the glass. Jasper's body bounced off the doors, before he tumbled on top of me. Pain shot through my stomach from the dead weight of a two-hundred-pound man. I pushed him aside with my hips and the hand holding the knife.

Water quickly filled the bottom of the car. The repetitive click of a seatbelt clasp and screams for help from the driver filled the top. Jasper was still unconscious. I unwrapped my hand and kneeled on the seat behind the driver. My upper body rested against the back of it.

I took the butt end of the knife and thrust it against the back of the driver's head. He slumped forward over the steering wheel. "I am sorry." The back end of the car collided with the water and I was flung backwards. My head hit the seat cushion of the opposite bench. Jasper's body rolled to the floor.

I rolled down the window closest to me and water billowed in. I waited for the car to fill with water so that I would not have to fight the current on my way out. Jasper still wasn't moving, and the water had risen to above the seat of the car, so his face was under water. Tiny bubbles escaped his mouth.

My life depended on his death.

I pulled Jasper's arm, his wrist just above the water, and checked for a pulse. It was faint but it was still there. The water level rose and his raised arm was completely covered. Would I risk leaving him here, not knowing if he would survive?

The water was close to the roof. There was no time. I dropped Jasper's arm, which slowly fell through the water, and filled my lungs with air. Just as the water covered my nose and mouth I pushed myself down off the ceiling and towards the window.

I grabbed the window frame and pulled myself through. Halfway through, a hand grabbed my ankle and pulled me back towards the car. I tightened my grip on the car and wedged my free leg in the window frame. With all my strength, I fought Jasper's grasp and I kicked my entangled leg free. The force pushed me away from the vehicle.

Jasper struggled to get his large frame out of the open window. My lungs burned but I swam back to him. I gripped the door frame of the car and kicked him in the head as hard as I could. He slumped forward and hung over the door. The car continued to sink to the bottom of the lake, while I pushed myself up off the roof.

I could see a faint light break through the surface above me. I swam as hard as I could towards it. Each stroke and kick moved me a little bit closer to existence. Below me nothing but darkness. The car, driver and Jasper had been eaten by the depths of the lake.

My lungs screamed for air and my arms were tired, adrenaline not a propellant. My brain would not accept *just a bit further* as motivation and panic took control of my body. I thrashed around, and without thinking, opened my mouth. It was filled with water. My chest burned from the intrusion.

I could see the crest of the water but my strength was gone.

CHAPTER THIRTY-SEVEN

My ears were filled with bees. My eyes fluttered, to adjust to the sunlight. The blurred movements around slowly transformed into faces. I was startled by the fact that one of those faces was directly above me. Their mouths moved but the buzzing prevented understanding. Someone was at my legs, but I could not tell what they were doing. I tried to move my head but it was stuck. I reached up and felt foam around my neck. I was in a brace.

I was covered in a silver emergency blanket which sparkled in the sun's rays. The voices around me became clear.

"Ma'am? Ma'am? Can you tell me your name?"

My throat was dry and it burned. My saliva got caught on sandpaper. The eyes above me were kind. I dug my fingers into the wet dirt I laid upon and pushed through the pain.

"O...Olivia"

"Okay Olivia, glad to have you back. I am Yen, and this is Kurt. We are going to take care of you. I am going to hold your head while Kurt rolls you over. We are going to slip a backboard under you and then strap you onto it. Ready?"

"Ye..." Pain prevented the s.

"One, Two, Three."

As I was rolled onto my side, I saw William and Helen huddled with some officers under a distant tree, unaware I had regained consciousness.

Kurt gently rolled me onto the hard board. I heard the clicks of the familiar snaps. I understood everything they had to do, although I appreciated that they took me through it, step-by-step. I stared at the multitude of small fluffy clouds above me. One looked like the head of an elephant. Another a small heart.

Kurt's voice got my attention, "We are going to lift you up, put you onto this gurney and strap you to that as well. Then we will take you to hospital."

I reached out for his hand to stop him, but the straps restricted all movement, "Wwwait...The men in the car. What happened to them?"

"I am sorry, but they didn't make it. The divers pulled them out, but it was too late. You were lucky a passerby found you."

I closed my eyes and shed a tear for the unknown driver, and a sigh of relief for Jasper. It worked. I was safe, and one Hammond was out of the way.

William appeared at my side, "Are you okay?" He looked at Yen and Kurt, "Is she okay? Is the baby okay?"

Yen responded, "Sir, we need to take her to hospital, to have them both evaluated. You are welcome to travel in the back of the ambulance with her, if you wish."

William nodded and ran his hand along the length of his face and the back of his neck. With my head restrained, he was not seen again until he towered over me, inside the ambulance, on his way to a seat beside me. The ambulance doors closed and a large hand wrapped itself around mine.

Strapped to the gurney, and confined in the back of an ambulance, there was freedom. An observer would not know this, but I was invigorated from the conflict with Jasper. One down, two to go.

The familiar electronic whistle of a bird filled the cabin. My stomach muscles contracted, as though they had met someone's fist. The last time I heard that sound, Claire was alive. I had chosen the ring-tone of a chickadee, as it reminded me of her soothing whistle. Over time, the chickadee's song became more like a crow's squawk, a disturbing and incessant cry for drug money. The last time I heard it, I ignored it. Ultimately, that was why I was on my way to the hospital to find out what, if any, damage I had caused my unborn child. I had always been furious with Claire for leaving destruction in her wake, and yet I was no better.

"She seems to be fine. No...I don't care about the damn meeting! If it's that important, he can come to the hospital. If he can't understand that my child, and fiancée, are the priority, I am not sure we should be doing business with him anyways. Or handle it yourself! You've been doing it since your husband *passed*, no reason you can't keep doing it for a few more days." The call went dead. "How long until we get there?"

"It should be any moment Mr. Hammond. It's just past those lights."

"Good." I could hear his suit crinkle as he leaned over, then he whispered, "Olivia?"

"Hmm."

"Just checking." He squeezed my hand.

Was William's ringtone always a bird, or had he found another way to hurt me?

The ambulance driver expertly halted the vehicle, the back doors opened, and metal wheel locks released the gurney. Yen instructed William to get out of the ambulance. Someone I did not recognize climbed in and helped Yen lower me out. Blue light reflected off the metal canopy we had parked under.

The automatic hospital doors opened and I was hit with the distinctive aroma of disinfectant. The white lights on the ceiling were blurred by speed and heads around me. Bodies collided with a double door and the light got brighter. William was ordered to stay outside, much to his chagrin.

Buckles clicked, numbers counted and I was lifted from one gurney to another. Wheels skated across the floor. The crunch of scissors, followed by the cool kiss of air on my skin, told me my clothes were sacrificed in the name of medicine. Instruments clanged and a language I didn't speak was being batted around the room.

A woman dressed in green scrubs appeared beside me, "I'm Doctor Jones. Can you tell me your name and what the date is?"

"Olivia and.." I thought about it, but despite William's newspapers I had not paid attention to the calendar date. "I don't know the date. It's

Sunday though."

"Alright. We are going to see where you may be injured. Can you move your fingers?"

The fingers on both hands moved with ease.

"And your toes?"

I felt the toes on my right foot move, however I could not feel movement with my left. I tried again. Nothing. Dr. Jones barked orders in the same unfamiliar language that had filled the room since I entered. Cold metal ran along the underside of my right foot and it reflexively moved. I presumed my left foot failed the same test. The rhythmic beep of the heart monitor sang faster.

"Olivia, I need you to calm down. Stress will only negatively affect the baby, okay. It's alarming that you can't move your toes, but it is also normal after a car accident. Often there is a pinched nerve along the path to those muscles. If that is the case, once we find it, and fix it, your toes will move. Let's take a deep breath together shall we? Inhale...and exhale. Good, keep doing that, while I take a look at your baby."

Like a chorus, the medical staff around me all kept me on tempo with their own long deep breaths. I focused on the repetition of my task and the light panels above me. Beaches, palm trees and water invited me to calm dawn. I counted the large green leaves on the trees and had gotten to thirty when Dr. Jones' face appeared above me.

"Good news, your baby looks to be okay. Heart rate is good, he doesn't appear to be injured and is wide awake and moving. We are going to move you to radiology and see if we can figure out why your toes aren't moving."

A couple of orderlies wheeled me out of the room, at a slower pace than I had been brought in. That had to be a good sign, right?

From a distance, I heard Dr. Jones update William, followed by his vehement voice, "Do you know who I am? Let me be with her. She needs-"

Then, silence as the emergency corridor doors closed.

The next few hours were a blur. I was moved from room to room, and machine to machine. I was left in the dark as to the results of all the tests.

I tried hard to fight off the sleep that beckoned me. William would not let me be alone for long. I needed to get hold of Charlotte and find out what the police had discovered. If there was anything suspicious about Jasper's or the driver's deaths, would she be able to cover it up for me? My eyelids were heavy, I would only rest a moment.

CHAPTER THIRTY-EIGHT

W hen I woke, William sat in a chair beside me, his fingers rapidly typed on his phone. Unless I was mistaken, he wore a different suit then when I last saw him. The dark-blue, pinstripe pants were unfamiliar to me, but a white shirt with a few of the upper buttons undone, was not. The suit jacket hung on a hook on the wall.

How long had I been asleep? The rustle of my sheets alerted William. He glanced over, and when he registered I was awake, stopped what he was doing and jumped out of the chair.

"You scared the shit out of me. You have been asleep for the better part of two days. The doctors told me you only woke up, briefly, when they checked on you, but you were not coherent. Otherwise, nothing would wake you. Not even when they moved you around to treat you."

I looked at my foot, hidden under the blanket, and said a short prayer. I tried to wiggle my toes. The blanket moved. I tried again. The blanket moved even more. A squeal of joy got stuck in my dry throat. What came out was a muffled gasp.

Water trickled into a pink, plastic glass. "Doctor Jones stopped by yesterday and advised her initial assumption was correct. Your left side must have been hit pretty hard in the crash and pinched some nerves, but they were able to release the knots."

He handed me the cup, I finished it and held it out for more. William refilled the glass and settled into his chair. "What happened?"

I sensed more concern than curiosity in his voice, but not much more.

"Jasper had heard our fight this morning. The other morning, I guess. He held a knife to my throat and threatened to kill me and the baby if I didn't tell him why I said I would rather die than marry you."

"Describe the knife."

Great, one answer and he already suspected a lie. I closed my eyes and paid close attention to the knife as I replayed the incident in my mind. "It was a switch blade. The handle had a golden inlay, with some sort of pattern on it. His hand covered most of it so I didn't get a good look. Maybe a dragon?"

"Jasper's had that since his dad died. He was gifted it when he was ten years old, after his Dad returned from a trip in China. Continue."

"I knew he would take whatever he had heard to Helen, hell, he may have already. Has she said anything?"

"We will get to Aunt Helen next, how did you end up in the lake?"

"You know me, I wasn't just going to sit there and let him threaten me. I attacked him and we tossed each other around the back of the car so much the driver could barely keep the car straight. At some point, he must not have paid attention to the road, as the next thing I knew, I was falling backwards against the seat of the car. Then, we were in the water."

"What happened to Jasper? He was a tournament-winning swimmer. There is no way he wouldn't have survived the crash, unless something happened to him."

Of course he was a freaking medal-winner! "I struggled to get out of the car and he tried to pull me back in. I kicked him hard in the head, and he went unconscious. I wouldn't have been able to get him out of the car, let alone to the surface. Hell, I couldn't get myself to the surface. So I left him behind. And I don't regret it."

"I would expect not." William checked his phone. "Well, I guess that takes care of that problem. Now what about the driver?"

"The driver? I didn't pay attention to the driver. If he didn't get out, then he must have hit his head on the steering wheel or something."

"So you did not intentionally kill him then?" William held his stare.

He had knowledge I did not. Shit! I heaved a sigh, "Fine. He overheard what Jasper had said, so he was a liability. I couldn't afford him exposing me, us, to Helen. So I used Jasper's knife to hit him in the head and knocked him out. The water did the rest."

"I see. Why lie?"

"That death, I regret. Although, if he worked for you I suspect he may not have been the most upstanding citizen. Either way, he was in the wrong place at the wrong time. Besides, I suspected you would use his death in your mind games. Torment me with reminders of what I have done since I met you."

"Admirable of you; however, no need for regret. Danny had a list of wrongdoings a mile long. On top of that, he was going to help me with Jasper's exit, so he would have been dead later this week anyway."

The way William talked about the death of someone, as though it was incidental, chilled me to my core. A soulless murderer, whose DNA coursed through the veins of my child. A shiver ran down my spine and I trembled. William noticed, pulled up the thin scratchy blanket from the bottom of the bed, and continued.

"Is there anything else you want to tell me about the accident?"

"Why don't you just tell me what you know. We have no reason to trust each other, so trying to test me really isn't going to help you learn anything about me you don't already know."

"Alright, why were your fingerprints on the steering wheel?"

"My...what?" It was not possible my fingerprints had remained on that steering wheel. The water alone would have washed them off. He would know that I would understand that. What the hell was he playing at? "Fingerprints wouldn't have survived in the water. You know that and I know that. So what are you really asking me, William?"

He pressed his fist to his lips, leaned forward and put his head down. He said something but I could not make it out.

"William, I can't hear you."

"DID YOU TRY TO KILL YOURSELF?" He pushed himself out of the chair with so much force it toppled over.

An orderly opened the door and stepped inside, "Is everything-"

"LEAVE!"

Terrified, the woman looked at me.

"It's alright. He doesn't like hospitals."

She slowly backed out of the room. Her eyes asked questions I couldn't answer.

"What makes you think I tried to kill myself?"

"One of the maids found a razor in our garbage covered in blood. Apparently, our closet and the bathroom looked like a tornado had run through it. Not long after, you end up at the bottom of a lake. You needed CPR! Did you want to die?" His eyes glistened with tears. He rubbed them away before they could fall against his cheeks.

William's vulnerability always took me off guard, and now was no different. I said nothing. The frame of the bed creaked as William sat beside me. "I know I'm a monster. Even if you didn't keep reminding me of it, I would still know. But to do this. To our son." A volcano of tears erupted.

I took his hand, "I didn't want to die."

William looked at me, "She told me she didn't want to die either. Then she took the wheel and drove us into the ditch."

Wait, what? Had I heard that right? "Sharon caused the accident? You told me it was your fault your wife and daughter were dead."

"It is my fault. I was out of town for work when Adam stopped by the house unannounced. Without me there to protect her, Adam decided it would be the perfect opportunity to assert what little power he had. I came home to find Sharon bruised and battered beyond recognition. Penny's arm was in a cast as she had tried to protect her mother and got tossed across the room for her bravery. I couldn't even punish Adam beyond a few bruises of his own. Our father refused to expel him from the business because he knew too much and a dead son, even one he never wanted, wouldn't be good for business. If you can't trust your family, who will trust you?"

"Shit." I now questioned if William wanted to kill me back in Toronto as revenge for his brother, or if he was angry I did something he never could.

"My drinking became compulsive, similar to the way it is now. Sharon and I were having our usual fight after a Hammond family gathering, and, as we approached a corner, she looked at me and said, 'William I love you, but Penny and I can't live this life with you. You saw what Adam did. I thought we would be safe with you, but it's too dangerous. I don't want to die, but I know there is no other way out.' She unbuckled her seatbelt, lunged over at me, took the wheel and drove us down the embankment."

Words of compassion got stuck in my throat.

"Now you go over a bridge, with my child. You can see why I might have my suspicions."

This new information made the room spin. I laid my head back onto my pillow. When the furniture around me stopped swaying, I nestled up against the bed rail and tugged William's arm, "Lie down."

Without question, he climbed into a bed not made for two people, and rested his head on the pillow. His blue eyes had turned grey.

"I forced the car over the bridge." William raised himself on his elbow, "But not to try and kill myself or this child. Yes, earlier that day, I was in a really bad place and I wanted to die. I did. I was prepared to smash the bathroom mirror and slit my wrists. Charlotte snapped me out of it. Then, when I struggled to get to the surface of the water, I accepted the fact my fears would be realized and I would drown, so I stopped swimming."

"Why drive off the bridge?"

"I could not kill Jasper with his own knife. Helen would have been very suspicious. When I saw the bridge, your car kilometers ahead, and no one behind us, I knew it was the only way."

William laid back down. We stared at each other and I couldn't help but see a person who was broken and flawed, but still a person. I wondered how much of William was actually him, and how much was a facade to survive the Hammond clan. A family he could never escape from.

CHAPTER THIRTY-NINE

The crisp winter breeze crashed against my face as William pushed my wheelchair out of the sliding-glass hospital doors. Although I was perfectly able to transport myself from the chair to the car, William insisted he help. My arm wrapped around his neck, he lifted me into the back of yet another large, luxurious, black car. The Hammonds must have a fleet of them.

Did the new driver know what happened to his predecessor? I locked all negative thoughts and allowed myself to enjoy the winter landscape. Snow had not yet fallen and the land had become barren, but the countryside was beautiful. The drive was rather peaceful.

The peace was disturbed when gravel, dispensed from under the wheels of the vehicle, smacked against the aluminum undercarriage. Hammond Manor loomed ahead and all of the thoughts I had locked away rose up. Had William told Helen what I had done? I wanted to ask in my hospital room but the thick haze of tension had parted and I had not wanted it to engulf us again. I hoped he had learned to warn me of unexpected actions after the engagement incident; however, he had a tendency to hoard information.

I exited the vehicle before William could force his help upon me. The black curtain for the parlour flapped closed and I suspected Helen skulked behind it. Laughter filtered into the entry and William and I walked towards it.

William stopped abruptly and I dodged to his left to avoid impact with his back. I, too, was taken aback by the familiar, petite figure, dressed in a white pantsuit, littered with large pink flowers, who stood by the piano. Her face radiated joy, and she was about to speak when Helen stepped forward, from her place beside the window, her eyes full of suspicion.

"Karey heard about the pending nuptials and insisted on handling all of the outfits. Flew in from Barcelona to be here. Was that not nice of her, William?"

William's face had turned ghost-white, "Quite. Thank you."

Karey came over and took both my hands in hers, "Darling, it is my pleasure. I am just over the moon that you have found someone who makes you happy. I always liked this one."

Helen coughed and took a seat in the large chair across from the fire. "William, make us a couple of drinks. We have a lot to talk about while Karey figures out what she is going to do with Olivia."

William whispered, "Be careful," and then walked over to the drink cart.

I did not react, or say the "you too" that sat on my tongue. Karey put her arm through mine and led me out of the room. Sweat ran down my back, and my hands had become clammy. Karey knew I had worked for William. Is that why daggers flew from Helen's eyes, or were they just from her normal disdain? Karey had no loyalty to me, but was her loyalty to William or Helen? Either way, Karey's presence was not good.

Rather than taking me to my room, we entered the one beside it. The one Jasper had stayed in. There were no remnants of him anywhere. The room was spotless, the bed meticulously made and ready for it's next guest. Jasper appeared to have been wiped clean from the family.

"Alright darling, strip down to your bra and underwear, step up here and I will see what dresses I have that might fit you, in your condition."

"Um, shouldn't we be getting ready for a funeral and not a wedding?"

"Funerals mean grief, and grief means weakness. There is no room for weakness in this family."

"Really? They won't even bury Jasper because of their warped view of funerals? Wow."

"They make the rules, not me."

I followed Karey's gaze to three racks lined up along the pale green wall. Each rack was stuffed with dresses, all in different shades of white. The fabric, desperate to be released from its confines, spewed out as each dress tried to take over the space of the ones beside it. The sun reflected off the embellishments and created a rainbow on the carpet.

The sight of the dresses made my stomach turn. The reality of the wedding hit me like a hard wave hitting a sandcastle. I took a deep breath, centered myself, and focused on one task at a time. I removed my clothes, tossed them onto the bed, and stepped up onto the small wooden platform. Karey walked around me a couple of times, stood in front of me, her right elbow resting in her left hand, as she looked between me and the rack. I was momentarily taken back to L.A, when I first met Karey and she dressed me for my first night of *work* for William.

"The good thing is, you shouldn't get too much bigger before the wedding, so most of what I have here will work. Let's see..." Karey walked over to the dresses and mumbled to herself while she looked through the collection. "Ah ha, there you are, my pretty."

With a tug, the jungle of fabric released a large princess dress that would have swallowed Karey up if she put it on. The bodice was covered in sequins and pearls. I thought it was hideous, but I was tired, and I did not want to argue over a dress for a wedding I did not want.

With Karey's assistance I got into the dress and the woman in the mirror looked like a giant white bell. Thankfully, Karey felt the same way.

"Nope, that won't work. Okay. Let's see what else."

She pulled a dress off the rack, examined it, put it back, and selected another. Her actions repeated as she made her way down the first rack. My curiosity devoured William's warning. "Karey?"

"Yes darling?"

"I am glad to see you made it out of L.A. I had heard not many connected with that place had survived. How long have you been in Barcelona?"

Karey handed me another dress. "For a while. Once I heard about the fire I came over, stayed with Helen for a few weeks, and then was sent on to Barcelona. Beautiful city." She walked around me, "Nope not that one."

I shivered, practically naked, in front of floor-to-ceiling windows. The leaves on the estate had been kissed with frost, as the cooler weather brought a change of seasons. It would only be a matter of time before they would fall to the ground, wither and die. Without the protection of the leaves, the trees would be battered by storms, and yet most would stand tall and strong.

"How does Barcelona compare to the caliber of work in L.A.?"

Karey looked over the top of her eyeglasses, and she handed me another dress, "Honey, it's all the same everywhere. Although, they don't have anyone like you everywhere, that's for sure. Look at you, going from rags to riches, and having William's baby no less. That was a good move on your part. I knew you would do well."

"A good move? This baby was not planned, if that is what you are insinuating."

"Really? Either way, it worked in your favour. Especially if the rumours about L.A. are true."

"Rumours? What rumours?"

Karey's regular genial smile contorted into a surly expression, "It's being said that William didn't have a handle on his workers, like people trusted he did, and a few went rogue. Burned the place down in the hopes of masking his death."

"Who are people saying were the rogues?"

"Now, that is where it gets really interesting," I felt the sharp prick of a pin in my side and had a feeling it had been intentional. "Given Jack and Kevin are dead, it would be easy to suspect them. Most do. But, nothing in the Hammond organization is ever easy, now is it? Helen and I have a different theory." She let her words hang heavy in the air, as my eyes fixated on her at my feet. Pins pulled from a magnetic armband were inserted into the dress.

Karey and Helen had discussed L.A.? Why wouldn't they? Karey was there and had information Helen would want. I wondered how Karey reacted to the news that William was engaged to a woman named Olivia. Had she suspected it was me and told Helen about my history with

William? Or was the secret sealed inside her until her curiosity was quenched by a visit?

Karey looked up at me, "Since you were there maybe you could confirm or invalidate our thoughts?"

"I can try."

"You see, William has always had somewhat of a hero complex. Even as a leading man in the Hammond organization, he has always been pulled to broken people. He gets blinded by them and loses sight of what is important - the business. This blindness, if identified by the broken person or people, could be exploited. Get people into positions in this family they really shouldn't be in."

"Why would this person, or people, have exploited William just to burn down his house and destroy the L.A operations? If they wanted a position of power themselves, as you suspect, would they not want everything to remain functional?"

"Helen and I had the same questions. It wouldn't make sense, would it? Unless that person's goal was to close operations in L.A."

"What would that accomplish? Especially, since the police thought William had died in the fire. Wouldn't the exploiter need William? Or are you thinking that person wanted to replace him?"

"That is where our theory gets a little tricky. Had Adam still been alive, Helen and I would agree that he had planned William's death so he could take over L.A., or wherever a new operation would have been set up. Given Adam is dead, someone else would have had to benefit from the fire. Especially if they thought William had been killed. None of the men would have been trusted enough to run things. And they would have known that. Therefore, the only people to really benefit would be the women. The question is, how, after all this time, would the women be able to organize in such a way that they could bring down both brothers and the entire L.A operation without any suspicion? Unless, the infection of dissent ran throughout the entire house." Karey pushed herself off the floor, her small stature came up to the lower part of my chest. "Given you are standing here, and Helen was not aware you had worked in L.A., I would bet money that you, William's latest favourite, toppled the house of cards. What I now need cleared up is, was William privy to the plan? Is that why he brought you here, to the belly of the beast, in the hopes of ousting Helen? Or was it dumb luck that you are back within his clutches?"

Frozen in place, even my eyelids refused to blink. The words perched on the tip of my dry tongue jumped, "Dumb luck."

"Huh. Not much of a mastermind after all, are you? Although, your impact on this family has been far-reaching. Beyond what you can even comprehend." It was not only the Hammonds whose personalities changed rapidly, "Now let's have a look at you."

Karey beamed, "Gorgeous. You will be the envy of all of the guests."

All I saw was a white blob draped over my body. One that caused my ribs to tighten and my skin to itch. "I don't understand, is there still a wedding? If Helen knows who I really am, then there is no way she would condone this marriage. In fact, I will be dead by the end of the day."

Karey unbuttoned the back of the dress, "Helen doesn't know. Now get dressed."

"You didn't tell her?"

"I fully intended to. I love Helen, we grew up together, not to mention how I would be rewarded for the information. But I see it two ways. First, William is prized to take over this business one day, and if he seems to want your secret kept I might do better playing to the up and coming boss, than the one on the way out. Second, this old sentimental heart of mine feels for William. He has had a shit life. The expectations his father placed on him, his mother's suicide, and the death of his wife and daughter at his own hands. Not to mention, being forced into a business that churns out monsters. When I heard he had spent his days and nights by your side at the hospital, only gone a few hours at a time, I changed my mind. William deserves better than the hand he was dealt. I can't say I understand why he is marrying you after what you did. Although I suspect the person inside of you has something to do with it." She could not help but straighten the clothes I had just gotten back into.

"So that's it? Everything goes ahead as planned?"

"Not exactly."

CHAPTER FORTY

The heavy oak door took the brunt of my weight. The cool air did nothing to lessen the sweat that dripped down my face and body. I stumbled on hills as I ran. I paid no attention to where I was headed, I just needed out of, and away from, that hellish house. The mountain of lies and deception continued to close in on me, and Karey had just added more. What she asked of me was something I would never have considered before Claire was taken. But what choice was there now?

Shades of orange and pink painted the sky by the time I stopped at a small, freshly- stained wooden dock. A single red Adirondack chair was placed at its edge. The dock jetted out into a small body of water that nature had carved out of the rivers on either side of it. I sat in the chair and tapped my fingers on the flat arms.

The trees towered around me and their knotted eyes scowled. They, too, questioned whether I would be able to pull everything off. Jasper's death happened sooner than I had expected, and I needed to stay alert to any suspicions around my involvement. The closer I got to William, I not only tempted fate, but I carved a space in my heart for him. I hated myself for it. I hated the fact I initiated most of our episodes of congeniality. What was I to do? If I rejected William, he would shut me out of everything, and my life would be even more unbearable. If I continued to embrace whatever feelings I buried within myself, I would lose the real me.

I needed to pull myself together. William ordered Claire's death! Why did my desire to fix people have to include him? He deserved whatever MI5 had in store for him.

A twig broke behind me. My head spun around. Charlotte stood at the edge of the forest.

"I don't have long," she said. "But I wanted to see if everything was okay. I saw you run across the field and knew something had to have happened. You never leave the house alone."

"I'm fine. Everything will be fine. We just need to expedite the plan, if possible. I can't stay here much longer and I can't actually marry William. You need to help me."

"We are close, but we can't pull the trigger yet. We don't have the paper trail to tie Lady Hammond or William to any of this. The phone app you told me about was a dead end. You would think there would be a data trail, but, whatever Joe had found, vanished. We can't use what he gave us in court, so we are back to needing witnesses and evidence."

"What about the documents from the office? They looked promising. Or the deed to that property."

"They were, we are following up on leads from those, but I don't know how long that will take. We are watching the property and gathering good intel on workers and clients. But until we have the information we need to get these bastards and I can get you somewhere safe, we continue to sit on it. Like you said, if it's a trap there is no sense setting it off before we are ready."

"Jesus! You're telling me that I will be trapped here for the foreseeable future, and I will walk down an aisle to be chained to a monster. Please tell me we can pull this off long before I give birth. I am not raising a child here."

"I understand this isn't ideal-"

"Ideal! Ideal would be me back in Toronto with Whitney, muddling through all the shit we went through, as we tried to piece together some semblance of a life. No, this is not ideal!"

"A lot has happened over the last few days, but I need you to trust me. We are closer than we have ever been, since you started to help us. We will get there. You just need to be patient a little longer. Now, rather than us arguing over the progress of this case, why don't you tell me what Karey said. Has she told Helen she knew you in L.A?"

"No. Karey is just as conniving as the rest of them. She is keeping that information as leverage."

"Leverage for what?"

"She wants-"

Leaves rustled and snapped branches emanated from the forest. The sound was distant but I prayed my yelling had not been carried through the trees. The sounds got closer. A few moments later, William emerged and brushed off the dirt from his clothes. Two men in black followed behind him. I turned to Charlotte, but she was gone.

William waved the guards away, "We need to talk."

"Yes. We do."

The dock rocked as William made his way towards me. He took off his shoes, balled up his socks inside them, rolled up his pant legs, and dangled his legs in the water beside me. He sucked his teeth as the cold water washed over his warm legs.

"Not surprisingly, Aunt Helen was suspicious of the car accident. I tried to tell her you would not be stupid enough to intentionally put our child in danger, but she was adamant you caused the accident."

Slivers from the worn wooden chair pierced through my tight grip and into my hands. "How did you convince her otherwise?"

"I didn't. I told her what happened."

My jaw dropped "What! Why would you do that? And why are you smiling?"

"Aunt Helen knowing about Jasper's deception is good for us. For you. She and I will have to spend time investigating how far his reach was and clean up any mess he made. But it means she is looking away from you."

"But wouldn't she be even more worried about me, knowing I was working with Jasper?"

"She knows how Jasper worked and at least seemed to accept you were coerced. Although, for her to believe that, I did have to tell her that you and Jasper had met at a club during one of his visits to see Adam in

Toronto. She thinks that you two had slept together and you never told me, so he was holding it over you."

"And she bought that?"

"I guess only time will tell, but she was hyper-focused on Jasper, so she is at least distracted. For now."

"Well, I guess that is good, as we have a different problem. Karey." I loosened my grip on the chair.

"When Aunt Helen did not instantly lash out at me, I figured Karey hadn't said anything. How is she a problem?"

"As payment for secrecy, she wants $10,000 a month for the rest of her life and her wife killed. Discreetly, of course."

William's body stiffened and a scowl permeated his face. "She does, does she? Was she so kind as to advise you how, if we met her demands, we could trust she would not change them?"

"When I asked, she said we would have to wait and find out. However, she told me she wanted you to be happy and that was why she hadn't told Helen. Not the fact she apparently wants her wife killed."

"That's nice of her. Her reason for wanting her wife out of the way?"

"Death seems to be easier, or at least cheaper, than divorce."

"And now she found a way to make it happen without raising too many eyebrows. What did you tell her?"

"That I would need to talk to you, but, given the alternative, I didn't see how we could say no." I pulled my knees to my chest. A duck and a trail of ducklings swam by, oblivious to the perils of the individuals they passed. "Please tell me Karey's wife is a horrible person and that we are not committing to the murder of an innocent person."

William thought for a moment, "I can't tell you that."

"Of course not." I rested my chin on my knees. "I can't do this. Adam was one thing, he was a monster. Jasper was about to kill me. Hell, even the driver was bad. But, I would rather die than sacrifice an innocent person."

"I will take care of it."

"I don't want you to take care of it, that is my point. We can't. It's not...right."

"I will take care of it."

CHAPTER FORTY-ONE

C hristmas came and went without celebration or acknowledgement. Given Helen's propensity for parties, I was surprised, but then, she and William spent most of their time in Helen's office. Business trumped the holidays it seemed.

They only emerged for quick meals and a few hours of sleep. When I did see William we barely spoke, and I was given no indication about what they were doing. Whether they forgot, or I was given some leeway, I no longer had a chaperon when I was outside the bedroom. As I did not want to lose my new-found privilege, I dared not ask what happened behind the solid oak door.

It was nice to not worry about onlookers on walks or during time spent reading in the library. My last outing proved I could be found if the guards looked hard enough. However, even with the security cameras, I had a sense of freedom that I had not had in a while. I immersed myself in other worlds and tried not to think about the impending nuptials, or the imminent death of Karey's wife. Karey dropped off my altered wedding dress and I almost got sick when I advised her William had agreed to her terms.

Charlotte and I took tea together without scorn from William. There was no real news on her part. Joe and Sally were still safe, but the case was stalled until we could gather more evidence. With the office constantly occupied, we would have to wait until one of us could get back in there and try to find something else.

The weekend approached and thousands of flowers, in shades of purple, orange, yellow and red were delivered. Tents were erected in the yard and a tuxedo for William was dropped off. I found the top hat amusing. Charlotte informed me that one English wedding tradition was for the men to wear tuxedos with tails, unless they had a service uniform, and the top hat. Like the women, the men also wore white gloves. It felt very Jane Austin to me, but who was I to judge, the marriage was ornamental, just like the outfits.

With all of the deliveries, I presumed the wedding was nigh; however, it was not until dinner two days before that I was actually informed the wedding would be on January 25, two days before my birthday. I was not surprised I hadn't been advised sooner. I was a secondary thought, to both Helen and William. They knew I would be where I needed to be, whenever I needed to be there. A new year with a new name, but the same sad life.

Later that night, William climbed into bed and looked haggard. The long hours of work had painted dark bags under his eyes. His perfect posture collapsed, as if his arms held the weight of the world. He had become apathetic about cleanliness and nightly left his clothes in a pile on the floor beside the bed.

I put the book I was reading down, and turned off the bedside light with a simple, "Goodnight."

"Goodnight" he said. "Oh, I am flying to Barcelona tomorrow. I will be back before the wedding."

CHAPTER FORTY-TWO

W illiam had left before I woke up, and I paced my room all of Saturday worried about what he was up to in Barcelona. Part of me wanted him to get caught. Another part of me hoped he would be unable to return and the wedding would be postponed. A small part of me worried for his safety, the part of me that constantly needed to be reminded how evil William really was. After all, he was about to murder an innocent person the day before his wedding. Who does that? William.

The baby was just as restless as I was, and little sleep was had Saturday night. The perilous road that brought me here was littered with unwanted memories. Dreamland was within reach when Charlotte woke me up.

"Is William back?" I asked.

"Not yet, but he will be. His flight should have landed. Here, you need to eat something if you are going to survive the day. Hundreds of people are coming for the wedding and you will likely not have much time for food."

"Any chance you can find me a body double on short notice?"

"If only." She lowered her voice. "There will be a lot of staff around, preparing the food and decorations while everyone is at the church, so I doubt I will be able to get into Lady Hammonds office unnoticed. However, the guise of a party, and a bride who needs to keep up her appearance, may lend to opportunities for you to step away. They changed the locks so I will leave a lock picker under the vase by the office door.

Now, we need to talk about what you will do if you should find something."

There was a quick knock at the door and then William stepped through. He did not look shocked to see Charlotte with me, but without words held the door open for her. Charlotte took the hint and left.

As William's hand rested on the door, I saw that his knuckles were torn and matched the cut over his right eye.

"What happened in Barcelona?"

"I took care of it." He stuck his head into the hallway, "You can come in now."

A medium-built woman with frizzy hair, wearing a black, floor-length dress suit with gold buttons running down both sides of an open jacket, stepped into the room. She clutched a carpet bag close to her chest, her head swivelled around the room.

William closed the door. "This is Barbara. She will help you get ready." The stern look on William's face told me not to ask questions.

I stood up and walked over to the mystery woman and held out my hand, "Nice to meet you. I appreciate your help." Barbara hesitated a moment and then shook my hand.

"Well, I will leave you to it. See you in a couple of hours. Unless you ditch me at the altar of course." Barbara forced a laughed and I smiled.

"Would you like some tea or a bite to eat?" I pointed to the platter of assorted fruit and pastries.

"Tea would be nice, thank you." Barbara looked meekly around the room.

"Any cream or sugar?"

"One sugar, please."

She had not moved an inch while I prepared the tea, and started to put the bag on the floor, but thought better of it and set it on the bench at the foot of the bed. I handed her the tea cup and saucer, which rattled in her hands.

"Are you okay?"

"Hmm? Oh, yes I am fine. The tea is lovely, thank you. We should probably get you ready for your big day." She finished her tea and placed the cup and saucer on the tray with the teapot.

Barbara trembled as she curled my hair and burned herself with the curling iron a couple of times, but insisted she would be able to continue without addressing the wounds. She remained focused and quiet. There were only a couple of unintentional jabs to the head with the bobby pins used to style my hair. The make-up application was a little more treacherous with her shaky hands. The eyeliner had to be applied three times, and I put on my own mascara for fear that Barbara would stab me in the eye with the brush.

We walked into the closet and the wedding dress was hung, in it's bag, beside the trifold mirror. When Barbara opened the bag and removed part of the flowing white dress, she burst into tears. She ran to the bathroom and locked the door behind her.

I left her to cry for a while and then knocked softly, "Barbara? Are you okay? Can I get you anything?"

"I...I just need a minute. I will be out momentarily."

"Alright. Shout if you need me."

I walked back into the closet and removed the rest of the wedding dress out of it's bag and hung it back on the hook. I stepped back and stared at it for a while. It was stunning. The heart-shaped neckline was covered in hand-stitched lace, which then was carried up over the shoulders and it had short sleeves that capped just below the shoulder. A simple off-white satin belt separated the bodice from the sleek princess bell skirt. No embellishments were needed, as the sheen of the fabric glistened. I turned the dress around and started to release the buttons from their looped clasps when my hands were gently pushed away.

"No, no! I will do that." Barbara forced herself between me and the dress and continued with the buttons. She gently removed the dress from the hanger and slumped down, the open back towards me, so that I could step into it. We pulled the dress up and I gently put my arms through the sleeves, trying not to catch my fingers on the lace. Tears started down Barbara's face as she clasped the buttons. This time she wiped them away and continued at her task.

After she had placed the long lace veil on my head, she looked at me in the mirror and smiled. "You look beautiful."

"Thank you." I did look beautiful. I had to hold back my own tears as my thoughts turned to Claire. We had spent hours talking about our dream weddings. Even if this one was a sham, I wished she could have been here with me, not just in spirit. I turned to Barbara and asked the question I had wanted to ask the moment she walked into my room, "Barbara, how do you know William?"

She fiddled with her dress jacket and then said, "I'm Karey's wife."

CHAPTER FORTY-THREE

I was driven to the church alone, everyone else had already gone before. The white, open- Rolls Royce pulled away from the house, and the event staff took no notice. They ran around the yard to create perfection for my return. At that point I would be Mrs. Hammond. The thought formed knots in my stomach. January 25, 2020 would be added to the dates I would long to forget. I looked down at my abdomen and murmured, "This is all for you."

Ten minutes later, I was parked outside the front steps of a church that looked at least two or three-hundred years old. Its stature dominated the buildings around it. I did not have time to take in the full magnificence of the architecture before I was ushered out of the car. In front of me stood three young children I had never met, all dressed in white frilled dresses, pink ribbons wrapped around their waists. Each held a small bouquet of orange and yellow flowers.

Helen came over, inspected the children and lined them up under the arched entrance. Helen banged on the heavy wooden door and two gentlemen, dressed in dark suits with ear pieces, opened it from the inside. She handed me a bouquet of beautiful red lilies, the center of each flower darker than the edges. They reminded me of blood which had thinned out as it spread.

"Karey outdid herself, yet again. I hate to admit it, but you look very nice. I am impressed."

The compliment was almost sharper than the backhanded remark.

The organ music got louder, Helen's arm wrapped itself around mine, and we started up the church steps.

She continued, "It is no secret that, although I do not dislike you per se, I do not trust you. This wedding is a necessity to avoid a scandal. That's it. If you think you will weasel your way into this family in more than name, you are sadly mistaken. Especially, with your notions of turning the business legitimate. I will only continue to tolerate your presence as long as William is happy. But if you do anything to jeopardize him, myself or the Hammond name you will be sorry. Understood?"

I nodded.

Helen walked me down the aisle, a smile plastered on my face, and the flower girls behind us. The extravagant church interior distracted me from the unknown onlookers and their whispers as we passed. Portraits with gilded frames filled the walls in between the large, arched, stained-glass windows. The ceiling conveyed scenes from the Bible. Each one was hand painted directly onto the stone. The paint stopped at the altar, and was replaced by a dark blue canvas covered in hundreds of gold stars. My dress swept along a cream coloured marble floor that was lined with a similar stone that the church was built of. The only part of the church that was not opulent were the church pews, basic wood benches lined the sanctuary.

After row upon row of bodies, we made it to the altar. Emma was seated up front, lips pursed and arms crossed. Her sour look did not detract from the fact she looked more voluptuous than at the party. William stood, his back to me and the crowd, another odd English tradition. It was not as if it would be a surprise as to who he would marry. I stepped beside him, he turned to me, took my hand from Helen, and smiled. "You look beautiful." I prayed my veil hid my flushed cheeks. Helen stepped back and took the empty spot beside Emma.

William looked immaculate wearing dark-grey pinstripe pants, a light grey double-breasted vest over a white shirt and a black tie with white polka dots. This was topped off with a black tail jacket, and a pocket square that matched the tie, a single red lily boutonnière on his lapel. The cut above his eye had been covered with some concealer. His knuckles were still red.

The ceremony was dreadful with recitations and scripture spoken in the monotone voice of the priest. The only thing that kept me awake was the anticipation of a conversation with William about what happened in Barcelona.

With the exchange of rings, another prayer, and the pronouncement of William and I as husband and wife, came the very public "You may kiss the bride". It was all surreal. William lifted my veil, placed his hand under my chin and kissed me gently as cameras flashed around us. William stepped back, and he looked happy. But he had looked happy before and then he had my friends tortured. Happiness was relative in this world.

We exited the church and birds sang from the trees in the churchyard. William climbed into the waiting car first and sat directly behind the driver. I maneuvered the dress and myself into the car, careful not to get the fabric caught on the frame. Once I was settled, the car pulled away and we awkwardly waved to the people who spilled out of the church. I suppose in another life I would have felt like a princess, whisked away to a mansion on a hill and a life full of wealth. Instead, I was filled with dread at the thought at how quickly Karey had appeared to have been "taken care of" after blackmailing William.

We only had a few minutes until we arrived back at Hammond Manor and it would likely be the only time we were alone together for the rest of the evening. Driver or not, I had no qualms about inquiring about William's trip.

"What happened in Barcelona?"

"I took care of it."

"I gathered that. What happened to Karey?"

"The less you know the better."

"I know I am of little importance here, but you brought Barbara back here, so it would be nice to understand why, and what I can or cannot say around her."

With reluctance, William gave me some details, "I found Barbara at home alone as designed with Karey. She invited me in and I told her that her wife wanted her killed. Of course she did not believe me, but it did not take long for her to start to come around to the idea. I told her I was only after Karey, and we made a deal that I would do her no harm so long as she kept quiet about everything. When Karey arrived home at the predetermined time to find her wife, the shock on her face when she saw Barbara alive and well, washed away any doubt Barbara had. Karey tried to make a run for it, but only made it to the end of the driveway before I ushered her into my rental car, Barbara seated up front. I took care of Karey while Barbara waited in the car. That is all you need to know."

How easily William could kill was terrifying. The names of the victims I knew about were what I needed to keep in mind when feelings of empathy or affection started to rise within me.

"How do you know Barbara will keep quiet and not blackmail you like Karey did?"

"Aunt Helen is handling that."

The days in the office must have included planning the trip to Barcelona, not just cleaning up after Jasper. I needed to get into that office.

CHAPTER FORTY-FOUR

I had never liked weddings, and mine had not changed my mind. The receiving line alone lasted two hours. Word had gotten out that I was pregnant, so, of course, everyone wanted to talk about it. After an hour, Charlotte brought me a pair of slippers. My feet had swollen and the small heels I had been wearing had pinched my feet. The lush softness of the slippers kept my feet comfortable, as my cheek muscles screamed from the workout they received.

Dinner was five courses and took another two hours to serve. Aunt Helen sat beside me at the head table, where we said nothing. Emma sat beside William and I heard no restraint with the flirtations. William's rejections only fueled her campaign.

After the last course was served, I almost took the opportunity to break away from the party, but realized I would be needed back for the first dance right away. I would not have time to rummage around Helen's office. It would have to wait a little while longer.

William had told me he had picked the song, and I erupted with laughter when "Stay with me" by Sam Smith started to play.

"What's so funny?"

"Do you know what this song is about?"

"Loneliness and unexpected fulfillment."

"Huh. You do know. And you thought a song that specifically states the people are not in love was a good choice for a first dance?"

"I thought it would be ironic."

"Is Alanis Morissette up next?"

William laughed while the guests crowded around the dance floor. I was not sure if it was the song choice, or the fact we could barely dance due to fits of laughter, that had caused waves of commotion in the crowd, but I ignored them. With one final dip the song ended and the crowd cordially clapped.

"It's been a long day and well, I have to pee, so I'll be back."

"Alright, don't leave me with all of these people alone for long."

Rather than use the trailer of bathroom stalls that was brought in, I headed for the house. No one would blame the bride for not using an upscale porta potty. After five minutes without a solution as to how to use a toilet in a wedding dress, I gave up and just balled up the skirt of it the best I could and did what I needed to do. Helen would not approve of the newly formed wrinkles but my bladder and I could not have cared less.

Finally free of the pain of a full bladder, I focused my attention on Helen's office. I cautiously opened the bathroom door and waited until the hallway was clear before I exited. As I ran across the entry hall I was grateful for the soft-bottomed slippers. The only sound was the swoosh of my dress. I lifted the edge of the vase and pulled out the lock picker. I heard people in the kitchen and I worked as fast as I could. The lock opened with ease. One would think with all the other precautions the Hammonds took, a better lock would have secured the room.

Once I closed the door, the light from the entryway evaporated and my eyes had to adjust to the darkness. I put the lock picker in the bodice of my dress. Had I turned on the light, someone outside would have noticed, so I had to work in the grey light coming through the window. The last time I was in here the laptop was gone, but now it sat in the middle of the desk. I peered out the curtains and found Helen was distracted with guests and Emma had William on the dance floor. I had time.

I opened the laptop and stared at the password screen. I thought about what little I knew about Helen and hoped a potential password would jump out. I tried her husband's name, Jonathan. Incorrect. William's father's name, her brother, Douglas. Incorrect. I looked at the books on the shelves but nothing stood out. I rummaged through papers on the desk, but everything was associated with household or wedding expenses. I almost choked on the cost of tonight's food, $145,000.

Four songs had played since I had been in the office, time had become my enemy. Finally, I decided to try something on a whim. If all else failed, a fourth incorrect password notification would pop up and I would head back to the reception. I typed in the six letters. As my finger hovered over the Enter key I closed my eyes, said a small prayer and hit the key. I slowly opened my eyes and I stared at an open computer. Thank you Prince!

There were dozens of folders on the desktop alone and more within the computer itself. There was not enough time to go through them all. I picked the lock on the center desk drawer and retrieved a USB stick. I stuck it into the computer, it only had a couple of files so I copied everything from the computer. The green bar slowly made its way across the screen. I got up and looked through the curtains again. Helen had moved on to other guests, and Emma was at the bar with some women I didn't recognize. I craned my neck as I scanned the crowd. I could not locate William.

I had been gone too long. I ran back to the computer - 80% complete. Come on! 87%...92%. My ear pressed against the door, I listened closely but could not hear a sound in the entry hall. 96%. My heart beat raced as my leg shook to release the nerves. 99%...100%. I grabbed the stick and wedged it in the bodice of my dress beside the lock pickers. The boning ensured the shape of the dress was not altered with the additional accessories. I was about to close the laptop when I realized two things. One; I had access to email and could try to reach out to Joe. Two; the computer would have a security feature to report unsuccessful attempts to access the computer. I desperately wanted to try and contact Joe, but for once my rational thinking overtook my rashness. For his own safety, and mine, I decided I needed to ensure no one would know I had been in the office.

After I cleared the information, and the internet search history for the process on how to do that, off the computer, I wiped off my fingerprints as best I could with the skirt of my dress. I stood with my ear to the office door and listened. My hand rested on the handle and I had turned it when I heard voices.

"OLIVIA"

I released the handle and locked the door with a faint click.

My eyes darted around the room. I could hide under the desk, but if William checked the computer my large white dress would give me away. I would be noticed behind a curtain by both William and those outside. Where the hell could I hide? As I stood in the middle of the room I heard the jiggle of the door handle. There was a gap along the wall beside the floor to ceiling bookcases and the windows. I wrapped the skirt of my dress tightly around my legs and I pressed myself flat against the wall. I covered my mouth with my hand to hide my accelerated breathing which reverberated off of everything around me.

Keys jingled on the other side of the door. Metal ground against metal as a key slipped into the lock.

Click.

CHAPTER FORTY-FIVE

I made myself as small as possible, held my breath and hugged the wall. The hand not over my mouth clutched my dress. Light from the entry poured into the room like a flashlight in the dark. It slowly widened it's breadth the further the door was opened. I watched the light crawl across the floor and inch closer and closer to my feet. Then it stopped, inches from where I stood. William's shadow loomed in the light reflected on the floor. It was the only part of him I could see.

The expanse of light started to decrease and the dark devoured it with the sound of the door closing. I continued to hold my breath until the lock activated and the door handle rattled as verification.

Then I fell to the floor and gasped for air. William had only stood there for a few seconds, but it felt like an eternity. Adrenaline coursed through me. I took a few deep breaths and worked to regain my composure. I peeked behind the curtain, William had rejoined the crowd but constantly ran his fingers through his hair and over his face.

Once again, I leaned my ear against the door. No sound. I unlocked the door, slowly turned the handle and peered out. I exited and placed the lock picker under the vase. The flowers in the vase were artificial. I looked around once more, took the USB out of the bodice and dropped it into the vase. Charlotte would have to collect the lock picker before another member of the staff found it. Hopefully, there would be time to inform her of what else she needed to take.

I rejoined the party and located Charlotte at the bar. William was with Helen and Emma on the opposite side of the yard. All three stared at me. It would not be safe for me to ignore them, so I headed over to the group. I would find Charlotte later.

"Finally, gracing us with your presence again, I see," Emma said.

"After four hours of not going to the bathroom, and dealing with hundreds of people I don't know, I needed a sanity break. I did not realize I needed permission."

"The people are here to celebrate you and William. Which means they should see you and William. Not just William," Helen said.

"I wasn't gone that long, and none of these people know me so I doubt they care. Besides, since they all apparently know I am pregnant, let's just tell them I'm hormonal and tired. Which is actually true. Now, William, unless you have anything to add, I need a drink." William's smirk told me he was impressed I had called out Helen and Emma, but there was no objection.

"Great." I turned and headed towards the bar but Charlotte was no longer there. Damn it! I could not change my plan now so I continued to make my way over.

The guests lined up at the bar allowed the bride to move to the front of the line, and congratulated me along the way.

"Orange juice, please." The cold drink soothed my throat. "Do you know where Charlotte went?"

"No, but she'll be back to help. These guests could drink sailors under the table."

"May I have a pen?"

I discreetly wrote a note on the coaster under my orange juice.

Look inside the place you just visited.

I handed back the pen, and slid the coaster over the counter-top and wedged it under a glass. The bartender watched, without acknowledgement, and continued to serve the guests. He grabbed glassware from around the one with the coaster. I smiled, he refilled my drink and I headed back to William. Time to give the crowd what they wanted.

Another two hours went by on crowd control before the child inside me screamed, with uncomfortable somersaults, for me to sleep. I pulled William aside. "I need to go to bed. This child is getting restless and I am exhausted. Do you think you could do the rest of this alone?"

He smiled, "Do I have to?"

"You are more than welcome to join me, but I will pass out when I hit that pillow, so it's up to you."

"Let me say goodbye to a few people and I will meet you upstairs. We need to talk about where you went earlier." The smile was gone.

CHAPTER FORTY-SIX

I ran into the bedroom, stripped out of the wedding dress, and splashed some cold water onto my face.

After I had left William at the reception, I realized I would need help undressing. I found a very helpful woman on my way into the house who, for the price of hearing all about her prize- winning poodle, undid all of the buttons for me. I received some curious looks as I walked up the stairs with the back of my dress wide open, but I did not care. I needed out of the dress and either needed to be asleep by the time William got to the bedroom, or come up with an answer as to my whereabouts.

I scraped off the mountain of makeup Barbara had put onto my face and put on some comfortable pajamas. I found the bed covered in red and white rose petals, which I rushed to brush onto the floor. There would be no wedding-night bliss. I climbed into bed, but knew William would see through my attempt to pretend to be asleep or he would wake me. I needed a plan. Where could I tell him I was?

I ran through different scenarios in my head and none of them seemed plausible. He would have checked the bedroom and kitchen. Would he have checked the stables? Could I say I was out there? I doubt it, I had not had the smell of horses on me. I went through every room in the house and then my stomach dropped.

The surveillance cameras. If they checked the cameras they would know where I was! Is that what William meant when he said he wanted to say goodbye to some guests? Had he gone to look at the video recording?

My chest and jaw clenched, my legs had grown restless so I got out of bed and paced the room. How had my desire to get out of here clouded my judgment enough to not think about the cameras? The stomach that had been on the floor now made its way up my throat. I ran to the bathroom just in time.

I leaned back against the wall beside the toilet, the blood drained from my face and the contents from my stomach in the bowl. I would have to tell him the truth. I would have to tell him I had been in the office.

The bedroom door clicked closed. I pushed myself up off the cold floor and walked my hands up the wall to help me get to my feet. I flushed the toilet and swished some mouthwash to hide the stench of vomit. Then I trudged out of the bathroom to face my fate. I had no words. No lie believable enough to not be verified.

William was undoing his cuff links when he noticed me. "I was half expecting you to be asleep."

"It took a while to undo the remodel of myself. I still haven't gotten all of the pins out of my hair, but I am about ready to say 'screw it' and sleep like this. It's been a very long day."

"Yes, it has. Sit. I will help you with your hair." I had no reason to decline his offer, so I sat on the stool in front of the vanity. I watched as William slowly and carefully removed pin after pin. After half of my hair hung on my shoulders William looked directly into my eyes, through the mirror, "You were gone for a while tonight. I had started to wonder if you had found a way to leave."

"No luck there." I hoped my joke would lighten the mood, but William's face remained unchanged and stone-cold.

"Where did you go?"

I stared William down. "After spending way too much time trying not to pee on my dress, and surrounded by strangers full of fake congratulations, I went for a walk out front." I could not help myself from lying. I would be caught by morning. What was I doing?

"Is that so? Why is it that no one saw you? It is not like you were inconspicuous in your giant white dress." He continued to remove pins from my hair.

"I really don't think many of these people actually care to interact with me, let alone worry about my whereabouts. More than half were probably too drunk to see straight."

"You would be right about that." William gripped my hair and pulled my head back. "Now why would one of the servers tell me that they saw you go into Aunt Helen's office? The room that, I know for a fact, was locked."

Shit! Where the hell did a witness come from? Was William making it up based on a suspicion? I opened my mouth to speak, but William cut me off.

"I want you to think very carefully about the next words that come out of your mouth. They will not only affect you, but the server. If you do not believe me, look out the window." He let go of my hair, and my head flung forward.

More worried for the server than myself, I went to the window. Below knelt a young man, maybe twenty years old, dressed in an all-black suit. Behind him was a large man, also dressed in black from head to toe, but he had on a balaclava. He had a gun pointed at the back of the young man's head.

I gripped the window frame and rested my forehead on the glass. I took a deep breath and turned to face William, "Let him go."

"Tell me what you were up to, and then I might."

"What did that kid ever do to you? In fact, he tried to help you! And you're going to have him killed?"

William rushed over to me, spun me around to face the window and pressed my face against it, "Stop stalling and start answering!"

I tried to get out from under his grip, but he had me pinned, "FINE! You want to know where I was? Like you suspected, I was in Helen's office." No one moved for a moment and then William let go. He stepped beside me as I pried my face off the window.

"The room was locked."

"Hair pins are not just for holding up hair." I had never actually picked a lock with a hair pin before, so I had no idea if it could actually be done. I prayed William didn't know any better.

"What were you looking for?" William's eyes darted between me and those outside. He fussed with the buttons on his shirt. Was he nervous?

"Anything that would help me get out of here."

"What did you think we would have, that would help grant you your freedom?"

"It would be impossible to run this *empire* of yours without some sort of evidence. I am sure anything I could find would be helpful."

"Find anything useful?"

William appeared genuinely interested in my answer. He was not yet aware of what I had taken. I breathed a silent sigh of relief. "No."

"And who would you have given it to? It is not as though we let you leave the house." His eyes widened as soon as the word house left his mouth and he ran out the door.

I looked out the window. The people below had not moved. I ran after William. I looked over the railing and could not see him.

His voice filled the house, "CHARLOTTE!"

I ran down the stairs two at a time. The guests that had been in the house looked on curiously as I ran past in my pajamas. I headed towards the kitchen as I suspected that would be where William would go first. When I got there, a path of parted bodies had already been created. They all pointed outside.

I ran through the door and was hit with the cold damp air, the smell of freshly mowed grass and horses. William stood in front of Prince's open and empty stall, his hair knotted in his hands.

William turned and, although he was ten feet away and it was dark, I could see and feel his anger. His body seemed to take up more space than normal and his eyes glowed in the moonlight. He bolted towards me and I quickly backed away. My toe got caught on the stone pathway and I started to fall backwards. My fall was prevented by the body of someone who pushed me back onto my feet.

I looked back and it was the large man dressed in black. I still could not see his face, but I did not need to in order for my body to fill with dread.

The man grabbed my arm and motioned, with his gun, for the young man he had brought with him to march forward.

William took me from the man. His grip strangled my arm. I wanted to fight him, but I doubted the masked man would hesitate to kill the young man if I did anything.

"WHERE IS CHARLOTTE?"

"I don't know."

"Just like you didn't know what happened to Adam? How did that work out for everyone? Once again you have other people's lives in your hands and you are choosing to lie to me?"

"Seriously, I don't know where Charlotte is." I looked at the young man, tears and snot streamed down his face. "Please don't hurt him. He did nothing to go against you or your family."

"If you don't know where she is, you better tell me what she has."

"I...uh-" William used his other hand to grip my neck.

"SPEAK!"

"Everything. She has everything."

William went ghost-white and released his grip. Unprepared, I fell to the ground. I could hear William mutter to himself. I kept my eyes on him while I tried to assess how I might be able to get myself and the young man to safety. Now free of William, I could get the gun, but it would likely discharge in the process and draw the attention of the guests. All of whose allegiance was to the Hammonds. I saw no way out. I slumped even closer to the ground. Defeated.

"Deal with him, away from the party, and put him with the others," William ordered.

I crawled to William and clung to his pant leg, "William, please. He didn't do anything. You don't have to do this."

William kicked me away, my lip cracked open. "I would not have to do this if you had not snuck around where you should not have been. I thought you had learned your lesson by now. His blood is on your hands!"

He was right, but I would not let him know that. "If you didn't run this evil thing you call a business, that kid would live. So, no, his blood is on your hands, not mine!"

William grabbed my hair and dragged me across the stones. I tried to fight his grip, and screamed as hair follicles released their contents. He tossed me into Prince's stall. William grabbed a black leather riding crop off the wall and whipped me with it. I rolled away from him, curled into a ball on my knees to protect the baby. With each lash came a hardened cry that escaped from me. After five lashes, William stopped. Blood trickled through my pajamas.

The leather riding crop hit the ground and footsteps shuffled away from me. Fear kept my body balled up on the floor. Unoiled hinges screeched and I lifted my arm and peered under it. The last thing I saw was William closing the upper stall door. Everything went black except for a ray of moonlight that seeped through the cracks in the door and the grates in the tops of the side walls.

A lock snapped.

CHAPTER FORTY-SEVEN

The stench of manure filled my nose while my swollen eyes adjusted to the darkness. I could just make out the grey stone walls and the wooden stall door, locked from the outside. I crawled towards the back of the stall, one hand up in front of me and the other entangled in hay, dirt and manure as I moved along. When I reached the back wall, I felt for the corner and placed my back into it. I wiped my filth covered hand on the wall and hugged my knees.

Despite my location, sleep overtook me as I thought about the young man who would meet a fate much worse than mine. I cursed God, if he was out there, for not saving him. Then I cursed him for Claire, Whitney and my predicament. Why was this happening? No matter how much I tried to help others I failed. I rested my head on the wall and let sleep win.

I was woken by hoof kicks and horse huffs from the stall beside me. The cracks in and around the door allowed in a red-hued light. I was exhausted, and suspected I had slept for no more than four hours. Thick, wood-slat doors slowed the cold morning air from entering the stall; however, it had permeated the stone walls and there was a chill deep in my bones. I would not find sleep again, and I needed to seize the opportunity to try and get myself out of here before the rest of the house woke up. The unease of the horse in the stall next to me would be perfect cover.

My back screamed after being cramped into an uncomfortable position all night. Even with some daylight I could not see very well and ran my hand along the wall to guide me towards the door. I stepped in something wet and squishy that filled the space between my toes. I knew what it was, ignored the repulsion and moved forward. My foot stepped on something hard. "Fuck." I bent down, felt around and found the riding stick. I picked it up. If nothing else, I was now armed.

A few more steps and I reached the door. It rattled when I pushed on it but would not open. I used the riding stick to pry the gaps in the door, to no avail. They were too small for my hands and there was no feasible way that I would be able to get at the lock on the other side.

My eyes, now adjusted to the small glimmer of light, looked around. Was there a way to get into an adjoining stall? At the top of the stall were some bars, but they were the size of small grates. Even if I could manage to climb up to them and get them loose, I would be unable to fit through.

I went back and sat crossed-legged in the corner I had slept in. I had become accustomed to the aroma around me enough that it only moderately gripped my senses. The gold band on my left hand itched and strangled my finger. I desperately wanted it off, but no matter how hard I tugged, it kept its hold on me.

My skin was warm to the touch. I had backed myself into a corner with no escape. I hated myself for allowing William's charm and vulnerability to confuse me enough to believe I could survive this family. Again. How could I have been so stupid? Waves of emotion rolled over me as I recalled our night together in the closet. The hospital bed. I had initiated both! How could I have wanted him to be that close to me? What was wrong with me? Had I been a participant in a ruse on the path to freedom, or had I longed for some connection with this horrible man?

My thoughts turned to Claire and how, in the end, she and I had not been so different after all. She chose a man addicted to drugs who took her down the dark and retched path of desperation and destruction. I was, for some reason, enamored with a man who created worlds of destruction and desperation. A man who made his victims feel they had some semblance of power, then, when they thought they could win, he would bite the head off the snake. What did that say about me? How disgusting was it that I succumbed to his manipulative nature? If Claire was alive today, would she have hit the ignore button if I had called?

Between the exhaustion and hatred, I cried so hard there was no sound. I slammed the sides of my fists against both walls until the pain in my hands overtook the pain in my heart. Eventually, the throbbing in my hands subsided. The ache in my heart did not.

The disparaging thoughts continued as I waited for William to make his next move. I was powerless. I questioned what type of mother I could be, when I could not protect Claire, or myself. No child would love me enough to see through the choices I had made. Provided I lived long enough to be a mother.

Behind the clatter of horse hooves, I heard boots stomp on the cobblestone. The steps got closer and stopped in front of the stall. Some of the sunlight which had shone through the cracks were blocked by the visitor's body. I gripped the riding crop, and was ready to run at whoever it was. My stomach grumbled and I realized I had not eaten since dinner, which I had thrown up. I would not have the strength to get past the number of people required to get off the estate. My battle would have to wait. I hid the whip under some nearby hay. Metal scraped along metal as a single latch was unlocked. Huddled in the corner, I shielded my eyes from the blaring sun that cascaded into the stall through the opened top half of the stable door.

"I said I did not trust you." Helen's voice emitted from a darkened silhouette.

Caldwell tossed two plastic containers and a metal bucket towards me. The clang of the metal on the concrete floor reverberated around the stall. I had to protect my ears from the racket. Caldwell started to close the door but Helen's hand stopped it's progression. "You should consider yourself lucky. William has spared your life. For now. But as soon as that thing is out of you, I will be more than happy to show you what the Hammonds do to traitors." She removed her hand, the door closed and I was enveloped in darkness.

I waited until I could no longer hear voices or footsteps, and went to inspect what I had been provided. The bucket, I knew, was my new toilet, which I did not hesitate to use after hours without a bathroom, and the weight of a child on my bladder. I found the two containers; one a bottle of water. I restrained myself to only half. I needed to ration myself, at least until I had a sense of when more would be provided. The second container held raw vegetables and cold chicken. Unlike the water, I devoured everything. If I was to be kept alive until the birth of this boy, I suspected food would appear at regular intervals.

It was this thought, and the realization that Helen called me a traitor, that gave me hope. William still had not told her who I really was. Above all else, he worked to protect himself. With the food and water settled in my stomach, I buried the self-loathsome feelings that had bubbled up moments earlier. I paced the small stall as I worked out my plan.

The length of the stall was seven steps. One, two, three, four, five, six, seven. Back and forth. I spun around on my heel and lost my balance on the slick, feces-covered floor. I wobbled, but my outstretched arms could not beat gravity. My body crashed hard onto the concrete.

A sharp pain shot around my stomach. Then another one.

CHAPTER FORTY-EIGHT

The pain increased in intensity every time I tried to move. The tiniest movement sent shards of pain up my back and around my torso. I stared up at the dark ceiling and pushed through the pain. I tried to roll onto my side but I could not handle it. After all the beatings I had taken, a fall was to be what kept me down.

The spasms had become unbearable. I screamed for help. Repeatedly. No one answered.

I managed to stretch my arm out far enough that I could reach the handle of the bucket. I pulled it towards myself. The contents spilled down my arm and around me. Not only was I covered in dirt, straw and manure, I now had my own urine mixed in.

I gripped the handle and smashed the bucket against the concrete. It did not take long for the horses in the adjoining stalls to become upset. They stomped their feet and raised their own voices. They may have muffled mine but I hoped someone would care enough to come check on them. They would be considered more valuable than me, and receive proper attention for their cries.

My suspicions proved correct. It was not long until voices spoke outside the stalls. Once the horses had calmed down, I screamed again. "Please help! The baby might be hurt. Please, I'm in a lot of pain!"

The voices stopped. I yelled again, "Please I am begging you, get help!" Nothing. Another shot of pain filtered up my spine, and I gritted my teeth, "What will happen to you if William's baby dies because you did not get help?"

Feet clamoured, followed by shouts for help. Moments later the stall filled with light and people circled me. The gardener, who had come upon Jasper and me by the river, checked my pulse, as if my convulsions of pain were not enough of an indication I was alive. The cook, who turned up her nose at my stench, balled up her apron, lifted my head and put it under as a makeshift pillow.

An unknown man dressed in a grey jumpsuit said, "We should get her out of here, so we can see her better." All three took positions around my body. The man continued, "One...Two.."

"Do not move her!" boomed William's voice from outside the stall.

As if I was on fire, all three backed away. They scrambled to be the first one out of the stall. After they exited, William ordered a light to be found, and the cook and stranger scattered, while the gardener remained. William's large frame entered the stall. His figure loomed over me and cast a shadow that engulfed me. I would have liked to have thought it was the sight of him that caused the pain in my abdomen to increase, but I knew it was my body's rhythmic cycle of fierce pain. Thirty seconds of calm, pain, repeat.

William crouched down beside me. Emotionless. "Are you really hurt, or could you not even spend one day outside the luxurious bedroom I had provided you. Which you deemed detrimental to your life."

"William, please. I slipped on the shit that is all over this floor. I landed on my back and can't even sit up. The baby could be hurt."

"The doctor has been called." He placed his wrist on my forehead, "No fever." He looked to the gardener and pointed to the back corner, "Pass me that water bottle."

The gardener obliged and climbed over me to retrieve it. William placed his hand under my neck and I winced as he raised my head. Water trickled down my throat and my chin. I closed my eyes, and William lowered my head back onto the apron. I tried to keep calm and heed the pain. I heard William stand up, but the few footsteps told me he had not moved far.

A while later, rushed footsteps approached. Doctor Harrison made her way into the stall. "Good God, the smell." She covered her mouth, "This was not how I wanted to spend my Sunday, young lady. Quickly now, where does it hurt?"

"Everywhere."

"That's not helpful. Where does the pain start?"

"My lower back, then it spreads up my spine and around my front."

"Can you move your toes or legs?"

"Yes, both." I bent both legs at the knees, which created a burst of pain. "Argh!"

She felt my neck and moved it, "William, come help me. We are going to roll her onto her side, towards you. Take her shoulders." They slowly, and painfully, rolled me over. "Hold her like that. Does this hurt?"

"FUCK, YES!" Doctor Harrison had pressed hard at the top of the crevasse of my butt cheeks.

"You have a fractured tail-bone. I am going to need better lighting, and electricity to check on the baby. We need to move her."

William swapped positions with the doctor and placed his arm under my back as he rolled me back over. He positioned his other arm under my knees and lifted me up off the damp, dirty floor. I wrapped my arms around his neck, but I avoided his gaze.

With caution he walked me into the kitchen and eased me on top of the table we had sat around and planned Jasper's death. He stepped back, leaned against the wall with his arms crossed, and observed doctor Harrison.

Ultrasound gel was squirted onto my skin. If it was cold, my body did not register it, as it was too consumed with the heat of the pain that radiated throughout my body. The massage of the wand spreading the gel around only aggravated the discomfort. Doctor Harrison circled my stomach three times and said nothing. No sound came out of the machine. Fourth time around and still nothing. William fidgeted with the collar of his shirt.

"What's happening? Is the baby alright?" William asked.

Without any consideration for bedside manner, Dr. Harrison stated, "I can't find the heartbeat."

CHAPTER FORTY-NINE

It was as if the breath had been sucked out of everyone, me included. Silence crowded around us. A sour taste filled my mouth. Whatever feelings I had towards the life inside me didn't matter anymore. With the baby gone, I dreaded how torturous William and Helen would make my own death. I was also overcome with relief at not having to raise William's child, and for this to finally be over. So this was where my road would lead?

The incessant click of buttons nagged at my ears. My eyes were drawn to the candelabra chandelier above me. The way the light danced on the ceiling reminded me of fireflies entangled with each other amongst the trees.

Thump.

Claire and I had loved to chase fireflies, during the hot summer evenings, when we were young. We could never catch one on our own, and begged our parents to help. It only took Mom a few minutes, and one would be in a mason jar. It bounced off the sides as it fluttered around. Dad scolded us for the entrapment of a creature meant to fly. Looking back, I wondered if he commiserated with the firefly, confined within a family he did not want.

Thump. Thump.

Hums of cheers broke through the wall of memories I had encased myself in. I looked away from the light and back to the doctor. William now stood beside her, his hand pressed against his heart.

Thump. Thump. Thump...

"Well, now that is better. I must have had the volume turned down," Doctor Harrison said.

The glare William shot at the doctor spoke louder than any words.

"Well, everything looks fine with the baby. As for you, you will want to sit on a foam donut for the next 8-12 weeks as you heal. Which means you may want to consider a C-section, as birthing a baby with a fractured tail-bone would be excruciating. You can take some acetaminophen to help with the pain, every four hours, without harming the baby, but no more than 500 milligrams." She turned to William, "Unless there is anything else, I will leave you all to it."

"Thank you," William said. "I will walk you out. Olivia, do not move. Sam, you are with me." The gardener scurried behind.

When William returned, Caldwell and a couple of his footmen were with him. Like everyone else who had encountered me today, they turned up their nose at the smell. The footmen hesitated to approach, took a deep breath, lifted me up off the table, and placed me on my feet. The pressure soared up my legs and settled at my tail-bone. Each footman put one of my arms over their shoulder and walked me, on my tip toes, back outside.

We stopped in the middle of the stable block. I was turned around to face the house. Helen had now joined William and Caldwell. A satisfied look on her face as she stood in the doorway, the two men on the steps below her. The rest of the estate staff formed a circle around me. All of them had the tattooed H on their wrists.

"Remove her clothes." William ordered.

My desire to avoid William's gaze ceased. My defiant eyes met his as the footmen tore off my clothes. I stood naked in front of the crowd. I could have tried to cover myself with my arms and crossed my legs in shame. Instead, I stood tall and proud.

"Sam." William said.

Sam held a long green garden hose, the nozzle pointed at me. His eyes were apologetic as he released the trigger. Pellets of ice-cold water hit my skin, and it felt like a thousand wasps stung me. The added pain made my head spin, but I stood my ground. I would not show weakness. I would not give William or Helen the satisfaction. Without being ordered, I raised my arms to shoulder height and turned around slowly. The crud that had seeped into my pores dripped down my body. When my back was to Sam, he was nice enough to avoid direct contact with my lower back. After I had completed my rotation, I cupped what water I could in my hands and tried to wash my face. I had not gotten very far when William's quiet, yet powerful, voice filled the yard.

"Enough."

Gravity pulled the droplets of ice water down my exposed body. My eyes found William's, anger mirrored in them. William turned to Caldwell, who had a pile of neatly folded clothes in the palms of his hands. A pair of black runners sat on top. Caldwell strutted towards me, cold dark eyes looked above my head, and he tossed the clothes at my feet. He looked as though he had plenty to say, but kept his mouth sealed shut. His eyes spoke plenty.

I picked up the clothes and hugged them to my body. The footmen retook their positions on either side of me. This time their hands rested at their sides. William nodded his head in the direction of the stall I had been removed from earlier.

I stayed where I was. "You're going to keep the woman pregnant with your child in a horse stall, in the middle of January? I see you are starting fatherhood off well."

William looked like I had sucker-punched him, but he recovered before Helen observed his reaction.

Helen stayed stoic, took a long draw from her cigarette and addressed Caldwell, "Just a small lesson might do her some good. William, go inside. I will handle this. You have someone else to worry about." William hesitated, but obeyed. Helen stepped down from the doorway and nodded to Caldwell, "You know what we need." With that he left the stables without a word.

I presumed Helen's comment about William having someone else to worry about, referred to Charlotte. I hoped that meant they had not found her. I prayed that, wherever she was, she was safe, and that justice would soon meet the Hammonds.

"Just because you are pregnant, does not mean you get to live a life of luxury. I am not sure you understand your new status here." Helen sauntered in circles around me, "Now, I should thank you for the injury you inflicted on yourself. It gives me great pleasure to see you in pain. But that is not punishment enough. You need something to remind you that you are not better than us. That you did not win. That you are but a speck of dirt on our path to our greatness."

I looked straight ahead. While Helen paced around me, my eyes only met hers when she chose to stop in my line of vision. Even then, I looked through her.

"Sam, come take the clothes and put them in the stall. You there, whatever your name is, get a chair and some rope." Helen flicked the butt of her cigarette away, "I am going to enjoy this." The large grin on her face matched her words.

After a struggle, the footmen and the woman, who brought the chair and rope, got me seated in the chair. The pain was insurmountable, so that I could not help but scream, which only added to Helen's visible pleasure. I kicked the footman who had tried to tie my legs. Helen ordered more of the onlookers to help and they managed to tie my wrists and ankles to the chair.

When the crowd around me parted, and moved back to their spots in the wider circle, I saw that Caldwell had returned. The object he carried caused my eyes to widen and my heart rate quicken.

CHAPTER FIFTY

T he black metal rod hung just away from Caldwell's side. The
furthest end glowed a bright, whitish-yellow, with a few flickers of
orange. With everything I had experienced at Adam's hands, I was still
shocked at the lengths this family would go, to torment someone. I
clenched my jaw and fists as Caldwell passed Helen the scalding hot
branding iron.

In slow motion, Helen's fingers wrapped around the grip. My eyes fixed
on the diminished space between me and the iron. A large hand placed
itself against my forehead, pushed my head back and to the left. The wet,
stray hairs stuck to my neck were pulled out of the way.

Helen held up the iron to reveal an H, one larger than the scars I had
seen the servants or workers at the Welcome Home party. "You are ours,
and, for however long we keep you alive, this will remind you of that. You
are no one, to anyone."

She stepped to the side. Even with the rope as tight as it could be, both
footmen held me down. Caldwell's grip on my head tightened. I took a
deep breath and gritted my teeth. There was no reason to fight. It would
only hurt more and Helen would take too much pleasure in it. The
onlookers stared at the ground.

The searing iron collided with my neck, right under the back of my jaw
and my eyes filled with water and a loud scream erupted out of me. The
pain from sitting on my broken tailbone paled in comparison to the fire

against my skin. Helen pushed the iron deeper against me, my nose filled with the putrid smell of burning flesh and hair. Nausea rose from the pit of my stomach and up my throat.

When Helen finally removed the branding iron, she stepped in front of me and I saw blackened chunks of flesh dangle from it. Caldwell and the footmen released their grips. My neck throbbed and I raised my eyes to Helen, as wells of tears streamed down my face.

"Now, where is Charlotte, and who is she working for?" Helen asked.

"I don't know where she is. She wasn't supposed to leave."

"How nice of her to leave you to take the fall."

"I'd rather her leave, and protect whatever information is in her possession, than to have stayed just for me."

"Very noble of you. I doubt you will feel that way long. Now, where is she going?"

"I don't know."

"I can brand the other side as well, or maybe the inside of your arm." She turned my strapped left arm over and held the branding iron above it, threatening another scar.

"Honestly, I don't know. Everything happened fast and she did not provide me with any of those details."

Helen's eyebrows scrunched to meet the top of her nose. She let go of my arm and twirled the iron like a baton, "Who is she working for?"

"I don't know that either. She only told me she could help me get out of here."

"And you believed her? I thought you would have been smarter than that."

Dark clouds had rolled in and a splash of lightning filled the sky. I counted one Mississippi, two Mississippi, three Mississippi, four...deafening thunder crashed above us. The crowd around me shuddered and Helen's eyes raised to the sky.

"Caldwell, untie her and put her in the stall."

She walked back to the house, tossing the branding iron to a woman in the crowd, who caught the hot end of it. She screamed, dropped the iron and clutched her hand, the cry of pain ignored by Helen. The man beside her helped her into a nearby shed.

The footmen untied me while Caldwell supervised. The release of my limbs brought faint relief. I teetered towards the stall, each step more painful than the last. Caldwell towered behind me. Now that Helen had left he spoke freely. His deep voice was as terrifying as his stature.

"If it were up to me, you and that baby would be buried in the pasture. Never to lay your eyes on Helen or this house again."

"I guess it's a good thing it's not up to you." A hard shove pushed me into the stall. I tripped on the cobblestone, but grabbed the wall to prevent another fall.

"Watch your footing."

The footmen closed and locked the stall doors.

I straightened my back and realized the closure of the doors had not drowned out the light. My eyes would not have to fight the shadows. All remnants that a horse had once occupied this space were gone. In their place, a camp light sat on top of an apple basket, which had been flipped to become a table. Beside the lamp was a bottle of water. The basket stood beside a one- person cot, made up with a pillow and sleeping bag. On top of the sleeping bag, Sam had laid out all of the clothes, with the shoes placed on the floor below. There was a hook I had not noticed on the wall and a blue fleece jacket hung in it's grip. I looked down beside me, the metal bucket remained.

I surmised my new living arrangements would not have been Helen or Caldwell's idea. I also knew a more livable cell meant I would be here a while.

CHAPTER FIFTY-ONE

I bolted upright, hands gripped to the edge of the cot. Drenched in sweat, my heart palpitations punched me from the inside. Every morning I woke up the same way. The nightmares never left me alone. When I wasn't visited by Claire or Whitney, I relived the beatings and rapes, or my mind was filled with a nightmare of the future. Scenes of a dark, unknown figure looming over my faceless son and instructing him how to torture and kill someone.

When the prison of my dreams released me, I faced the one in reality. Exhausted, I fought hard to not go stir crazy with the very little contact I had with others. My only companions were my son, and the horses on either side of me. I received two meals a day. Each meal was brought by two people, who were different from the ones who gave me my previous meal. After five days, I figured out there was a rotation of ten people, with another rotation within that group so that they were not always with the same partner. A chance for me to build trust was eliminated by the eyes of the partners. Along with food and water, I received prenatal vitamins and the doctor-recommended acetaminophen. The painkillers did nothing to numb the agony of my situation.

My only comfort was a tattered copy of *A Little Princess*. The spine cracked with the turn of every page. A sound that pulled me away from the incessant thoughts of self-hatred, which filled the sluggish passage of time. Sara's journey in the book was not unlike my own: the loss of someone turns a life full of love and happiness into turmoil and torment. Unlike Sara, the end of my journey was yet to be written.

A few hours after the incident in the courtyard, the cook-who had always refused to give me her name- had visited me. She was doused in raindrops and handed me a towel-wrapped package. She refused to speak to me, avoided my gaze and left just as quickly as she had arrived.

The package contained ointment and bandages for my singed skin and the book.

I had no way to see how the H on my neck was healing. My fingers told me the skin was wrinkled, rough and raw. I changed the bandages often and hoped whatever scar I had would not be as noticeable as my mind had made it out to be.

The damp cold storms of winter came late, but they came just the same. I was thankful an English winter rarely meant a temperature below zero. However, the concrete absorbed and retained the cold, which meant it felt much colder than the weather outside my prison.

I received wool blankets and, as an afterthought, a better solution to ensure I was at least tolerably warm was devised. Sam and Caldwell discussed potential options nearby and I rested my ear on the stall door.

"What about a small wood-burning stove? We have an unused one in the shed." Sam said.

"She would try to burn the stable block down."

He was not wrong, I would have considered it. A voice I did not recognize suggested using a coal warming pan.

"That idea is ridiculous. A pregnant woman breathing in burning coal might not bear a healthy baby. Do you want to face William's wrath if that happened? I do not."

The voices faded in the distance and I was notified of the solution to the debate the next morning when, at gunpoint, I was told to stand at the back of the stall. A medium electric heater was brought in and placed in the front corner where my bathroom bucket had been. It now lived at the foot of the cot. The black heater reminded me of the bottom half of a colonial wood stove. The cord was pinched under the stall door and must have been plugged in somewhere on the other side. The electric heat cut the ice cold air and made the temperature bearable. I was thankful for the small consideration for the child. My best interests would not have factored into the decision.

I spent most of my time on my side on the cot, as every move I made sent pain searing through every nerve in my body. Using the bucket to go to the bathroom was especially difficult, as I had to hold myself up against the wall, which put enormous pressure on the muscles around my tailbone.

Once I was able to move, without my lower back feeling it had been stabbed with a hundred knives, I climbed on the cot and tried to loosen the grates in the top of the walls. I would not be able to fit through any hole left behind, should a grate become free; however, maybe I could make a weapon. The riding crop had been removed with the redecoration of the stall. On my tip toes I yanked as hard as I could but the grates would not budge. They must have been secured into the concrete when the wall was built.

With little to occupy my hands but a book, I found myself slowly picking away at the stone wall beside the cot. My nails had been shredded down to my fingertips, which were torn and scabbed. Smears of blood adorned the wall where I dug.

Otherwise I spent hours watching the spiders weave their webs, or dance round the walls of the stall. It was not nice of me, but some days I would pull down the webs just so I could watch them rebuild.

Neither Helen nor William had visited me. I had not expected to see Helen, as she would rather pretend I no longer existed. However, I thought the shred of decency tucked away in William would have surfaced on occasion. Maybe it did. Every now and then, late at night when I tried to fall asleep to the words of Frances Hodgson Burnett, I thought I had heard William meander outside the stall. The familiar click of his footsteps paced back and forth. There was never a knock, word, or acknowledgment.

I would continue to read and when I closed the book the footsteps faded into the distance.

There was no news about Charlotte, which I hoped meant she was safely back at MI5. Helen would have flaunted any information about Charlotte's capture, if it had occurred. I also hoped that something useful had come from all of the information I had copied onto the USB stick. Whatever that something was, it needed to be found soon. I needed to be found soon. It was only a matter of time before I would lose my usefulness. Or my mind.

I didn't know how long it took for a fractured tailbone to heal, however it was not healing fast enough. From the ear-dogged pages of my book, I counted I had been in the stall for ten weeks. I was certain the weight of an extra person was hindering the healing process.

Even confined to such a small space, pacing the stall was painful and most days I wanted to give up trying. But I pushed through. I didn't know when, or if, I would be given the opportunity to escape but I had to be physically ready. Even if that meant just being prepared for the pain that may come with it.

Every day I placed my thumbs on each hip bone. I stretched out my middle fingers and each time the gap between them was larger. I was eight and a half months pregnant. Before I knew it there would be a baby in my arms.

The boy inside me was a fighter. Or an acrobat. He tumbled and kicked as if his life depended on it. Did he know how imperative those skills would be to survive this family? This world?

If I could not get him free of this place, my son would grow up in a world where those around him fed on the fear of others, and each other. Helen would always despise him, because of me, and I suspected William would, a little, as well. He would hide it, but it would lurk in the shadows.

Or would the boy be smart enough to get out from under Helen and William's thumbs? Embark on adventures around the world? Or would he find it easier to become a version of his father, broken to the extent where happiness would never be an option?

CHAPTER FIFTY-TWO

D espite the rising and setting of the sun, the cold made the days seem never-ending.

"Well, my child, if we don't get out of here soon, I'm afraid we may freeze to death." My hands were millimeters above the heater in a desperate attempt to stay warm.

Footsteps neared. Keys jangled and the locks on the stall released.

I grabbed the bucket, stood and readied myself to pounce on the unexpected visitor.

The meager camp light had not prepared my eyes for the bombardment of sunshine. I was temporarily blinded and averted my eyes from the large, dark figure that approached. Before I could reorient myself, the bucket had been removed from my hand. My weapon was gone.

The stall came back into focus and so did the figure. Caldwell stepped out of the shadows and into the stall. I looked around for anything I could use to fight my way free.

"I wouldn't if I were you. Although, I am tempted to let you try and fight me. The pain I could cause you would be nothing in comparison to what you have caused this family."

"The pain I have caused! Me? The network you support has resulted in damage beyond recognition. But what do you care, so long as your precious Helen is protected?"

Caldwell's grimace signaled I'd hit a nerve. I continued to poke it, "Don't think I haven't noticed how you look at her, as you follow her around like a puppy. So tell me, how does it feel to be the man who will be no more than a servant to her Ladyship?"

Muscles bulged in Caldwell's neck and his hands were clenched into fists. He lunged towards me, but was pulled backwards by the collar of his butler's jacket. He gripped the door frame in order to stay upright and looked behind him. The figure was masked by Caldwell's body.

"Patience Caldwell, it won't be long before we can take care of *this*."

Caldwell didn't have to move for me to know who stood behind him. The familiar voice, which I had not heard in months, was hard to forget. Caldwell fixed his collar and left, angry huffs trailing behind him.

"What is with your incessant need to anger people who could cause you serious harm? Especially being pregnant. It's as if you feed off another's anger." William's voice was not accusatory, rather calm and gentle. It was unnerving.

"Do you expect me to treat him with some sort of respect he doesn't deserve? You know what, don't answer that. Instead, why are you here? It's not like you have had any interest in my well-being, since I have resided in my humble abode."

William didn't answer, but took the three steps needed to look around the stall. A couple of weeks ago, someone had rolled a handful of coloured pencils through the gap under the stall door. They left a few pieces of paper tucked under as well. I quickly used up the paper and then moved onto the dirty grey cement walls. I had created vignettes around the stall. Some peaceful, others a little more violent. Thankfully, my artistry had not been reported by those who brought my food. Their looks of indifference on each visit had morphed into pity. They hadn't started to talk to me, but I knew it was only a matter of time.

I had suspected the gifter was the cook, given she was the only one to show an ounce of kindness towards me. However, William was unsurprised to see the walls adorned with colour. Could he be the bestower?

William peered at a drawing of a body sprawled on the ground, an empty cavity in the center of it's chest. Beside it was a knife pierced through the middle of a heart. "Is that supposed to be me?"

"Yes."

"The hair could use a little work, I don't think I style mine like I have been electrocuted."

I couldn't help but laugh, "Ha. An artist's interpretation is their own. Although your temples have been peppered with grey since I last saw you. I will have to incorporate that into the next one. But, if you don't like your hair in that one, don't look in the corner, you don't have any hair at all."

The side of William's mouth rose slowly into a half-smile, "Do I at least look good bald?"

"Not really." Unsure what was happening, my nerves started to take over and, to distract myself from them, I fiddled with my jacket, "You still haven't answered my question, why are you here?"

"Honestly, I don't know." William sat on the cot, his back rested against a scene of a mother pushing a child on a swing set. "I guess I just wanted to make sure, despite Doctor Harrison's reassurances, that everything was okay, given how close you are to the due date.."

"Okay? Really, how do you think I am, because it's not okay."

"Calm-"

"Don't you dare tell me to calm down! You have me locked away in here for months, with not a word from anyone who sees me. Barely enough food to keep my strength up, and the mental anguish of knowing that as soon as I give birth I'm dead. Oh yeah, I'm doing just great!"

William remained silent and I eyed the open stall door. Could I make it before William could rise from the cot? If not, would I be able to fight him off of me and get away fast enough?

"Have you made up your mind?" William asked.

"About what?"

"If you are going to try and run?" How he always seemed to read my mind baffled me.

"And if I did?"

"The men have orders to shoot if you step outside this stall unaccompanied."

"I see; I bet Caldwell is standing right outside waiting for me himself."

"Likely. Now, why don't you sit and actually tell me how you are doing."

As much as I didn't want to be any closer to William than where I stood, I needed to get this over with, so he would leave. I longed for the company of another person, just not him, and the longer he stayed the more havoc he played with my emotions.

I slowly bent my knees and with my hands behind me to catch my body, I lowered myself onto the cot, "I don't know what else to tell you. Life is shit and in a matter of weeks I'm dead. What more do you want from me?"

"Since you're resigned not to elaborate, how is our son?" His blue eyes looked to my stomach and then to me.

"He's fine, as far as I can tell. Doesn't Doctor Harrison tell you anything after her weekly visits?" William had suffocated my life for too long, I would not give him anything.

For a split second, William's eyes widened slightly. Had he been caught in a lie? Were his intentions for being here different? "May I?" he outstretched his hand.

"No you may not!" I slapped his hand away, "Your hand will never touch me again, or this child if I have anything to say about it."

William closed his eyes and, when they opened, fury painted them, "Well, I guess it's a good thing that you will have absolutely no say about anything that has to do with my son." He pushed himself off the cot and marched out of the stall. He turned around, "You know, I came here thinking that maybe you would have come to your senses by now. Not be so quick to anger. I considered having you moved back into the house, it would have been an uphill battle with Aunt Helen, but I could have made her see reason. But I guess you haven't learned your lesson so here you'll stay. Just remember, it's your fault you are out here and live the barren life on the road to death. Not mine, yours."

The upper and lower stall doors slammed shut and I was ensconced in darkness, the camplight seemed to barely break through the shadows of my past.

My blood boiled over and I released my anger with a long, loud scream, unacknowledged by anyone outside the stall.

My situation was not my fault, was it?

As a storm started to move in, I replayed the events, from the past four years, that led to this moment. It wasn't my fault Claire became addicted to cocaine, or that she was sold to Adam Hammond. If those things hadn't happened, I wouldn't be in this stingy cell. But, what stood out in my memories was the constant stubbornness I displayed. Each act resulted in the tortuous events that followed. Maybe William was right, if I had kept my mouth shut, would I be in this mess?

Sleet pelted the roof as thunderous echoes filled the stall. As secure as the stall door was, it rattled in the wind. If my thoughts would not keep me awake, the storm would.

I moved my cot as close to the heater as possible, however the warmth had little impact. My toes, fingers and nose tingled from the cold. I stared into the heater's fake flames and watched them dance the same pattern over and over. I was mesmerized. My eyelids became heavy and I prayed my mind would be silent for the night.

Before I could fall asleep, the stall doors flung open, ice cold wind pelted me and two large men in black walked in. Without words they each grabbed an arm and pulled me off the cot and out of the stall.

CHAPTER FIFTY-THREE

The storm clouds had drowned out the moonlight, and the fog and sleet muted the light from the windows of the house. Only a pale glow from the lamp above the kitchen door could be seen. Everything else was doused in darkness.

The two men rushed me inside, a trail of puddles left in our wake. I was hustled through the kitchen and into the reception hall. We stopped beside the stairs, in front of a door that blended so well into the underside of the stairs, I had not noticed it before. Only now, directly in front of it, did I see the rectangular outline of a secret door. One of the men waved his hand over a section of the door and a digital keypad appeared. He shielded it with his body and typed in a code. The door unlocked and I was dragged down dark stairs, lit by a small blue hue embedded in the back of each step.

Lights flickered and cracked along the narrow basement hallway. The dirty grey walls curved at the top and the bottom and formed a tunnel. Everything was a stark contrast to the clean, modern decor of the house above.

I was dragged inside a room at the end of the hall, and the hairs all over my body stood on end. The walls, ceiling and floor were covered in thick, murky plastic. On a raised platform, in the center of the room, was an old, rickety, white, metal hospital bed. Some of the white paint had chipped off and revealed crusty orange rust. Arm and leg straps were attached. A metal table, with a leather instrument case rolled out, revealed a multitude of scalpels and other sharp objects. Two large circular surgery lights, encircling the bed, emitted beams of white light.

I struggled to free myself from the men's grips. They were unfazed by my kicks. "You can't do this! It's too early."

The men said nothing. My limbs flailed as they removed my clothes and forced me into a hospital gown. They lifted me onto the bed. One of the men climbed on top of me and kneeled on my arms, and then my legs, until the straps were done up. I tugged hard but they would not loosen. I tried to get my mouth to the buckles, but they were too far away.

The men watched me struggle from their posts on either side of me. A faint scent of cheap cologne wafted through the room. Otherwise, the room was odorless. Each man's stature and vacant expression reminded me of a stone statue. No matter what I did, or said, their faces remained cold and locked.

Footsteps echoed in the tunnel. Doctor Harrison and William walked in, both dressed in green scrubs, caps and gloves. My chest was heavy and I was too scared to speak. This had to be a nightmare. Surely, I would wake up before I was flayed open.

My eyes followed William around the room, but he refused to look at me. I needed him to see me. Then, maybe whatever decency he had inside would help him stop this.

"Please, William don't do this."

My existence was left unacknowledged.

Doctor Harrison held up a long needle with black markings evenly spaced along it. I was hit with a wave of nausea at the thought of it being stabbed deep into my body. "I am going to give you an epidural. It will take about twenty minutes to fully numb you."

"What's going on? Are you inducing labour? It's too soon!"

"You are at thirty-seven weeks, which is considered full term. The baby will be fine." Doctor Harrison said.

"Are you fucking kidding me? I may not have had a child before, but I know that one generally waits a little longer, say, until the baby itself is ready. Or at least not the moment week thirty-seven arrives." I fought with the straps wrapped around my limbs.

"We are going to get the baby out, and we will do just that. William, turn her back towards me, and hold her still. One small slip and the needle may end up somewhere it doesn't belong." Vengeance flashed in Doctor Harrison's eyes.

I heeded her warning, and tempered my desire to struggle, as William contorted my strapped body to expose my back. The needle pierced my skin, and I bit my lip, as I felt it slide deeper inside of me. I was about to hurl questions at Doctor Harrison about the safety of the baby, and myself, but her phone rang. My skin stretched as it stuck to the side of the needle now being withdrawn from my body.

William gently rolled me back over, as Doctor Harrison removed a glove, answered her phone, and walked out of the room. She had seen me as an inconvenience, one which would come to an end tonight. The slip of a scalpel would ensure I had been *taken care of.*

I turned my head to William. He was situated at the foot of the bed, some of his hair strayed from under the cap. "William, please what is going on? Surely, this cannot be good for the baby."

Without a glance in my direction he responded, "Doctor Harrison assured me this is perfectly safe at this stage in the pregnancy. Knowing her life's at stake, she would not lie to me." He looked to the gentlemen standing guard, "Leave." They dutifully obeyed.

"Why now? What is so urgent?"

"You don't need to know, or worry, about the why. You need to stay calm so that everything goes smoothly."

"STAY CALM! I am strapped to a hospital bed that looks like it came from a boarded-up asylum, in a slaughterhouse wrapped in plastic. All to remove a child that is not ready to be brought into this world, and you want me to stay calm. You-"

"Doctor Harrison can always give you a sedative if you refuse. I just thought you might want to be awake and see the baby before..." he rubbed his neck and turned away.

"Before what, you kill me? Enough with these childish games. Whatever power you think they give you, they don't. I know my fate. But we are talking about the well-being of this child. What if he is not fully developed yet? Are you prepared to raise a child who may not be up to the Hammond standard?"

William looked over his shoulder and leered at me. "My son will be fine."

"Oh, so you are a doctor now? Great, well as long as you know that he will be fine, I guess that is enough for me." I flailed in the restraints to release some of my anger, and then stopped my battle with them. William had made his decision, and would not yield; my pleas would only make him more steadfast.

Numbness spread across my body. I steadied my voice, "Have you found Charlotte yet?"

William's lips pinched, his eyes narrowed, but he did not take the bait. I tried again.

"That is what all this is about isn't it? You haven't found her yet, and your high-powered friends won't be able to protect you from whatever information is in her possession, will they? Ha! Now you want to up and run, but don't want the hassle of having to deal with me, wherever it is you end up. Oh, how scared you must be."

Within seconds, William's face hovered over mine, contorted in anger. His large hands gripped my neck, my ability to breathe cut off. My hands trapped, I could do nothing but gasp.

"If I had not needed you alive to bring my son into this world, you would have been dead a long time ago. Just like all of your friends from L.A."

I went cold where the epidural had not spread its reach. The water that had built up in my eyes, from not being able to breathe, turned to tears. William released his grip enough to let me inhale, and then tightened it again. "Did you think I would actually let everyone get on with their lives? Leave witnesses? You cannot be so naive." Satisfaction at my astonishment joined his anger. This time William's grip blocked off all of the air.

As I stared into William's devilish blue eyes, I saw Jessica. Rayna. Saria. Fay. Lily. They were not survivors after all.

A dark, blurred mist encroached my vision. William's face and my surroundings went hazy. The remaining oxygen inside my body dissipated and contorted my vision. The anger in William's eyes transformed into panic and he let go of my neck. I choked on the air my lungs rapidly inhaled. Light started to surround me again.

I swallowed saliva to moisten my throat. "You bastard. You couldn't just let them try to be happy? After everything you and your family had done to them. Why are you so fucking cruel?" Sadness enveloped me and I choked on my tears.

Doctor Harrison returned, took in the scene, but did not address it. She put on a mask and handed one to William.

"Alright, let's see what we have." She pressed her hands around my exposed stomach, and advised William what parts of the baby were where.

"William, roll the table to the foot of the bed, and pass me the basin with the sponge and sanitizer."

William complied. The sharp smell of antiseptic hovered over me. My entire stomach had been dyed a dark orange and brown. Light reflected off the metal cart and danced around the room as Doctor Harrison readied for the first incision.

Now masked, I could only see William's eyes, which were laser-focused on my large, round stomach. There was no sign of fear, anger, or uncertainty, only confidence. Has he assisted in other surgeries before? I did not know if that gave me comfort, or added to the growing list of attributes that terrified me.

I looked up at the plastic-covered ceiling. The shadows of my surgeons loomed above me in a large, dark arch. The shape of a scalpel disappeared into the shadows and I closed my eyes.

Lord, whatever happens to me, please keep this child safe. Protect him from becoming his father. Guide him to a life where he can help, not torment, others. Show him how much I tried to save him and that Your love is what matters.

When I eventually reopened my eyes, blood seeped out of a newly-made hole in my body. The gloves on the hands that caused the unrequested damage had turned from green to burgundy. A mountain of blood-soaked gauze formed on the floor.

Instruments clanged on metal, the sound pierced my ears as knives pierced my body. Diamonds of light danced on my stomach and the surgical gowns on either side of me. Hands disappeared inside of me. My large stomach created a wall, but I pieced together the events of the procedure.

Then, movement stopped. Doctor Harrison stood up from her hunched position, her arms bent at ninety degrees. A single blood drop released itself from the tip of her finger and hung in mid-air, before it fell onto my arm. It joined other blood droplets which had congealed on my skin.

William continued to hover over my stomach. Eyes widened and breath quickened, his hands moved towards my stomach and back to him. He looked up at the doctor, who nodded. His hands disappeared inside me.

A small head with thin, dark hair, covered in blood and bodily fluid, was lifted above the screen of my stomach. I tried to pull myself up as I strained to see if he was okay; however, the restraints kept me horizontal. William turned the child's feet towards him and positioned the body along his arm. Through the mask I could tell William was smiling.

The baby, on the other hand, was not. Shrill cries erupted from the tiny body. Doctor Harrison wrapped him in a blanket and pointed to the scissors. Despite the circumstances of the birth, there was still time for ceremony, and William cut the umbilical cord. The part of the cord attached to me fell away and hung outside of my stomach.

The baby was returned to William's arms. He walked past me and I craned my neck to follow his movements. Plastic crackled, and William entered another room I had not known existed.

The creak of taps being turned, running water, and more cries seeped through the plastic around me. When William returned, the baby's face was a bright pink and he was wrapped in a new blanket.

"William," I whispered. "May I hold him?" I reached up but was hindered by the straps.

William stood beside me and turned the baby so that I could see my son's beautiful, wrinkled face. I was filled with more love than I had ever known. I tried to reach out to him, my fingers spread wide, even as my wrists remained restrained.

"No, you may not."

William's back was all I saw, until he was gone.

"WILLIAM!" I fought the restraints, the room filled with my anger. My hair tousled in front of my face. The thickness obscured Doctor Harrison from view, until she hovered directly over my head.

"Now, there is no need for that. Here. This will help."

A small prick in my arm and a wave of calm came over me. My head fell back against the pillow and I turned to the doctor. Voiceless.

"When you wake up, you will be in a lot of pain. An infection will develop in a few days, if you don't bleed out first."

My eyelids became heavy and I fought to keep them open. I felt a hand brush the hair out of my face and grip my chin.

"You wanted revenge for your sister. Now, it's my turn. No one goes after Helen and gets away with it."

CHAPTER FIFTY-FOUR

Flames ripped through me. Every inch of me burned, but no spot more than my stomach. The glare from the surgical lights filled the room, and my eyes. The signal from the heart monitor blared in my ears. I went to move and was reminded, by the restraints, that I could not.

How long had I been asleep? I craned my neck and surveyed the room. I was alone and there was nothing that could help me. The clamps, which had kept my stomach open during the c-section, peered out over the hump. Pressure surged with every breath.

Was it William's or Helen's idea for me to die slowly and alone? Or Doctor Harrison's?

Had the sedative contorted her last words to me? Was she Helen's sister? There was no portrait of the doctor in the dining room, with the rest of the family. If Doctor Harrison was a Hammond, why had she not been invited to the welcome home party, or the wedding? The more questions I asked myself, the more I realized there was only one answer.

Only Doctor Harrison was aware of her relationship to Helen.

An explosive crash above me created new questions. I closed my eyes as I tried to hone my ears in on whatever sound I could. The heart monitor faded into the background.

Light taps. Rubber on stone. Fabric scratched against itself. The sounds got louder. Closer. I hesitated to make a noise, fearful William had sent someone to finish the job. I opened my eyes, and a thin light darted on the other side of the plastic. The light pierced through and landed on me.

"Tiger has been located, I repeat, Tiger has been located. Fourth room in the basement. Medical attention is required immediately."

The light dropped to the floor and revealed someone dressed in full-black military tactical gear. Plastic shuffled behind me and then "Clear."

The same voice who announced my location, now addressed me, "Olivia Beaumont, I am Agent Rosenberg. We are going to leave you restrained for a few moments longer while Doctor Olsson puts you back together enough that we can move you, okay?"

I nodded.

"We are just going to give you some..."

"No! Please, no drugs."

The fact Rosenberg had introduced herself as an agent, and spoke in a British accent, did nothing to ease my suspicions. William very well could have sold me to someone who came to collect their merchandise. I wanted to be coherent, and prepared to fight, if I had to.

Doctor Olsson detached a pack from his back and placed it in the space on the bed between my sprawled legs. The sound of a zipper was quickly followed by the sanitation of himself and me.

"Without anything to help with the pain, this is going to hurt a lot. I need to repair the damage done by the c-section before we can move you.

The clanking of surgical instruments was drowned out by my screams. Those around me had no reaction.

Agent Rosenberg took off one of her thick, leather gloves, folded it in half, and put it between my teeth. I bit down. My screams only muffled.

Doctor Olsson moved quickly, and yet, what felt like an eternity in hell ended when the buckles of the restraints clanged against the metal bed.

I was wrapped in a warm blanket, and moved to a gurney which must have been brought to the basement during the surgery. Pain still coursed through every fibre of my body.

Weapons were drawn, the agents on high alert, as we made our way towards the exit. The darkened entry floor reflected the throbbing blue light that seeped in through the wide-open front door. We emerged from the house and I saw four black cars and a large blue truck with the word Police in large letters across its front. I heard sirens and saw flashing lights of more emergency vehicles, as they made their way towards us.

People were huddled around the trunk of one of the cars with their backs to us. A small young blonde, whose safety I had prayed for everyday, ran over. She threw her arms around me, I winced, and she let go.

"Oh, sorry. I'm so happy you are okay." She looked me over, her blond hair was not in the familiar bun, but hung down on her shoulders. "Well, relatively okay, I see."

There was no time for pleasantries. "They have my baby. We have to find him."

"I know. We have a lot of people on this and we will find them. We got close in Bristol. They can't hide for long."

"William eluded LAPD for months. How can you be so sure you will be the ones to catch him? How long has the alert for my abducted child been out? Have there been any tips?"

"I need you to trust me. No alert has been issued. We do that, and the Hammonds know we found you. We can't risk them, or their allies, being updated on the situation. We have a plan and it's going to work. But, for now we need to get you to hospital. Once you are properly cared for, then we will fill you in. You have to promise me you will not go rogue before that, okay? Only a few more hours."

"We don't have hours!"

"You do, if you want to be alive to see your child again. You see that stocky man over there, holding the radio? The one wearing glasses? He's my boss, and he will ensure that the work doesn't stop. He's more determined to find the Hammonds than you know, and has barely rested in four years, in order to do it right." Her eyes were serious and yet pleaded with me to not do anything rash. She took my arm, "Come on, I will stay with you the entire time."

She walked beside me as I was wheeled towards the waiting ambulance. I stared at the man she had pointed out, as we walked. His dark skin was illuminated in the emergency lights, which shadowed the wrinkles and white stubble on his face. The crowd around him had grown to include the agents who had found me, and everyone paid avid attention to every word the man spoke.

The crowd dispersed, some returned to the house and others headed for different areas of the estate. Locked in place in the ambulance, those who had rescued me dispersed. Charlotte sat beside me. Charlotte's boss looked over at me, placed his hands into his jacket pockets, and with straight-back shoulders, walked over. What he lacked in stature, he made up for in demeanor.

"I'm Director Chaffin. I am sure you have a lot of questions, and we will get to those later, however I have a question of my own. In all your time with the Hammonds, has anyone ever mentioned Noah?

CHAPTER FIFTY-FIVE

P ain shot through my body with every bump the ambulance hit. I continued to refuse drugs. I needed to be coherent as long as possible. Charlotte sat beside me, her topaz eyes not hiding her concern.

"Please tell me what's being done about my son."

"I told you, I would inform you after the surgery. The one done in the house was a quick job to ensure you could travel. We have to make sure you are properly taken care of. I don't want you thinking you can power through and run off to find him."

"But-"

"Pick another subject."

"Fine. Who is Noah?"

"Director Chaffin's son. He got caught up with the Hammonds. They groomed Noah so well, he believed it was his choice to sell himself."

"And your boss never noticed?"

"He had thrown himself into his work after his wife died. He trusted Noah when he said he was a driver for a legitimate service. After a few months, Noah had come home with more money than a typical driver would earn. Suspicious, Director Chaffin searched his son's room and found high-end clothes in the closet and a second cell phone taped to the bottom of a drawer in the dresser. Director Chaffin hacked into the phone and found naked photos of his son, in an assortment of poses."

My heart broke for the Director. Even after what I had been through with Claire, I could not imagine how it would feel to stare down at my child on that phone.

Charlotte continued, "When confronted, Noah told his father that an 18-year-old could make their own life choices, he was fine, and he made more money in one night than his father did in a month. Noah also used the Hammond name as a threat, as he believed they would protect him from any attempts his father made to remove him from the business."

"They brainwashed him well, poor thing."

"It is heartbreaking. Even the fact that any funds he made were provided back to the Hammonds, and he only got a monthly allowance, made no dent in his logic."

"How long has he been gone?"

"Four years. Without a trace."

"And Director Chaffin has been after the Hammonds ever since?"

"Tired of the corrupt reach the Hammonds had into every aspect of society, the Director had spent his personal time trying to assemble a case against them. However, when Noah disappeared, he went into overdrive. Director Chaffin spent even more time at the office, kept a cot in his closet and, within a year, was rewarded for his dedication. He was made Director of an off-the-books team into the family's organized crime, drug and trafficking operations."

"The Director has to know that the Hammonds' grasp on a person is never released. Unless that person has no life left in their body."

"He knows, but he doesn't stop hoping that this time it will be different. In the end, he just wants closure. Even if it comes in the form of a body."

"I hope he finds some closure. However life-shattering it may be."

I too hoped my son could be returned to me, untainted by the Hammonds.

CHAPTER FIFTY-SIX

My eyelids fought my desire to open them. I could smell potent disinfectant, mixed with a trace of stale urine. There was something else in the air I could not place. Something sweet. Fruity.

I felt heavy and yet light at the same time. Although I could not see it, the bedding wrapped around my body tucked me into a suffocating cocoon. My arms were heavy planks beside me. My head was the opposite. It was filled with fog and there was a tugging feeling at the tip of my skull, like a balloon that tried to move just a little higher than its current position.

The last 24 hours replayed like a movie, the back of my eyelids the movie screen. The makeshift surgery room. Doctor Harrison. William. My son. My insides turned to my outsides. My son. The swarm of agents. My son. Charlotte and Director Chaffin. My son.

My breath became heavy. Last night's replay faded into darkness as the sides of the bed closed in around me. As suffocation neared the more muddled the faces became. Doctor Harrison morphed into Charlotte. Agent Rosenberg turned into a black bear. My son transformed into a monster. A monster named William.

Adrenaline burned through my veins, like hot lava. My son would not become a monster! I would do whatever I could to prevent that from happening. The adrenaline's intensity caused the narcotics to release their grip. My eyes shot open and my arms, no longer stuck at my sides, propelled me to sit up.

Dizzy from the quick change in altitude, I steadied myself as I surveyed the room. The lights had been dimmed, but bright sunlight poured in through the small window. Unimpressive beige walls surrounded me. There was another bed in the room, empty. To my left sat the source of the sweet, fruity smell.

A bull-necked woman, in her fifties. Arms crossed. Chin to chest.

I eased myself off the bed with caution. Pain shot through my stomach. I winced but continued. My feet hit cold tiles. I grabbed the rolling stand with the IV. The wheels sang as they rolled along the floor. My jaw clenched tight through the pain.

The woman in the chair remained motionless.

The curtains on the window that looked into the hallway had been closed. Unafraid of what may await me, I placed my hand on the doorknob.

"Going somewhere?"

I looked at the woman. There was no change in her position. Eyes closed. Body hunched. I looked around. Had I missed that there was someone else in the room. No. Had the drugs played tricks on me? I shrugged the question off and started to open the door.

"You need to stay here," the same voice said.

This time, when I looked at the woman, she had unfolded herself and now stood tall and towered like a giant. How had she fit into the chair?

"Ma'am. Please get back in bed." Her eyes darted between me and the bed.

"I need to pee."

She pointed to an open door within the room. The toilet was clearly visible from where I stood. "I will need to help you. There is no way you can do that on your own."

"Right. well, given I don't know you, maybe I will just head back to bed. I can pee later." I slowly made my way to the side of the best but stopped before I tried to heave myself back onto it. "Is there any news? Have they been found?"

"I am just here to make sure you are safe. I do not know the status of anything or anyone."

The breath I did not know I was holding released itself from my chest. The guard was not going to let me leave. She could easily blockade the door and, even if I was not in a diminished state, I wouldn't get past her. I was stuck.

Door hinges creaked and my attention, and that of my guard, turned to the front of the room. The guard had somehow managed to make herself appear even larger. Her hand rested on her holster and she stepped between me and the door. Her body blocked my entire view.

When the guard's hand fell to her side, I knew whoever had entered was not a threat. With a nod of the head she left the room. Charlotte replaced her, and the energy of the room shifted to one of hope rather than apprehension. Charlotte looked at me with concern, but had a smile on her face.

"Why am I not surprised to find you out of bed?" She brought over a chair, "Sit."

I moved the IV stand to one side of the chair, grabbed the arms of the chair and, inch by inch, lowered myself, in the same manner I had done only a few days ago when a round, hard, heavy mass had protruded from my body. I looked across at Charlotte.

Her fingers, on both hands, rapped against the side of her legs. Given the smile I surmised it was an excited tick, not a nervous one. "We found them."

Charlotte was right to have given me a chair. The blood drained from my body, and the fuzziness I had felt when I first woke up returned. Had I heard her right? The man, who had eluded the LAPD for months, was caught within hours of fleeing Hammond Manor? I gripped the arms of the chair and braced for the bad news. William would not go down without a fight.

"Alive?"

"Yes."

Tears released themselves from their ducts and poured down my face. The love I felt for a child I had never held was inexplicable. It filled more space than the room I sat in. He was safe. I had so many questions but none of them mattered. I needed to see my son.

"Where is he?"

"Here. He is being looked over by the doctors, but he will be brought up to you soon."

"Was he hurt?"

"He was fine, as far as I could tell. I'm sure he's okay. It won't be long now." Charlotte came over and wrapped her arms around me. I unloaded all of the anger, frustration, fear and sadness into tears soaking her shoulder, until a nurse walked in with a blue bundle in his arms.

Charlotte stepped back. Tears had kissed her cheeks as well.

The bundle was placed into my outstretched arms. "Everything looks good. No concerns from the pediatrician. Congratulations, you have a healthy child."

Despite the last 24 hours. The last five and a half months. An unforced smile filled my face. Swaddled in a blanket, my son looked so peaceful. Unaware of what the start of his life entailed.

The weight of my responsibilities as a mother weighed a thousand times heavier than the person in my arms. The room around me disappeared, as my vision tunneled on the beautiful face in my arms. Any dislike or disdain I had felt during my pregnancy fell away. An old skin shed.

The sound of Charlotte's phone brought me back to the hospital room.

"Yes sir. Just waiting on the doctor to give her the all-clear. He should be around shortly. Yes sir." She hung up and put the phone in her jacket pocket. "We have a safe house ready for you two. We have taken a lot of precautions to make sure none of the Hammond's connections could find it."

It only took one word to puncture the balloon of happiness. Hammond. The family sucked the life out of those around them and my fight with them was far from over. I held the one thing William would fight harder than anything to get back.

"You said you found them. All of them?" I asked.

"The staff were easy to find. They had returned home to their families, unaware of the reason for the sudden departures of Helen and William. They were told they were not needed for the foreseeable future. Helen had boarded her jet, with a flight plan to Poland, but we got there before it took off. We were lucky. There's no extradition treaty and we could have lost her forever." Her phone beeped. She ignored it.

"What about Doctor Harrison? In all of the commotion last night I forgot to tell you she's Helen's sister. Can you believe that? No one had ever mentioned a sister, only Douglas the brother."

"That's because no one knows."

My eyes fluttered, "What do you mean no one knows?"

"Not even Helen."

"How? Helen knows everything about the people who work for her."

"It was even hard for us to trace the lineage. Doctor Harrison had covered her tracks pretty well. Fake information was everywhere and Helen likely fell into the trap of believing what she was seeing. Turns out the're half sisters. It seems the Hammond males are not big on monogamy and Helen's father had a child he kept a secret right up to his death."

"Then how did Doctor Harrison earn the trust of the family, if no one knew who she was?"

"My guess, she made herself invaluable and trustworthy in some way neither you or I want to think about."

"But you've found her right?"

"No. She has completely fallen off the grid. We will keep looking, but she is proving to be the most difficult person to track down."

"More difficult than William?"

"He was particularly easy to find, shockingly. We watched one of the credit card accounts that was found on the USB stick, and found a purchase for some diapers, formula, baby clothes and then a charge at the Gonville Hotel in Cambridge. We picked William up not long after." Charlotte seemed pleased with herself.

For a man adept at hiding, why had William used a credit card? Why stay at a hotel where he would be seen? Would none of his connections harbour him? His tactics made no sense. In Toronto, William said he would rather die than go to jail, he had to have known he would get caught. Was that his intention?

CHAPTER FIFTY-SEVEN

I was finally released from the hospital a week later. The drive to the safe house took awhile as we circled back on streets we had already traveled. We looped round-abouts numerous times, changed routes and ended up, what I believed was, only a few blocks from the hospital I had been discharged from. I understood the need for vigilance and I enjoyed my time in the back seat of the vehicle with my precious cargo.

We parked out front of a nondescript brownstone. Nothing about it made it stand out from the rest in the long row of attached homes. Suspiciously, there were no other vehicles, or people, on the street. No nosy neighbours stared around curtains. The only sound, the cooling car engine. Desertion surrounded me. Even the smell of smog seemed to avoid the street.

The inside of the house was as uneventful as the outside. The entry hallway was long, narrow and cramped. Agents emerged from the second floor and the back of the first. Their shift was over and their car engine ignited and puttered out in the distance.

I was ushered into a small living area. A pink couch, single green chair with torn arm rests and table sat around the opening of what once was a fireplace.

"There is a crib in the room at the top of the stairs and to the right. Along with clothes for both of you. Two of us will be inside with you at all times. Others are posted within range. No one will go in or out that is not authorized. The kitchen is stocked with food and formula." She pointed through the alcove on the other side of the living room. "Would you like to rest?"

"I'm fine. I would rather understand what is going to happen now." The bundle in my arms squirmed, but then settled himself.

"Right." Charlotte sat in the chair.

I remained upright and swayed to keep the baby calm.

"Helen and William face numerous charges and you will remain here throughout the trial. We await news as to who the judge is; however, the Hammonds have quite a few in their pocket, so the statistics are not in our favour. Although you are not obligated to testify, it would significantly help the case if you do. Especially if the judge turns out to be dirty. It would be hard to refute the testimonies of multiple victims."

"More people have come forward?"

"Not many. A few who worked the party you attended at Helen's, the cook and a few from the house in Germany you told us about. We are hoping the more media attention the case gets, the more victims and witnesses will come forward. On the flip side, that does raise the threat level to your safety. Which is why we have heightened security measures. We cannot take any risks. This is our one shot at these people."

"What was on that USB drive?"

Charlotte's eyes sparkled. "Gold! Account records in code. It took our analysts about a week to crack it, but once we did, it was a mine of information. We followed money all over the world. A lot of work will be required to actually persecute those outside of our jurisdiction, but it is underway. On top of that, we found records of legitimate employees. Partial victim records. It seems only some of the houses kept records of who they trafficked, background checks - like your own - while others had no records at all. Sadly, we still haven't tracked down Noah."

"Will any of that be admissible, given the way the information was obtained? I didn't exactly have a search warrant."

"I have good news on that part. Thankfully, William had the laptop on him when we found him. He had not deleted any of the information. So although work was underway, based on what you provided, we can rebuild that part of the case file with legally obtained information. Otherwise, yes, we likely would have been fucked."

"I don't understand. William would have known using a credit card would get him caught. He would also know the laptop in his possession would be utter destruction to his world. For someone who is usually steps ahead, he was five steps behind. Has he said anything?"

"He is still being processed. Director Chaffin and the Crown Prosecutor are going to speak with him later this evening."

"I doubt he will say much."

"Even if he wanted to, I doubt his Emma would let him."

"His Emma?"

"His lawyer."

"Right. William has not been in the UK long. And have most of his crimes not happened in L.A.? Are you even going to be able to go after him for anything? Anything that comes with a long sentence, at least."

"This is where I have to hand it to Helen. Almost every asset was transferred into William's name. The only things left in her name were the jet she was about to fly away on, and a house in Kensington. Everyone we talk to, although they are not saying much, point the finger at William being the mastermind behind everything. They say Helen was only a figurehead."

I had to pick my jaw up off the floor. "That sneaky little bitch. When did she do all of this? If it was recently, you should still be able to hold her accountable, no?"

"The records say the day of the fire in L.A."

"What? That makes no sense. Why transfer everything to a man gone into hiding and the rest of the world...oh. She didn't know he wasn't actually dead. Helen probably wanted protection if, by chance, international authorities came looking." I shook my head. The elaborate plans this family erected were well thought out. "But that only covers activities over the last seven or so months. That cannot be enough protection for her?"

"Again, it depends on the judge. Helen is a really good actress. I see her playing up the I found God card and saying she tried to change the ways of the family, but William refused. She could say that discussions occurred with William months prior to the fire but that all of the legal matters did not get finalized until last August. The harder she pretends she is rehabilitated, the more likely she will get no more than a slap on the wrist."

"A slap on the wrist! For keeping me captive in a horse stall? For branding me with a hot iron." I pulled my hair away from my neck and exposed the scar.

Charlotte walked over to me, "Jesus!" she shook her head, "Their system is just as backwards as our society. If she acts like a helpless woman-"

"Helpless? That woman is evil!" My yelling startled the baby awake and his shrill cries hurt my ears. I laid him against my chest and bounced to settle him down. The cries were muffled but still there.

"This is where your, and the others, testimonies are key. Even with that, her case is going to be hard to win. I have seen it before. Murderers turn on the charm and the jury eats it up."

"Great. She walks free. Flees and continues to traffic people, no harm no foul. Not to mention she will come after me and my son. This is utter bullshit!" The baby went into full lung- heaving cries. "Great, even he knows we will be living in fear the rest of our lives, if Helen goes free." I pulled a soother from my pocket, sucked it clean, and slipped it into the baby's mouth. The cries ceased.

"We will figure this out. If legal means don't work..."

Charlotte's eyes held a gleam I had not seen before. It wasn't evil. But it wasn't nice.

CHAPTER FIFTY-EIGHT

A week after our relocation to the safe house, my son was still nameless. Names that came to mind were tossed away like coins in a fountain. I hoped the next one would be better. I called him 'Honey' or 'Bud'. Something one would call a pet, or a spouse.

Charlotte and I never spoke about what illegal means she had referred to, with respect to handling Helen, or even William, if necessary. There was no need. Even if she was not a spy, she was smart and resourceful. I trusted she would find a way to keep everyone safe. Having worked inside the Hammond home for four years, I was certain Charlotte was high on Helen's payback list.

Doctor Harrison was nowhere to be found, but I was assured people were looking.

The sun room, at the back of the house, was where I spent most of my days. Today, the baby slept in my lap, and birds swooped down onto the wet grass and emerged with fat worms hanging from their beaks. Despite April's spring weather, the cold from the horse stall had yet to leave me. I sat bundled in a thick, wool sweater and wrapped in blankets every day, surrounded by the sunroom glass.

I was once again trapped inside, the difference this time was it was for my protection and I felt less constricted. Some days, I mindlessly watched television, the content unregistered. Instead, my mind grappled with everything that had happened and the possibility of what was to come.

Sleep was difficult. On top of caring for a newborn at all hours, I was having nightmares that gripped my mind. The quietest footstep of an agent put me on high alert. If I had looked fatigued from life in the stall, I look battered now.

Another bird hopped along the grass. A "ping" sang behind me, the signal of a text. I ignored the sound and focused on the bird, grass dangling from its beak, now accustomed to the monotonous conversations that occurred around me.

Four loud clicks signaled the front door had been opened. Down the hall were Charlotte and Director Chaffin, coats spotted with raindrops. Charlotte wiped the rain off her face and smiled. Director Chaffin followed her on their way towards me. Charlotte took the white wicker chair beside me and Director Chaffin the wicker love-seat across. The floral cushion hugged his hips. His vacant expression put me on edge.

"How are you?" Director Chaffin asked.

"As good as can be expected, I guess. Alive."

"Thank God for that. Look, I'll get right to the point. We need your help with a couple of things. One is not so difficult. The other, we are pretty sure you are not going to like. Which one do you want presented to you first?"

"It's been months of things I don't like, so why stop now. Let's start with that one."

"Alright. I want to preface our request by letting you know, your agreement to help will make William's persecution happen more quickly and almost painlessly."

"You have my attention."

"William has agreed to plead guilty to all charges of human trafficking and money laundering."

I laughed, "He wouldn't do that." Charlotte's face was serious so I continued, "Why would he do that?"

Charlotte leaned forward in her chair, "Maybe he understands he can't win. Whatever it is, we do not want to waste this opportunity."

"No, he's just playing another game, luring you in, and then he will take his shot when the opportunity arises. He has to have an escape plan. There is no way he willingly becomes a caged animal. I don't believe it." I ran my hands over my face.

"Anything is possible," Director Chaffin said, "But we have to take that chance."

"Okay, for argument's sake, let's say he's willing to plead guilty; one, where are the murder charges? The grounds of Hammond Manor have to be strewn with buried bodies. Two, what does that mean for sentencing? Will it be more lenient because he cooperated? Finally, what does this have to do with me? I have already agreed to testify."

"One, we haven't found any bodies, yet. Nor have we found evidence to tie William directly to the deaths of any missing persons. His time in Los Angeles, and Jasper's propensity to do the dirty work, would be good alibis should we find any. Sentencing depends on the judge, but the minimum for each charge of human trafficking is twelve months' imprisonment. Money laundering is two to fourteen years. Even with good behaviour, William will die in prison. Even if the Hammonds have the judge in their back pocket, they would be hard-pressed to not issue at least the minimum, if not more, due to the press coverage. Otherwise they tip their own hand that they are corrupt and likely to lose their seat."

"So William is willing to risk going to jail forever. For what?"

Director Chaffin and Charlotte exchanged glances, neither wanted to deliver the news. Director Chaffin ran his hand along the back of his neck, "Visitation with his son."

I stared at him, my eyes blinked in quick succession. Had I heard him correctly? "I...but..."

"We were just as shocked," Charlotte added. "I think Emma was too, given the look on her face after William proclaimed his terms."

"So I let William see his son, and he pleads guilty. Simple as that?" I was skeptical. Nothing with William was simple.

Charlotte continued, "He wants to see you as well. But, given you would be bringing the baby, I figured that part was evident. There is one catch."

"Aha. Always a catch. What is it?" I took a deep breath as I braced myself.

"You are to remain in England after the trial. Relocate to the area he will be held and bring his son to see him no less than twice a month."

Astounded, I almost allowed the baby to roll off my lap as I stood. I noticed what was happening just in time. "Stay here. Allow him to be a part of this child's life. Has he lost his mind? Have you lost your mind? No! No! My son will have nothing to do with his father or this horrific family. I won't allow it!" My blood boiled. I held the baby as close to me as possible. Under no circumstances was William going to get what he wanted.

Charlotte looked to Director Chaffin, "Could you leave us alone?" He nodded and left the room.

"Charlotte, I am not doing this. You can't ask me to do this." Anger turned into sadness and tears filled the pores on my cheeks. "Do you know how hard it is to look at my son and not already see William. To look past who this child's father is, so that I can try and love it as much as possible. Having to see William...No. I can't."

"What we are asking is hard. Very hard." She looked behind her and lowered her voice, "But if you do this, we get a conviction and William is locked up. In a dream world, we get him to testify against Helen. All he is asking for, in exchange, is to see his son. You may be right, this might be too easy, but what happens if we don't? He could walk free, then what?"

She stepped in to console me, and I pushed her away, "My son is not a pawn!" She followed me to the corner of the sunroom, where I picked at the leaves of a small plant.

"It hurts, but the truth is, that is exactly what he is. Trust me. William will not actually get what he is asking for. He only needs to think he is."

"Won't there be stipulations in the conviction. Legally enforceable ones?"

"Yes-"

"Then how?"

"Do you trust me?"

"Yes."

"Then have faith."

CHAPTER FIFTY-NINE

Director Chaffin re-entered the sunroom, his dark skin wrinkled with worry. "How is it going in here? We don't have much time. William wanted an answer, and his first visit with his son, by two this afternoon. There was also that other matter I wanted to talk to Olivia about."

Charlotte looked at me, "Are we good?"

"Fine. I will agree to his terms."

"Thank you." She squeezed my hand.

Director Chaffin's hand rested in his pocket. "When we met, I asked you about my son, Noah. You didn't recall him. I was wondering if you could look at this picture? Maybe he, or they, had changed his name."

He pulled out a photo of a teenage male. He wore a white sports shirt, with a red Liverpool Football Club logo, the smile in his eyes as big as the one displayed on his face. Director Chaffin was also in the photo, arms wrapped around his son, wearing a matching smile. They were in a large stadium. A crowd of white and orange surrounded them. My eyes welled with tears.

The photo shook, "You know him?"

I nodded. I stared at the young man who had been held at gunpoint outside my bedroom window. The young man who now laid dead and buried somewhere on the estate.

"When did you see him last? Was he alright?" He spoke quickly, so many questions were thrown at me I could not keep up. After a while he stopped and allowed me to speak.

"Sir," it was the first time I had called him that and I could tell it put him on edge, "I'm sorry, but I think Noah is dead."

Director Chaffin's knees buckled from under him and he slammed against the stone floor. Screams of despair erupted from the huddled mass. The agents on the main floor ran into the room, hands on their holsters. Charlotte ushered them back out as tears fell from the Director's eyes.

I grabbed my glass of water and handed it to him. Hands shaking, he took it. "How? When?" he mumbled.

"The night Charlotte fled. William tried to get me to turn on her, and used your son's life as leverage. I'm so sorry. I thought he had believed me when I said I didn't know who Charlotte worked for. He said if I told him what information I had retrieved, he would let Noah live. Blame me. I could have saved him but I didn't."

The Director brushed away his tears, pushed himself up off the floor, and rested his hands on my shoulders, "You are not to blame. The Hammonds are. Now, let's go get this son of a bitch!"

"Your son is somewhere on the estate. William ordered him to be put with the others. It was not long after I heard a single gunshot. I doubt they would move him far when they have all of that land."

The Director nodded, Charlotte took my hand and we walked towards the front of the house. We gathered coats and the diaper bag and were given the all-clear to leave the house.

I had hoped the only time that would necessitate the sight of William would be when I testified. Even then, I planned to divert my attention as much as possible. Now, we would be confined in a small space together. One I would be unable to leave, for fear he would rescind his offer to plead guilty. I only hoped whatever plan Charlotte had up her sleeve would be enacted soon. My desire to see William dead was strong and I would not be able to contain myself for much longer.

CHAPTER SIXTY

The large, stone fortress filled the horizon. The central building was made of shades of red and dull, yellow brick. A bricked pentagon, with five glass windows, protruded outward beside the main entrance. Four of the five had a closed shutter, one remained open. Along the perimeter of the complex stood towering cement walls.

The front gate reminded me of a castle gate. A half-moon brass metal grate on the top, and a thick metal door that slowly slid into the wall as it opened. The door was as thick as my body.

I was guided through security. A cursory review of the diaper bag was completed and a quick scan of my body with the metal detecting wand, and I was through. The fact I had MI5 agents as escorts likely made the processes easier. One of the prison guards led us down a hallway marked with two yellow and black lines, each about four foot away from the wall. Unlike prisoners, we were not relegated to walk between the lines and the wall. Instead, we proceeded down the center.

We passed by the communal meeting area, where prisoners in blue or grey jumpsuits sat with their visitors. One of the children present looked scared and hid behind, what I presumed was, their mother. They were huddled as close as possible to the woman's back. Hands covered their eyes. The male prisoner tried to coax the child to him, without success.

We stopped, a loud buzz preceded the clank and churn of a metal door. We stepped into a crisp white room, with two wooden chairs with black vinyl seat bottoms and backs, and a rectangular metal table. The three of us walked in, but no one sat down. I placed the baby carrier on one of the chairs and faced the opening away from the door. I left the canopy down. William would only see the child when I wanted him to.

Another loud buzz, we all turned. A guard stood against the far wall of the hallway outside the room, arms crossed in front. They were immediately obscured by a tall figure in grey. My heart stopped at the sight of the shaggy, greying hair. The laser blue eyes, now a little dimmer, landed on the carrier. William's hands were cuffed in front, a silver chain hung from his wrists and connected with the cuffs at his feet. He shuffled into the room, head slightly lowered, but eyes fixed on where my son rested. The guard followed behind, unlocked William's hands and attached the cuffs to a thick metal bar welded to the top of the table. William's feet remained secured.

Silence filled the room. William stared at the car-seat, a blue blanket the only visible item. My crossed arms tightened.

Director Chaffin broke the silence with a cough.

"Mr. Hammond, as you can see, Olivia has agreed to your terms. Before she allows you to hold your son, you need to sign these." He placed a burgundy briefcase on the table, clicked open the locks and placed a stack of papers and a pen in front of William.

The calmness Director Chaffin displayed was remarkable. If I was him, the pen would become a weapon and William would have one less eye.

Coloured tabs indicated where signatures would be required. Director Chaffin's small stature loomed over William. William's hand hovered over the documents.

"What guarantee do I have that our agreement won't be breached?" William asked, his voice like a knife to my heart.

"Anything signed here today is enforceable." Director Chaffin looked at me, "Olivia is aware of this and has agreed. You get what you want and we get what we want. The only real loser here is, well, Olivia. She has to see your ugly mug for as long as you live on this earth. You should probably thank her for that. I know if I was her, I would want to be as far away from you as possible. Remember that with every visit. If I hear about any mistreatment, or indication of mistreatment, solitary confinement will become your permanent home. Those prisoners do not get visitors."

William looked at me. I looked away. A pen moving on paper drew my attention back to him. I watched papers flip and signatures added, until all tabs contained the ink they required.

The Director picked up the package and removed the pen from William's hand. "Fifteen minutes." He glanced at me, "We're right outside if you need us."

The loud buzz startled me. My heart wanted to dance itself out of my chest. The clank of the door created knots in my stomach. My fists clenched themselves so tight my nails dug into my palms. Charlotte's face filled the small window of the door. She nodded. I uncrossed my arms and walked over to William.

SLAP.

"I deserved that." William's hands remained in his lap.

"You deserve...a lot more than that." My anger erupted and my fists collided with any part of William that was in view. Face. Stomach. Chest. Arms. Only the legs tucked under the table escaped my wrath.

William sat there and absorbed each punch. An occasional huff came out of his mouth when I hit him particularly hard. Otherwise silence. Out of breath, and strength, I backed away and stood beside my son. I pulled a water bottle out of the diaper bag and chugged half of it.

"May I see my son now? Or are you getting ready for round two?" William asked.

"I'll save round two for another day."

"I don't doubt that."

I put the bottle back into the bag, and opened the carrier's canopy. I unbuckled the bundle, cautious not to wake him. Gently, I removed the sleeping baby. With gritted teeth, I lowered my son into William's arms, and spiders crawled up mine as my hand brushed against William's chest. I stood over them, afraid to step even two feet away from my whole world.

William's apathetic demeanor evolved into contentment. Enamored with my son, our son, William eased his finger into its palm. "He's beautiful."

William looked up, "What is his name?"

"I...uh...I haven't chosen one yet."

"Any particular reason why?"

"I haven't found the right one."

"Do you mind if I suggest one?"

I rolled my eyes. I would not use a name William recommended, but humoured him. "Sure."

"Calvin."

"Calvin? Why Calvin?"

"I thought it would be a nice representation of the 'Cl' from Claire's name and the 'vi' from yours, add the 'n' to transform into a boy's name and it's Calvin." William searched my eyes. The struggle I had inside myself stayed hidden. I loved the name, and hated that William was the one who thought of it.

"Your lips are not worthy of Claire's name. And how is it you want to honour her, when you are the reason she is dead?" I reached for my son but William stood up and turned away from me.

"I have five more minutes with my son." The baby squirmed and cooed behind William's large frame.

"Fine." I dropped the carrier on the floor beside the chair and took its place. William retook his seat.

If I was going to be stuck here I would get answers. "Why did you make a deal?"

Focused on the child, William answered, "It was time."

"Time for what?"

"Time to stop. I'm exhausted with all of it. The lies. The death. The hurt. So much hurt. I can't do it any more, now that he exists."

"That's it? Just like that? A child has you give up everything you have worked for. Suddenly you are Mr. Friggin Rogers? I don't buy it. Nothing with you is that simple."

"You don't believe that I would want a better life for my son?"

"Ha! If you did, you wouldn't have literally ripped him out of me and run. You would not have left his mother behind." I could not hit William when he held my son so the table received my anger and rattled in response.

William stayed silent.

"I know you, Mr. William Hammond. I don't want to, but I do. Yes, that boy is important to you. Yes, I believe you are tired. But what I don't believe is that you would give up. So, what happened? Did you realize Helen had gotten the better of you?"

William glared at me. Lips pursed. I had him.

"You were not aware she had transferred all her assets to you? Let me guess, you were both supposed to head to the airport, until she came up with a better plan. Split up. She takes the plane. You go by, oh I don't know, car and then train? To where? Scotland. Meet up with some of your allies. Then she handed you the laptop, as, of course, the allies would need the information in order to keep the business afloat until things died down a little."

The sides of William's mouth twitched and he rubbed his thumb against the back of the baby's soft hand.

"I bet you had a feeling something was off, but her men outnumbered you. So you went along with the plan. She drove towards the airport, and you in the opposite direction. When did you open the laptop? It had to have been before you got to the hotel. You would have driven all night to get as far away from Hammond Manor as possible. Come on, you have already signed your life away, what do you have to lose by telling me what changed your mind? What made the ever-strong and domineering William Hammond fall?"

If smoke could come out of a person's ears, it would have filtered out of William's. He looked at the bundle in his arms, and took a deep breath. "When Aunt Helen and I went over all of the records, everything was in her name. There was no indication it had been transferred to me. You're right, Aunt Helen's sudden change in plans alerted me that something was wrong. When I unlocked the computer the same documents I had seen were there. However, hidden in the depths of the computer was the evidence that she had long ago planted, for me to take the fall. That, on top of Charlotte, and I knew it was only a matter of time before more than the LAPD would hunt me. As you know, I am very adept at hiding. But not with a child."

"No. He did not make you stop. He may have contributed, but, like you said, you have a talent for hiding. I am sure you would have been able to manage, even with a baby; even make a game of your trips around the world. There is more you are not telling me."

William's familiar mysterious grin made its appearance. "You do know me well." He looked up at the clock behind me, kissed the top of the child's head and motioned for the carrier. I placed it on the table. William gently put the child in, wrapped him snug in the blanket and clasped the harness. A loud buzz and a guard walked in. Charlotte stood in the doorway.

The guard re-attached the handcuffs and moved William towards the door. Before I could protest, William turned back, "Two weeks. I will tell you the rest in two weeks."

CHAPTER SIXTY-ONE

L ater that week, Charlotte walked into the living room and slumped into the tattered chair by the unusable fireplace, which had inherited a bright green plant in a gold pot since our arrival. Exhaustion and sadness enveloped her. I gave her the space she needed and turned back to the television. She would speak when she was ready.

A commercial for dish soap was interrupted by the gurgle of a throat being cleared. I turned to Charlotte, her topaz eyes duller than when she arrived. "It was horrible, just horrible. I knew the Hammonds were evil, but I never...what we found today would make the skin of the most hardened person crawl."

I had experienced enough trauma at the hands of the Hammonds that I really didn't want to hear any more horrors, but Charlotte would need to heal, and if I could help with that, after the help she'd afforded me, I would.

"What did you find?"

"It took all day, and ground-penetrating radar, but we found a couple of mass graves. Each with, the techs expect, at least twenty bodies, if not more. The most recent grave was easily recognizable with the fresh mound of dirt, but the other one seems to have been there for years. Unnoticed. A small tree was trying to grow on top."

"How long had the bodies been there?"

"We won't know for sure until all of the bones are removed, but the Hammonds have owned that property for a long time."

"Noah?"

Charlotte nodded, "He was the most recent body added to the pile. We were able to carefully remove him, and a few others, whose bodies had not started to decompose too badly."

"How is Director Chaffin?"

"Devastated, naturally. But I think after the two of you spoke he had come to terms with how he was going to find his son."

"I feel like we should do something, but I also know that nothing anyone does will ever fill that void."

"I think all we can do is pray that justice is served to William. A miniscule consolation for the lives he has taken, but something, nonetheless."

"Will Noah's death be added to the charges?"

"William has already signed his deal, so, as hard as it is, Director Chaffin said he won't try to renegotiate and risk the guilty plea. Not when the only evidence we have, so far, is your statement that William ordered Noah to be killed. He will go after William separately for this."

"I suspect Director Chaffin has many more nights on the cot in his office."

"Likely. If he will sleep at all." Charlotte opened and closed her mouth, and did it again.

"What is it?" I asked.

"I know I haven't been doing this job long, but I don't know how long I can keep it up after seeing all of those bodies."

The pink couch cushion under me sprung back into place after I stood up. I wrapped my arms around Charlotte, "This job spotlights the darkness that lurks in the world. Sometimes, it can seem unbearable, but you can't let that darkness overtake you. Trust me, it tried to devour me numerous times. You are a strong and smart woman. The job will be hard, but look at what you were able to accomplish. I suspect you will be able to make a big difference in a lot of peoples lives."

We sat like that until the baby monitor on the coffee table emitted small, quick cries.

I kissed the top of Charlotte's head, and, my heart full of pain, left her to her tears.

The thought of what Charlotte, and the other MI5 agents, found today haunted each creaky step I took up the stairs. No amount of evil that I had seen had prepared me for the Hammonds.

Judgement day was coming, but William and Helen's fate rested in the hands of men.

The question was, would the men be outside the Hammond's reach, or firmly grasped within it?

CHAPTER SIXTY-TWO

With William's confession and agreement signed, his court case moved swiftly to sentencing. News of the forty-eight bodies, and counting, found on the Hammond property had remained front page news for the last three weeks. Although the investigation was in progress, it did not stop the media from speculating on the impact on William's sentencing and Helen's trial.

Media reports would likely have no bearing on the next few hours. Without actual charges being laid, any sentencing made on the basis of media conjecture could allow for a mistrial. I hoped the judge would be smart enough to not be influenced by journalists, or the Hammonds.

Ten of us had agreed to testify before the plea deal was signed. One by one, our witness impact statements were presented to the judge, reporters, the Crown Prosecutor and Emma. Ever the loyalist, Emma's reaction to the horrors experienced was that of indifference.

Strategically, I was the last one the Crown Prosecutor called forward. I stood and brushed the wrinkles from my suit pants and straightened my jacket. Charlotte squeezed my hand in support. The other hand held wrinkled notes. Notes I was not sure I would need, given how fresh the wounds of torture, rape, confinement and death were.

I stepped around the baby carrier seated beside me on the floor. The occupant was completely unaware of what was happening around him. The wooden barrier between the gallery and officers of the court prevented William from laying eyes on his son. Intentional? Yes. Conniving? That too, but I was allowed to be. William would not see his child between scheduled visits. He did not deserve the luxury.

Our second scheduled visit was called off when the prison had to go into lock-down, after a riot broke out the day before. The rest of the story, as to why William surrendered without a fight, resided behind the prison walls.

A glass of water sat on top of the wooden lectern positioned between William and the Crown Prosecutor. From my work with the Toronto Police Service, I had testified in court on multiple occasions, and nerves were not something I had battled back then. However, this was different. This was my life I would speak about. My hands shook as I unfolded my wrinkled notes and tried to flatten the papers against the lectern. I took a sip of water and waited to be instructed by the judge to speak.

The judge's beady eyes, framed in round spectacles, stuck to his papers. He pointed at me with his pen, as if a conductor of an orchestra. He had done the same with the others.

"My name is Olivia Beaumont. I am originally from Toronto, Ontario, Canada and I am a human trafficking victim of William, Adam and Helen Hammond. Today, I share with you the horrors that I experienced at the hands of this family in the hope that somewhere in your heart, Judge Moore, you can come to terms with just how monstrous this man before you is."

Time stood still as I recounted each day of my story. One dreadful event after another. I told the stories of the voiceless victims who helped me escape Los Angeles.

Sobs filled the gallery, and echoed through the courtroom. However, the noise escalated immensely when I removed my hair from my neck and revealed the large H.

"Now, here I stand. Unable to sleep due to nightmares. Certain smells trigger unwanted memories. I am a sister, without a sister. I am a Detective who jumps at the sound of a car exhaust backfiring. I am a mother to a child I had not planned to have, and yet love immensely, despite who his father is. I am tormented by the eyes of a monster looking up at me from my son's face. I am a person who is repulsed by the thought of a man touching me intimately. I am skeptical I will ever trust anyone. I am more broken than I ever thought possible."

I looked at William, slumped in the prisoner's dock. "I am all of this because of what William Hammond, and the empire he and Helen Hammond commanded, did to me."

Judge Moore, using his pen like a baton, tapped his desk and motioned me to step down. "Ten-minute recess and then I will have my ruling." He rose from his seat, the side of his mouth raised a little when he looked at William, and then he headed into his chambers.

Back at my seat, I received reassurances from other survivors. Hugs were exchanged, even though none of us felt comfortable with them. The notes in my hands felt like they were on fire, so I pushed them onto Charlotte. I never wanted to see them again.

Reporters in the gallery whispered about Judge Moore having already decided the verdict. I agreed. He had not acknowledged a single person who stood before him and shared their difficult story. Ten minutes was also not enough time to fully comprehend what we all went through. As Charlotte and Director Shaffin alluded to, Judge Moore was suspected of being a Hammond supporter.

The judge walked back into the courtroom after exactly ten minutes. I wondered if he watched the minutes on the clock tick by.

The one thing I was grateful for, was minimum sentences. No judge, in the Hammond's pocket or not, would be able to argue extenuating circumstances.

All eyes were fixated on Judge Moore.

"Mr. Hammond, please rise." William obeyed. "After considering all of the statements made today, Mr. Hammond's plea of guilty, the evidence presented by the Crown Prosecutor, and the defense, my ruling is as follows: On the twenty counts of trafficking a human you are hereby sentenced to ten years."

Gasps erupted around me. I couldn't breathe.

"On the three counts of money laundering, you are hereby sentenced to three years."

The onlookers' disbelief became audibly louder. "Order. Order or I will have you all removed."

Judge Moore handed down sentences below the minimum. I was not shocked by the blatant corruption, but I was dismayed.

"Mr. Hammond, after all of this, you are sentenced to a total of thirteen years, minus time served. With good behaviour you could be released in as little as ten years. Do you understand?"

"Yes, Sir. I understand." William looked at me and smiled.

CHAPTER SIXTY-THREE

I held it together until the bailiff had removed William from the courtroom, and then I grabbed the baby carrier, and ran as fast I could to the bathroom. I had barely touched the breakfast Charlotte had brought me, but whatever remained came back up into the closet sink. I washed the vomit from my face, and swished water around my mouth to get rid of as much of the horrid taste, and smell, as possible.

William knew this would happen! He knew he would be able to manipulate the system. Bah!

I punched the mirror and it shattered. Blood dripped down my hand, but I let it run. What did it matter anyway? Any life I had seen, in the minuscule shadows of my future, no longer existed. William had clouded over all of it.

His plan to see his son twice a month meant a bond, however twisted, would form. One that could be expanded upon when he was released and the child was still young. There would be ample time to groom him.

Why did I agree to this? I hated myself for thinking I had a chance, however small, to win. The master manipulator outdid himself. He, pretty much, managed to get away with fucking murder, human trafficking and money laundering. The corruption was blatant and without a truckload of evidence, MI5 would never be able to get William in front of a court again. Even for the murder of Noah. William hadn't pulled the trigger, so the Crown would not waste their time.

A guilty plea meant William would not have to face a jury. A jury that may not have fallen in line. With the judge, there was only one risk. A risk they mitigated. How could I have been so stupid? I should have known when William had, too easily, agreed.

Shit! Helen! They both had this all planned before they fled. William had not just found out that she transferred all of the assets. He knew. And with any conviction, the assets would either be forfeited or transferred to his next of kin, when there was no evidence to support they had been obtained via illegal means.

They would transfer to me, his lawfully wedded wife, or my son once a divorce was finalized. Once out of prison he would take back everything, as if nothing happened. Just an extended vacation in a cell block full of new contacts. Fuck!

The bathroom door slammed against the tiled wall. Charlotte's rage projected from her eyes.

"That shit judge just sacrificed himself for the Hammonds. He will be disbarred, but they will take care of him, I am sure. Fuck!" The rage turned to concern when she noticed the trails of blood around the room. "Jesus, Olivia! Give me your hand. She wrapped it as best she could with the scratchy brown paper towels available. "Let's get you fixed up and then we drink."

"I might need more than a drink."

She grabbed the carrier, the child still asleep through all the commotion, and led me to the first aid room on site. A nurse stitched me up, as I explained to Charlotte the realizations I had come to as I bled all over the bathroom.

"Now I really need a drink," Charlotte said. "I knew they were smart, but damn it, that was a good play. Director Chaffin is going to lose his shit, if he hasn't figured this out already."

I declined the painkillers I was offered, as tempted as I was to numb today away, I would not jeopardize my son. If the Hammonds genius plan included a case I was an unfit mother, I would not help them.

My stomach dropped to my feet. "Everything I said today. About being broken and how William has affected me. Could that be used against me, to take my son away?"

"I...well...I...no? I mean it is a public court record but...Shit!"

I jumped off the patient table, "That bastard is going after my son! He can't have him Charlotte. Not again! He always wins. God damn it!" I collapsed into her arms, her jacket drenched in my tears.

She rubbed my back, "It's okay. It just means it is time for Plan B."

CHAPTER SIXTY-FOUR

William requested he receive a make-up visitation, since his last one had been canceled. I thought it would be poetic to dress in all-black. After all, my life was pretty much over.

With William's sentencing complete, and the results as the Hammonds wanted them, the safe house was no longer needed. We were relocated to one of the many Hammond properties around London that now had my name on the land title. MI5 could not trace the money used to purchase the properties to illegal activity and therefore had not ceased them. At least not yet.

At first, I refused to use anything I had gained from William, but Charlotte was quick to point out I had no money, no job, another mouth to feed, and the government would no longer cover any of my costs.

I chose what I felt was the simplest property, all four thousand square feet of it. I swore it would only be temporary, until I was comfortable enough to go back to work. Director Chaffin had offered me a job but, like I was upon my return to Toronto, I doubted if police work was right for me. I wanted to get away from all of the politics and corruption. Find a small town somewhere and live the simple life.

I rested the baby carrier in the crease of my elbow and looked at the smile on the face within it. He, too, was dressed in a cute black suit. Charlotte poked her head in the doorway, "Are you ready? We're going to be late."

"Ready."

William was being moved to the prison where he would carry out his sentence. Charlotte had worked her magic and arranged for the visit to occur on the way there. No other prisoners were to be transported, which made the exchange of the regular guards with MI5 agents easy.

Charlotte drove, and London pedestrians, and buildings, passed me by. Landmarks and monuments I had only seen on television and in movies towered over us like we were ants. In another life, I would probably have come to love this city. In this one, I loathed it. Hatred and fear were the only things I received from this place.

Forty minutes after we had gotten into the vehicle, Charlotte pulled over on the shoulder. Under a large beech tree. Despite the sun, I turned up the collar of my jacket to protect my neck from the cool May wind.

The road was deserted, except for a large armoured transport that came up over the ridge in the distance. The closer it got, the quicker the beats of my heart pounded against my chest. I leaned against the passenger car door and watched as my dapper young man tried to shove an entire giraffe into his mouth. Drool covered his suit. Despite who I was about to see, I smiled at the happiness a baby found in a simple toy.

The grinding of the armoured car's brakes drew my attention to the other side of the road. The pot-bellied passenger got out and conferred with Charlotte. Both walked to the back of the truck. I opened the car door and released the clasps that had secured my son. He was only two-and-a-half-months old, but every day he looked more like me.

I bundled him up in a blanket, and put the toque he'd pulled off, back on. My grip tightened on the carrier and I stepped around the open back door of the truck and stood beside the guard. Charlotte had climbed inside and sat opposite of William, who was chained to his bench. The guard helped me up into the truck.

"You look nice, going somewhere after this?" William said with a smile. His grey jumper looked new, and prison life did not appear to have affected him.

"I have a hot date."

"Really?"

"Yes, with a bottle of Merlot. Let's get this over with. Here."

William's hand's were still shackled, but I managed to wedge my son between his arms and sit him on his lap. It wasn't perfect but it worked.

"Could you at least undo my hands? I can't hold him properly."

"Not today," Charlotte glared at him. "We don't want you getting any bright ideas out here in the middle of nowhere, now do we?"

The veins in William's neck pulsed, but rather than lash out, he focused on my son, cooing like most adults do with babies. I was disturbed to witness the monster transform, the moment the baby was in his possession.

An awkward five minutes later Charlotte announced, "time's up!".

"Our agreement says thirty minutes a visit, after sentencing."

"You can't honestly expect us to keep to that when we are seated on the side of the road. It is too dangerous out here, exposed as we are. You're lucky to have gotten the time you have." Charlotte said.

"Dangerous? Are you afraid the wild life will come after you?"

"In a manner of speaking."

I stood up and struggled with William to remove my son from his arms. Finally, he relented. Charlotte jumped out of the truck with ease and helped me down.

A light, but damp, mist had started to move in, since we had been inside the truck. I handed the baby to Charlotte, who walked back to the car. Chains jangled inside the truck.

"Out!" the guard instructed.

I turned back towards the truck and saw the colour drain from William's face. I smiled. The guard, baton at the ready, pushed William forward. I backed up and gave them both room to descend the stairs. With chained feet, William took each step slowly and with caution. His eyes, filled with fire, locked onto mine. Fear stayed at bay. Plan B was all I needed today.

The guard pushed William towards the ditch. With limited movement, William was unable to steady himself and rolled to the bottom. He managed to get himself into a seated position along the opposite slope. He tried to stand but gravity fought him and he decided to stay down.

I proceeded down the embankment, shoulders back, posture tall. One hand rested on my lower back. I reached the bottom and cocked my head to the side, as if I pondered what to do next. I knew exactly what I would do, but William had played so many games with me, it was my turn. William squirmed.

I stood on my side of the ditch, removed my hand from the small of my back, and a ray of sunlight broke through the dark clouds and reflected off the silver barrel in my hand.

William's eyes enlarged. He must have expected another beating. Not a gun. "You can't do this. Aunt Helen will..."

"Helen's dead."

The breath got stuck in William's throat, but not his breakfast. He clamored to his knees, vomited and used his arm as a towel to wipe his mouth. "She...how?"

"It's funny what happens when the general prison population believes Helen not only trafficked men and women, but children."

"But she...we...never."

"I would argue eighteen is close enough to a child, but either way. Even hardened criminals don't appreciate that someone around them harms children. Whether the stories are true or not. I'm pretty sure Helen didn't enjoyed her last shower too much. " Adrenaline coursed through me. This was it.

William tried to climb up the bank of the hill below me, but slipped on the damp grass. "You little bitch!"

"Oh yes, I'm a bitch. The bitch holding a gun, so you better watch what you say. Unlike whatever took place in your and Helen's courtrooms, I have the only thing needed for justice."

"You won't get away with this!"

"Pretty sure I can and will. You see, people in high places, with morals, made this happen." I turned off the safety, and cocked the gun.

"Olivia, you don't know what you are-"

BANG!

"FUCK!" Blood oozed out of William's right knee cap. "You don't understand what you are meddling in. This won't end well for you."

William clenched his jaw as he tried to hide the pain he was in.

"Aww, are you worried about me? How sweet."

BANG. Another knee cap.

"ARGH! Jesus Christ!"

"What? You don't like the monstrous tactics of your brother? The one thing I won't do is rape you repeatedly before I kill you."

BANG! An arm.

"What a shame." William muttered.

BANG! The other arm.

My enjoyment in the torture terrified me, but he deserved what he got. For Claire. For Whitney. For all of them. And for me. I crouched down, at eye level with William who had leaned back against the ditch.The life blood drained out of him.

"I love you, you know." William said.

The words knocked me over like I was a feather. "Wh..what did you say?"

"I love you. This was all for you. I was going to do my time. Then we could be a family."

"Are you kidding me? That was your plan? For all of us to be one big dysfunctional family. Built on what, trust and loyalty? Stop feeding me your bullshit."

"I'm serious. Biweekly visits were not only about watching our son grow up. It was about showing you how I could change. About how you could love me again."

"Again? I never loved you!"

"Only love would allow you to bring me into your hospital bed. Love created the laughter we shared."

"Shut up! Shut up! Shut Up! That was not love." Was I telling him, or myself? "Your time to talk is over. You can't weasel your way out of this. You have caused me too much pain, for me to love you. You have beaten and killed. You're a monster. Unchangeable, unlovable!"

"Am I?"

"YES!"

"I love-"

The smell of more sulfur tickled my nose.

CHAPTER SIXTY-FIVE

Smoke trailed up towards the clouds, and William's eyes followed suit after his head had fallen back against the hill. Blood trickled from between the glassy blue eyes that now stared at the grey clouds above. Raindrops hit his face, and trickled back into his wavy brown hair.

Keys jangled beside me. "Ma'am. We can take it from here."

I crawled towards William's body and checked his pulse. Call me crazy, but he had risen from the dead before, I was going to make sure it did not happen again. Nothing.

I pushed myself up to my feet and stumbled to get my footing. William needed to die, there was no other option. I needed to be the one to do it. So why did I feel empty? In a haze, I walked back to the car. Charlotte leaned against the hood of the driver's side. My son was asleep in the back, oblivious to the fact his mother had just murdered his father. I stowed away thoughts of the trauma that knowledge would cause if he ever found out.

Charlotte removed the gun from my hand, removed the last bullet and put it into her jacket pocket. The gun in the other. Without words we both got into the car, put on our seat belts, and Charlotte pulled out onto the deserted road. London became another shadow of my past that I would fight hard not to revisit.

The luggage in the trunk ricocheted, when the car tires collided with some railway tracks. Screams erupted from the backseat and he would not be settled until I found that damn giraffe. I had to climb in between the passenger and driver seats, into the backseat, to locate it. I spent the rest of the drive beside my son, enraptured by his innocent eyes.

Twenty-five kilometers later, we pulled into the loading and unloading zone outside a large train station. Charlotte grabbed a trolley and pulled the luggage out of the trunk while I removed the entire car seat.

With everything stacked so it would not fall, Charlotte handed me a train ticket and a key ring with five keys attached, two of which were skeleton keys. The ring also contained a picture of a young girl in a white vintage dress, and straw hat with blue ribbon, about to walk through a door covered in green vegetation, a beautiful garden on the other side.

"I called my Aunt to let her know you were coming. Her place is just down the street from mine, now yours. All she knows is, you are a single mom who needs to start over. Quietly. She had to do the same thing, so she likely won't ask too many questions. She agreed to hire you at the bookstore, part-time to start, until this little cutie can go into care. Then, likely full-time, after that. She's been looking to retire, but didn't want to give up the shop, so this works out perfectly."

"Well, I don't know if I would use the word *perfect* to describe my predicament, but I do appreciate everything you have done for me. I pull the money together somehow and pay you for the place. Market value and then some."

"You have paid more than enough. You just need to take care of yourself. I will come up to visit when I can. I wasn't one for seeing my Aunt, she's a little weird for my liking, but now I have a better excuse to come visit the coast, don't I?" She pinched his cheeks and he giggled.

A loud whistle echoed, "You better get going. Don't want to miss your train. Not in this rain."

We hugged each other as though we would never see each other again. "Thank you," I whispered in her ear. Charlotte smiled, and got back into her car.

With the baby carrier propped on the front of the trolley, I maneuvered my way around the station. I found platform four, with twenty minutes to spare before departure. The station worker helped me load everything into the luggage compartment, and assisted me to my seat. Charlotte had purchased two tickets, which was fortuitous as the train was almost full, and it would have been uncomfortable to have the baby carrier on my lap for the six-hour train ride.

With both of us settled in, and with no passenger across from us, William's final words started to echo in my ears. They got louder, and I looked around to make sure I was not actually hearing someone else talk. William had a way of coming back from the dead. I shook my head. He could not come back this time. I made sure of that. Just like I had made sure to see Helen's lifeless body.

My already strained heart tightened further. I had never seen Jasper's body. What if he...No. He would have surfaced by now, if he had managed to survive. That man was too cocky to let anyone think they had gotten the better of him.

My fears were drowned out with the return of William's words to my ears. He had been wrong, I hadn't loved him. Right? Everything I did, I did to survive. Not out of any sort of affection.

The engine of the train started to roar. A whistle blew, and the familiar "All aboard" was announced. I rested my hand on the carrier and closed my eyes. A body plopped into the seat across from me, and I opened my eyes.

Their face was obscured by a blue, plaid scarf and their head by the hood of their black jacket. Dark brown, almost black eyes, peered between the tiny gap. Was that black hair under the hood? My heart started to pound. The last time I thought I was safe, William showed up at my door. I looked warily at the stranger. They pulled back their hood to reveal short black hair. They unwrapped their large scarf. One. Two. Three. Four. Five rotations and the face revealed.

Relief.

"Did my get-up scare you, darling? I am sorry. At my age, even the slightest chill will have me in bed for days, much to my daughter's dismay." The old man smiled at me. "That's who I am going to see in Wakefield. She just had her fourth child and I have yet to meet him. I see you have one of your own." He sat on the edge of his seat. "A boy? You can rarely tell with babies" I nodded "Isn't he adorable. What's his name?"

"Calvin."

EPILOGUE

Large pellets of rain streaked across the glass windows of the train, as we sped along the tracks. Calvin slept beside me, and the man across from me was engrossed in a tattered novel, whose cover was half-missing while the other half was held together with yellowing tape.

Ever since we left the train station, my gut gnawed at me that something was wrong. Had I forgotten anything? I ran through a list of all the essentials I needed to pack and matched them to their locations in the luggage. Nothing was missed. I checked on Calvin, he looked peaceful and unaware of the hustle and bustle of the passengers around me.

A group of teenagers across the aisle joked loudly with each other. Diagonally and across from me sat a family. Dad typed on his phone, Mom stared blankly out the window and a young girl watched a video on a tablet. Her bright pink headband had cat ears on top.

Many of those around me mimicked the father, heads down and eyes staring into the light of a phone. I wondered if anyone ever took in their surroundings anymore, or was everyone just happy to stay in their little box of personal space.

The hairs on the back of my neck stood on end. I swore I could feel someone watching me. I stood up and the train door at the back of the car clicked shut. A figure in a tan trenchcoat disappeared into the other train car.

I stretched, and observed those passengers behind me. No one seemed suspicious. I ran my fingers through my hair and told myself that my fears about the Hammonds were getting the better of me. Calvin and I were safe and starting a new life.

I inhaled and exhaled a large breath, and, satisfied nothing was wrong, I sat back down. The train door behind me slid open and clicked closed. A fruity smell drifted down the aisle. My arms prickled and goosebumps rose to attention. I rubbed my arms and looked behind me. I didn't even try to be casual about it.

I didn't see anyone new.

"Everything all right?" the man across from me asked.

"Oh, yes. You know how you get that feeling that someone is watching you? I'm just being paranoid, that's all. I'm fine."

"I swear I feel my ex-wife's eyes burrowing into the back of my head all the time. But then again, she did that every day for thirty-five years, so it's probably one of those phantom feelings. You know, like when people lose a limb and can still feel it."

I laughed, "Maybe that's it. I've been so used to having someone around, it feels like they are here, even though I know that can't actually be the case."

"I am sure the feeling will go away. It just takes a bit of time." The man didn't press further and returned to his book.

The hairs on the back of my neck remained at attention. The clickety clack of the wheels turning along the track seemed to grow in intensity as I focused my attention on them and the rapidly passing scenery of fields and towns.

There was no one here. No one was watching me.

What I hadn't noticed behind me, was that the person wearing the tan trench coat had returned and taken their place on the aisle directly beside the door. Eyes forward and on me.

Acknowledgments

Writing involves long hours tucked away, alone, in a room where one tries to bring the scramble of ideas to life on the page. Many cups of tea fueled my brain as I battled the voices in my head with the story I hoped to write. Most often the voices won and the story changed from the inceptual concept to what the characters wanted. I think that makes the story even better!

Outside of the tea, I could not have completed this book without the love and support of my husband, Brian. His constant encouragement to explore ideas and actually write them has made Olivia's journey possible.

Thank you to my editor, Lisa and my advance readers; Candice, Megan, and Kim for your invaluable insight.

A special thank you to my fourth advance reader - my Dad! You have always encouraged me to follow my dreams, and it may have taken 38 years to listen, but I am finally doing it. But hey, I listened to your feedback about the book so my inaction time is reducing ;)

My mom and my sister are some of my biggest fans and advocates, I don't know what I would do without you.

Lastly, and most importantly, thank you to you, the readers, for taking time to enter into this world. I hope you enjoyed the journey!

About Author

N. L. Blandford is passionate about creating awareness around social issues through fictional stories. Her cunning and fearless characters take readers on thrilling journeys rooted in truth.

N.L. Blandford donates a portion of the proceeds from *The Perilous Road to Her* and *The Perilous Road to Freedom* to a charity who supports survivors of human trafficking and/or victims of sexual assault.

N. L. Blandford resides in Calgary, Alberta where she has built a life of dream exploration with her husband, mild mannered dog, Watson, and stubborn but loveable cat, Sebastian. When she is not writing, she works full time as an investigator of fraud at a financial institution.

www.nlblandford.com
nl@nlblandford.com
Instagram.com/nlblandford
bookbub.com/authors/n-l-blandford
Twitter.com/nlblandford

The Perilous Road To Her

In book one of The Road Series, *The Perilous Road to Her*, N.L Blandford takes us on a woman's harrowing journey to find her missing sister.

Olivia Beaumont, a Detective in the Toronto Police Service, finds herself dreading calls from her older sister Claire. Olivia's attempts to help Claire fight her drug addiction have only been met with refusals. Ready to walk away, and let Claire hit 'rock bottom', Olivia is drawn back when she learns Claire is missing.

Determined to find Claire, Olivia goes on the hunt for those who have taken her. However, the perpetrators have other plans. Suddenly, Olivia feels the prick of a needle in her neck and her world goes black. When she wakes up she has been transported into the underworld of human trafficking. Greed and sex surround her as she is forced to work for the monsters who have built an empire on the desperate and unlucky.

COMING SOON

THE PERILOUS ROAD TO HIM

Book Three: The Road Series

Olivia Beaumont has built a quiet and peaceful life with her son Calvin. But her past will soon threaten their future.

WANT MORE

Newsletter

Want the inside scoop on what's next from N. L. Blandford and receive exclusive content?

Sign up for the monthly newsletter and to receive the free novella "On The Perilous Road". The story is not available for purchase, is a prequel to The Road Series, and explores the backstory of William Hammond. The character everyone hates to love!

Sign up at https://www.nlblandford.com/

Reviews

I hope you enjoyed Olivia's journey so far. If you liked the book and can spare a few minutes, I would really appreciate a short review on whatever website you purchased the book. Reviews are invaluable to an author as it helps us gain visibility to new readers.

Thank you for reading The Perilous Road to Freedom. Without you her journey would be incomplete.

BOOK CLUBS

The Perilous Road to Freedom

1.Olivia battles a new set of Hammonds, who is your favourite addition to the story?

2. Olivia risks the life of her child every time she confronts William and during the battle with Jasper. How do you feel about this?

2. The book is full of struggles. For example, struggles of/for: freedom, power, family rivalry, and the loss of loved ones. What struggle resonated with you?

3. What struggle did you wish the author explored deeper?

4. William is a complex character, humanized by the author. Does the fact William is not a stereotypical villain, without any emotions, make it easier or harder to not like him? How do you feel about the character overall?

5. How do you feel about how the story ended for William?

6. How much visibility did you have of human trafficking before reading this book?

7. What did you learn?

8. What are you unsure about, but intrigued to research more?

General Book Club Questions

1.What part of the story stuck with you? Why?

2. What character(s) do you love to hate? Hate to love?

3. What issues do you have with the story?

4. What resonated with you?

5. Where do you see yourself reflected in the story?

6. How is the story a window into another world or life experience?

7. What details or patterns did you piece together to create a new understanding?

8. Does the author get the ending right? Why or Why not?

9. How has the story changed you or your perspective?

10. What would you edit for the big screen?
Who would you cast?

11. How does the story portray gender, race, class, sexuality?

12. What feelings did this book evoke for you?

13. If you could hear this story from another character's perspective who would that be?

Want N. L. Blandford to attend a virtual book club session about her book(s)? Visit nlblandford.com to contact her.

RESOURCES

To help stop human trafficking become knowledgeable about the issue and take action. There are extensive resources available. Below is only a selection.

Learn More

The books and resources by:
Rebecca Bender
(https://www.rebeccabender.org/resource-list)
Timea Nagy
(https://www.timeascause.com/),

<u>Canada</u>

• Not in My City (https://notinmycity.ca/)

• Public Safety Canada (https://www.publicsafety.gc.ca/cnt/cntrng-crm/hmn-trffckng/index-en.aspx)

• Canadian Human Trafficking Hotline (https://www.canadianhumantraffickinghotline.ca/)

<u>United States of America</u>

• The Polaris Project (USA) (https://polarisproject.org/)

• U.S Department of Homeland Security ((https://www.dhs.gov/blue-campaign/what-human-trafficking)

• United Nations -Office on Drugs and Crime (https://www.unodc.org/unodc/en/human-trafficking/what-is-human-trafficking.html)

Reporting/Get Help

If you have been a victim, or might know a victim, of human trafficking please contact:

• Local law enforcement

• Social Services

- Licensed mental health practitioners
- In Canada, the Canadian Human Trafficking Hotline at 1-833-900-1010
- In the United States of America, the U.S. Immigration and Customs Enforcement (ICE) Homeland Security Investigations (HSI) Tip Line 1-866-347-2423

Manufactured by Amazon.ca
Bolton, ON